Track of the Giant

WILL BAKER

Track
of the Giant

A Double D Western

DOUBLEDAY

New York   London   Toronto   Sydney   Auckland

A DOUBLE D WESTERN
PUBLISHED BY DOUBLEDAY
a division of Bantam Doubleday Dell Publishing Group, Inc.
666 Fifth Avenue, New York, New York 10103

A DOUBLE D WESTERN, DOUBLEDAY,
and the portrayal of the letters DD
are trademarks of Doubleday, a division of
Bantam Doubleday Dell Publishing Group, Inc.

Library of Congress Cataloging-in-Publication Data

Baker, Will, 1935–
   Track of the giant   /   Will Baker.—1st ed.
      p.   cm.—(A Double D western)
   I. Title.
PS3573.E199T7   1990
813'.54—dc20   90-3084
CIP

ISBN 0-385-41397-1

Track of the Giant

[1]

ONE BRIGHT DAY in April, arriving on the new horse-car from Boston, Willard Starkwether Evans was unexpectedly early. So when he saw the little crowd under the trees in Brattle Square, he tarried at its edge to eavesdrop. A makeshift table had been placed on the greensward, and beside it were a young woman, seated in a straight-backed folding chair, and a tall, swarthy man. He stood a little in advance of her, but turned so as to regard her easily while he addressed the crowd. As Willard approached, the man's quick black eyes acknowledged him, then darted off hungrily around the circle of faces.

". . . the various faculties of the soul. To say this young lady is of sanguine temper would not astound you; to remark her nobility of carriage would likewise be to belabor the obvious." Here the man cocked an eyebrow at one of the students who had pressed to the forefront. "Would you not agree, sir, the young lady is extraordinary?

The youth swept off his hat and turned pink, and a gust of laughter swept through the onlookers.

"No, all this and more is given us by the merest common sense. Indeed, much of what the great doctors of the Science of Phrenology have discovered by painstaking measurement is only confirmation of what any shrewd judge of character might observe. *However*"—here the man's easy smile vanished, and he stepped back swiftly, placing his hand on a small metal box in the center of the table—"eminent scientists have combined their knowledge of Phrenology with another great principle of our age, the active principle that moves all things, the essence of every impulse, indeed, the prime mover itself unmoved, which the philosophers of Antiquity sought high and low— Yes, I speak of the fount of life: *electricity!*"

The word was punctuated by a sharp click as the lid of the box sprang open. With a deft movement the man removed and held aloft a thick glass bottle, from which protruded a rod topped by a small, glittering ball. For several moments he said nothing, his look held steadily, reverently, on the little ball. The crowd of students had fallen silent. Willard could hear, with unnatural clarity, a trolley rattling by on Harvard Square. He cleared his throat. The man gave him one swift look and continued:

"Electricity! Or 'animal magnetism,' as the great Mesmer christened it. That subtle force, mysterious and powerful, whose presence we can scarce detect, whose absence is still, cold, numb *death!*" He paused, and again there was silence. "For, gentlemen, without the vital spark we are but clay. Yet, charged with electrico-magnetic forces, our puny frames may perform the most astounding feats—or commit the most execrable crimes. Magnetism by itself is but an immensely potent force, without moral direction. The magnetic currents of the brain are like a great river, capable of turning a mill but also capable of flood."

His voice growing ever more commanding and resonant, the man took a second bottle from the box and brought it gradually nearer the first. When the two balls were only inches apart, his knuckles grew white. Over his temple a vein started forth, sudden as a snake. Fascinated, Willard watched it pulse softly. Then there was a small but distinct snap, like that of a carriage whip, and a little blue spark sizzled between the balls. Sighs, whispers, and exclamations ran through the crowd. Two or three of the zealous began a hesitant applause, but ceased in confusion at one look from the experimenter.

"Similarly, the great Dr. Grimes saw clearly the need to implement our phrenological principles through application of the immense power of electromagnetism. He developed this Magnetizer, the Grimes *Phrenomagnet,* to perform that amazing task. Now"—the man bowed slightly to the woman seated beside him, his exceedingly white teeth flashing beneath a glistening moustache—"let me assure the young lady —Miss Elizabeth, was it not?—who has so bravely volunteered to demonstrate the effectiveness of the Phrenomagnet, that we shall observe the strictest propriety in our experiment. Please be at ease, madam."

The young woman—slender, erect, and most striking, Willard thought—nodded shyly and arranged her hands in her lap. Directly before her in the front row stood a large, coarse-featured young man, whose slightly officious manner suggested that he was the young lady's beau.

From somewhere the man had now produced a little chart on a stand. The chart showed the outline of a human head, which was divided into numbered and labeled segments. Using the bottle and rod as a pointer, the man touched certain of these segments to illustrate his remarks.

"The faculties in the ideal type are displayed here. In most of us, the centers of Hope, Faith, Conscientiousness, and Magnanimity are not so developed, and those of Amativeness, Acquisitiveness, Cruelty, and so on are more so. Of course in the female type there is greater development of the Philoprogenitive and Protective portions of the brain, and a corresponding want of rational power. However, we can enhance, by scientific application of positive electricity, certain of these faculties, and inhibit the growth of others by means of negative electric charge."

The man stepped nearer the woman, and Willard saw her eyes lift to his face just before his back blocked the view. There was fear in her look, but also a kind of yearning. The man spread his arms and spoke more softly, so that the onlookers held their breath and strained to overhear.

"Permit me to observe, madam, you are very near the ideal type. If anything, you are perhaps too modest, too little thoughtful of yourself. Beauty and grace need not so hide themselves. We intend now only to stimulate briefly those strong and righteous sentiments becoming to your nature. You need only be your true self, think of nothing, forget everything—troubles and trials—but hear my voice. The magnetism of this rod is no more than that of your mother's hand when you were a child. You remember her touch?"

Holding aloft the bottle, the man turned again. His audience swayed back a little, as if embarrassed at having listened so intently. Willard was frowning. The fellow had amused him at first with his ridiculous theories, but the rapt attention of the students—young men supposedly training to be scholars and scientists—had begun to disturb him. He remarked, too, that the magnetist had placed himself so as to block the young woman's view of her beau, and the young man was glowering in agitation.

"We shall attempt to stimulate first the portion of the brain where Hope resides. Hope, the weaver of dreams, the alembic of the future, the cloud which bears us fearless into the unknown . . ." He whirled about and reached out with the peculiar wand. The ball flashed in a splinter of sunlight coming through the trees. It touched the woman's temple. Her body stiffened. The rod retreated, and she slumped a little in the chair.

"The magnetic force must be applied in gentle dosages, so as not to overbalance the mind," the man intoned. "Softly as a mother's hand . . ."

Again the ball flashed. Swiftly, yet gently, it moved in and out, grazing the woman's hairline. Her face grew flushed. Her eyes brightened, then suddenly spilled tears. She gave a small, sharp cry.

"Yes, Elizabeth?" The magnetist crouched slightly before her, arms now aloft. He looked like a great crow spreading and shaking its wings. "What is it you wish? Do you see? Is it . . . someone?"

The woman half rose from her seat, as if linked by an invisible wire to the Phrenomagnet. "My brother!" she whispered. "He was—is—my brother. I shall see him . . ."

"Your brother. He was in the war? Is that it?"

"Yes, he . . ."

"He did not come back? But you know now you shall see him again! You are full of hope. He *shall* be with you once again!"

"Yes! Oh yes! I shall, I *shall!*" The woman clasped her hands to her breast and sobbed with joy. The wand moved to a point a scant foot from her nose and held steady.

"You are now the eldest of your family? Yes, as I thought. To you has fallen the labor of a mother. A tender grace, no higher task in human-kind—but in one so young! Maidenhood has also its claims, its right." The man wove closer, and all eyes remained riveted to the shining orb at the tip of the wand. "Think now not of others but of thyself. We shall stimulate the centers of Self-Regard, of Acquisitiveness and even Vanity, for some measure of self-interest is necessary to organisms, for their survival and the evolution of all things." He touched her forehead, and instantly the woman's expression changed. The laughter that bubbled through her tears quieted. Her hands unclasped and crept toward her hair. "Is it not right for youth—and beauty—to wish for something for themselves, Elizabeth? Elizabeth?"

Elizabeth was gazing upward now at the light shimmering on the leaves. A half-smile on her lips, she appeared to be in a deep reverie. Her fingers probed in a leisurely way through her coils of bright, auburn hair, and she uttered something between a long sigh and a groan of relief. "Mmmm," she said, "of course. I want . . ." She stopped and glanced slyly around.

"What, Elizabeth? What do you want? You should have it, you *must* have it."

"Stop that! You let her be!" The sullen young man took two quick strides, clapped a hand on the magnetist's shoulder and spun him around. Cries of disapproval erupted from the audience, which pressed forward around the table. The magnetist pushed the other man away and gestured with the bottle and rod as though with a talisman. His dark face was convulsed with rage and consternation.

"Get back!" he thundered. "You will ruin the treatment, destroy this young woman's—"

Elizabeth cut him short with the sound of some small rodent in mortal pain. Willard saw her face for a moment through the jostling crowd. It was rigid with terror. Her squealing arrested the movement around her. Then it ceased as abruptly as it had begun, and Willard saw her go limp and begin to slide from the chair.

"Doctor, doctor!" he heard someone shout. He shouldered his way to her side.

"It's Professor Evans," one of the students exclaimed. "Make way, make way!"

The young man and the magnetist hovered over Elizabeth, glaring at each other, their fists clenched.

"Stay back," Willard said firmly. He whipped his handkerchief from his pocket and turned to one of the students. "Find the nearest hydrant or horse trough and soak this thoroughly. You, there, go fetch a constable." He bent over Elizabeth and began to loosen her shirtwaist at the neck. With one careful thumb he lifted an eyelid, and saw that her pupils were rolled back out of sight, contemplating something within her own skull, though rapid, her pulse was regular and strong.

The magnetist was beside him, hissing in his ear.

"Be careful, man! Her brain is charged. She—"

"You may explain your absurd notions to the constable when he gets here," Willard said with a chill smile. "Your charade has gone on rather too long. Sensible men ought to laugh you out of town without assistance from the law. Unfortunately, the ignorant and the gullible—"

Elizabeth moaned softly. Her lids trembled, opened partially, and he saw that her eyes were a cold green, like seawater. She focused on his face and her lips moved.

"Yes . . . someone . . . like you . . ."

"Madam," he said gently. Her body twisted again, as if in some delicious dream, and Willard was momentarily unsettled by the swell of her white throat. "You are in a state of shock, I believe. Be very quiet, and let us assist you . . ."

Deliberately ignoring the magnetist, he beckoned to one of the bystanders, and together they eased the woman onto a pile of coats that solicitous gentlemen had spread under a tree. His dampened handkerchief had been returned, and Willard now pressed it to her temples. He was about to dispatch another student to the apothecary's shop around the corner, when he felt a tug at his sleeve.

"He's gettin' away." The young man's expression was one of doglike expectation. Indeed, the table, the chair, the chart, the bottles and metal box had miraculously disappeared into a suitcase, which the magnetist swung jauntily at his side as he strode down one of the paths across the square.

"All right. Stay by her and keep everyone back." Willard sprinted away down the path. As he approached, the man grinned broadly at him over his shoulder, but did not slacken his pace.

"Ah! Dear Professor Evans!"

Out of breath and taken aback, Willard was unable to reply with the tone of stern authority he had expected of himself. "You . . . I say . . ." he heard himself stumbling. "You shall be brought to account for this. That was despicable. You caused that young woman to . . ."

"Myself, a mere charlatan, *caused* a woman to faint, Professor?" The man laughed. "Surely a learned man like yourself, a disciple of the great Baum, can cause her to recover!"

Willard tried to seize the man's shoulder but found himself clutching at thin air. The magnetist had slid under his arm; then Willard felt a sharp pressure at his side. He looked down and saw the naked blade laid against his ribs. The other was so close he could smell a cloying cologne.

"Be a good chap, Professor. Rather say, as gentlemen, we have a difference of views? I wouldn't advise trying to hold me . . ."

Willard felt, not fear, but a strange giddiness, as if he stood at the brink of a rushing river.

"You have your game, Professor. I have mine. We are closer than you think. The human mind is a power and a mystery. You should not play with it idly."

With one glance of light the knife vanished into the man's coat. A small card was pressed into Willard's hand. He watched without moving as, in a few swift strides, the man gained the border of Mt. Auburn Street and turned down it. In a moment he was gone.

W. Miller

Willard read the card slowly as he walked back through the square. The sight of cold steel, he realized, had not perturbed him so much as the remarkable effect of the electric bottle. As a close student of progress in every field of science, at a time when, in his view, the path lay open to rational mastery of the universe, it was disturbing to see a quack of the worst sort achieve such results using only a silly toy. He was resolved to question Elizabeth, in the hope of gaining some understanding of the man's trickery. And how had the rascal known he was Baum's pupil? However, when he regained the site of the demonstration, Elizabeth and her beau were nowhere to be seen. He was told that the two had gone off in a cab. No one remembered hearing an address. Now only a handful of spectators remained under the trees, milling angrily about.

There were, it appeared, several wallets missing.

[2]

WILLARD MADE HIS HABITUAL DETOUR through the Quadrangle on his way to the intersection of Kirkland and Cambridge Streets, thence to Divinity Avenue and the new Peabody Museum that housed the treasures of his profession. Today, though he had arranged to spend the afternoon boating on the Charles with Lydia Braddock, he was absentmindedly retracing his usual route, dawdling along under great maples, intent on the incident in Brattle Square.

The existence of men like Miller the magnetist disturbed him. There was no further excuse for such superstition. Everywhere Darwin and his disciples looked—pigeons, orchids, cucumbers, sea urchins—all was cold purpose, clear design. Natural Selection, manifestly, had triumphed over that threadbare ghost, the soul. Yet, for the masses of men, the absurd doctrines of the Church persisted—special creation of each species, the denial of fossil evidence, belief in the Flood. And these were by no means the full measure of human gullibility.

Every kind of trickery, trumpery, and tomfoolery seemed to prosper in this age. There were palm-readers, seers, faith healers, phrenologists, vitalists, theosophists, and snake-oil merchants. Worst of all—from Willard's point of view—were the pompous frauds like Miller who tried to disguise their chicanery in the rigmarole of pseudoscience. They took some of the vocabulary of respectable thinkers, even some of the ideas in crude form, and made of them hobgoblins that terrified the ignorant. Even here, at one of the oldest and finest colleges, Willard now and then found a student who thought the sun spun about the earth.

Willard glanced up and found himself before Appleton Chapel. His eye traveled up the single spire, then lingered on the high and narrow arched windows. The sandstone was bright in the overhead sun, the glass somber in shadow. He could make out "Christo et Ecclesiae" and "Veritas" engraved above and below the main rose window. Truth! His mouth writhed in disgust. As the Church saw it, truth would have man prostrate, sniveling over his sins, dreading an invisible avenger. Still, he reflected, when it came to architecture, the believers had a sure instinct for an awesome kind of beauty.

On a finger of vine exploring the base of the spire he caught sight of a small brown bird. It uttered a surprising cadenza, then darted from sight. Willard smiled and glanced about appreciatively, but there was no one near. In a moment the bird reappeared and repeated its complex, plangent song. The odd notion came to him that the bird was calling him, inviting him into its leafy nook. He thought then of the girl in the park, as she looked when she drew the pin from her hair. He frowned. Of late he had been bothered by daydreams, reveries, and a seductive, summery idleness that without warning disrupted his active mental life. It was time for him to begin rigorous research on new material. Insects perhaps, or fish.

With a start, he realized he had wandered quite out of his way. The Braddocks' elegant and spacious home was on Bow Street, just off the campus. It was of brick, with a mansard roof of slate and an oeil-de-boeuf. Braddock was, like many of the older faculty, independently wealthy. He was also a professor of Greek attached to the Divinity School, and did not, therefore, entirely approve of his daughter's engagement to a penurious young scholar in the disquieting new science of paleontology. It would not advance matters to be tardy. Willard had already turned about and set off at a smart pace when he was hailed from behind.

" 'Fessor Evans! Message, sir. Message!"

It was a student he vaguely remembered from a prior semester, a gawky lad with straw-straight hair. Willard accepted the envelope and, conscious of the boy's anxious, curious look, broke the seal and took out a single sheet of notepaper. In a small, contorted hand was written the following message:

Come immediately. Urgent. Here is the end to arguments. You will be a great man.

BAUM

"The devil take you!" Willard expostulated.

"Beg pardon, sir?" The boy looked injured.

"No, not you, for heaven's sake. I say, do you know Professor Braddock's house? On Bow Street?" Willard patted his pockets and found a pencil and the card the phrenologist had given him. He began scribbling on the back of the card.

"B'lieve I do sir."

"Then take this to Miss Braddock, Miss Lydia Braddock." He crossed the *t*'s and dotted the *i*'s in "irritation" and "trial" and handed the note to the boy, along with a silver coin. Then he turned and marched purposefully back across the Quadrangle, ignoring the glances and whispers of the young sports who idled there. The day, which had dawned clear and carefree, was in shambles. Sometimes, in his innermost self-questioning, he encountered the uncomfortable suspicion that the courtship of a delicate, fair, and highborn woman was not in the end compatible with a passion for old bones.

"Beautiful, eh?"

The skull was anchored on an iron pin at the center of Professor Baum's worktable. It grinned up at Willard like a child encircled by macabre toys—calipers, compasses, bowls of plaster, cartons of bird shot, and cloth tapes.

"Indeed." Willard bent and traced a finger along the heavy superciliary ridge. "An excellent cast. It is quite as Fuhlrott's photographs represented it." He peered into the black caverns of the eyes. "Hello, Fritz," he said. "I do wish you could give us an account of the last"—he cocked an eyebrow playfully at Professor Baum—"fifty millenia."

"Forty. And deprive us the pleasure of all most supreme, to expose these . . . these *Gimpel?!* Much better he is locked in the silence of ages. We shall unravel his secret for ourselves, eh?"

The professor had flushed pink above his great white beard. Eyes blue and clear as summer heaven watered behind his spectacles.

Willard looked back at the skull. He did not want to inaugurate another harangue on the learned dolts who failed to grasp the professor's eccentric theories. As Baum's protégé, he would be allowed to make his own measurements and draw his own conclusions. Now he was anxious to learn the reason for the scribbled note that had spoiled his afternoon lark. At the thought of Lydia, a pang of some dangerous feeling struck him, and then was gone like the shadow of a swift bird.

"Sir, what is the urgent matter you mention in your note?" He masked his bluntness by pretending still to examine the rear molars.

"Ah! Yes, of course. I told you last week of the outlaw and murderer, the giant aborigine—most interesting case. You must pack immediately and go West. To Idaho."

Willard swayed, but managed to sustain himself against the worktable.

"When they catch him you must be present. We must have both the head and feet. Also, if possible, the femur. Most supreme, of course, the cadaver entire."

"Really sir," Willard began. "Really . . ."

Baum paused, quizzical. "What is the matter? Can it be you do not see the opportunity?"

"Sir, I am not at liberty . . . my fiancée . . ."

"Take her, for heaven's sake. Have the wedding immediately."

Willard laughed. "That is out of the question, Professor Baum. You don't know Lydia. Anyway, my position would not allow such a step now. The Braddocks . . ."

"Of course I know her. Ah, you're right, Willard, Roland would never allow it. I am not thinking. Leave her. Afterwards marry." Baum began to pace around the table. Willard knew the tirade he had hoped to avoid was now irreversible.

"You must have a chair—Paleontology or Anatomy, no?—to satisfy Professor Braddock. Otherwise no wedding, eh? So. You shuffle about the library and the museum for five, perhaps ten, perhaps more years at such research as I must do because I am an old man with dyspepsia." Baum threw out his arms as if to wrestle a giant. "Or you go to secure measurements of this Big Foot bandit, a contemporary specimen of a rare pithecine ancestor. And in a few months you are the most famous scientist since Humboldt. Of course, the library is the safe way. Since I fled for my life from my own country, it has been my way. You are in that case not to blame . . . but I would be disappointed. Your preparation has been so brilliant . . ." The old professor turned away.

"Sir," Willard replied carefully. "Surely it would be possible to preserve the remains in a hogshead of alcohol, as was done I believe in Lord Byron's case. And also for the Patagonians studied so productively by Huxley. Then we would have all of our records here for convenient reference."

"Who would supervise such work? Not the ruffians who put a price on the creature's head. Not any reputable scientist. There are none in these savage regions, my good man. None. We can appeal to no one." Baum gestured irritably at the skull on the table. "We are on the brink of great discoveries. But fools and charlatans have muddled everything. Herr Schaafhausen and Fuhlrott have provided the world with the bones of the devil! They cannot say so, of course, men of science, but it is so! He was there, near Düsseldorf—there in the valley of the Neander, doing his evil work already fifty thousand years ago! They know not what they have found!"

"I know, sir, I know. Quite." Willard edged toward the door. "Clearly their prejudices have influenced the evaluation of the facts. But . . ."

"See here!" The professor scurried across the room to a desk stacked high with books. The pile looked like the forlorn, crooked staircase of a house that had itself vanished in flames. He jerked out one volume and the rest collapsed in a thudding, flopping jumble. "Folly upon folly!" He shoved the volume under Willard's nose. "It was not enough that Lyell and Huxley must put him down as some kind of Negro savage, and speak of the occipital depression as the certain mark of brutality; now this charlatan has denied him all semblance of humanity!" Following the professor's trembling, stubby finger, Willard read:

Taking into account the recessive jaw to be inferred from the La Naulette discovery, and the extreme dolichocephalic properties of both the Düsseldorf and Gibralter skulls (cf. the glabella-occiput axis in proportion to the lambdoidal apex), it is possible to conclude that the creature is not at all a hominid, but a giant chimpanzee, perhaps suffering from brain disorders . . .

"Eh? Eh?" Baum slammed shut the book. "A hypothesis so mad it ought to be laughed out of every scientific society in the world, and men —men of science, they call themselves—are discussing it seriously . . ."

Willard smiled. "Ingenious, you must admit. But to make Fritz here not merely an ape, but a mentally degenerate ape—that is rather a stretcher, isn't it?" Baum drew a mighty breath, his face aflame, but Willard hastened on. "On the other hand, Professor Baum, the mystery remains, and that is why the hypotheses grow more erratic. We know that Fritz—"

"I wish you would not call him so," Baum interrupted. "My grandfather . . ."

"I beg your pardon. Homer? Yes, why not? We know Homer walked erect, was shorter but markedly more robust than ourselves, had immense eyebrows and no chin; was an excellent hunter and perhaps the best maker of stone tools and weapons of his time . . ."

The professor uttered an outraged squawk of protest. "Best? What means best? The most murderous . . ."

"The most precise, sir, the most *elegant.*" Willard had forgotten his strategy of escape, his hope of salvaging at least a stroll in the college square with Lydia. His hazel eyes were narrowed with the intensity of a man pursuing dangerous quarry. "There is nothing like his spearpoints until we reach the reindeer hunters of—yesterday, so to speak. And he was strong, very strong—a kind of diminutive Hercules—capable of subduing the woolly rhinoceros, the cave bear, and the giant hyena. But, sir —and in that 'but' is all the controversy—he disappeared. Vanished. The giant was replaced by . . . our own kind—legs too long, arms too short, head too big, belly exposed, and teeth too small to serve for anything but cracking nuts."

"But the soul of man, damn you! You forget!"

Willard smiled ruefully. "We shan't agree on that, Professor Baum, as you well know. But both of us know we will not shirk the responsibility of testing hypotheses exhaustively. Hence . . ."

"Hence the important business to expand our research to include living specimens! That is why we must see that the skeleton of this mythical brigand is available for measurement." Baum leveled a forefinger at Willard's chest. "You have now of your lifetime the greatest opportunity of ever! Think of it! We know from our dissections and measurements of students that so many characteristics of *Neanderthalensis* appear in modern man—the prognathous jaw, enlarged femur, the thick occipital—especially in the criminal type—"

"Not at all!" Willard protested. Then he realized the professor had paused deliberately to allow this outburst, so much had this dispute become a ritual between them. He smiled in spite of himself and Baum continued.

"—and we are convinced this type has interbred with Cro-Magnon strains. Now, suppose a *pure* throwback! A being so like our Homer that we could hardly with our skill of many years tell them apart. A great, lumbering beast-man! The size of Cro-Magnon and the bulk of Neanderthal! The hunter of mastadons is now robbing stagecoaches! What a piece of evidence with which the great learned societies to approach? Eh?" Baum was scarlet with hope.

"Perhaps."

"Ah, so now it is 'perhaps,' is it? Then you admit to me the desirability? You will bring back across this large country this skeleton?"

Willard drew a breath, about to declare his resounding refusal. The notion was mad. How could he abandon his research, his strict regime of reading and note-taking, to say nothing of his courtship . . . The older professor was watching his face with the alertness of a great, fat robin in a meadow after a rain. Before Willard even realized what his own answer would be he saw the white beard tremble with delight.

"Good for you!" Baum bounded back to his desk and seized a massive folder wrapped with red string.

"I don't know, Professor Baum," Willard objected. "It upsets everything. How am I to afford the expense?"

"Of course I have thought of that. Foolish I am not. Money I know. Take this." He pushed the folder into Willard's hands. "It has all the information I have collected on these specimens, especially this Nampuh, the Big Foot. Money? You have heard of Mandrake Stoneman?"

Willard looked at the old professor in amazement.

"No!"

"But yes. He is *very* interested in our researches, my good man. You know he has many times taken voyages to India and Jerusalem and such places of exotic grandness to discuss with kings and emirs and chiefs."

The information that the expedition might be paid for from the Stoneman fortune was enough to throw Willard into confusion. Starting with coal, steel, and railways, Stoneman had moved into shipping lines, manufacturing, and land companies. He had been instrumental in driving the French from Mexico, and he elevated and deposed senators. It was known that he had himself coveted high office, in the period of turmoil after the war. Wisely, he had finally abandoned such open campaigning. For there were disturbing rumors. Stoneman had tried to interfere in the Reconstruction, offering to return to Africa in his ships all Negroes who volunteered. He had openly called for closing the United States to immigrants, though his own grandfather had arrived from a debtors' prison in England. He had personally threatened the leader of the Workingman's Party. It was said he secretly favored monarchy.

Even his reputed interest in history and science had a peculiar cast. Willard had once read a vicious lampoon of the man in which it was suggested that his quest for a proved, lineal descent from Moses was misdirected, since, the satirist ventured, "the paternity of Lucifer might more easily be charged." Still, he had liberally endowed Harvard, and in recent years had maintained an Olympian reticence on public issues.

"Why is he interested in our work?" Willard asked.

"Stoneman has heard of my theories. Especially this part, where I say the legends of the Titans, and Cyclops, and old Celtic giants are rooted in evolutionary fact. If there was—or is—a species more huge and strong than Homo sapiens, and lacking also, most important, a moral sense . . ."

"I know the theory, Professor," Willard said gently. "And you know my alternative: he was not only stronger but smarter, and unfortunately outnumbered . . ."

"Yes yes yes." Baum waved impatiently. "We make a mistake to argue what we so well know already. We at least have agreement that he was probably uglier." Both of them smiled at the old joke.

"Stoneman interests himself in the possibility that now alive are a few descendants of some mongrelized form of this monster—*ach*, you object —well then, of a degenerate subspecies. If we can determine the measurements of this type—"

"Then you can spot him in our midst, and deport him or imprison him." Willard glanced at the skull, which was still grinning fixedly at them.

"So, Willard, you are extreme." Baum seemed hurt. "But let us suppose there were correlations between these measurements and some criminals, some aberrations. Would it be so foolish to forbid to this type reproducing itself?"

Willard returned the gaze of the honest, heaven-blue eyes for a moment and then looked away. He could not answer directly, and that upset him. He had determined to give his life to science, to uncompromising conclusion based on fact. Yet sometimes those conclusions ran head-on into some stupid but disconcertingly powerful feeling he had not even known he had. He found himself in the ludicrous position of defending a squat, beetle-browed creature already dead for fifty thousand years, a creature whose descendants, if any, would have tarred and feathered him for suggesting such ancestry.

"Anyway, we do not yet know if such correlations exist. We gather measurements. That is all. I have said to Stoneman we know nothing yet, can predict nothing. Still he gives us the money." Baum turned back to his worktable, picking up a pair of calipers hooked like great claws. He fitted them carefully around Homer's temples, adjusted a thumbscrew scale, and, pursing his lips, penciled an entry in a notebook. Then he looked up swiftly over his spectacles with an air of innocent inquiry. "Eh?"

"All right." Willard sighed. "I'll consider it."

[3]

ABOARD A STAGECOACH, Willard found, it was much harder to make entries in his journal. In fact, since leaving the train at Salt Lake, he had found everything more difficult. Some of the stations beyond Omaha had been closed because of rumors of hostile savages. Near Medicine Bow they had broken a wheel, and had to wait until the blacksmith was sober enough to repair it. The pass over the Divide was impassable due to a cloudburst. He had been advised to take another stage line—an altogether dustier, creakier, shabbier enterprise—north to Salmon City and from there over the mountains to Boise, where he could catch a freighter into Silver City.

As he penetrated further west, his clothing and his books seemed increasingly out of place. He had gotten a plain wool suit and sturdy brogans for traveling, and in his trunk aloft were canvas trousers, a blue spencer, heavy boots, and an overcoat. These were packed around his photographic materials, his dissecting kit, a revolver, an umbrella, and a plaster cast of Homer's reconstructed skull. But the stiffness of this new gear stood in sharp contrast to the sweat-stained and patched apparel of the drovers and miners who hung about the road stations. Holding a book, or entering notes in his journal, he was immediately conscious of stares and whispers. At the moment, in fact, an old man stinking of rum —one of the two passengers who had stumbled into the stage at Buffalo Gap—gazed awestruck at the pencil poised over the page. With an effort, Willard ignored him and, jabbing at the page between jolts, went on with his account.

He was larger than I expected, and much younger as well. Surely not over fifty, and with a boundless, ruddy vigor. In our conversation over brandy—excellent French spirits—he allayed some of my earlier fears, but aroused new ones quite as formidable. Thinks Baum's work will provide the evidence necessary to begin the reform of society—chiefly by means of selective breeding! Hopes to develop a strain of man built out of the physical dominance of the pithecine type, but subject to the moral superi-

ority of a pure caucasoid. Baum has tried to caution him against expecting too much, but Stoneman is obviously a headstrong, masterful sort. He is fascinated with the notion that legendary giants may in fact be an offshoot of the extinct race from the Neander, and is determined to have the Big Foot from the Owyhees as a contemporary specimen.

What bothers me about the man is his intensity of purpose, and a flicker of derangement in his eye when he speaks of the Negro, the Indian, or the Irish—especially the Unionists. The reputed strength and virility of these types is coupled, Stoneman thinks, with an inherent depravity. I was tempted to refute this ridiculous position, but Baum was signalling me furiously with his eyebrows to be still. At any rate I was treated to an elegant dinner and a cigar that cost at least fifty cents. And Stoneman assured me that he would send a personal note to old man Braddock to explain my absence.

It was not of course so easy to justify the matter to Lydia. She pouted prettily for an hour. By dint of fervent vows that I would finish this business in three months or less, and bring her back a nugget as big as her fist, and cover myself with glory as discoverer of homo idahoensis, I managed to earn a reprieve. God grant I can keep my word!

Everything here seems to exist on an enlarged scale. These plains are endless. When mountains finally rear skyward, they are like none I have ever seen: naked, rock spires ridged with snow, running from horizon to horizon, tearing holes in the clouds. The rivers boil down canyons— jagged fissures in the rock, often fantastically carved by erosion—like unleashed demons.

Distances between habitations have likewise stretched inordinately. Ask a driver how far we are from the next settlement. He rolls his "chaw" about and expectorates with great skill at the backsides of the wheel team and says "a piece." That could easily mean forty miles. Chicago, it appears, qualifies as a "fur piece."

I have been studying the newspaper articles Baum collected on Nampuh. Apparently, the plaster casts of his footprints are in Boise, where I hope to be within the week (barring storm, war parties, or lame horses!) I shall try to collect copies of these casts, and outfit my expedition into the Owyhee mountains, which according to my map are not more than two days hard travel from Boise. I am to locate the sheriff of the territory, one David Updyke, to assist me in forming a posse to pursue the dread Nampuh. Exciting indeed to picture . . .

"Hain't there."

Willard looked up, frowning. "I beg your pardon."

"Said hain't there." The man nodded at the notebook. "Updyke hain't."

Willard barely controlled his temper. The man had somehow deciphered his script, even upside down. "May I ask where the gentleman is, then?"

"Well, mister, the *gentleman*—is planted."

"Planted?" Willard looked startled. "What do you mean, 'planted'?" He snapped his notebook shut. "And how do you know of his whereabouts? And may I ask you to introduce yourself?"

"Weel . . ." The man started to scratch his head, but as this skewed a filthy, battered hat down over his eyes, he abandoned that location in favor of an armpit. "Best take all them questions back'ards. Name's Pee Wee Sullivan. Now, how I know his whereabouts is because he has took up residence permanent-like. Six feet under." He grinned. "That's what I mean."

Willard was dumbfounded. He had counted heavily on having the guidance of local authorities, and Stoneman's influence had produced from the Territorial Legislature a guarantee that Updyke would be readily available for such assistance. "Why?" he muttered, almost to himself.

"Why? Well, person starts to stinkin' if you don't plant 'em purty soon."

"No, I mean . . . I'm sorry Mr. . . . Sullivan, was it?"

"Pee Wee."

"Well, my good sir—"

"Lookahere, mister." Pee Wee fixed Willard with a stern look. "If you like bein' 'mister' that's fine by my lights. Or if you don't want no name that's fine too—lotta fellers don't. But I go by just plain Pee Wee. Everybody knows me thataway. Ketch my drift?"

"Yes. Yes, of course. Allow me to introduce myself. My name is Willard Starkwether Evans. Now—Pee Wee—may I ask if you know the circumstances of Mr. Updyke's death?"

Pee Wee was stricken by a wheezing cough that failed to disguise his mirth. "Circumstance? Circumstance was he tried to stretch a lariat with his neck, and he fell 'bout two foot short of the grass. Danced mighty hard to span it, but never made 'er."

Willard was pale and unsmiling, but the other man seemed not to notice. "You mean he was hanged?"

"Hung. Beggin' yer pardon, Willy. Hung, we says out here. Yessir, hung by the neck until goddamned good and dead. Hung fer bein' a murderin', thievin' sonofabitch. Ever see a man hung, Willy?"

"No."

"No? Mighty interestin'. Mighty. Bunch of miners and roustabouts and jackleg lawyers gits holt of a sidewinder and sends out the news they're fixin' a necktie party. And there ain't no news travels like that news. No sir, like berries through a bear. Next thing a fella knows they's ever prospector and shirttail drover, and all the other thieves which ain't been caught yet in the en-tire territory, waitin' around under the tree, drinkin' cheap whisky and swappin' yarns about all the other hangin's they seen, and layin' bets on whether or not this one will holler. Pretty soon here he comes, and for a while everybody shuts up, to see how he'll go. Usually one feller's got a rope and another's got a box, and if it's a big town like Virginia City or Denver then maybe they got a preacher to do a little prayin'.

"But if the man don't break down and howl, the boys start proddin' 'im. 'How far you gonna stretch, Jake?' Or, 'I bet any man here a dollar the sonofabitch'll shit his pants.' Or, 'What's yer girl gonna do tonight, Mr. Desperado?' And sometimes the feller'll holler back and tell 'em all to go to hell. I seen Bert Casey hung over in Orofino ten year back, and he cussed everybody there right up till the rope cut off his wind. But most times they git a mite pale around the gills. Some start to shakin' and you got to have two men holdin' 'em up. Some start cryin' and beggin' for a pen and paper to write their dear old mothers with. That always riles up the boys, and they dillydally around then and take their time, makin' fun. Then they stick the box under 'im and throw the noose over a stout limb and cinch 'er up pretty tight—you got to use a high box and a cured rope or he'll hit bottom on you. Then sometimes one of the old-timers gits the privilege of kickin' out the box, and he'll give kind of a little speech, like, 'This man was thief and murderer and judged guilty to be hung, by we his peers. Therefore, you sorry, worthless, cowardly sonofabitch—so long!' and boot the box away and down he goes.

"Once they drop, they all act alike. You got to tie down their arms and legs to keep 'em from thrashin' around, and slit their trouser leg, case they might be full of shit. Lot of times they curl up, back'ards, till you'd swear their heels would touch the back of their heads, and 'course their eyes bug out and they bite their tongues, and sometimes their peckers stick up, but after two, three minutes they just sag, like a old sack of spuds, and their heads nod over, like they was starin' at their toes. They look real peaceful then, turnin' round real slow, then turnin' back." Pee Wee stopped, staring into the space above Willard's head, lost in reverie.

"You're goin' to ask next, tell by your face, how come we hung the sheriff. Well, I dunno about back East, maybe it's different. Out here, all the old desperadoes that was throwed out of Californee want to be sheriff or senator or the like. They git an edge on the young fellas thataway. They catch a few of 'em fer show and then they got the claim to theirselfs. Politicians here is crookeder'n a dog's hind leg. But it's just like any other kind of outlawin'. Git caught and you swing. If'n you don't git caught, or you can lie like sixty, you maybe git to be governor."

"I see." Willard's voice was subdued. He managed a smile. "Things in the East are rather different. We try to avoid the problem by electing men of adequate means, who would scorn to raid the treasury."

Pee Wee cocked his head. "Don't yer rich fellers fall to stealin' from each other?"

Willard's smile broadened. "It has happened. And such theft may lead to vying for public office. Perhaps things are somewhat the same."

"Truth, ain't it?" Pee Wee wheezed in delight at this rediscovery of a principle he held to be universal. "So you aim to git a posse, do ye? To chase ol' Big Foot? How come a gentleman like you to be lookin' for that murderin' Siwash?"

Briefly, in simplified language, Willard explained his mission.

"Lordy. Pale-ee-tent-ology!" Pee Wee was clearly impressed. "Well, you're dealin' with an ape all right, I tell you that. Them newspapers don't tell the half. He ain't like your reg'lar outlaw; he don't do it fer money on account of he ain't got nowhere to spend it hisseff. Man seven feet tall comes to town, everybody *knows*. Be dead 'fore he got to the door of the first saloon. But anyway he don't do it fer liquor neither, like a reg'lar half-breed. You know he was a breed? Folks say so. He just does it for plain damn meanness. And all them Shoshonis and Bannocks and Paiutes that was run out by their own people, they hang around him just for devilment. It ain't no tribe, like the paper says. It ain't nothin' but a bunch of butchers." Jerking the window curtain aside, Pee Wee spat angrily into the cloud of brown dust rolling past. "You got yerself a tall order, Willy, to run down them dogs."

Willard was sobered. "I had hoped to get help from Updyke. But if the officers of the law aren't dependable . . ." He paused, and looked inquiringly at Pee Wee.

"My advice, don't trust nobody." Pee Wee removed his hat; his few strands of hair were the color of old planks silvered by weather. "How-somever, you are shore in need of somebody with a little savvy about this yere country. You got to hire packers and git yerseff a camp set up and all. I take it you got the jack to handle that?"

"Jack?" Willard frowned. "Jack who?"

Pee Wee laughed politely. "Money, Willy. U.S. notes, or dust?"

"Oh." Willard flushed. "It seems I need a translator. Yes, I have money for the task."

"Ain't carryin' it with you, are ye?"

"No. That didn't seem wise."

"Sure as shitfire ain't, not on this yere route. Plummer used to hold up damn near ever stage that went through. Ain't quite so bad now, but it ain't no Sunday School, neither. Yessir, you do need a little helper. Somebody with some savvy 'bout the Owyhee country, like where the springs is, which trails is safe, pickin' up cheap feed in Gilvray's store in DeLamar, and the like." After a moment or two he picked up his hat, regretfully, like a man departing from a funeral. "Otherwise, Willy, ye ain't got a Chinaman's chance of ketchin' that big ape."

Willard pretended to speculate, but could not repress a smile. "I don't suppose a person of *your* wide experience would be interested in such a position?"

"We-e-ll, as a matter of fact, you happen to ketch me when I ain't engaged, though I was jest last month workin' for Sam Johnson's drayin' crew on the new road to Idaho City. Howsomever, at the moment I ain't engaged. What might you be thinkin' of, Willy, as it comes to pay for this job?"

Willard shook his head. "I really cannot say. I don't even know what the job is, you see. At the moment, it appears, just your common sense could save me a good deal of grief. A manservant in Boston might properly expect his keep and perhaps five dollars a week."

Pee Wee laughed. "You ain't had much experience in minin' camps, I guess. Five dollars would buy ye just about as many eggs."

"Perhaps if you told me what your previous employer paid?"

"Board and two dollars and four bits a day."

"Shall we say two dollars a day and meals and lodging?"

"Done." Pee Wee beamed. "You ain't easy to skin, Willy. You got yerseff a pardner." He stuck out his hand. Willard took it, and then, even as they sealed the compact, there was a tremendous jolt of the whole coach. Above the twang of bursting rawhide, the splinter of wood panels, and a terrible squealing of horses, Willard heard the sharp, distinct explosion of gunshots.

[4]

THE THREE OF THEM sat stiffly in the drawing room while Skillings snipped twine from the package. Inside the cloth bag was a paper wrapping, and inside that a box of thin wooden slats. Here Skillings stopped and ventured a look of inquiry at Professor Braddock, who moved his head a fraction of an inch. Skillings stepped back.

"That will be all, Skillings. Take the wrappings with you when you go."

When the door had closed softly, Professor Braddock remained silent for a moment, as if concentrating his strength. He was a tall, narrow man with heavy brows and a severe mouth. When he spoke again his voice was measured, the tone of the practiced lecturer. "Would you be so kind as to unpack the contents, Dieter?"

Baum approached the box reverently, removed its top, and took out a leather pencil case.

Lydia Braddock, sitting on the edge of an armchair, took a sharp breath; her small, firm bosom rose suddenly. Under a great mass of black curls, her oval face was a pure blank of pain.

Her father turned to her, solicitous.

"My dear, perhaps you should withdraw, until Dieter and I . . ."

"No, I want to know everything."

Baum had paused during this exchange, but at another nod from Braddock he gingerly removed the remaining contents of the box. There were, besides the pencil case, a large manila envelope with an official seal, a broken shaving mug, some badly twisted photographic plates, one stained and cracked shoe (which caused Lydia to turn away and press a handkerchief to her mouth), and a clothbound notebook.

"His journal," said Baum. He held the notebook awkwardly in his small, plump hands. There was a long silence. "In such matters, I know not to do what. I . . ."

"His mother is confined, and not in possession of her faculties," Braddock said with magisterial incisiveness, "and his sister has not been located. I believe he has no other living relatives. You were his closest professional associate. Lydia was his intended, and I, therefore, his prospective father-in-law. It seems to me no infringement upon his memory for those nearest him to peruse his last words." Braddock paused and turned to Lydia, who lowered her eyes and spoke softly.

"He would want it so."

Braddock settled back in his chair and sighed. "I suppose we had best begin with the letters."

Baum put down the notebook and took up the manila envelope. He broke the seal, removed two letters, and began to read the first.

My Dear Sirs:

As commanding officer of this post, I am under the obligation to perform the regrettable duty of forwarding to you the personal effects of one Willard S. Evans, along with a brief account of the tragic circumstances of his disappearance and, we may assume, demise.

I must speak first of the unfortunate incidents which led us to issue a warrant for Mr. Evans' arrest—

"What?" Braddock straightened in his chair.

"Beg pardon," Baum murmured, staring at the letter as he moved it various distances from his spectacles. "But yes . . . 'arrest.' Ah! Wait . . .

The warrant has of course been withdrawn, as the grounds for it were clearly a case of mistaken identity, but we profoundly regret this misunderstanding, as it seems to be among the events which precipitated the young man toward his doom.

Baum stopped, perplexed between melancholy and relief, and blew his nose in a rumpled kerchief drawn from his pocket. "You see? A mistake."

"Go on," Braddock urged, still frowning.

On May 25 I received a report of stolen stock from four ranchers who had tracked the thieves from the Wind River range all the way to the lower Snake. At Thousand Springs, two men mounted on stolen horses had apparently separated from the others and were making their way into our district. We kept a watch on livery stables in the area and on May 29 located the horses. They had been left by a "Mr. Evans" and his companion. No one imagined that this "Mr. Evans" could be the distinguished professor, of whose impending expedition we had been apprised some weeks earlier.

Officers were dispatched to apprehend the criminals (as we yet believed them to be). There was an altercation, and a deputy was shot and wounded. Evans and his companions—an elderly man and also a young woman—

"So," Professor Braddock said, "he had not the fiber to withstand the godless West." He turned slightly toward his daughter, without looking at her. "I think you had best retire and leave this business to Dieter and myself."

Lydia remained seated, ramrod straight. Her voice was barely above a whisper. "Papa, I should prefer to hear."

After a moment the professor spoke again in an even, dry voice. "Proceed then. And leave nothing out."

Baum flushed, adjusted his spectacles, and resumed reading.

. . . a . . . a young woman, took flight, and we subsequently learned that they had hired Frank Billings, a local freighter of no good repute, to transport them and their baggage to Silver City. At Lyons Camp, however, they encountered bad weather, and Evans changed his mind. He sent his companions back to Boise while he set out, accompanied only by Billings and the pack string, apparently to locate by himself the notorious Indian outlaw Nampuh. He was clearly distraught. Foster, the freight agent at Lyons Camp, attempted by every means to dissuade him from so dangerous an enterprise, but Evans persisted, talking wildly of the posse he would form, the reward for the giant outlaw, and the advancement of science.

On June 1 Lieutenant Murdoch, in command of Troop F, was sent to investigate a report of robbery and murder. A badly mutilated body and two dead mules were recovered from Succor Creek canyon, as well as a few items discarded as worthless by the assassins. Foster identified the corpse as that of the packer Billings, and the savagery of the deed left no doubt that it was more of Nampuh's terrible mischief. Some of Professor Evans' equipment was salvaged, but there was no sign of his body.

On June 4 a man calling himself Harry Sullivan and the young woman, who identified herself as Mrs. Elizabeth Evans, the young man's bride—

Professor Braddock brought his fist down on the arm of his chair with an impact that rattled small objects on the mantelpiece. "I will not have you subjected to this, Lydia! The man was an out-and-out—"

"Father!" Lydia rose from her seat. "Whatever he has done—and you forget what *he* has been subjected to—I deserve to know. I was his—"

"Don't speak of it!" Braddock half rose from his chair. "It was a colossal mistake, I knew from the outset. That scoundrel—"

Baum cleared his throat loudly and extensively, and Lydia shot him a grateful glance.

"Roland," the old professor went on, "this is perhaps but a fairytale story made up by this woman. No evidence, my good man, no evidence yet!"

"Or perhaps he was tricked somehow, Papa. Willard is . . . you know how he is. He . . ." Her voice wavered and she put a hand over her eyes, then turned with a sharp rustle of linen and went back to her chair. "Anyway, we cannot even be sure he is not alive. It appears they have not recovered . . . anything."

"You forgive the scoundrel?" Professor Braddock's tone was cold, remote. "Then I am troubled for your own moral soul."

"Let us go onward," Baum interjected, "and hear the evidence, eh?" He shook the paper and ran a finger along a line to find his place.

" '. . . who is a woman of great beauty' . . . uh . . . mmm . . . charm and so forth . . . 'claims to have known Evans in Boston, though they were married only two days before his disappearance.' "

"Here?" Lydia whispered. "In Boston?"

"I think that is enough," Braddock said. "And more than enough."

"Wait!" Baum looked wildly about him, as if other, invisible listeners crouched in the gathering shadows of the room.

However, it is known that this woman arrived in Boise a scant two weeks ago in the company of an itinerant "doctor" of phrenology and theosophy, a palm-reader and magician, named Miller, who, she said (when I pressed the inquiry), was her brother . . .

"Preposterous!" Braddock exploded.

"Phrenologist?" Baum appeared to demand an answer from the paper in his hand. "Willard, with a *quack?*"

"A small enough matter," Braddock said, "for a horse thief and philanderer."

"Who can this possibly be?" Baum looked stricken.

"Wait!" Lydia stood up abruptly and hurried to a small, cherry-wood secretary beside the fireplace. "*I* know!" While the two men exchanged a look of wonder, she opened a drawer with a little brass key and removed a bundle of envelopes and note paper. From these she plucked a white card, which she handed to her father. "That Saturday we had planned to go boating, last spring—the very day you proposed this expedition, Dieter—Willard sent me this. Look on the back."

Professor Braddock read the card rapidly and handed it to Baum.

"Electrophrenology!" the old professor roared. "Meddling quacks! It is incredible!"

Professor Braddock snorted. "Not in the least."

"But could it have possibly been the same man he met in this Boise?" Lydia frowned. "What was the name?"

". . . Miller . . . Müller! Great God! Could it be . . . ?" Baum collapsed into his chair and the card fluttered from his hand to the floor.

"Send for some water!" Lydia hurried again to the desk and returned with a small amber bottle. She uncorked it under Baum's nose and he reared back, sneezing.

" 's brennt die Schnauze! Genug! I am all right!"

Skillings had answered the bell and now swiftly returned with a pitcher of ice water, to which Lydia added a few drops of the liquid in the amber bottle. Baum drank a few swallows and seemed restored. He sat staring at the card, alternately nodding and shaking his head.

"Could it be? They could not know! How?"

"What is the matter with you, Dieter?" Professor Braddock was impatient. "Know what?"

"It is the name—Miller, perhaps changed from Müller. In my field of study, Roland, you would know it immediately. We were students together at Bonn, and rivals later, and finally political enemies . . ."

"I don't see what that has to do with this electrofabulist or whatever he is."

"Müller had a son—Wolfgang, I believe—who took up medicine and had at first a brilliant career, and then went into the dogs. He was using the mad theories of Mesmer to debauch respectable women, and so embarrassed the family was that they granted him some money in exchange for him coming away here to America."

"And changed his name to Miller!" Lydia exclaimed.

"It is often done. But that is not all, I fear." Baum shifted in his chair.

"What do you mean?" Professor Braddock spoke sharply.

"Of course you know of my love for Willard. He has become more than my student, my right hand. I think about him as my . . . as my son." Baum's voice dropped to a barely audible murmur. "*And* as my heir. You see, Roland, like you I have private incomes, the interest from my small fortune. Small, but a fortune, if undivided—and I have no more family. Müller and his kind, the believers in savagery—they took care of that!" Baum paused, swallowed, and then continued. "I put most of this money into a legacy for Willard, to come to him . . . upon his marriage." The old professor cradled his head in his hands and moaned. "Would God I had better brains!"

"There, there, Dieter." Lydia patted his shoulder. "You could not foresee this."

"I was afraid that if he knew, he would not be in his work so dedicated. He is a young man so bright, but also . . . vulnerable. And you, Roland, would forbid marriage until his career was established. I wanted him to make great discoveries, not be like Müller's boy, a none-too-well."

"Ne'er-do-well," Braddock corrected.

"But if this Miller is Wolfgang Müller," said Lydia, "I don't . . . Ah! Yes! I do too." She smiled, as if at the sudden unhinging of a lock-puzzle. "They found out somehow. They followed him with some scheme to get his money. Perhaps kidnap him." She turned from the two men and spoke as if to herself. "Or perhaps degrade and blackmail him."

"It is possible, yes? It seems otherwise too much coincidence. Müller must have known my name."

"Even if he knew Willard was your student, how could he discover what none of us knew, that he was also your heir?" Professor Braddock frowned. "Unless you told *someone?*"

Baum blinked and a moment later swallowed audibly. "Stoneman," he whispered. "I remember now, someone in his office, hair red a little— auburn is this, no?—a woman."

"Striking?" Lydia spoke between clenched teeth.

"I . . . I think. Yet vulgar, you see, a—"

"Whore." Professor Braddock glared at them. "I do not beg your pardon, Lydia. You insisted on staying. Your young man was taken in by a whore. Dieter, why, for the love of heaven, did you tell anyone?"

"But you see, *I* paid for the expedition! I wished to forward Willard's career, but without betraying my fortune. I heard of Mr. Stoneman's strange hobbies, I contacted him and arranged all to appear as a millionaire's whims, no more. Yet of course I had to explain to him this devious approach."

"So you told him of the legacy?"

"No, not at first." Baum's brow furrowed mightily. "I said only that I wish to assist this young man, to advance his prospects . . . then, yes, I go back and I tell about the estate that is coming when he marries." He threw up his hands and his head drooped in despair, his white beard nestling into his shirt front.

"So we must suppose," said Lydia, "that this woman, this Elizabeth, wormed her way into Stoneman's affairs and learned of Dieter's fortune and its disposition, so as to relay the information to Müller."

"So it must be. Perhaps Müller even came here to cheat an old man, to regain his father's favor, and saw how to do it through this temptress. My family—gone! Now Willard too . . . I am alone in this terrible country!" Baum was racked by a throttled sob.

"You are not alone, Dieter!" Lydia said, her eyes shining.

"My daughter speaks for both of us," Braddock added, a little uneasily. "But I have one further question. What did you give Stoneman in exchange for this favor?"

"You will think me a foolish old man, but I was obliged. I promised Stoneman two things. The money—the legacy—I agreed to put it in the form of stocks in a railroad he controls. I forget which."

"*Railroad!* Good God, Dieter!" Professor Braddock exclaimed in exasperation. "You should have confided in me."

"And the second promise?" Lydia leaned forward intently.

"I promised him"—with a supreme effort Baum met her gaze—"the head of a giant!"

She recoiled, and for long moments no one spoke.

"And Willard was . . ." Her whisper trailed away in the darkness.

"Yes."

She curled slowly at the waist, her hands over her face, and the others heard the small, muffled sound of her sobs.

"That is enough." Braddock rose and placed a hand on her shoulder. "Leave the rest of it."

"The letter says no more," Baum muttered, "but there is this other letter from the Sullivan fellow and of course the journal—"

"I shall have it!" Lydia cried out abruptly, tearing her hands from her eyes. "Everything!"

"Enough!" Professor Braddock's voice was sharp as a nail. "I shall have our physician here tomorrow, and you are to rest—"

"No! Papa, please . . ." She twisted away from his hand and ran to the table, seizing the letters and the small notebook. She clutched them to her breast and backed toward the door, her face dark but for two glistening ribbons of tears.

"After such corruption you will need strong physic, my dear—to rid yourself of any memory of that damned pup! Burn the notebook, Lydia!

Destroy it!" Braddock's tall figure was silhouetted against the gray evening sky squared in by the window, his arm extended to receive the notebook. His daughter reached for the door latch with trembling fingers.

"Papa . . . please, no, I don't want medicine. I want . . ." The rapid, shallow sobs overcame her; she jerked open the door and fled from the room, bent and hobbled in the sad parody grief makes of old age.

[5]

IN HER ROOM Lydia wept steadily for the greater part of an hour, until she heard a tread on the staircase. Then she choked back her tears and mastered her voice sufficiently to inform her mother, through the heavy oak door, that she was indisposed and would not take supper, only a pot of tea. After a series of plaintive offers of additional nourishment or comfort, her mother grew pettish and retired with an angry thumping of heels, and Lydia turned to light a small oil lamp at her writing desk.

The glass shade adjusted and wick turned up, she unfolded the second of the letters. It was written on cheap foolscap, with many ink-blotches and scratched-out words, and the characters were crude, like those made by schoolchildren. A notch in her usually smooth brow, Lydia began the painstaking work of deciphering the narrative before her:

Too Willys Foks,

I am sur Sory to be the Bearur of Bad Newes, and am hopin You do not mind a Stranger takin the Libarty of writin to You to ecspress his Sorow and All, so havin in Mind to tel the Storey of the final Howrs of yor Beluvud.

I am sory about how I rite, having very Litle Edgucashun, but I am 67 yers old and Too old to lern.

Withowt mor Malarky then here is the Story. I clum on the Stage at Laramie heded for Pokytello wher I was hopin to git on as Bulwhaker or els in the Wagon Yard, as I am a Fare Smith. Mister Evans was a Pasenjer on this Stage, and as fin a Jent as I hav seen comin down the Pike, tho a little Stiff.

After a Spel we got toogethur on a Deel. I was hird as Gide and Packer and allround Rowstobowt for Mr. Evans Outfit. We was shakin hands on it when Hoopseedazy! Al Billy Blu Hell bustid loos. We had Harnis and

*Hors raped round our Neks and that Stage was no mor than a Heep of
Kintlin. I got fowld in the Tugline and Willy was throwd under an got
kiked by a Hors. A Hors kiks you, you dont kno anithin for quit a Spel.
Ither yor branes are noked out or you are luky.*

*This was the cas with Willy. For 3 days he dont rekogniz me. He cood
walk and talk wel as ever, but never had no Idee how he come to be with a
Herd of Horsis. How com was we round a corner and run plum Smak into
a big Herd bein run by Art Cole and his Boys overland to the Humboldt,
and the Gard lost his Hed and cut loos on the riders. They shot bak naturl
enuf, a Person cood hardli do no Les, and next Thing we know our Driver
and Gard is Ded as Stons, and Arts Boys is in a fix. They mite hav finishd
there Job an put Willy and Me under the Sod, but I knowd Art from sum
Biznes Afears of sum Yers past, so insted they dicided to hawl us along,
sins they didnt Trust to tern us loos. Then we was in a Fix, becaws to al
Intens and Purpuses we was herdn 40 hed of Stoln Stock with a Passl of
Killrs.*

*Wel after sum mity clos Shavs we did exskap and git to Boise and I was
nevr mor Glad to see a White Man and wet my Whisl, I can tel You that.
Willy got a Leter of Credet at the Post Ofis which he took to a Bank and
we had Plenty of Jak. I am not Prowd of the next 3 days and I imajin
Willy aint niether, but we had cum thru the Vally of Deth and cood be
forgiv for Bustin loos a litle bit.*

*Lik lots of Fellrs when they bang Heds with Whisky the first time
Willy tride to drink it al up at onct. Then we run into a Fellr he knowd
and his ladyfrend. This Fellr was a Sliker, and the Lady was a Looker. She
took a Shine to Willy, and He plum cum apart at the Seems. She fed him
a Bushel of Bull Hocky, about how this Sliker Fellr kep her by Fors and
whopped her. Next thing I knowd, she talkt him into gittin the Judge and
hitchn the 2 of em.*

*The next Mornin Willy was jumpy as a Stud in Flytime and talkt
Foolish as I evr herd a Man talk. We was sposd to git a Packer to Silver
City, an Plenty of Suplise, so I went on the Prowl and run into Ethan
Mills who tolt me the Sheruf was lookin for us.*

*I lit out to find Willy, a Wantid Man now. A Mite to late. A Depity
Sheruf found him an the Lady whos name was Elizabith, and tride to
arest her first and Dang if Willy dint paist the depity in the Eye and nok
him Flat, and then the Depity who most likly workt up his Corage at the
Saloon al mornin tride to draw his Colt and shot hisself in the Foot. Wel
ther was a Fix. I found em at the Hotel and we throwd Everthin in our
Mantees an hird Frank Billings who was al we cood git to hawl us to*

Silver. Then when we got to Lyons Camp Willy went Loco an sent
Elizabith and Me bak to Boise on account of cold Wether and run off
with Frank, fird up about Big Foot an his Mezurments and Redempshun.
It was to Bad becaws He was a Dam Fin Fellr and I wisht I hadnt set bak
an let him go. Also I wisht I had see that Depity go Tale ovr Tincup.

Ever remanin Yer respecfil Servint,
Harry Sullivan, esk.

Lydia was unnaturally pale and the letter between her fingers shook
from the heavy blows of her heart, but she scarcely paused before throwing aside the foolscap and opening Willard's notebook. She glanced over
the first several pages, full of anecdotes of the railroad journey and theo-
retical speculations on certain fossils, until she reached the entries that
corresponded with the events described in the two letters. These were
made in a hurried, uneven hand, and with a pang Lydia noted small
smudges—traces of her beloved's own touch—on the creased pages.

May 22—
I reread the preceding and laugh like a madman! How blandly I as-
sumed I would be in Boise within the week, would have brave peace
officers to assist my investigation, would ride after our specimen as a
gentleman rides to hounds! And where am I, in fact? One of a pack of
cutthroats skulking through the "Badlands" (Western nomenclature is
charmingly direct) with a herd of stolen horses!
On the route here I met a meddling old rascal who, I now suspect, was
an associate of this disreputable pack of "rustlers." I have ever been gull-
ible, and was charmed into engaging this personage—vulgarly known as
Pee Wee—as manservant and general factotum. Hardly was the compact
made before our coach was ambushed and wrecked, and I was stunned
into a light coma by a blow to my medullar scarp. I and my new employee
have since been, at least by association, cohorts of this nefarious crew.
Cole, the leader of this band, is a squat, foul-mouthed creature with a
rather small, bullet head. His neck is so thick the occiput scarcely projects
at all, and his brow, though low, is not prominent. Some of the others are
long-headed—one has the high, clear brow of a great scholar or states-
man. Except for their vicious oaths and an ugly scar on one man—blade
or bullet surely—you might not distinguish them from any ordinary citi-
zen. Of course they are yet members of the White Race; however de-
bauched, they do not betray, as would the Negro or Aborigine, a clear link
between flattened skull, low coronal ridge, and an inborn childishness and
sensuality.

May 23—

The young man with the high forehead has at least born out our preju-
dice. While the others were out as sentinels or with the herd, he warned us
privately that we had best slip away. Apparently my language and demeanor has offended or rendered suspicious Master Cole. We are taking
his advice. Pee Wee has collected a small sack of dried apples and jerky,
even as I scribble these lines. We shall set out on the hundred-odd mile
journey to Boise, through country infested with savages. God grant us
good fortune!

May 25—

Twice we had to cross the river, at great risk of life, to avoid scouting
parties. Pee Wee, scalawag that he is, has nevertheless great skill in finding paths and springs and so on. We are now eating a root he calls camas
—very starchy and bland.

May 26—

I cannot think from hunger. The last of our dried fruit is gone and there
is no more camas. We are on sage plains that shimmer like water in the
heat. We travel now only at dawn and dusk.

May 27—

Same. I do not care what happens with the experiments or if I ever.

May 28—

Tonight we struck the Boise River, and both of us cried like babies.
One more day.

June 1—

Everything is asunder! My God, my God! What have I become? My
mind is such a ghastly upheaval I no longer trust even what I say here to
myself! I have betrayed everything—everything sacred to me! My profession, my family, my beloved Lydia—Yet I intended to save a poor soul—
Bewitching, too—Damn! I must get down here some record of what I have
undergone—So—

We plunged into the roiling mudhole of this boom city with tears still
on our faces. As dirty and starved and sunbaked as we were, we looked
better than half the poor devils here. It is sheer bedlam. Wagons are
jammed end-to-end across town, axle-deep in the mud, and more arrive

each day. Some of the miners returning from Idaho City are so gaunt they look like walking cadavers; others have struck it rich and are transformed overnight into ridiculous parodies of New York dandies. A man has built a mansion on Warm Springs Avenue, with cut glass windows and cupolas edged in gold leaf. A few steps away, in hovels made of crates and feed sacks, the Chinamen sit, stupefied with opium. There is no standard here but raw gold, no thought unconnected to gold, nothing that cannot be bought for gold. In this turmoil, half delirious with relief at having survived, I became unbalanced.

Probably my will had been undermined by the long, hard journey. Nor did Pee Wee's example help. Perhaps, also, I was not yet recovered from the blow from the horse's hoof. I am not used to whiskey and— Oh my God, what is the use of explanations? Nothing—Nothing!—of honor remains to me, except the duty of finding the cursed Shoshoni giant who has led me on this wicked way. I shall have the reward and send the specimen to Baum—or die in the attempt! Tomorrow I begin the search—I shall send Elizabeth back with Pee Wee to await word of my redemption—or my wretched end!

My wife! All thoughts scatter again on that reef! It happened so quickly I cannot find the hidden spring or gear that hurled me over this tremendous and terrible precipice. I remember the gambling-hall where I reeled, howling in the wild joy of survival, and finding myself suddenly face-to-face with her, looking deeply into those peculiar sea-green eyes, amazed— nay, confounded utterly—to recognize the woman I had once inadvertently held in my arms in Brattle Square . . .

Lydia's body was rigid now, the notebook steady as a rock between her hands. Without breath enough to utter even a whisper, her lips nevertheless moved to form the word silently: *inadvertently.*

. . . on that day in April when, I now realize, my entire life balanced on a fulcrum point. She was in the company of that leering charlatan, the phrenologist, a man she called Wolf—I saw in a flash how he had used her then as a kind of bait—but on some pretext he abandoned us, and then I remember only her hand in mine and her voice, so stricken with suffering—though I can recall little of the tale except an impression of horror and disgust at her panderer's excesses. A voice so full of secret yearning for salvation, a yearning that called forth vibrations in all my being. The rest has the peculiar quality of a play, or nightmare, where actors are fated to pitch through their parts—Wolf slinking from my fists, the champagne, the room where I fell into a kind of swoon and awoke in

the harsh light of morning, with her beside me, her soft, white, ample bosom against my heart where already an awful dread stirred amid the dregs of desire—oh Hell!——

The entry broke off with a slash of ink, a gesture of haste or despair. Lydia shut the notebook carefully and stared for a moment at its cover, at Willard's neatly printed name. Just then a board in the hallway creaked and there was a gentle tap at her door.

"Tea, ma'am," Skillings called hopefully.

She rose and admitted him, nodding at the writing desk. He deposited the tray and fussed for a moment over the napkin and spoon.

"Will there—"

"No, thank you, Skillings." Acknowledging his look of sympathy, she closed the door behind him and returned to the desk. Attempting to pour the steaming tea, she saw on her dresser across the room the framed photograph Willard had taken of himself with his new portable camera a year ago. He was smiling broadly, the panama hat held over his chest nonchalantly. He looked affectionate, carefree, without guile.

The spout had strayed and she saw that she had spilled hot tea on the corner of the notebook. She bit her lip hard, her breath catching, and then suddenly, swinging it by the handle that imitated a twisting vine, she hurled the delicate bone-china pot at the photograph. It smashed the glass front and tumbled the frame to the floor, and the pot exploded in a shower of white fragments. For a long moment she stared at the scatter of debris on the floor. Then she dropped to her knees and picked up the dripping picture. Holding it to her breast, she rocked back and forth as the image of the man she loved began to swell and discolor.

[6]

WHEN WILLARD AWOKE he knew he was freezing, and the fact filled him with petty irritation. It was June, and one did not freeze in June; yet, in the gray predawn light he saw broken fangs of rock above a collar of snow on the horizon. He closed his eyes again, trying to withdraw into sleep as into a cave. For an instant he teetered on the brink of oblivion, and then the wind cut at his face. His limbs underwent a feeble convulsion and he felt something clutching his foot. He groaned and sat up.

A rope was knotted to his ankle, the other end tied to an iron stake driven into the ground. A second rope ran from the stake to a still form a few feet away. He recognized the freighter's plaid coat, now dark and stiff with blood. Behind the two of them, on the banks of a small ice-rimmed creek, was a cluster of makeshift huts made of light poles bent hooplike and covered with deer hides, old blankets, and strips of canvas. Between and around these shelters were packsaddles, pots and pans, and trunks broken open. A foot protruded from the doorway of one hut.

Willard groaned again and, threshing his limbs like a turtle, managed to inch toward one of these trunks. The rope was long enough to allow him to retrieve a small heap of clothes, among which were his two pair of woolen underwear. He wrapped the garments clumsily around his body and huddled into them. The wind, rising again, struck tears from his eyes.

It grew lighter. The sagebrush slopes began to emerge from shadow in tones of pale green and yellow. The jagged tips of mountains reddened. A few clouds in the west showed suddenly white. All at once Willard saw that one boulder on a low bluff above the creek was not a boulder at all, but a man. He was perfectly immobile, wrapped in a buffalo robe, a rifle across his knees. But Willard knew the sentinel was awake, had heard his groans and seen him crawl to the heap of clothing.

Someone stirred inside one of the huts, and in a few moments a man crawled out. He stood, blinked, yawned, and began to rummage through the gear and refuse strewn about the campsite. He came up with a bottle and tipped it straight up to empty the few swallows left, then hurled it across the creek to smash on the rocks. He glanced toward the other man on the bluff, and they exchanged gestures. He was Indian, but except for braids, a feather stuck in the crown of his hat, and ragged moccasins, his appearance was no different from that of the prospectors and freighters Willard had seen. He wore miner's iron-pants with leather patches, a homespun shirt, and a filthy vest with three gold watch-chains adorning the front. After staring at Willard opaquely for a few seconds, he walked to the still form of the freighter and kicked him in the legs. When the freighter did not move, the Indian kicked him in the back, and was rewarded with a low moan.

Another Indian, this one in buckskins and without hat, emerged from a tipi, and after a fruitless search—for another bottle, Willard guessed—began to drag the twisted, gray skeletons of sagebrush into a heap. In a few moments yellow fire licked high and more men crawled out into the warmth, muttering now in harsh, unfamiliar syllables. They made coffee in a blackened stewpot, and began frying some kind of cakes in a skillet. Willard saw that the two doing the cooking both wore skirts, which were hiked up and stuffed in their cartridge belts, exposing heavy boots and a stretch of bare leg. He also noticed that at least two of the band were white, or very nearly so. One of these, a short, burly man with a beard, finally approached him, bearing a cup of steaming coffee, and squatted in front of him. He smiled, revealing large, even white teeth.

"Allo," he said. "You man? *Hombre?* You sheet? *De la merde?*" He sipped very slowly, smacking his lips. With great effort Willard managed to keep his gaze from drifting after the cup. The man watched him, smiled again, and held out the cup. Willard made no move.

"*Vas-y,*" the man said. His voice was gentle. "Eez all, my fr'en."

Willard's fingers twitched, and he was about to raise his hand to accept the offering, when there was a commotion around the fire. Two of the Indians had stepped before one of the tents and begun to shout something. Listening closely, Willard realized it was a kind of chant, accompanied by an occasional stamp of the foot. The sun had just reached the valley, and the band of men, turned to bright gold, cast immensely long shadows on the plain. As the flap over the entrance stirred, the two singers turned away toward the east.

The shape that emerged was large and cumbrous, like a plough horse, until the man stood erect. Then it was as if the whole scene shrank before Willard's eyes. The men standing about the campfire were suddenly boys; even the snag-toothed mountain beyond seemed smaller. The tips of the three eagle feathers in Nampuh's hair were nine feet from the ground, and his back was much wider than an ordinary door. He was deep-chested, long-armed, with unusually large hands and feet. When he grasped the bottle one of the men reverently handed him, it disappeared in his grip; he seemed to be drinking from his clenched fist.

"*N' regarde pas.*"

Willard obeyed the soft command and stared at the ground. He heard the Frenchman get up, and a second later he knew Nampuh had looked his way. He felt the giant's glance as a kind of heat, as if the door to a furnace had been thrown open. When he finally looked up, Nampuh was crouched by the fire stuffing the fried cakes in his mouth, grunting orders between swallows. Some of the men left at a trot down the creek. They returned in a few minutes on horseback, driving a herd of ponies before them. Others spread out a blanket and piled on it what had been stripped from their victims the day before: rings, watches, money, clothing, some hand mirrors and razors, and his battered trunk of photographic gear.

Then a series of similar vociferous arguments broke out. A man would seize an item, gesture with it, make a speech, and put it beside him or between his legs. Another man would object, shaking his head and fist. At a word from Nampuh the first man might restore the item to the pile and then the whole process would repeat itself. At one point two Indians, one stocky and very dark, the other tall, lighter-skinned, and hawk-nosed, sprang back from the blanket and drew knives. The taller one held also a razor with a silver-inlayed handle. Nampuh spoke once and held out his hand. The two hesitated, then sheathed their blades sullenly, and the tall one dropped the razor into the huge, outstretched palm. Without pausing, Nampuh tossed the razor into the fire and resumed his eating, whole cakes disappearing into his mouth at once. The bargaining went on, but at a more subdued and decorous pace. In the end, nothing was left on the blanket but the case containing his photographic equipment. This was shoved aside, as no one seemed to want it.

One of the Indians said something that brought a silence, which was interrupted only by the roaring of the fire and the whickering and squealing of horses. All at once the whole group—Willard had counted twenty-three—turned to look at him. After an intense stare that nearly stopped his heart, they looked again at the fire. Nampuh said something, and a small, wiry man, his leggings black with grease, rose and moved toward the captives. An argument broke out behind him. Two other Indians, one wearing a heavy necklace of claws and teeth, seemed to appeal to Nampuh. He listened, then stopped the man moving toward Willard with a word. After some discussion, the Indian with the necklace and his companion dragged one of the trunks to the fireside and pointed within, their heads averted. Nampuh peered into the trunk, fascinated. Again he glanced up at Willard, and the sensation of a sudden, hot wind recurred. Others rose and walked over to look inside the trunk. A murmur arose, perhaps of awe, perhaps of anger. Nampuh spoke, and the Frenchman got up and walked toward Willard.

"Eh, my fr'en, they no *sabe*. How you geet theez head?"

"It is the head of a man of long ago. Our ancestors." He took a deep breath. "Nampuh's ancestors."

The Frenchman flashed his wide, mirthless grin. "Sheet. You lie. Say dat, he keel you."

Willard lay back down and looked up at the sky. "He will kill me anyway."

He heard the Frenchman laugh and walk away. When the chorus of angry voices broke out, Willard readied himself for death, perhaps preceded by torture. But there was a note of doubt in the uproar. The discussion went on; it seemed interminable. At first he could understand none of it. Then, with a shock, he realized that Nampuh sometimes spoke English words to the Frenchman and one of the other half-breeds. In fact the language used by the whole band seemed at times to be a pidgin, scraps of French, English, and Spanish sprinkled through a guttural aboriginal tongue.

Something was resolved, for he heard sounds of packing and the horses began to stamp. The chill was gone from the air, and the sun was even hot on his brow. Footsteps approached, and in a moment he was jerked to his feet. The Frenchman gripped his arm while another man untied his leg.

"They theenk you air medicine man. *Muy malo.* Nampuh keel you but Shoshoni say bad luck. So you *allez* weez us." He shoved Willard toward the fire. The other man, the Indian with filthy leggings, grabbed the freighter by the hair. Though small, he leaned forward, dug in his heels, and began to drag the body. The freighter's eyes opened and he uttered a low sound. The whole front of his coat was caked with dried blood from the stomach wound. The Indian looked around, surprised. Someone said something and the others laughed. When he reached the edge of the fire, the Indian jerked the freighter to a half-sitting position and drew from his belt a huge, broad-bladed knife. He held it six inches in front of the freighter's face. His other hand was knotted in the freighter's hair, and he shook the man's head until the eyes seemed to focus on the bright steel.

The Frenchman leaned close to Willard, giggling like a small boy.

"He poot out the far now."

The blade flashed like a mirror as it turned and, in one quick, hard stroke, it passed across the freighter's throat. A thin line opened suddenly into a maw that vomited a cascade of blood into the embers. The Indian released his grip, and the freighter dropped face down into the cloud of steam and ashes that boiled up. There was a loud sizzling and the knees curled up, the body jerking as if attempting to get to its feet. There was no head, only a dark plume of smoke.

Everything receded for Willard. He heard, as from a great distance, hearty laughter. His body was utterly numb, and he expected it to fall, but it did not.

"He fonny, eh?" Willard felt the Frenchman's breath in his ear. "Nex' far, maybe you poot heem out, eh?"

[7]

PROFESSOR BAUM fidgeted in the lobby of the grand offices of the Mohawk & Massachusetts Railway. Brokers, bankers, messengers, and petty speculators milled about under the cut-glass chandeliers, arguing and dropping ashes on the carpets while they waited for an audience. Whenever a runner arrived with new figures from the Exchange, the babble rose to a crescendo. The hubbub over stock-watering, bear raids, and the new Bessemer rails addled Baum's thoughts. He was relieved when the Pinkerton agent who had taken his card returned and escorted him through oak doors to the secretary's anteroom.

Fairfield, a fleshy young man with corn-blond hair, received Baum with enthusiasm and an ill-concealed fascination.

"Ho ho! You're the feller who's after us to hire apes, eh?" The secretary flipped open a box of cigars and pushed them at Baum. A red jewel glinted in his tie. "We could use 'em, Perfesser. These Irish won't work, you know, without sugar. And they're stupider than an ape."

"No, no," Baum began. "These things—"

"Mr. Stoneman—Mandrake—is interested in your ideas, Perfesser, very interested. Don't say no, whatever you do. This is not the age for no to anything. Go ahead, help yourself." Fairfield selected a cigar, nipped off the end with a tiny silver tool, and poked it between Baum's teeth when he opened his mouth to refuse.

"No sir. A great age, sir. Fortunes made every day. Look at Mr. Stoneman. Began with a flock of turkeys. Only twelve, he was, a baby. In ten years he was worth a cool twenty thousand. And now—" Fairfield winked conspiratorially. "Who knows? And look here."

He took a broadside of cheap yellow paper from a stack on his desk and dropped it in Baum's lap.

LAND!!!   WEALTH!!!   FREEDOM!!!

Fabulous opportunity in the Idaho Territory!
For men with Enterprise, Gumption and 200 Dollars
Cash Money!

The Mohawk & Massachusetts Railway and the Snake River Land Company two months ago sent Mr. Thomas Fletcher, formerly of the United

States Surveyor's Bureau, to examine the site of a new line along the Northern Route into unexplored parts of the legendary Idaho-Montana Territory. Mr. Fletcher's reports have amazed Wall Street and launched the biggest stock boom ever! Look out Commodore Vanderbilt! Look out Mr. Softshoes Gould! These discoveries put your Minnesota tales to shame! Emerald pastures for cattle, tall timber for hotels and hostleries, warm valleys where cherries, peaches and some say oranges grow bigger than any. Mr. Fletcher also collected ore samples of gold and silver to rival the Comstock. The Mohawk & Massachusetts stands ready to sell land for farms and mines in this Eden at values from two dollars the acre to four dollars the acre, and for townsites at five dollars the acre to ten dollars the acre. Some smart investors have bought townsite property on our Eastern branches and sold it one week later for *twenty-five* dollars the acre! This is no place for the weak or timid, but if you are man enough to aim for riches, with some hard work and adventure thrown in, join up for Idaho! Minimum purchase is 200 dollars' worth.

Baum blinked behind his spectacles and nodded. "It is a very large country. Yes, a wonderful thing . . ."

"Perfessor," Fairfield said, "Mr. Stoneman ain't an ordinary man. He's a king, and I wouldn't be surprised if one day he owned 'er all, the whole kit and caboodle, from here to Californee. Tell you a little secret. You read there that the smart spec'lators sold out for twenty-five an acre? Now, who bought 'em out? Stoneman himself. Not direct, of course. He's no fool. When the boys on Wall Street heard, they bought it up to *forty* an acre. See?" Fairfield laughed triumphantly.

Baum flushed. He understood nothing of all these figures and strategies. He had come to report the failure of their expedition and the mystery that surrounded it. It was a sad duty, not only because of the sacrifice of a promising young scientist, but also because not a scrap of information had been collected. He also intended to ask Stoneman to assist in providing for a further investigation, especially into the whereabouts of the red-haired woman. Everything possible must be done to ascertain Willard's fate.

The conversation with the secretary was seeding in Baum's mind an uncomfortable suspicion that Stoneman's motives were not those of scientific inquiry. Already in recent months he had felt inexplicable shudders and convulsions in his adopted country. The great war had not touched him so much as this new atmosphere of feverish excitement, the talk of rushes, booms, crashes and panics, the constant clatter of construction, the throngs of foreigners, the flags of smoke from the iron horses creeping along the horizon. Baum felt himself adrift in the tiny eggshell craft of his science, on a surging tide of lawless energy.

Even as he pursued these reflections, Fairfield kept up a torrent of grandiose prediction, imprecations against competitors, and cunning hints of political influence. It was understood that Baum had already made certain investments—substantial investments—with M & M. He, Fairfield, was also a broker in a small way, and advantageous prices could be arranged for cash purchases, fifty thousand or more, in a land deal out Wyoming way. The secretary seemed to have forgotten the reason for the interview. Puffing energetically on his cigar, the jewel at his throat flashing as he sermonized, he took on the appearance of a locomotive himself, rushing down upon the plump little professor until the latter at last gave a cry of alarm and threw up his hands.

"Nein! Nein! Das ist . . . that is too much! I do not want the town, only to see Mr. Stoneman now. My loved friend, Professor Evans, has died! You hear, died! We do not have apes for work on your railroad! Nonsense! If you make locomotives and towns, why are so many bad? Eh? So Willard, he went to this Idaho and now he will never come back! I am here to submit this to Mr. Stoneman. I wish to be shown to him!"

Small and plump as he was, Baum had an imposing stance, developed in the lecture hall and at the podiums of scientific societies. When occasion demanded, he could increase his stature and girth until his waistcoat and bib stretched taut as a sail, and his beard jutted like the prow of a sturdy little freighter breasting a gale. Fairfield was arrested; he sat silent, mouth open, his cigar for once held steady at the root of a long stalk of smoke. They remained this way for some seconds, immobile, and then a bell above their heads jangled violently.

The secretary was out of his chair and across the room before the sound died away. He went through a door into an inner office. Baum heard whispers and grumbles inside, and then the secretary reemerged. He bowed with a mocking flourish and signaled Baum to enter. Looking neither right nor left, the professor tacked, tilted, and drove forward into the current of authority that raged out through the narrow doorway.

[8]

THE MOUNTAINS tumbled upward all around them, and the juniper and sage were thinning out. Briefly the day had warmed, but by mid-afternoon they felt the cold blowing down from the snow-skirted fangs of rock above them.

For some miles, Willard saw and heard little. The execution of the packer had numbed him. He sat with head bowed, his pony tethered to the tail of one of the braves' mounts. Whenever scouts returned, they stopped in a wooded spot or in the shadow of a bluff and there were consultations. Sometimes they changed direction, or doubled back over trails they had already traveled. Once, near midday, the man leading him had thrown him a strip of dried meat. It was almost black and crusted with mold, but he had wolfed it down.

Licking the last traces of grease from his lips, he was shaken by a wave of self-disgust. He knew that hunger and fatigue were eroding his sense of outrage. In spite of himself, he would eat, he would sweat, he would drink. At the end of the day, he knew he would groan with relief to dismount, yearning for the warmth of the fire, the smell of coffee, even the company of these men whose sleeves were still spattered with the blood of his companion.

There had been nothing in his life to prepare him for this revelation. He thought bitterly of the laboratory and sunlit study where he had spent so many pleasant hours examining and cataloguing bones and bits of chipped rock, complacently toying with dates and devising clever explanations for a collection of firestones, tools, and skeletons. The memory of his learned chatter with Baum on the "amorality" and "brutishness" of primitive man—this struck him now as utterly ludicrous. With what blithe, condescending detachment had they discoursed on infanticide, incest, cannibalism! Over fine port and cigars!

Detachment. His smile was a mirthless wince. Pee Wee had already seen to that. Pee Wee and the stolen horses. And hunger and dirt. And whisky and Elizabeth. The man he had thought he was, the only man he knew himself to be—trustworthy, honorable, rational—had crumbled away in a matter of hours.

There was a high-pitched sound to his right, like that of a rusty hinge.

Then a shadow flickered along the ground; above glided a bird with broad wings and a fanned tail, also the color of rust. It hung for a moment to examine him, then lifted away, as if falling into the bottomless pit of the sky.

It was near dusk. They had climbed a steep slope that, near the top, abruptly flattened before rising sheer again for the last two hundred feet. The narrow, grassy bench was fringed with the last of the junipers, and a small spring ran from the cliff behind it to form a series of clear pools. Here the band halted and began to unpack their horses. Willard swung down at a nod from the Frenchman, and staggered when he tried to walk. His feet felt like wooden knobs.

There was a low laugh just behind him, then a sharp blow at the back of his knees, and he went down. Instinctively he rolled, covering his face with his hands. Someone else, aiming for his head, kicked his shoulder, and the man behind struck again in the small of his back. There was a chorus of whoops, and he felt the thud of running feet on the earth. There was a powerful spasm in his belly, curling him up like a hedgehog. The blows redoubled, lifting and turning his whole body so that, without any effort on his part, he was being rolled to the brink of the steep slope. He knew, suddenly, that he had to get to his feet immediately or he would never walk again.

[9]

"YOU DON'T IMAGINE, do you, Professor, that I had anything to do with this woman's schemes?" Stoneman drew on his cigar, nearly a foot long.

"I cannot think so," Baum said. "But how unfortunate, how regrettable that she learns of the legacy. And now an inheritance she could claim."

Stoneman's eyes, which had the pale brightness of steel, regarded the professor with weary amusement. "The woman had the appearance of a lady," he said. "And of course Fairfield is a fool for a pretty smile."

Baum shook his head. "But my dear sir, I asked for strictest confidence. All discretion of gentlemen. My fortune—"

Stoneman uttered a kind of coughing bark. "For God's sake, Baum. A few thousands. A proper little pot for a young man to come into, get a start with, but I sign drafts for twice that much every week. I never thought it worth a special messenger."

"Two hundred and ninety-three thousands," Professor Baum retorted, lifting his chin a little. "A little pot?"

Stoneman shrugged. "Could push a stock a few points one way or 'tother. No more. But let that be. It was useful, I admit."

"But these railroads. If you will pardon, sir, people say—"

"To hell with what people say!" Stoneman removed his cigar and his eyes glittered. "You ought to know from your own business, Professor, that people will say any kind of nonsense. Your preachers, now, trying to tell us man is an angel. Little darky angels right along with the rest in God's own heaven! Love your brothers. Well, we know a little better, eh Professor? Mr. Darwin showed us." Stoneman grinned suddenly, and was silent for a moment. "And your Willard. The big ape got him, eh? Too damned bad. But let me tell you about *my* business, Professor. I can call Fairfield in here and give him a note to the editor of the *Post,* sign one bank draft and have a boy take it to our office at the exchange. Tomorrow morning you'll read in the paper that investors have confidence in rails, because of the Bessemer process, and the smart money is moving that way. People say what I pay 'em to say."

As he spoke, Stoneman's irritation dissipated into a benign lecture. "People are not much evolved, Professor—the majority, that is. Look at 'em, in the street, when you go back out. Watch the way the workers walk, the old women. You can see the monkey in 'em, especially these emigrants." He puffed contemplatively, glanced at Baum. "No offense, Professor. Gentlemen like yourself are an exception. Breeding shows. A man with a straight back and a shave, a refined lady stepping into her carriage—that's as far removed from these bohos and hunkies as they are from their uncles still swinging on vines. Evolution is a pyramid; so is the nation. Look here." One hand, like a large, lightly furred gopher, darted into his coat and came back with a wallet. Stoneman pulled out a bank note and tossed it on his desk between them.

"You see that emblem on the bill? The pyramid and the eye? You know what it is?"

"Isis, the Egyptian god, and of course the Rosicrucian—"

"Don't give me a lecture, Professor." Stoneman rapped on the bill with his knuckle. "Are you a Mason?"

Baum shook his head.

"Then I can only tell you some of it, leaving out the Highest Mystery. But the All-Seeing Eye has made the world in this shape so that one superior man may lead all the rest, from the top down. At the bottom are the animals, Professor, the dumb brutes. Powerful but in need of"—he swallowed and cleared his throat—"domination. The ape is king over the lion because of his cunning. The nigger is king over the ape, in his own country. The Chinaman and the Arab are king over the nigger— Ever been to that part of the world, Baum? Africa?"

Baum shook his head again.

"Your Chinee owns the stores, or the Mussulman. Superior on that scale. But away over all these is the white race, the most advanced, which is divided up with the Irish and the bohunks and Italians at the bottom, your French and Spaniard in the middle, and the English and Germans"—Stoneman winked and nodded at Baum—"on the top. And the English go from commoner to king, of course. It's a wonderful principle, Professor, a wonderful—"

"Please!" Professor Baum's hands were pressed over his eyes. "It is not like that. Evolution—"

"A wonderful principle," Stoneman went on. "Of course it's like that. Oh, I know you scientists have to have every jot and tittle in place before you will risk committing yourselves. No matter. But anyway it's a damn shame about young Evans. You say he fell into rough company? Wouldn't have guessed it, to look at him."

"He was captivated by outlaws, robbers, murderers. He had no experience. He was brave, but . . ."

"Foolish. They go together sometimes. Any chance, Professor, somebody else could go after this giant? You could measure the head, maybe put it in that exhibition we talked about?"

"No," Baum said coldly. "No one would do such a thing. Now, about the stocks—"

"Don't trouble yourself." Stoneman waved one of his large, furry hands. "Your investment is safe. You own two thousand shares of the Silver King Railroad and Snake River Land Company, secured by my personal bond. This woman—the so-called widow—might complicate matters, but leave that to the lawyers. In six months, Professor, those shares will be worth twice what you paid for them. Believe me."

"I want to sell them now. I care not for twice. I shall trouble you no more."

"Not so simple, Professor. Not so simple. Sell now and you won't get half."

"What?" Professor Baum's beard lifted like the bowsprit of a schooner in a sudden gale.

"Don't worry, man. Your money is as safe as the U.S. Mint. And I'll tell you a little secret." Stoneman laughed out a great cloud of smoke. "The U.S. Mint is only as safe as I am."

Baum opened his mouth to remonstrate, but could not organize the English words into a thought. Willard lost to him forever, his fortune threatened, an ancestral enemy gloating over his downfall—the sum of his woes struck him mute.

Stoneman rose and came around the desk to him. "You're over-wrought, man. Nothing to be done now. The boy's gone. But I'll do this for you." He placed a hand on Baum's shoulder and without knowing quite how, the professor found himself on his feet and gliding toward the door, as if pulled by a great magnet. "I've got a good man I'll send out to Idaho territory. He can be there in two weeks. He'll make inquiries. I'll let you know."

In a moment Professor Baum found himself again in the outer office, where Fairfield leered at him, stickpin flashing.

"Well, Perfesser, how's your exhibit getting along?"

"I . . . I have had no time," Baum said.

"I want to see it," Fairfield boomed. "Tremendous poster idea. All them ape heads lined up."

Baum stared for a moment at the grinning Fairfield, then strode out of the office.

When the professor was gone, the bell rang immediately. This time Fairfield lifted a brass horn from beneath his desk and held it to his ear. His employer's voice echoed as if in a vault.

"Get hold of the Finn," the voice said. "Send him up right away."

[10]

WHEN HE LURCHED to his feet, Willard saw that the men had formed a semicircle about him, pinning him at the edge of the bluff. One of their number moved into the enclosed area, crouching on the balls of his feet. A short, wiry man with a cast in one eye, he was grinning, talking in the soothing tone used with frightened animals. This soft cajolery chilled Willard to the marrow. The other faces in the ring were no longer expressionless, but tense with anticipation. One of the men fumbled with his belt, and others called out in excitement.

The crouching figure advanced a step or two. Willard took a deep breath, then shifted into a stance of balance and readiness. He had boxed a little in college, and acquired from his tour in Europe a knowledge of *savate*, the art of combat with the feet.

"Très bien, ver' good," he heard the burly Frenchman call, "Thees gurl like to fight."

Willard's assailant darted suddenly toward him, one hand grappling for a hold on his legs. Willard danced backward and, kicking swiftly and high, drove his pointed foot at the man's throat. His aim was off; the boot caught the Indian at the shoulder tendon and spun him. Willard kicked again and felt his boot toe drive beneath the man's rib cage. When the man tried to turn back, emitting a grunt of surprise, he was off balance, sagging over the hollow of pain in his side. Willard adopted a prizefighter's pose, fists curled up before him, and punched rapidly two, three, four times, driving the blows straight from his shoulders as he had been taught.

The Indian fell, blood streaming from his mouth. Willard stepped back, holding his posture of bent knees and cocked arms. A silence had fallen over the spectators, and he could hear only the ragged, blubbering breath of the man stretched on the ground before him. The Indian raised his head, eyes bleary, then struggled to prop himself up on one elbow. He had lost a tooth, and twin rivulets of red ran now from his nostrils. No one spoke or moved, and the stillness was peculiar. Willard glanced swiftly around the ring of faces, all of them regarding him intently, expectantly. The Indian tried to roll over on one side and get a knee beneath himself, but fell back with a groan.

"Keel him," the Frenchman said, and Willard heard a note of urgency, of apprehension, in the command.

He took another step away and dropped his hands to his sides. All at once, as if at a signal, the men broke into exclamations and excited conversation. The ring they had formed began to disperse rapidly outward, leaving him alone beside the groaning man. The Indian called out in a low, hoarse voice, then groaned again. Willard heard something like a sob, what was surely a curse, and finally a cry that raised the hair at the back of his neck. He turned away and hurried after the others, who seemed to be fleeing away.

The flap of the tent was thrown back, and Nampuh's great head protruded through the opening. He said something, and one of the men answered briefly. Two of the Indians moved then to escort Willard to Nampuh's tent. When he stepped inside, the giant was already seated on a bear hide. Willard's trunk and photographic gear were placed to one side, and a few tote sacks and baskets occupied a far corner. From rawhide thongs attached to the ceiling pole hung a deerskin bag and the withered claw of some large bird of prey.

Nampuh gestured to indicate a spot before him, and Willard sat down at the edge of the great pool of black, glistening hair. For a long time the giant regarded him, while outside the camp was quiet except for the snorts and stamping hooves of horses. Weak and out of breath after his struggle, Willard found himself nevertheless calm within, as if desperation had reached a point of such intensity that it formed an icy, obdurate surface where he could now walk with firmer tread. He felt the pressure of Nampuh's stare, but sustained it, and took note of the man now at close quarters.

The giant wore a deerskin coat tailored to his extraordinary dimensions; under this was a homespun shirt that had been split at the seams and patched with strips of canvas and deerskin. On his lower body he wore a breechclout, leggings, and moccasins of buffalo hide through which protruded great toes with horny nails the size of silver dollars. About his throat hung a necklace of drilled bone, cheap glass beads, and bear claws. A thong bound a fistful of his lank, greasy black hair into a topknot that held aloft three broad eagle feathers.

The mass of hair on the great head made impossible any fair estimate of its dimensions. Willard could see that the skull was brachycephalic, Mongol, and the fold at the corner of the eye pronounced, but he detected also an uncharacteristic flattening of the nostrils, and, even allowing for layers of smoke and grease, he found Nampuh's skin unusually dark. Calculations were difficult to make because of the man's size: his features were more like slabs of stone than the planes of a human face; the nostrils and eye sockets were dark and thicketed as crevices in a cliff.

Willard found it difficult to concentrate for other reasons. The odor in the tent was the rank, overwhelming scent of a large animal in its den—a stew of rot, excrement, sweat, and wild sage. And the steady stare unnerved him: Nampuh's eyes shifted without warning from the dull opacity of basalt to the glitter of flint, though the rest of his countenance registered no change.

All at once the giant reached to one side, flipped open the trunk containing Willard's effects, and after rummaging within for a moment, brought out the plaster cast of Homer's skull. He tossed it onto the bear hide between them and spoke one word, in a voice at once hoarse and resonant.

"Shame."

Willard could not conceal his astonishment. "I beg your pardon," he said, and immediately felt ridiculous.

Nampuh gestured again, as if at something outside the tent. "You shame not kill him. Shame twice. Big shame."

Willard closed his eyes for a long moment. He was not used to searching for words so simple and bare.

"I did not kill him," he said finally. "He is yours."

The eyes turned to dull stone and Nampuh shook his head slightly. "Not mine. *Personne. Nada.*"

"Yes," Willard ventured. "So I leave him alone."

"Except kill. I kill you, you mine. He kill you, you his. You not kill him, he nobody now. Have to kill himself. *Malo.* Bad shame. *Acai-tyn.* Bad luck."

Nampuh pointed at the plaster skull. It was one of those Baum had carefully modified for verisimilitude, tinting the wet plaster with a yellow wash, incising and chipping to imitate the cracks of the original, blotching and staining with sepia inks to represent the ravages of time.

"Grandfather?"

"No."

"Why here?"

"This one," Willard pointed to one empty eye socket, "bad man. Very bad. A long time ago. He killed many people."

Nampuh gestured again at the skull, his eyes glittering now. "Your enemy?"

Willard opened his mouth to assent, but the other raised a hand suddenly and closed it into a mighty fist, and words died in his throat.

"No," the giant said, "no lie." He grinned suddenly, a row of fine, white teeth slashing across the dark face, and brought the clenched fist down upon the plaster skull, which shattered into a dozen fragments and a small cloud of white dust.

"One lie, you stranger." Nampuh leaned forward a little, and the force of his look was like a hand upon Willard's face. "Two lie, you enemy."

He waited then, and it seemed to Willard the whole camp outside had fallen silent. There was nothing but the sound of the giant breathing, and the rank odor of the place, foul as a bear's den.

"Three lies," Willard said, "you die."

Nampuh threw back his head and laughed. A horse whickered outside, and a pot clanged. A mutter of voices was audible, and all at once the routines of life, having been momentarily suspended, were resumed.

"Ver' good." The giant grinned again, swift as a blade in the sun. *"Très ben.* You ketchum." He took a pinch of the powder from the crushed skull and sniffed it. *"Ai-pin-ta,"* he said. "White rock." He stared again at Willard.

"My grandfather," Willard said evenly, "gave it to me. Another one, far away, is the real one." He paused. The giant's eyes had gone opaque again. "The other one . . ." He pointed at the bones of the necklace. "Like these. True. Very good."

"Genoowine."

"Yes." Willard could not suppress a smile. "Genuine. The genuine is very . . . very much money. *Dinero.* Understand?"

"Sabe. Gold."

"Very old. *Very* old. Many, many grandfathers. This one is the oldest. First grandfather."

"White man?"

Willard hesitated. "I don't know. *No sabe."*

"You grandfather, where he ketchum?"

Willard concentrated, then pointed east. "Far away. Many miles. A land over a great ocean—water—"

"You-rope," Nampuh said. "White man's land."

"Yes!" Willard was startled. "You—"

"How ketchum? This old grandfather, all bones?"

Willard shook his head. "Skull. Head bone. All broken. My grandfather put pieces all together." He picked up two fragments of the plaster and demonstrated assembly.

"Where?"

Willard gestured again, using one of the shards to scoop up a bit of earth. "Dug up."

The giant sat back, straightening his spine. "He dead, Old Grandfather. You grandfather dig bones?"

Willard nodded. Again a silence fell. Nampuh watched him without expression.

"You ketchum Nampuh's head?"

Again Willard found himself without voice. *Two lies, I am his enemy,* he thought. *But the truth? The truth is worse. Surely he knows of the price on his head.*

"Plenty gold," the giant said softly, as if he had heard the thought. "You ketchum Nampuh's head."

Willard took a long breath. "Yes. Plenty gold." He felt the blood drain from his face. *Now he will have me. And I deserve it. I came to collect his head. To buy a woman. I am as much a blackguard as these savages. I deserve . . .*

Suddenly the giant laughed again, and nodded vigorously. "Good. Ver' good. You like ketchum Nampuh's head. No lie." He reached out then and picked up the camera, its bellows partly extended and wrenched from the metal track.

"You ketchum picture? Nampuh?"

"I—I don't know. Some things are broken. I need—"

"Ketchum picture." Nampuh set the camera on the bear hide. "Pronto." He called out, and in a moment one of the men parted the tent flap and stood while the giant gave commands in Shoshoni. The man came into the tent then, lifted the bag of equipment, and departed. Nampuh moved his head slightly in a gesture of dismissal, and Willard got quickly to his feet.

"I will need fresh water," he said, "and clean pans . . ."

"He help you." The giant took from the basket beside him a small sack of soft leather, from which he shook a handful of bright beads, buttons, and coins. He began examining them, and did not look up when the tent flap dropped behind Willard.

[11]

"IF THE CEREMONY WAS LEGAL, you bring her back—alive. The man she travels with, this quack doctor, you may handle as you wish. If he is troublesome . . ." Stoneman shrugged. The Finn continued to look out the window, without expression. "If the whole thing was a put-up job, and there is no record of it, then you impress upon them—so that they do not forget it—how inconvenient their little game is, and how bad for their health it will be if they ever meddle in my affairs again."

There was a considerable silence, broken only by the distant knock of horses' hooves on cobblestone, and the shouts of cabdrivers.

The Finn had said nothing since his entry. He would go unremarked in a crowd, for he was below average height and dressed in a plain, dark suit. But a nearer view would reveal peculiarities. He had almost no neck, so that the high collar of his shirt nearly enveloped his very small, delicate ears. A powerful build was evident in the broad hands with their short, blunt fingers, and the wrists, solid as fenceposts, emerging from starched cuffs. The face was Asiatic, a Lapp's face; the cheeks high and tight around almond eyes, and the mouth merely a thin cut above a round chin. Across the room it might appear a benevolent face, a brown, man-in-the-moon face; but a pace away it became a countenance from which many blizzards had scoured all trace of human feeling.

"What money?" The Finn turned from the window at last. His voice was soft and heavy, like a late snowfall.

"As usual. Thirty dollars a day and your expenses. Five hundred in advance. If there is a special circumstance—the fellow is troublesome— then of course a thousand on top of that. And of course the brigand has a price on his head." Stoneman spoke evenly, then moved with swift efficiency to open a drawer and remove an inlaid wooden box.

Despite their long association, he still did not like to be in the Finn's company any longer than was necessary. It was not fear or revulsion that made him concentrate on the box, the canvas bag inside, the exact counting out of gold coins (the Finn accepted only gold); it was an emotion as powerful as these but alien and unnameable. He was aware that the Finn felt it too. The man always left as soon as their business was completed, disappearing through a side door that led down a stair-way, and through two more locked doors to an alley.

The Finn made no move toward the six stacks of five coins each. "The rest—the hundred—is for tonight?" The thin mouth bowed suddenly into a smile. "A new duck?"

Stoneman nodded once and slapped shut the lid of the box. "An hour. Two cabs in the alley. Take one of your boys with you."

The Finn plucked a heavy wallet from inside his coat and unlaced one of its compartments. With one hand he held the wallet at the edge of the desk, and with the other he sent the coins crashing into its mouth. When the bulging purse had disappeared into the coat again, he turned and walked away. At the side door he spoke without looking back. "One hour," he said. "My pleasure."

Stoneman lifted a speaking tube from a bracket on the desk and turned a crank to sound the bell. In a moment Fairfield's voice answered.

"He's gone," Stoneman said. "I'll be going out myself in an hour. To the theater. Have the barber come up here, and send a boy with a note to my wife. I'll be quite late. Now before the Exchange opens tomorrow find out from Trembath the earliest quotes on silver, you understand?"

"Oh, that's a good one! Shift to silver. Oh sir, that will show the Commodore, that—"

"That will show nothing, Fairfield. I have said nothing about shifting. I want the quotes, that's all."

"Yessir." There was a respectful silence.

"And Fairfield, that red-haired doxy you were sporting with in the spring—she bamboozled you, you know. That fat little Hun with the white beard was in here trying to draw out his chips, raving because she fleeced his boy, who lost his scalp in the bargain, too, and I wanted to see the proof of that outlaw ape. A personal desire of mine, you understand?"

Fairfield whispered something.

"If that happens again, Fairfield—"

"Oh no sir, no sir. Never again. That woman—"

"I don't want to hear about her. Now, another thing you can do. Send Bell around tomorrow, and tell him I want to know the lawbook on intestate settlements for widows."

"Yessir. Widows. Yessir."

Stoneman hung up the tube and for a moment stared at the portrait of himself on the opposite wall, over the marble fireplace. Then he placed his heavy gold watch on the desk before him, removed a sheaf of papers from another drawer, and looked through them until he heard the faint rap at the door. He grunted and the barber slid into the room, bag in hand and fresh towels over his arm.

They retired to the washroom at the rear of the grand office, a washroom—so it was bragged about on Wall Street—as large as the headquarters of many a company. It contained Oriental rugs, paintings of dogs and pheasants, an antelope head, a gigantic porcelain tub, a row of washbasins with plated spigots—gold for hot, silver for cold—a dressing table of oak and ebony with a great oval mirror, an armoire, a medicine cabinet, a chaise longue of dark velvet with lace antimacassar, and a barber's chair with calfskin headrest and panels inlaid in ivory.

The barber, a rotund Italian in a smock of dazzling white, entered the room talking, and continued talking as he twirled the taps to dash steaming water into the bowls, then drew from his bag scissors, brush, comb, strops, and assorted razors with handles of brass and bone. He spun the chair and eased Stoneman into it, pumping handles to tip and elevate. He talked of the wonder of emigrating to this amazing country, of the telegraph, gaslights, and closed sewers. He spoke of the great men who conducted this gigantic enterprise, the future. In and through all this he wove his own humble story, his wife and his children and his countless relatives, their little triumphs and foibles. His voice ran like an ebullient brook in and around the sound of the brush whipping froth in a mug, the light slap of hot towels, the thwack and hiss of the blade on leather. Stoneman's eyelids drooped. With plump, soft fingers the barber pried and stretched the skin of neck and jawline. The razor glided—now slow, now quick—but always with a flourish at the end of the stroke that left a smear of suds, speckled with dark nubs of beard, on the towel over his arm.

When the sideburns were trimmed and darkened with henna, the barber returned to the theme of gratitude for this great land and its leaders. Then, with a spray of cologne and a slow spin of the chair, he fell silent. Stoneman considered himself in the mirror, touched one temple, then grunted and dug in his pocket for a dollar, which the Italian took with a low bow and a soft expression in his own tongue. His paraphernalia was packed up swiftly in the black bag, and he padded ahead of Stoneman, out of the washroom and straight on to the main office door. He opened it just far enough to slide through, and was gone.

In the outer office Fairfield held ready Stoneman's coat and cane, and when the coat was adjusted and buttoned he ran a brush lightly over the shoulders. Stoneman said nothing, but, before turning to the side door that led to the alley, he lifted the walking stick and placed the heavy gold head gently against Fairfield's lips. Fairfield nodded vigorously. "No sir," he said. "Nary a word." Stoneman dropped the cane into his hand, turned, and left his offices.

Two cabs were drawn up in the alley. The larger, a coach and four, was directly in front of the narrow doorway from which Stoneman emerged. When he climbed in, the driver kept his eyes straight ahead, the reins held ready. The blinds went down, and at a rap from within the driver clucked and the horses stepped out smartly, taking up the slack in their harness. Twenty yards behind, a light phaeton pulled away from the curb to follow; the Finn drove, one passenger beside him.

They traveled for perhaps a half hour, the horses working up a creamy froth around their collars. They were in an older section of the city, where the stone steps of high, narrow houses were worn smooth, and where the trees behind wrought iron gates were half-dead. The gaslights in their sooty cases left doorways in shadow. Finally they halted before the entrance to a once-elegant small mansion, whose grounds were now ill-kept. A man and a woman stepped from the darkness and came quickly through the gate, leaving it ajar behind them. The man rapped the door of the cab and it swung open immediately.

"Glad to see you, Mr. Smith," the man said, and helped the woman up into the coach with a rustle of many petticoats. There was no answer, and the door closed immediately. The driver slapped the reins over the rump of the wheel team, and as the cab drew away the man stepped back through the gate and disappeared into the gloom.

In a few minutes the two vehicles drew closer together, bumping and rattling now on narrower streets. Here streetlamps were rare, but some light came from open doorways and storefronts beneath soiled and tattered awnings. They turned at last down an alley, barely navigable, and stopped at an unlit doorway, the phaeton now drawn up just behind the coach.

The Finn and his companion, a man in a workman's jacket and boots, sprang from their seats and moved toward the narrow wooden door. Before they reached it a Negro child stepped out to greet them with an awkward salute, like a miniature soldier. The Finn shot a word at him and the boy nodded, standing aside to reveal a dimly lit hallway. The two men stood then by the coach door, one on each side, each with a hand in a pocket. The coach door sprang open and the two passengers, hidden in their wraps, hurried out and vanished into the dark wall of the building. At once the coach rattled away, only to halt at the end of the alley. The man in the rough jacket sauntered to the other end of the alley and took up a position there. The Finn disappeared inside the building after the coach passengers, and the Negro boy shut the door and put his back against it.

The room was lit poorly by a single lamp nearly black with neglect. Stoneman helped the woman remove her cloak, then shrugged out of his own greatcoat and tossed the wraps on a chair, placing his cane atop the heap. The room contained only a rude table, upon which rested a basin and pitcher, a divan covered in faded velvet, and an odd structure of roughly sawn planks against one wall. The planks made up a three-sided enclosure, a stall with its gate missing. An iron ring was bolted to a rail along one of the planks and from a post hung a few coils of leather strap. The floor in and around the stall was covered with two inches of clean sawdust.

The woman lifted a hand to her hat and moved toward the divan.

"No," Stoneman said. "Not yet."

The woman resettled the hat and smiled slightly. She was tall, very fair, and full-figured. The gown she wore was of wine-dark satin,

trimmed in expensive brocade, and the brooch at her throat was a glittering cluster of gems. From her sash she took a small fan. With a quick
snap of her wrist she spread its ivory blades, and behind its first flutters
she hid an artificial yawn.

"Mistuh Smith, I do *so* enjoy these evenin's," she cooed. Her throat,
fine and muscular, undulated with her words, the vowels enduring like
the notes of a flute. "The theatuh and then a little strollin' about the
grounds." She moved to his side and slid a white hand into the crook of
his arm. "He'p me ovah this path." She leaned against his shoulder, the
brim of her hat brushing his neck, and uttered small sounds of surprise
and satisfaction as they walked in a circle twice about the room.

"Beautiful," she breathed. "The trees and the rivuh."

He stopped, his face unsmiling, eyes turned toward a windowless wall
as if seeing through it to an infinite horizon.

She gave a little cry of delight. "Ovah theah, Mistuh Smith, by that
hossbahn. Show me the livestock. Ah know you are a breedah!" She
folded the fan and tapped it, ever so lightly, on Stoneman's forearm.
"And blood tells, don't it Mistuh Smith? Blood always tells."

Stoneman glanced down at her and his lips drew tight in a kind of
smile. "Now, now," he said gruffly, "a barn is no place for a lady."

"Of co's it is! Ah been fond of stock all mah life." She undid a ribbon
under her chin, pulled off the hat, and swung it by her side, releasing a
cascade of pale curls.

"Oh surely," Stoneman murmured.

"Come, now." The woman raised the fan and brushed its tip along
Stoneman's jaw. "You be good." She rapped lightly.

"Again," he whispered hoarsely. The ivory blades flicked sharply and
left a faint, rosy welt on his cheek.

"I odah you, you heah?" She uttered a little laugh, squeezed his arm,
and pointed imperiously at the stall.

Stoneman broke away from her, his face darkening with blood, and
strode across the room. He picked up the cane from the heap of coats
and struck the gold head in his hand, then against the door, which
immediately opened a few inches. A plump black hand gripped the latch
and they heard a low voice, unintelligible but full of urgency. Then the
hand shoved open the door and withdrew.

For a moment the doorway yawned empty; then a hand crept over the
threshold, a forearm, then another hand, and finally a head, a dense mass
of black hair. A mulatto girl, crawling on all fours, entered the room. She
was clad in a loose shift, her legs and arms bare. Stoneman lifted his cane

and with its tip pushed the door shut with a clap. Then he prodded the girl's buttocks, at the same time making with his lips the sharp sucking noise, the reverse kiss, that teamsters employ to settle a draught animal into its traces.

The mulatto girl uttered a squeal, then attempted, without great success, the grunt of a heavy beast. She tried to move quickly across the room, her haunches rocking and hands slapping against the floor.

"Why, that's a fetchin' little sow, Mistuh Smith! Ah just knew you had fine stock heah." The woman tossed her hat on the divan and then half reclined onto it, lifting her feet from the floor with a sudden flash of petticoat and ankle.

With prods and a few quick cuts, the cane hissing through the air, Stoneman followed as the girl backed into the stall. She glanced up only rarely, her oval face calm except for an occasional, uncontrollable twitch of pain. She did not look higher than Stoneman's belt. When she was inside the wooden enclosure, he leaned the cane against one of its slats and seized a handful of the dark hair. With the other hand he took down the coils of leather strap hanging from the post and shook them out. One end of the strap was braided into a loop, which he slipped over the girl's head. The other end he passed through the iron ring, so that with a jerk he could pull the girl forward, snubbing her against the rail of the stall.

He uttered more of the little sucking sounds and, keeping the strap knotted in one fist, recovered his cane. He stroked the thin wood smartly across first one ham, then the other, bringing forth more squeals of pain, and these seemed genuine.

"She is just mah-valous," said the woman on the divan. "Spiruht and bone." He said nothing, but slashed twice more with the cane. The smock was riding up on the brown haunches, and with the cane's tip Stoneman hooked the hem and tossed the garment up around the girl's waist. She wore nothing beneath it. He ran the cane between her legs and slapped it back and forth to spread them, at the same time hauling on the strap to bring her head to the iron ring.

Stoneman's face was dark as old brick and his breath came rapidly. He kept the cane between her legs, the tip of it quivering. "Come here," he commanded hoarsely, and the woman on the divan swung her gleaming slippers again to the floor. Her mouth twisted once, swiftly, but it was not a convincing smile. "Come here," he repeated, his voice almost breaking. "Undo my buttons, damn it, hurry! Whoa! Whoa!"

She glided across the room toward them, the gown rustling, and her laughter was as perfect and metallic as the notes of a music box when the cover is sprung.

[12]

ONLY SIX of the glass plates remained undamaged. Seventeen were badly cracked, and seventy-three shattered to bits. One of the plates, by a happy miracle, was the ground-glass focusing screen. A bottle of collodion had also been broken and the contents had dribbled over a box of prepared printing paper. The small jars of alcohol, acetic acid, and varnish had been stored in wooden racks with a leather cover and appeared intact; and the dry chemicals—protosulphate of iron, nitrate of silver, potassium cyanide and hyposulphite of soda—had been stored in metal canisters wrapped in waxed paper. Two quarts of distilled water in a brass-bound flagon of heavy glass had also miraculously survived.

Then, at the bottom of the trunk, Willard made a discovery that thrilled him: a new pencil and a booklet for field notes on exposure and development times—he would be able to resume his journal! He knew that these humble but precious tools would give him—as they always had —a small but dependable purchase on the universe. But he had at the moment a more immediate task, so he hid the pencil and booklet beneath the rack of chemicals.

The portable dark tent, made of heavy drapery material, was stained and covered with fragments of glass, but when Willard shook it out he could see no rips. His tripod also functioned, after he bound up a splintered leg with twine. The camera was another matter. The brass tube containing the lens was safe in its reinforced cabinet, but the main body had been wrenched from its base, and the leather pleats of the bellows were torn in two places.

The Indian who had been assigned to assist him withdrew, reappearing a few moments later with a farrier's tool and a leather pouch. He elbowed Willard aside and with a careful pinch of the tool bent the cleats of the guide track into position. Then he removed a hooked needle and a coil of fine gut from the pouch, and began to stitch the torn seams of the bellows. Willard remarked other needles, a pair of steel clamps, and a surgeon's probe and lance. His new assistant was evidently the band's physician, with a kit stolen from some hapless victim of an earlier raid. Gnarled and dirty as the man's fingers were, they worked with deft speed, and, when Willard removed the dark slide and peered into the main chamber of the camera, he could see no telltale pinpoints of light.

He had removed the trunk to a small outcropping of rock fringed by a few large sagebrush, taking advantage of a narrow strip of shade. The trunk was designed to serve as a developing laboratory: panels at the ends were actually enamel-lined trays in which the nitrate solution was prepared, and two telescoping brass rods at the back corners extended to hold up the dark tent; this fit over the rods and fastened snugly to the rim of the trunk top. Willard erected the tent, then by pantomime and gesture instructed the Indian to fetch clear water from the spring above the camp.

As Willard worked, laying out the pans on the trunk top, measuring powders to make the fixing and developing solutions, the Frenchman and another Indian, a young half-breed, came to watch, squatting on their heels.

"Ver' good." The Frenchman laughed without sound, showing his white teeth. "Nampuh not keel you yet. First theeng, make photograph, eh? Photograph." He nodded. "That eez French, you know dat? My peeples. Daguerre. He make it."

Willard had selected one of the good plates and was cleaning it with a soft cloth. He looked up in surprise, and the Frenchman grinned again.

"Ver' good, you bet. I know dat. A Franchman, he make dat photograph first theeng, eh? I got one photograph, *moi.*" He lifted the flap on a beaded pouch slung under his arm and began a search through its contents.

Willard picked up the one remaining bottle of collodion and unstoppered it. Holding the clean plate by one corner, he tilted the bottle over it until the liquid dribbled onto the glass surface. When the collodion had pooled, he tilted the plate first one way, then another, until the entire surface was coated.

The Frenchman stood and held out his discovery, a small tintype set in a cheap oval frame. "Me. *Moi.* Jacques Beaufort. I waz preety fellow, no? *Très beau!*" He smiled proudly and the half-breed grunted his admiration and approval.

Despite himself, Willard glanced at the picture. Then he looked again more closely.

"You were a soldier," he said, his tone a mingling of surprise and accusation.

"Sojer," the half-breed repeated, and spat.

"I scout for Eenglish," Jacques said, "keeling *Gros Ventres*, beeg bellies. Also for bluecoat, keeling Crows. Plenty times, you bet."

Willard, coating a second plate, pretended disinterest. The photograph had revealed the Frenchman in a uniform coat, with epaulettes and a military cap, though below the waist he wore deerskin leggings and moccasins. Jacques Beaufort grinned happily into the camera, his moustache full and carefully combed. Treachery, Willard reflected, in no way seemed to interfere with the man's good humor.

"Ketchum Crows," the half-breed said. "Plenty Crows, plenty Shoshoni." He grabbed himself between the legs and made a sawing motion with his other hand.

The Frenchman laughed loudly and restored his picture to the beaded bag. "Ketchum soldiers now. Keel ever' god-damn one!"

The half-breed laughed too, a sound like some large bird hooting. They slapped each other on the shoulder, Jacques losing his balance and sprawling on the ground.

Three plates were now in the wooden rack and Willard had poured the panel trays full of distilled water. He was aware that his mouth had curled into a smile and a bubble of laughter had caught in his chest. He was startled, then appalled. The sight of the two grown men laughing and rolling in the grass had struck him off-guard.

"What you theenk, peek-chur man? I waz good scout, no? Fight good." The Frenchman rolled to his feet. "Ketchum new peek-chur?"

"Yes. Ready." While Jacques and the half-breed set off for the campground, Willard ducked inside the tent and adjusted the flaps to keep out all but a dim glow, then began to mix the solution of silver nitrate in one of the pans. When the bath was ready, he dipped each plate in the sensitizing solution and removed it quickly to the wooden rack. From a drawer of the trunk he selected three dark slides. He placed one of the prepared plates in each slide, securing the thin wooden covers with brass clips.

When he emerged from the tent, the whole company gathered around him, whispering and staring in unabashed curiosity. Quickly he mounted the camera on its tripod and secured the focusing screen to the back. He selected a spot where the outcropping of rock slanted into the grassy slope; a single gnarled sagebrush served as backdrop, breaking the line of the sky. After inserting the lens in its socket he threw the black hood over the camera and peered at the screen. A hush fell and he knew that Nampuh was approaching. The scene before him—the rock and brooding bush—grew sharp, then blurred, then sharpened again as he spun the knob. He tried to estimate the intensity of the sunlight, and calculate the time he would have to keep his subject immobile.

When he threw back the hood and looked up, blinking in the sudden brightness, the whole band was waiting, expectant and hushed. Nampuh stood with arms folded, staring impassively at the black box.

"Ketchum photograph," Nampuh said, and a murmur went through the group.

Willard nodded and walked in front of the camera, gesturing toward the slope of rock. "Here," he said. "Some of you sit on the ground." He squatted to demonstrate. "The rest behind. Nampuh . . ." He indicated the spot in the back row at the center, where the huge figure would dominate the composition. He noticed that the giant had added more necklaces and wore a bright blanket about his shoulders.

Nampuh stalked to his position and turned to face the camera. As the men gathered about him they plucked at and nudged each other in excitement.

Willard shook his head and frowned. The men looked at him with sudden smiles. A few laughed aloud. He felt ridiculous, to be chiding these outlaw killers as if they were children. He looked pleadingly at the Frenchman.

"Tell them they must be quiet, absolutely quiet. They cannot move a finger. *Pas un sourcil.*"

Jacques said something to Nampuh, who then uttered a single word. The men turned motionless as stones. The rows of eyes bored into him, and Willard was unnerved, confused. He smiled weakly and nodded approval, but not an expression flinched.

He retreated to the camera, adjusted the focus once more, removed the glass screen, and placed the brass cap over the lens. Then he slid the first dark slide into its slot and swung away the inside cover. The uncanny silence endured. He stepped in front of the camera and drew a deep breath, placing one hand on the lens cap.

"All right," Willard whispered, and pulled off the cap. He counted, trying to maintain a steady rhythm. Usually he would use his own pulse as a timing mechanism, but his heart was hurrying out of control. The group before him might have been a carving, but for an indefinable force —the odd pressure of Nampuh's gaze multiplied to an almost unbearable degree.

When he thought the necessary time had elapsed, he recapped the lens, jerked the exposed plate out of the camera, and jammed in the next slide. When he had exposed and removed the second plate he found himself trembling. It occurred to him to keep the last slide unexposed until he knew the fate of the others, so he spoke up, in the croak of a man whose voice has gone unused for a long time.

"All right. It's over. Tell them they can move."

Nampuh shifted his shoulders under the blanket and stepped back, and immediately the men moved too, some breaking into whoops, springing to their feet and swarming toward Willard. They watched the dark slides, curious yet wary, and pressed about him in postures of supplication. A few seemed puzzled or fearful and hung back near the rock. Nampuh stood uncertain between the two groups.

Willard realized that the band was unsure what their comportment should be in this ritual, so he indicated by gesture that they should all again be seated and remain silent. When they had hunkered down, he withdrew into the dark tent to begin processing the photographs.

He nearly collapsed with relief when, under his careful coaxing, the images started forth from the glass plates. He fixed and washed them, then exposed sensitized print paper through the new glass negatives. Finally he had two adequate prints, every countenance visible. When the paper was dry, he emerged from the tent, sweating and in shirt sleeves. The band regarded him, waiting for a signal. They had squatted in the sun for nearly an hour, patient as a church congregation.

This notion acted on Willard as an inspiration. He had intended merely to hand over the prints, wash out his pans and bottles, and fold up the trunk, but now he saw an opportunity. Nampuh still appeared uncertain of the next step in this process, and the members of the band glanced restively back and forth between their leader and the stiff paper rectangles in Willard's hand.

He strode to a place in front of the band and nodded at Jacques. "I have something to tell them," he said.

The Frenchman rose and, after a glance at Nampuh, sidled away from the group to stand expectantly beside Willard.

"These are like a mirror," Willard said, holding up the photographs. "All of you are in here. In here forever. You cannot get out." He surveyed the dark, somber faces as Jacques repeated the message in Shoshoni. Some of the men murmured, ill at ease.

"If any man wishes to know who are Nampuh's people, who has been with him—here you can see them all. Nobody can leave his side."

He walked to the end of the row of seated warriors and handed the last man one of the prints.

"Do not touch the faces," he cautioned. "These faces will not grow old. When all of you are dead, these faces will be just as they are. The rock and the bush there, they will always be the same."

The photograph passed from hand to hand. Each man held it gingerly, and stared intently before giving it to the next in line. Willard strode to Nampuh and extended the other print.

"Yours," he said. "Ketchum all your people."

The giant reached forth and, a little hesitantly, took the picture. He gazed at it for a moment, then looked up with a grunt of approval. For the first time Willard saw a glint of some new feeling in the opaque black eyes. It was recognition, perhaps even respect.

The giant slipped the photograph carefully into a pouch slung from his shoulder.

"More," he said then. *"Otro."* He jerked his head, the eagle feathers flashing, toward the black heap of cloth over the trunk. "Nampuh. My goods." He said something aside and the men began to rise to their feet, groaning over stiff joints. Four of them set off toward the main camp.

"Only one left," Willard said, holding up a finger to represent the plate remaining. For a moment Nampuh considered. Willard kept his finger extended, for it seemed to him the giant was counting, and he thought of their exchange concerning the three lies.

"Today." Nampuh nodded again. "Me, plenty goods."

Indeed, the envoys were returning, bearing saddlebags, wooden crates, an armful of guns, and a pair of battered cavalry swords. They arranged this gear about their leader, who then assumed a position of dignity: erect, unsmiling, arms crossed.

Adjusting the focus and composing the photograph, Willard had time to examine the stack of possessions, and was alternately appalled and touched at what he saw. Besides the swords and carbines, revolvers and old-fashioned single-shot needle guns, there were a few items of clothing, some with ugly, dark stains, and a motley collection of horn-backed combs, razors, gilt buttons, watches, lockets, leather pokes full of gold dust, a broken stagecoach lantern, and a few parts from a dismantled sewing machine.

A poor harvest, he thought, for a bandit king. The lot, except for the raw gold, could not be worth more than fifty dollars. And how many had been slain for this pathetic booty? In a vision as sudden as a lightning-lit landscape, he saw the packer again tumbling face first into the fire, and his heart lurched.

He righted himself by concentrating once more on the business of picture-taking. Nampuh held himself motionless for the exposure, then retired to the shade of the rock while the porters carried his goods back to the tent and Willard withdrew under the black hood. The balance of light and shadow was correct, and in the developer he saw the complete and miniature scene, every detail etched clearly. Nampuh was an imposing figure, his size apparent in relation to the rifle barrels, which barely surpassed his waist. Willard made three prints, keeping one in the trunk for himself.

When he handed over the others, the giant examined them with pleasure and again Willard caught a flicker of warmth in the Indian's features. He determined all at once to take a chance.

"Good," he said. "For Nampuh. You send one picture to Silver City, maybe Boise. Then everybody know Nampuh, his goods."

There was a silence. Then Nampuh smiled and put the prints in his shoulder bag. "Maybe so. Maybe show white people."

Willard looked down, controlling his expression carefully. If the picture reached Boise, the territorial authorities would know that he was alive. No one else could have taken the photograph; no one else in the territory would have the proper equipment and knowledge to use it. And if there was the slightest hope of his release, then his work must go on. With the pencil and notebook, he had at last all the tools of his trade. He took a deep breath.

"For Nampuh I have worked. Now I would like . . . ketchum heads." He stopped, fumbling for a clearer phrase.

Nampuh regarded him, puzzled at first, and then he laughed, a great, booming bark. The giant shifted his shoulders under the bright new blanket and seized Willard's arm with one hand.

"You ketchum Nampuh's head?" Again the rolling laugh. "No knife?"

Willard was lifted nearly off his toes; the strength of Nampuh's grip pulled him like a magnet.

"No!" He shook his head violently. "Measurement!" He made an awkward circle with his hands around his brow. "How big."

Nampuh released him and considered him, questioning. Willard stepped back hastily, his arm tingling. "Wait!" He took a handkerchief from his pocket, rolled it tight, and demonstrated a measurement of his own skull. "How big," he repeated. "Only how big. How little."

"How many head?"

Willard gestured at the camp, where a few men still looked their way. "All. Everybody."

The giant watched him carefully for several moments, mouth twitching and nostrils flaring in amusement. Then the eagle feathers bobbed in assent, and he shouted something toward the camp. Other men in the band laughed, as Willard set out briskly to recover the little kit that contained his calipers, tapes, and casting clay.

[13]

LYDIA had gotten three hundred dollars for the pearl necklace, two diamond and sapphire brooches, and a gold bracelet. She cried when the man at the shop scooped her jewelry into his strongbox. The necklace was her favorite and had belonged to her maternal grandmother.

As it was, the enormity of her transgression would leave Professor Braddock devastated. She had heard his arguments with Baum, at first only passionate but in the end bitter, as he tried to dissuade his colleague from pressing the inquiry further. Willard was surely already dead, as the Army's report implied, and Professor Braddock hinted, with intense scorn, that the young man more than deserved his fate.

She simply did not believe it. That Willard could have wed a stranger, a common tart and trickster, was beyond credence. Through some impersonation or clever business with papers he had been duped, she was sure. Otherwise . . . but she could not contemplate an otherwise. Something strong stirred deep within whenever she hesitated in her faith, and she had at last determined that even if Willard was lost to her, to this life, she must go to the scene of the tragedy, discover the truth, and so preserve his honor. And of course her own.

A single rap at the door roused her from her reverie.

"Ma'am?"

It was Skillings, come to fetch her trunk and two carpetbags. She composed a demeanor of blithe and idle gaiety, the manner of one off for a midsummer visit to a cousin in Philadelphia—where, indeed, everyone in the household except her own maid thought she was going.

"You must have quite a round of balls and parties in store, Miss B.," Skillings remarked, estimating in a glance the heft of her trunk.

"A different gown and slippers for each one," she answered with a laugh. "You know vanity is our weakness. Do be careful with your back."

She picked up her parasol and one of the carpetbags, the one containing her money, Willard's notebook, the maps and train schedules, and a duster—all items which might give away her real destination. As she followed Skillings down the stairs, there was both terror and exhilaration in her heart. Even as she imagined her father tearing open the seal on the letter brought by her maid—reading at first with an impatient frown, then with a rush of blood to his cheeks—she found that through her grief and apprehension ran a thin but bright thread of delight.

At the station they mounted the iron steps through a boil of steam, and Skillings found her compartment and settled her there. The aisles were swarming with passengers, most of them with no more than a purse or handbag, for the train was a local to New York; from there she was to transfer to another local bound for Philly.

"Mind yourself, miss," Skillings said from the doorway. "You have all manner of riffraff abroad these days." He spoke with avuncular solicitation, his cadaver's face reforming itself with difficulty under the influence of real affection.

Lydia pressed his hand and said, "Don't worry, Skillings. I shall be perfectly all right."

They heard the conductor shouting. The aisle outside the compartment was a-clatter with heels, and the train underwent a little jolt, its joints clashing.

"Good-bye, miss."

"Farewell, Skillings."

He had begun to shut the door to the compartment, but hesitated for a moment, surprised by the taut formality in her voice. She held her cheerful smile heroically until he nodded and slid the door panel completely closed.

She saw him once more, through tear-filled eyes and a window fogged with smoke and flecks of cinder; he stood, vaguely puzzled, one hand raised in the gesture of parting. Then the train jerked out of the station, passing rows of coal and freight cars, and began to pick up speed.

Lydia settled back with a shuddering sigh. It was done. As agreed with the maid, it would be four days before the letter was discovered on her dressing table and brought to Professor Braddock. By that time she would be almost in Boise, the Idaho Territory. She would have gone through such places as Omaha and Cheyenne. The names had an exotic, savage character; they evoked lurid rumors of the red man, feathered and bestial.

But she had her money, and the names of the military men who had signed the reports of Willard's fate. By careful and discreet inquiry she had obtained the name of a distant relative, a great uncle, who had a store and hostelry in Virginia City. Even so, the magnitude of her under-taking—the deceit and the danger involved—almost overwhelmed her. The turbulence in her heart sometimes grew unmanageable; several times in the last weeks, she had inexplicably excused herself from the table, and had pled female indisposition so often that her father had insisted on a physician's advice.

The kindly old man had prescribed laudanum and sulfur in a tincture of alcohol, for nerves and restoration of the blood. She had feigned a recovery and seized the opportunity to prescribe for herself a visit to her Philadelphia cousin, a girl her own age. A letter written three days ago to the cousin warned of a postponement of the visit and confirmed a new date. It was unlikely her father would telegraph to ascertain her safe arrival, since she had made the journey often and without mishap.

They were racketing by the squalid settlements of the back bay—the weather-beaten shacks and sheds of the crabbers and codders, and a few clusters of brick tenements inhabited by the workers from the Neponset and Quincy mills. The reeds and sedge grass along the track were more gray than green; gray, too, were the coats and caps and faces of the children who looked up from their games in the mud to observe the train, which they had seen too often to bother waving at. This mournful landscape always depressed her, and usually she pulled the blind and immersed herself in a romance. But now she stared, thinking that, if she was to survive the rigors of travel westward, she would have to accustom herself to such sights.

She knew also that the Braddock wealth derived in part from invest-ments in the textile mills and in property not distant from this very region. To her naive inquiries as a girl her father had replied with an indulgent smile, telling her that such matters were not for pretty heads. If she persisted he remarked shortly that the lower orders, as he called them, were content with their lot, that for those without refinement and intelligence, comfort must be earned through hard labor. For their own class, he added, there was not only arduous labor, but also the duty of perfecting higher faculties, of advancing humankind, of compassion and charity toward lesser beings.

But Lydia had never thought of herself as belonging to the silly, addle-pated throng of young people that made up Boston society. For one thing, although it made him uncomfortable, her father permitted her access to most of his library. Excepted of course were certain indecent Greek and Roman works. She also read a little in fashionable, highbrow magazines, where she encountered modern thinkers and poets. Some of this material, like the poems of Thompson and that terrible old man, Whitman, she thought ridiculous or debauched, but here too she knew a strange, remote turmoil, very like the feelings that had rushed in on her when she first conceived her plan to make this voyage into the unknown.

Over the rhythmic clattering of the rails she heard the voice of the conductor as he made his way down the aisle.

"Attleboro! Pawtucket! Attleboro, Pawtucket! Next Sto-o-op!"

She pulled from her handbag the small gold watch given to her by her father two birthdays ago. It was not yet noon. All at once she was grateful to the modern world of steam and steel that could hurl her into the future at fifty miles an hour, too fast for reconsideration or compromise. By late in the day, she would be in New York boarding a night express westward; and sometime the day after tomorrow, or perhaps the day after that, barring unforeseen delays, she would be in Nebraska. Nebraska!

[14]

THE MESSENGER kept his eyes lowered while Stoneman dug in his waistcoat for a coin. The lad's cheeks were ruddy, as from fever or a cold wind, and his breath came in short gasps. It was an effect he had on young men, Stoneman knew, when they stood for the first time in the presence of one worth so many millions. Once a novice had fainted dead away on the carpet at the sight of the open safe and its glittering stacks of twenty- and fifty-dollar gold pieces.

When he dropped the coin—a generous twenty-five cents—into the youth's palm, he smiled a little. Those who knew him would remark that this reward was even more generous, for Stoneman's smile was a rare thing. Men who had seen him almost daily for years could count on the fingers of one hand the times they had heard him laugh outright.

After the lad's hushed expression of thanks and swift exit, Stoneman broke the seal on the letter and began to read, his look leaping from figure to figure. He took a pencil from his desk and began to jot more numbers on a pad.

He heard a soft noise and looked up, nettled, to see Fairfield's round, pale countenance at the open door. The man had never before entered without a preliminary knock and a polite silence before his employer's acknowledging grunt. Stoneman was startled beyond outrage, and taken aback by the intensity of Fairfield's manner.

"Sir, I must speak with you, if you please, sir." Fairfield moved across the carpet like a puppet lifted by strings. Then he sat, suddenly, in an armchair, like a man just shot.

"What the hell is wrong with you, man?" Stoneman reared away from his desk, planting his feet more firmly, as if to rise. For an employee to sit unbidden in his presence was also unheard of.

"It's about everything, sir, and involves you . . . a tremendous opportunity. I believe, yes, I believe I have seen a way out for us, sir—"

"Goddamn it, Fairfield!" Stoneman roared. "Will you stop calling me 'sir' every other word and tell me what in Christ's name brought you crashing in here like this?"

"Yes si—" Fairfield stopped, blinked, and swallowed. Then the spots of color in his face spread together into a uniform flush, and he began to speak rapidly.

"It's this way, and let's put the worst of it up first, and maybe you'll kick me out right now but I wouldn't sir—I'm sorry, I mean I wouldn't because there is a chance to recover a great deal of boodle. The woman —that confounded red-haired trollop—and her boyfriend are here in New York again and . . . and I must beg your pardon sir, they know about the visits to the . . . theater." Fairfield closed his eyes and again the color drained from his cheeks, for he heard Stoneman reply in a new voice, a hiss.

"Who told them?"

There was a long pause, and Fairfield seemed to shrivel in his very clothes. But finally he blurted out the words, as if addressing a crowd from the scaffold.

"I did."

Stoneman's hand, still holding the pencil, began to tremble a little, but he still spoke in a rasping whisper.

"Did you, Fairfield? How did you do that? Tell me how you did that."

With a wild, incongruous smile, Fairfield looked into the space just above Stoneman's head.

"I couldn't help myself and you'll think I'm a lunatic and a fool but I swear to God it's the truth, sir, the God's truth. I was mesmerized by that damned devil of a German. I never saw such a thing, sir, you've got to believe that. Of course I'd never clapped eyes on the gent before, so I didn't know what he was after, you see. I was drinking a drop at the Boomer's Club—a little place on 10th Avenue where young sports have their whisky and talk trade, you know—and met this fellow and he was damned charming. The damned slickers from over there, they know the book on bamboozling a fellow! He had traveled a good deal and he knew a fair lot about rails and coal and silver and land, along with God knows what manner of hogwash about what cognac a sport should drink—we drank a good bit, too, I admit—but he knew the standing of Mohawk & Massachusetts stock, and the Snake River Land Company too, which ought to have made me cagey, but like a fool I bragged a bit about what I've done to be clever at watering a stock or selling short and so forth. Oh, he was all ears, he was! The damned slicker!"

"Fairfield." Stoneman's hiss was now barely audible. One look at his face and the blond young man cringed as if before a fire. "Stop driveling and tell me *how they know about the theater.*"

"Sir, I can't explain that very well." Fairfield's voice had also sunk to a whisper. "You'll have to believe what the doctors tell us. The man had a devilish way of persuasion, and he is a doctor himself or so he says, and an inventor too. He said he wanted to show me one of his inventions, some kind of magnet or electrometer or something, so we went off to his quarters, both of us still in our cups a bit and leaning on each other—and he began to demonstrate the cursed thing . . ."

"Go on," Stoneman said. He was now partly in shadow, for the afternoon had waned; the sun poised on the horizon for its plunge into darkness. The last light from the window was a heavy, dull gold with a hint of red, and fell directly on the portrait of Stoneman on the opposite wall.

"The room had hardly any furnishings, a table and chairs and a light and mirror—something odd about the light—so I should have known there was some damned bilk afoot, but anyway, he brought a box with a battery gadget inside. It was all about electricity and regions of the brain and our faculties and so forth. He was damned infernally persuasive, and he went on and on about the power of steam and gold and how I looked upon you, Mr. Stoneman, like a father. All the while he told me to keep watching the light in the mirror, and after a while I just drowsed off. Just for a moment, before I shut my eyes, I thought it was your voice talking to me in a dream, telling me to be a good son and shoot the works for I knew more than I thought I did." Fairfield's voice caught in a small sob. "I swear to you sir, until I opened my eyes again I had no notion I said anything more, anything at all. But in the morning that woman—the redheaded one, Elizabeth—was there with us, both of them smiling at me like cats . . ."

"And?" Stoneman breathed.

"I was flabbergasted, discombobulated. They told me bold as brass that I had spilled everything, and the woman had already gone out to the theater and talked to those nigger devils. Got them to sign something, gave them money, I suppose. Those two already knew all about the old perfesser's legacy to the young fool who went off to measure Injun brains, and damned if they didn't skedaddle to Idaho and get this Evans fellow married—"

"I know all that. Fairfield . . ." Stoneman stood slowly. "Fairfield, you are a fool, a colossal fool, and a jackanapes as well. I will crush you like a bug. If the Finn were here—but you know of course I sent him off to take care of this very matter. Fortunately for you. But I shall see to it that you never show your face on Wall Street again, that—"

"Wait! Wait sir, for the love of God!" Fairfield waved the paper in his hand like a flag of surrender. "Hear me out, please. These people—vile as they are—they know who they are dealing with, they know your reputation. They propose something interesting, very interesting. Please."

Stoneman stepped from behind the desk and loomed over the man in the chair. "What do they propose, Fairfield? That I pay for your incompetent meddling?"

"No, no." Fairfield shook his head violently. "Listen, sir. They have a scheme. Listen. This Silver City, the mines, the whole shebang is going to peter out, according to Miller, but they've hit a side vein that tests out good—good enough to last for a few months. The owners are putting it out as a big new boom, but they know things are bound to plunge, right to the bottom. What they don't take account of, sir, is the copper there —common as dirt, a mountain of it! Miller has a notion of what it's worth. He's a sharper, sir, and no mistake. Damn it, sir, the man is right. If we put out a bit of cash to prime the pump, and perhaps run a rail line to the town site, we can drive the price of silver up for a while, and investors will flock in. When we've got 'em, and the vein is near out, we start dumping, first the silver and then the rail stock and then the town. The price will hit bottom again, we'll buy it back cheap, and in a few years that copper will pay—copper's coming, sir, electricity and all—and we'll make a very considerable profit."

"We?" Stoneman said. "We, Fairfield?"

"I mean, sir, primarily you and Miller and Elizabeth."

"You mean you want me to use my money to make them rich? A complicated form of blackmail. Is that what they told you to work out of me, Fairfield, you despicable—" Stoneman raised a hand, considered, then lowered it slowly again. "Get out," he said tonelessly.

"No, wait. You don't understand, sir. They're willing to match you, dollar for dollar. A joint investment. Of course they need an . . . advance."

Stoneman paused, then gave another of his rare smiles, this one knife-thin and bitter as gall. "How much do they have, Fairfield? Ten dollars? A hundred? A thousand?"

"Elizabeth will inherit Evans' fortune," Fairfield supplied quickly. "And it would be easy to do if a man like yourself acted—indirectly—in the matter. I realized, sir, when you asked me to check on property disposition for widows that . . . you might be considering a way to recover that legacy."

Stoneman turned suddenly and walked to the window. His employee heaved a long sigh, sagging a little in the chair. "But it isn't an ordinary business now. It appears, sir, that . . ." Again Fairfield's confidence deserted him and his voice quavered. ". . . that young Evans may be alive."

Stoneman turned in the gloom, a dark shape against the window. "What did you say?"

"He may be alive, that young fool. Look here." Fairfield fumbled with the paper, removing a smaller square clipped to it. "May I light a lamp, sir?"

"Light it."

Swiftly Fairfield took a small box of matches from his pocket, lifted the shade of the lamp, and turned the gas jet. With a snap the room was full of yellow light. He reduced the flame so that the desk was illuminated, but the corners of the room remained in shadow.

"You see, there is a photograph of that giant—the papers in the Idaho Territory got ahold of it—and they figure Evans must have done it. He took photographic equipment with him, and this is a professional job. The Injuns couldn't have done it."

Stoneman walked to the desk and looked at the small square of paper. Without picking it up, he read the few lines of print beneath the smudged photograph. "What a brute," he said quietly. "What a magnificent brute."

"So you see, Mr. Stoneman, we don't know if Elizabeth is a widow or not yet. But Miller assured me that she's bound to be one soon. The authorities figure this outlaw gang is boxed into the territory, and the savages will probably kill Evans when they have to run or fight for it."

"Probably," Stoneman sneered. *"Probably?"*

"Well," Fairfield shrugged, "Miller suggested also that a special posse —a posse bent on taking care of these fellows one and all—couldn't pick and choose its targets. You see, sir, if Evans turns up alive the old man will want his fortune settled on him right away, and—"

"For the love of God, Fairfield, you don't need to babble everything— you see where it has got you." Stoneman circled the desk and sat down again. His features were knotted into a frown, and he picked up the pencil and rapped it on the photograph. "How do you know this is authentic?"

"An Injun brought it into Fort Hall. It was a print already processed in the field. But there's another angle, sir, which I have been thinking of. This big ape or whatever he is has stirred up a lot of people, got into all the papers out West. We could make quite a splash with that sort of thing. Something like"—he pretended to cudgel his brains for a phrase —" 'Land of the Giants' or 'Where Colossus Walked,' and if we sent in a posse to take this fellow—I understand you and the perfesser were interested in his head—we could display 'im, pickle 'im or stuff 'im, and I'd wager we could sell mining stock and land like taffy at a church picnic. I've got a little sketch of that sort of blarney on the paper there, sir. I hope you'd take a look. Please?"

Stoneman was staring into the depths of the office, where his own image brooded from its canvas. He appeared not to have heard. "That brute," he said, as if to himself. "Animal."

"Sir?"

Stoneman started, then spoke gruffly. "Pickle him, Fairfield? *Pickle* him?"

"Well, sir, I've seen such at fairs. It's quite a sight, sir. These niggers and Tasmanians and so forth." The blond young man detected that his ideas had at last registered, and a tiny, tremulous hope for salvation took root in his heart. "It might be possible to get the perfesser in on it, sir, and give the thing a scientific flair."

"Alive," Stoneman said, "alive. Maintain the size, but breed out the savagery." He was again looking at something far away, or maybe deep within himself. "Trained to work and fight, to conquer. A new type." After a moment he frowned again. "How am I to respond to this proposition from your friends?"

"They're not my friends, sir. Oh no! They were too smart to give me an address. They said they were leaving again, right away, for Idaho, and I should wire them a response in Boise, and then send a courier with the proper papers and some funds. Fifteen hundred." He cleared his throat. "I've been frantic, sir, and I've thought about it every which way. Their plan does seem the best because the alternative, you see, sir, if the Commodore's newspapers knew of the theater . . ."

"I understand the alternative," Stoneman broke in acidly. "For the time being I shall go along. I will accept their personal note for one half the amount necessary to move into the Silver City prospect. Wire them and make out the papers."

"Thank you, sir," Fairfield said constrictedly. "Thank you. If I can be of assistance—"

"You?" Stoneman gave the young man a look that made Fairfield shrink again into the chair. "You, Fairfield? Your simple task from now on is to keep your mouth shut. Any more blab and you are through, understand? No more cigars, no more cognac at the Boomer's Club, no more *anything.* Do you understand?"

"Yes, sir." Fairfield's voice had almost disappeared.

"As for the business of dealing with this . . . specimen"—Stoneman laid a finger on the photograph and traced an outline delicately—"I shall deal with the matter myself. You may go."

Fairfield rose again with his jerky, puppetlike quality, and swiftly floated to the door. It closed with a click, leaving Stoneman to study the image on the desk before him.

[15]

THE WATER LINE had broken again at the end nearest the spring. Sections of conduit, made from logs split lengthwise and scooped out with an adze, had slipped and sunk; the old man was pounding stakes to realign them. The midday brightness made him squint, and the sledge missed its stroke and caromed off his shin.

He cursed at the top of his lungs, but the sound was instantly absorbed into the bare humps of encircling mountains and the profound blue sky. The canyon below wavered in the hot air, and at the far end of their water line he saw his partner look up from the stone circle of the mill, then look down again and continue plodding beside the horse.

"Sonofabitch," the old man muttered, rubbing his leg. He swung the sledge at his side for a moment while he pinched the sweat from his eye sockets with finger and thumb. Then he removed his battered hat and slapped the dust from its brim.

It was near time to take their pokes and ride out, before this hell of a place drove him crazy. The undependable pipe sections, the ribs showing on the horse, the diet of beans and dried apricots, the deerflies and rattlers, and the boy's endless repetitious, inane talk were wearing him down. They had already stayed a week beyond their original plan, having found at last a main seam. It was high grade, but locked in a feldspar and quartz aggregate, difficult to extract.

Still, thinking of the heavy deerskin pouches concealed in a flour canister, the old man replaced his hat, smiled and licked his dry lips. They would soon have a swank room, clean sheets, roast beef, whisky, women, and good cigars. Some of the roustabouts and drifters in Silver City would get an eyeful. They just might drop a few hints, send the whole lot of those no-accounts over the mountain into Big Foot's country.

He sighed heavily, tapped the stake one more time, and set off for the mill site. It was a dry, hot fall, and after lunch they would move to the shade of a grove of aspens to retort yesterday's concentrate. Then, at sundown, they could weigh and divide the day's dust. The old man then thought of their table fare, and felt both the gnawing of his hunger and a wrench of revulsion. Merely the odor of stale beans nauseated him now.

As he approached, his partner looked up once more, then clucked at the horse and prodded its behind with a slender willow switch. The animal was harnessed to one end of an eight-foot post, whose other end was shackled to an eyebolt driven in the center of a ring. Three granite boulders, attached to the post on short lengths of chain, were thus dragged over a floor of flat stones; this pulverized the ore. The water line ended in a long, narrow sluice box tilted down the slope beside the rasting ring.

The old man cupped his hand into the stream coursing through the box, and dashed a few drops over his face. He watched the last few chunks of ore knocking and skittering under the dragstones. His partner's face, the color of tallow, was blank and intent, a ploughboy's face. Hair like straw showed beneath the wide plainsman's hat, and over his shoulders and arms was a layer of gray dust. He put one heavy boot after another in rhythm, now and then touching a hand to the halter. Stupid as an ox, the old man thought, and just as strong. He would have preferred a partner who could tell a story or play the mouth harp, but at least the boy was honest and could stand the backbreaking labor and rotten victuals.

"Tie 'im up," the old man said. "Let's eat."

The young man pulled the horse to a halt and muttered a word or two in its ear. The animal inflated and then collapsed its dusty sides in a long, wet sigh, and its head drooped, followed by a cloud of flies.

"Mite left," the boy said, with a reproachful look.

"Hell with it." The old man took a flat scoop shovel from the ground and stepped into the ring.

"Rastin's hard work," the boy said, unhooking the horse's halter. "Mighty hard work."

"Got to rast it," the old man replied. "Out in the goddamned wilderness thisaway. Lord Jesus, I wisht we had a wagon track in here and could set us up a proper stamp mill. Git the goods and git out of this hellhole." He scooped up the crushed rock, now like fine sand, and pitched it into the sluice box.

"That would be somethin'. A road. Yes sir, a road." The boy unbuckled the harness and brushed some of the dust from the horse's back. The old man glanced briefly at him, then returned to shoveling with more vigor. The boy's habit of repeating things, pursing his lips in an empty show of thought, irritated him. He thought again, almost desperately, of the chandeliers, oak counter, and bright glassware of the saloon below the Pioneer Hotel.

They heard then neighing and stamping from the clump of aspens where their saddle and pack horses were kept. Both men stopped and listened intently. They heard hooves crack against the corral poles.

The old man straightened. "Sonofabitch," he said uneasily. "Somethin' after the stock. Git down there with that horse and see what's a-stirrin' 'em up."

The boy nodded and set off downhill leading the tired horse, his feet raising small clouds of dust. The old man turned back to his work. As he straightened to fling a shovelful into the bin, he stopped, quite still, a tiny avalanche of sand pouring from the lip of the iron scoop.

Down the slope toward him rode three men, cantering smoothly. For an instant the old man's legs twitched with the impulse to run, but then he saw that they were white men. He propped the shovel carefully against the sluice box and walked toward the little pole shelter that housed their goods, their grub, and the carbine, shotgun, and two revolvers. He busied himself with the coffee pot and kicking up the fire coals, glancing down at the aspen grove, but his partner was out of sight; all was still, except the leaves quivering in the sunlight.

One of the group, a short, barrel-chested man, lifted a hand in greeting and reined in his horse. "Howdy, mister," he called out genially. "Mind if we set a spell?"

The other two men fanned out on either side. One looked Mexican, the old man thought, and the other had a long, irregular scar on his cheek. He rose from the fire and, exaggerating slightly his arthritic crouch, walked to the open door of the pole shed, the coffee can in his hand. Once more he looked swiftly toward the aspens, and the leaves flashed silently back at him.

"What's yer business?" he asked brusquely. "Ride up on a man like that all of a sudden, fright a person awful bad. Me and my pardners thought you was maybe old Big Foot."

The leader and the man with the scar laughed.

"Well, we been chasin' a couple of them thievin' siwashes. Run off some horses of ourn. You ain't cut any sign of a herd?"

The old man shook his head and reached into the shed to replace the can on its shelf.

"Thought we was Big Foot," the man with the scar said and laughed again. When the old man turned back to them he saw them grinning, their guns swinging up in their hands.

[16]

THE CAMP WAS SILENT except for the desultory rasp made by a man sharpening his knife on a flat rock. Men and horses drowsed in the sun, and the mountains around them shimmered a little where the broken rocks gave off heat. Willard crouched behind his crude lean-to—a frame of poles covered with branches—under which he had dragged his trunk to serve as a kind of table. Littered on the trunk top were his tape, calipers, and a few sheets of paper covered with figures. He was writing in a steady frenzy, taking no notice of the flies that alighted on his shoulders and cheeks.

August 17—

The mad ironies of this business! For days I measured the crania, mandibles, and occipital cavities of this entire band of cutthroats, and threw a glance at their molars and incisors as well. Ostensibly to test your hypoth-esis: is there or is there not a brutal type, representative of an earlier evolutionary stage?

And then—a new kind of experimental verification! I was obliged to accompany three of my new brothers on a raid! Nampuh forced me to go, just as he can, with a single look, impel any of us. Dirty and ragged as the rest, I found myself skulking through the wilderness like the degenerate breed I had come to study. And worse! I witnessed murder again, and this time I was hardened to it. I myself—ah God! I cannot yet write the word. Objectivity! Angel of true science! Thou was not meant for such trials!

The measurements at any rate revealed nothing conclusive. The sample is far too small, and I have no museum specimens for comparison. Yet even without proper method, without hope of publication, this effort com-forts me, provides a scrap, however pathetic, of the life I once knew. Nampuh has promised to permit me to take his measurements—though we must "talk" first—so even a poor remnant of our marvelous science commands some respect here, among the lowest of humankind.

Now the raid. Jacques was given the charge of overseeing me, and this grinning homicide told me unequivocally—three times, the key to making bargains in this band—that he would slit my throat if I uttered a word or moved a finger during their assault. Then, paradoxically enough, he pre-sented me with an old rifle, a .45-70 that must have weighed twenty pounds, two cartridges, and a hunting knife. I was mounted again on the packer's pony, and we set off at dawn.

We travelled most of the day over these bleak, bald mountains, as forbidding a land as God ever created. There are some awesome canyons, where streams are visible far below, no wider than silver threads, where the scrubby juniper trees and small pines give a narrow, green relief to the eye, but we kept for the most part to trails just under the brow of ridges and promontories. Periodically one of the men would dismount and creep to the top and watch, I suppose for smoke or dust that would betray human presence.

There was little talking. The thin, muscular Indian who had helped me with the camera, a friend to Jacques, and another man—squat, sullen and graced by a tremendous wart on his cheek—took turns riding ahead for a few hundred yards every hour or so, while Jacques remained always at my side. He questioned me a little about the measuring session, and bragged about the conformation of his own skull. It verges on the exceptional—no surprise, stuffed as it is with evil humor—but as far from the dimensions of his countryman, the peerless Baron Cuvier, as he is from that great scientist in culture and sensibility. I wonder what Professors Broca and Gratiolet would think of this specimen, posed alongside the great skulls of Swift, Byron and Napoleon?

None of these intriguing points could be raised with the subject in question, of course, and Jacques fell into a fit of hilarity when I told him that men's abilities and character might be figured in the weight, volume and proportion of their brains. When he informed the other two of this proposition they too could barely contain themselves and rode by me with little whoops, slapping my shoulder. I asked the reason for their mirth and he told me, smirking, "You thank mens air strong with theez brains? Brains?" He repeated the word and the others joined him in sustained laughter. "We air strong here and here!" He thumped himself on the chest and gripped between his legs obscenely; the others did likewise, and they all laughed at my discomfiture. They literally have no notion of what intelligence is, as we understand it: the power of those, like Cuvier, to conceive abstract principles and pursue their demonstration or refutation.

But had I seen any opportunity to enlighten these savages, by even the smallest margin, there was still too little time to attempt it. We rode steadily, mostly uphill, and stopped only once in mid-morning for a mouthful of their dreadful dried meat. They kept looking to the west and talking their gibberish, until we veered that way for a mile or two, and then I noticed, indeed, the tiny flecks of black—much like particles of ash—turning in the sky. Vultures, I presumed. When we were close enough to see the pinions of these gruesome creatures flashing in the sun, we dismounted, and left Wart (as I privately dubbed him) with the horses while we crept through the rocks.

August 20—

I had not time to finish the above account before being summoned to Nampuh's tent for the promised (or threatened) "talk," and immediately thereafter we moved the whole camp a day's march deeper into the mountains, apparently to avoid reprisals for the raiding party mentioned earlier. It is colder here, and we are quartered in a stand of pines—these mountains have a scattered covering of these larger trees—whose great boughs form a gloomy cavern beneath. The wind through these boughs makes a tremendous, roaring dirge as well, so I am compelled to write in circumstances that perfectly suit the Gothic tragedy that this journal must now recount.

The talk with the giant began with questions about my "grandfather bones." This time I perceived that Nampuh understands and even speaks more of the language than he lets on. I tried to tell him, in a most rudimentary way, about the descent of our kind from ape-like primates (which he has of course never seen). He insisted that these creatures may be the white men's ancestors—they are a hairy breed anyway, he remarked with a great bark of laughter—but as for his people, they were created by a coyote. I could make no more headway in my efforts to provide him with some notion of the scale of geologic time. The argument from rocks made no impression; he refuted it, curiously, quite as Agassiz and Gosse did, claiming that this coyote created the world just as it is—the lava and sedimentary formations already in place!

I placated him with the statement that there were many disputes among my people over God's designs, and the words he had spoken through his Prophets were sometimes obscure. This he seemed to understand. I feigned also a student's interest in this coyote, and pursued questions of my own about the creature's place in the scheme of things. Finally Nampuh seemed satisfied, and told me that they would teach me how to walk (!) and ride and eat; he said that I had fought well, and the others had decided to let me live—for a while at least—even though I had committed a great mistake, apparently, by not killing the Indian who attacked me, who was the least of the warriors among them. Now, it seems, I must take the man's place. I questioned him about the fate of this worthy, as I had not seen him since the day I took the photographs, and the giant merely shrugged and said the man had gone "into the mountains" to die. With this grisly information, our interview was completed.

Now about the raid and its terrible outcome. Over the ridge, where the vultures circled, we found a terrible, bloody spectacle. Two men who had been operating a crude mine and milling operation had been murdered a day or two before. Their swollen corpses lay where they had fallen, the heads only bloody knobs, as they had apparently been scalped. A few clothes and shovels, empty flour tins, and a broken dish were scattered about, all that remained of the camp. Jacques and the thin Indian inspected the area, sometimes on hands and knees, gesturing and arguing.

Jacques explained to me that other white men had carried out this massacre, attempting to make it appear the work of Indians, probably Nampuh's people. He showed me, in fact, a dim indentation of a boot heel near one of the bodies, and a series of tiny furrows in the dust which he said were made by an uprooted sagebrush dragged over the area to obliterate tracks. The two of them calculated the number of attackers at six, and guessed that they had stolen the miners' horses and gold. After a brief parley, it was determined that we were to continue in pursuit of this alien outlaw band—an irony which I could have appreciated more, had Jacques not impressed upon me that I would have to join their party as a full-fledged avenger.

So as soon as they had picked up the trail, we rode hard for a day. The band was not hurrying, Jacques judged from the tracks, because the area was so remote they had little fear that their crime would be discovered before winter. And possibly, it was speculated, there were wounded. At dusk Wart spotted a tiny glimmer of flame across a vast canyon, into which the trail made by the horses disappeared. We retreated from the bluff we had attained and rode at a gallop toward the head of this canyon. When we reached a point where it narrowed, we dismounted and led the ponies in darkness down the rocky slope, across a brush-choked rivulet, and up the other side.

We moved silently and swiftly behind Wart, who seemed to have an uncanny knack for finding animal trails that zig-zagged along the forbidding slope. At the top of the far canyon wall we paused, and my three companions held a long conference that was sometimes heated. The dispute seemed to be over whether we should simply steal the horses, as Wart thought best, or kill the whole lot of the thieves, as Jacques maintained. Once they turned to me and Jacques outlined these positions and asked my opinion. I was helpless to answer, except to say miserably that I thought both courses of action were wrong. They registered first disbelief and then disgust, and went back to their arguments.

Jacques won out, and we spent the next hour, under a heaven full of the brightest, most numerous stars I had ever seen, staking out the horses in a small meadow in a side-canyon, far enough away so that their scent would not disturb the horses of our enemies. I suppose, to be perfectly frank with myself, I had come to think of them as enemies. A justified assumption, as matters turned out. Then the lean Indian, whose name Jacques had translated for me as Broken Arm, slipped away in the darkness on foot.

We waited perhaps two hours, while I dozed fitfully and Jacques and Wart conversed in low tones. Then, all at once, Broken Arm was standing among us—an unnerving apparition. It is true these people can move in their homeland like ghosts, making no disturbance at all. He gave the situation to be as follows: there were but five of the robbers, all but one of them white men and the other a Mexican. One was suffering from fever. Broken Arm drew in the sand a map of the camp, including the disposition of the horse herd, which he said numbered twenty-three head. Wart gave a greedy grunt at this information.

For another hour they discussed their strategy, at the end of which

Jacques communicated my duties to me. The outlaws were camped on a knoll skirted by sparse timber, and the horses were picketed among the trees. Jacques and I were to circle the knoll and slip through the timber to positions on the downhill slope. Because we were white men, Jacques remarked, our smell might not be so unsettling to the stock. Wart and Broken Arm would descend the ridge to the knoll just before dawn and creep as close as they could to the camp. At a signal—Broken Arm demonstrated here his talent for mimicry of the owl's hoot—we would advance and fire upon the enemy. My target, it was stressed, would be the sick man, since he could not flee like the others, and Jacques supplied me with two more cartridges, saying, however, that if I missed with the first three I had best save the last one for myself.

I had of course fired fowling pieces and pistols before, but the unwieldy rifle I now carried seemed a great handicap to accuracy and mobility. Jacques rolled his eyes when I took aim, and advised me to prop the barrel on a branch or log. He told me—three times—that I must not hurry and must not be afraid, or I would be a dead man in two hours' time. "Beeg mark, un homme," he said. "Beeg belly. Shoot for belly."

I had not time to remonstrate, for we were off over the steep and broken ground, Jacques in the lead. We circled very far beyond the perimeter of the outlaw's camp, it seemed to me. I never glimpsed the fire again, and concentrated mostly on maneuvering the heavy rifle through the underbrush and on keeping my companion's form, continually dissolving into the shadows, within sight. As I calculated the time, we walked for the best part of two hours before Jacques halted and I nearly collided with him. We stood together beneath a large, dead pine. Looking further uphill, I could see dark shapes moving in the faint starlight between trees.

"Cheveaux," Jacques whispered. After a few moments he crept very carefully and slowly ahead for perhaps ten yards, then crouched in a stand of saplings. I watched him pick up a pine cone and pitch it gently ahead toward the horses. There was a startled snort, and I saw one of the dark shapes rear alert. After an excruciating wait, Jacques tossed a second cone, and at the small, dry impact there was a brief trampling of hooves, then silence.

Jacques stepped slowly forward, approaching the glade, and two of the horses trotted away, neighing nervously. A third animal extended its nose tentatively, and after a moment took a hesitant step toward us. Jacques advanced too, and held out one hand. The horse came near enough to sniff at his fingers, then shied away with a little whicker. But when it returned to the herd, it resumed grazing, and soon the rest of the beasts did the same, apparently ignoring us.

Jacques jerked his head and made a slow, sinuous movement with one hand, so I moved as softly and calmly as possible to his side. He placed a rough hand briefly over my mouth, then made a slicing motion with the same hand across my throat. With another gesture he indicated that I should load the rifle, so I took one of the cartridges, a heavy brass tube as large as my middle finger, and, unlocking the breech gently, I slid it into the chamber.

We moved step by step through the trees toward the knoll, stopping in the shadow of larger trunks to wait and listen. The terrain gradually took shape in the dim light of the stars, and with a shock I saw finally a group of dark humps at the brow of the knoll. A lean-to, made of ponchos stretched from a branch, sheltered a square of impenetrable darkness, and scattered about the ring of firestones were saddles, wooden chests, and three bedrolls. Jacques led me to a position behind the trunk of a fallen log, and motioned for me to remain there. He withdrew to a spot behind a cluster of young trees, out of my sight.

We had been under the strain of travelling surreptitiously for most of the night, yet I felt no fatigue, only a greatly intensified alertness, apprehension and impatience. It could not have been more than half an hour before the eastern sky began to pale. I sat immobile, listening intently though there was nothing to be heard but the occasional moan of wind in the trees, or thump of a horse's hoof.

Once the stars began to disappear into a sky the color of skim milk, the scene before me grew rapidly more distinct. I could see an arm protruding from one of the bedrolls, two rifles leaning against a tree, and a blackened pot beside the fire pit. Birds began to cheep, intermittently at first, then in a gathering chorus. I knew a sensation of deep dread; the rifle felt like an anvil in my hand; my eyes skirted around the mute forms near the fire—I feared to see a movement, a sign of precious, human life.

A flicker of movement at the corner of my eye caught my attention. Jacques was gesturing at me elaborately, indicating that I must lay the rifle across the log and prepare to aim. My hands trembled and a band of iron locked suddenly across my breast, but I managed to swing the barrel into position. I had determined in the course of this long night that I would fire over the heads of our enemy, that I would not, for this gang of scoundrels, stain my hands with the blood of another human being.

We waited again, for interminable minutes, and then one of the heaps of bedding stirred, was still, and stirred again. A man sat up, his long hair in disarray, and after a moment stretched his arms. I had received a shock when the face appeared from the nest of blankets. I recognized the man as one of the cutthroats who had robbed the stage, slain its driver and abducted Pee Wee and myself. He bore a hideous scar, a clenched, irregular streak along his jaw, white as death.

Jacques' tale had not been a fabrication, then, and these ruffians had indeed committed their bloody crimes under the mask of savagery. A thrill of anger coursed through me, and at that very instant we heard the hoot of an owl. In my excitement at the discovery of our enemy's identity, I had quite forgotten this signal, and for an instant it did not register, but then I saw Jacques running up the slight rise, weaving through the scatter of fallen trees and boulders.

The man caught sight of him and dove with a loud oath for one of the rifles against the tree. Jacques stopped, took aim, and the dawn was shattered by the roar of his carbine. I saw the plume of smoke, and the man stumbled, then fell, a blanket still dragging at his legs. The others were scrambling from their bedding, arms flailing, their shouts hoarse with panic. Jacques fired agin, and I heard more shots in rapid succession from a distance—Wart and Broken Arm—mingled with the terrified neighing of horses.

A man rolled suddenly out from the lean-to and wriggled rapidly along the ground to the base of a tree. He had a revolver, and in a moment came a bright, fiery flash at the heart of a blossom of smoke. Jacques dodged, as if a stone had been thrown at his head, and dropped flat on his belly on the ground.

One of the men staggered to his feet and began a shambling run, holding one arm stiffly against his side. Jacques fired, but the man did not break stride, and as Jacques took aim again, I saw movement inside the lean-to. A squat form appeared at the edge of its shadow, and then the long snout of a rifle. I knew by the man's build, the small head, that it was Cole, the leader. By the direction of the gun barrel, I knew also that he was taking careful aim at Jacques.

The tiny, gold ball at the tip of my own weapon settled on the form in the lean-to. I hunched and squinted, edging the cradle sight on the breech upward until the spark of gold nestled in it. I pulled the trigger, and there was a terrific, bellowing roar and a great cloud of greasy gray-black smoke. I was stunned, and the gun scraped against the log and slipped to the ground from my senseless hands. I could not think, and only stared through the wreaths of smoke, as if into the pit of hell.

The rest of the battle I scarcely remember. I believe only the man with the revolver ever returned our fire, and he was first wounded, then killed in a hail of bullets from before and behind him. We sustained no wounds at all, except for a slight burn on my left hand from the breech of the ancient blunderbuss, which sealed imperfectly. My bullet had struck Cole squarely in the chest, and had taken his life instantly. I sat in a stupor while Jacques, Wart and Broken Arm exulted, tearing through the packs of their prey.

I believe I was near insanity during this time. Again and again I saw the man at the threshold of the shelter, the sight locating itself on his chest, the explosion; and the implacable work of my own hand and eye terrified me. Yet, even in my recognition of this awful crime, I realized that there was no choice: certainly Cole and his henchmen would have killed us, had our assault failed. Beyond all these concerns was a final, and horrible, realization. I had felt, faintly and obscurely, a pang of something like joy beneath my paralysis, at the instant the bullet sped on its fatal path. Now that pang had been replaced by an irrevocable dreadful knowledge—I was a murderer!

Jacques and Wart approached me, both of them grinning and chattering like monkeys. In Jacques' hand swung a limp, dark thing, dripping blood. He threw it on the log before me with a whoop.

"Scalp. Peau de chien!" he said, and clapped a hand on my shoulder.

"Ketchum scalp." Wart's broad face had quite lost its expression of sullen suspicion. He grasped my other shoulder and the two of them hoisted me to my feet and began to pummel me and hop about from one leg to the other in a kind of crude dance. Wart began to chant in his own guttural tongue.

"See-eeng!" Jacques shouted, grinning still like a madman. Somewhere within me the barricades around my suffering gave way, and I found myself uttering cries, tears welling out of my eyes. Shoved hither and thither by my companions, I stumbled through this dance, howling like an animal.

When the looting was completed, and the horses rounded up, Jacques insisted on tying the scalp—a ghastly, shriveled thing caked in blood—to my belt. Tonight, he told me with a foul wink, I should smoke it over the fire. Later in the day I rode with it dangling at my side into the main camp, and had to bear the whooping and coarse jocularity of the whole band. Mercifully, the thing is buried now in an oilskin wrapper at the bottom of my trunk. My reward has been the repossession of all my remaining equipment, and permission to have this miserable shelter by myself, removed from the others.

I have given the best account of these developments that time and circumstance allow, but if I had an eternity to compose, I could not effectively describe the avalanche of contrary and powerful emotions that I underwent in these few days. The light is failing now, the wind moaning ever louder, like the assembled demons of hell, and I can grasp at no hypothesis that would promise salvation, even redemption. I do understand, finally, that all my theorizing with Baum about our savage ancestors was the ridiculous babbling of fools.

[17]

LYDIA had found herself staring at an odd man in the dining car. He had remarkably small ears, vaguely Oriental features, and neat habits with napkin and fork. He ate like a cat, with a curiously refined avidity. And once he had turned swiftly—for no reason she could divine, and again like a cat—and caught her gazing at him, so she had thereafter allowed herself only a rare and discreet glance. There were, anyway, a hundred other fascinating subjects for her attention.

Since Omaha she had seen Indians actually board the train. An old man and woman, faces withered as turkeys', were allowed places in one of the last baggage cars after a discussion between the conductor and some of the passengers. She overheard the words "funeral" and "only son," but watching the couple amble past her window, backs bent under stuffed flour sacks and woven baskets, she could detect no trace of grief in their manner. Except for moccasins and braided hair, they wore nothing more exotic than an incredibly soiled muslin dress and a threadbare coat with missing buttons.

Lydia was disappointed. But the very next day they passed an encampment, the great, conical tipis stark against the horizon, and a group of youths galloped beside the train. These young men wore only breechclouts, and huge black and white feathers fluttered in their braids. They shook lances at the passengers who gazed out at them, and she could hear their demonic yells. She shrank back from the window at first, and then, realizing the riders were only feigning an attack, she leaned forward to watch again.

They were hanging at a breathtaking angle from the necks of their mounts, each with a heel hooked over an undulating back; one youth perched erect on his galloping pony, arms outstretched. The grace and daring of the exhibition caught Lydia by surprise, lifted her quite outside her usual reserve, and she gave small gasps of appreciation and delight. She laughed aloud finally, her face flushed, when the riders dropped from their horses, holding on by a handful of mane, and bounded from the ground again onto the running animal.

Then there were the traders and cattle buyers, men with faces like leather, wearing huge, high hats and clothes that were a queer mixture of broadcloth and doeskin. They were very polite, but in an unfamiliar, intense fashion. After an exchange of small pleasantries they would continue to stare, or alternately stare and look at their boots. She might reopen her book and read for some time, then glance up and discover that they were still regarding her with a kind of melancholy yearning.

Now and then, too, she encountered the more nefarious characters who could afford the price of a ticket. One man—probably a gambler, to judge by his silk vest and fancy kerchief—tried to ingratiate himself by pretending to discuss literature with her, having spotted the title of her book. She was reading a tale, fantastic yet true, told by a sailor who was captured and lived with the cannibals of the South Seas for two years. The author had written several books in this line, and Lydia had brought this one in the hope that she could acquire some knowledge of savage ways.

"A pack of lies," the gambler said. "You shouldn't bother your pretty head with such guff. These fellows will make up any sort of nonsense."

At first she had defended the book, which to her had the ring of authenticity, and possessed as well a vividness and eloquence well beyond the ordinary travel account. It soon became clear, however, that the man was only trying to invite himself to her table for lunch. She excused herself coldly, and thereafter avoided his hungry and glittering eyes.

This variegated cast of colorful characters became something else outside the station at Salt Lake. Lydia knew that the railroad could carry her only to Utah, whence she would have to travel by coach to the Montana and Idaho Territories, but she had no clear idea of what this second portion of her journey entailed. Seeing the single-minded frenzy with which the people here pursued their selfish purposes, she realized for the first time the enormous obstacles she faced.

The station platform was a mad hurly-burly of men and their trunks, barrels, and sacks. Carts trundled by in a chorus of warning shouts, and the train crews swarmed over the engine and cars, armed with wrenches, brooms, and oil cans. On an adjoining platform another train had drawn up a long string of cars heaped with a reddish earth, and sweating, bare-chested laborers were knocking loose the iron doors of these cars, releasing avalanches of the earth into wagons, whose eight-horse teams jostled each other and lunged finally away with a great groaning and creaking of wooden axles. A cloud of dust from this operation floated over the yard, and already Lydia could feel the fine grit settling on her face.

She made her way somehow through the throng, drawing her skirts close to avoid the hurrying men. They were a rough lot—booted, ill-smelling, and unshaven. Many tipped their hats or bowed, but the gestures were not courtly, were rather, it seemed to her, a rude advance; and others swept their eyes over her with shocking boldness. Even the few other women, some with children, stared at her with no sign of friendship or sympathy. Perhaps, she thought, these were the Mormons, who viewed outsiders as heathen enemies. Most were careworn, dressed in coarse frocks and aprons, and she felt, all at once, as if the velvet trim of her jacket and the satin ruffle at her hem were a badge of shame.

Finally she found a porter, an evil-looking old fellow with tobacco stains in his beard, and he heaped a small cart with her baggage. She was directed by a harried clerk to an office on the street behind the station, where a stage company could book her passage to Virginia City. She was overwhelmingly grateful, now, for the name of the distant relative there, and for the opportunity—though it be several days distant—of seeing a friendly face, finding a connection to her life.

They made their way across the street, through a stream of freight wagons and men on horseback, to the office. It was a poor affair, a dusty little lobby where a youth was sorting mail into sacks and an older man sat at a desk, making entries in a ledger. Through the open back door Lydia could see a yard of bare, hard earth, a ramshackle stable and coach house, and a forge.

Behind them came a few other passengers from the train. The man at the desk glanced up and heaved a sigh of exasperation. He picked up a ticket book and beckoned impatiently at Lydia.

She slipped her hand into her bag to clutch her purse, and stepped bravely forward. But when she spoke, her own voice seemed to her faint and tremulous, the voice of a mere girl.

"I should like to secure passage to Virginia City," she said. "As soon as possible."

"Them yours?" The man jerked his head at the baggage cart.

"Them's her'n," the scrofulous old porter rejoined. "This yere lady's."

"Overcharge for the trunk," the man said. "Thirty cents a pound."

He flopped open the ticket book and took a cheap steel pen from a drawer. The point of the pen hesitated over the paper after the word "Destination," which Lydia read upside down.

"Which 'Ginny?" he asked, and suddenly yawned.

"I beg your pardon?" Lydia hesitated too, her purse half withdrawn from the bag.

"*Which* Virginia City?"

Lydia looked at him blankly. The room seemed to tilt ever so slightly. "What?"

"Lady, do you wanna go to the Comstock in Nevada, or to Montana?"

The room tilted farther, and Lydia swayed against the counter. Behind her she felt, rather than saw, someone step nearer, and the clerk's eyes shifted to a point a few inches to her left.

"New to the territory," a voice said, almost in her ear. "This lady needs time to consider. You will allow that?"

It was a quiet voice, but there was a force in it that set the clerk back a little in his chair. "Surely," he said. "Surely, sir. You wanna rest a bit, lady? Come back, you don't hafta stand in line."

She felt a hand on her elbow, guiding her to one of the benches along the wall. It was the odd man with small ears, the man so quick and delicate in his table manners, who smiled now ever so slightly at her.

"Have a seat, ma'am. Take time to think. I can help you." He kept his hand, light as a cat's paw, on her arm until she had sunk to the bench. "My name is Baldo," he added, the voice soft and sounding to her slightly foreign. "An honor to serve you."

[18]

PROFESSOR BAUM could tell from Skillings' look, drawn and white even beyond his usual funereal aspect, that the matter was of the utmost gravity. The brusque urgency of Braddock's note had implied as much. Baum had donned his old-fashioned stovepipe hat, swept up his briefcase —purely out of habit, for it contained nothing but a ruler, some random notes, and the lower incisors of a gorilla—and taken a cab to the Braddocks', where Skillings now conducted him through darkened and hushed rooms to his colleague's study.

Professor Braddock stood before a wall of books, his back to the door, when Baum entered. For a moment, until Skillings had retired, Braddock remained so, facing away from his friend as if in shame. Then he wheeled suddenly, and with a shock Baum saw that Braddock had acquired, overnight as it were, the pinched and withered face of an old man.

"She's gone, Dieter!" he croaked.

"Gone? Who is gone?" Baum placed his briefcase on top of the desk and took his old friend by the arm. "What is this? It is too dark in here, man. Open the blinds wide open!"

"Dark? Dark? It may as well be Hades, Dieter! My God! Lydia has gone. To that lawless, infernal, degenerate . . ." Braddock put a hand quickly over his eyes, and his voice nearly broke. "That damned young Satan!"

"Lydia? Gone?" Baum looked wildly about, his white beard jutting at the corners of the room. "Gone where? What damned thing is this? What young man?"

"*Your* young man, Dieter," Braddock said bitterly. "That cursed Evans. It was not enough that he break her heart during his miserable life. Now he has driven her out of her mind."

Baum shook his friend's arm violently. "What are you saying, Roland? For the love of God, what is the matter? I know he may have done a wrongdoing, but the poor man is dead!" Baum's voice too was losing control, and his pale blue eyes shone with tears.

"Dead or not, he has worked his evil way with my daughter!" Braddock shook free from his friend's grasp and strode to the desk. He picked up a crumpled sheet of paper and thrust it at Baum. "Read! Read! Would to God he *were* alive, so I could have the satisfaction of shooting him through his black heart!"

Professor Braddock sank then into a chair and buried his head in his hands. Baum fumbled with his spectacles, jammed them on his nose at a skew angle, and squinted at the paper, turning it a little toward the faint halo of light around the heavy drapes. In a few moments he uttered a gasp, then a small, strangled sound. In one motion he lowered the piece of paper and his spectacles fell from his nose to dangle on their gold chain.

"I . . . Great God!" Baum stared again at the letter, shaking his head. "Idaho!"

"You see, Dieter? You see?" Professor Braddock looked up suddenly. His face seemed to the other even older, a caricature of death, yet rigid now with a new intensity and power. "You see what we must do?"

Baum could not speak. He shook his head and laid the letter gently back on the desk.

"We must find her. We must save her. If any human or divine power can be summoned for the task, we must invoke it. I want you to come with me."

Baum placed the spread fingertips of one trembling hand on the desktop. He looked at his colleague for a long time. Finally, his voice creaking as if with disuse, he spoke.

"To Idaho?"

"Yes, Dieter. Tonight. On the first available train."

Baum closed his eyes momentarily. All the trepidation, the uncertainty, the confusion he felt in this adopted country of his—which seemed to be hurling itself with a mad and terrific racket into the maw of destruction, a new Sodom—all his fears for the future of civilization could now be traced to this one sinister place, this Idaho, which had swallowed up the young man as dear to him as a son, and now had stolen his best friend's innocent and lovely daughter. He sagged against the desk with a sharp intake of breath. Professor Braddock half rose from his chair with a murmur of concern; but then, as a chevalier weary from the lists slowly raises the tattered pennons on his lance to meet the last and most heroic of challenges, the trimmed white beard lifted from Baum's breast, slowly but without hesitation, and the blue eyes took fire again.

"Yes," he said, and then again more firmly, more loudly, "Yes! To this Idaho! You and I, Roland, we shall find her and bring her again to home!"

Their train was inexplicably held up in Denver, and Skillings had descended in search of another bottle of Nervine, which Baum required as a restorative. Professor Braddock had purchased three newspapers, and now sat erect examining them with a scholar's care, while Baum fidgeted with his watch-chain and alternately glared at or ignored the throng on the platform. From time to time they engaged in desultory conversation, but Braddock was still so single-minded in the grim purpose that arose from his grief, and his colleague so overwhelmed by the barbarity of life in this unfamiliar region, that their exchanges soon expired in gloomy, uncomfortable silence.

But now Braddock gave a low exclamation of surprise, and tapped his friend peremptorily on the knee.

"Your giant ape has been playing havoc again, Dieter. See here." He shook the paper, folded it to emphasize one bold headline, then handed it to Baum. "A bloody business."

Baum donned his spectacles and read intently.

THE SAVAGE OWYHEE COLOSSUS MURDERS MORE!

Big Foot Attacks Innocent Miners

After a lull of several weeks, when little was heard in these parts of "Chief" Nampuh and his foul depredations, the Bloody Tyrant of the Owyhees descended from his mountain fastness to butcher and defile two independent operators of a remote mine near the head of Dollar Creek.

Slain were Thomas ("Hardrock Tom") Fletcher and Timothy Kirkpatrick, who had been working as partners on various claims in the Dollar Creek and Horse Mountain areas. Both were well known at stations on the Humboldt Trail. Their horribly mutilated corpses, and the wreckage of their camp, were found by George Williams of Boise. Williams rode at a lather for Silver City to warn every miner, freighter and cattle driver in the area of the monster's return.

Outrage is running high throughout the territory, and many of the foremost citizens are proposing a Volunteer Militia, if the United States Army cannot subdue the cunning Giant and his bloodthirsty crew. Big Foot's victims number at the present in the dozens, and no freight string or stage is safe from Boise to Elko. Only last month a young man of culture and learning was captured by this outlaw gang, and his awful fate is still unknown.

The time has come for all who possess an interest in Progress and Civilization in this land of wealth and potential profits to rise up and treat this band of murderous savages to a dose

of lead or good, three-quarter-inch hemp, which
they so richly deserve.

Baum pulled himself erect, the newspaper quivering in his hands, as
Skillings opened the door of their compartment and slipped inside, bearing a small parcel.

"It is Willard," Baum said excitedly. "Surely it is Willard. The young
man of culture. Here it says his fate is unknown! Perhaps he is a captive
—is alive still, even as we now are speaking!"

Professor Braddock frowned and recoiled slightly from the newspaper.

"A misfortune it would be," he intoned, "if poor hardworking men
were cut down and a scoundrel spared."

"Roland!" Baum removed his spectacles with a fumbling hand. "Do
not speak so!"

"How, Dieter, could I speak otherwise? Think what this . . . this
ne'er-do-well has done to my life! To Lydia!" Braddock turned abruptly
to stare out the window, indicating the subject was distasteful.

Skillings cleared his throat, setting the package carefully on the seat
beside Baum.

"Your medicine, sir." He coughed deferentially again. "About the
delay, gentlemen. I troubled to inquire and may suggest that we shall not
have more than a half hour to wait before departure. It appears that we
have a distinguished new passenger."

Professor Braddock turned back from the window. "What is it, Skillings?" His voice was abstracted, pettish. "What is this about a new
passenger?"

"Beg pardon, sir. I spoke with another manservant on the platform. If
you take a look from the window there you can just see the cars at the
rear of the train—private cars, sir, very elegant indeed. The personal
traveling suite of the financier Stoneman. The new passenger, sir. Mr.
Mandrake Stoneman of Wall Street fame." Skillings allowed himself a
very small but intense smile of pride.

[19]

THE PINKERTON CAPTAIN nodded through the window to the
conductor, who smiled, uttered a great oath under his breath, and then
signaled the brakeman, who relayed the high sign to the engineer. The

whistle hooted and the bell clanged, the great wheels spun, caught, spun another half-turn, and began to creep ahead, until all down the line coaches hitched and shuddered into motion.

Stoneman felt the shock of departure only faintly, since his private cars were double-sprung on a new hydraulic system that corrected for lateral as well as vertical displacement. These mobile quarters, in terms of design, were twins of the presidential coaches commissioned by President Grant, though their interior appointments were more opulent. They also had double iron doors and armored shutters, tastefully drawn out of sight behind the oak paneling, and the attendant car—where his servants and the Pinkertons rode—was equipped with an ice locker and complete kitchen.

He had dismissed Adams, the Pinkerton captain, and Fairfield to allow himself an untroubled few hours in which to reflect on the course of action he had determined to pursue. Wo Hang, the Chinaman who served as his personal valet whenever he traveled, had left him a whisky and soda on a heavy silver tray by his armchair. Stoneman settled back to sip the fine old liquor, an Ohio corn-mash bourbon that he imported by the keg, and to begin the slow, serpentine speculations that so often led him to his original—some said brilliant—strategies of the marketplace.

Now and then, one heard whispers of mockery, hints that Stoneman's policies went well beyond the blend of voracity and cunning so admired by his countrymen—that they bore the stamp of something unhealthy, possibly lunatic. The great man, these gossip-mongers sneered, still believed in branding thieves and beheading socialists, believed that the strongest—meaning himself—should rule with fearsome authority, perhaps even believed in absolute monarchy.

If these anonymous rumors stung him, Stoneman did not manifest any direct reaction. He had hired men like Fairfield to speak for him: genial, articulate, and calculating men who created, for the world of finance and for the curious public, a Mandrake Stoneman of imposing magnanimity, a titan whose only aim was to serve the advance of civilization by striking down the forces of darkness and chaos.

To Stoneman himself it seemed that he alone could face the unadorned truth about polyglot humanity—that the rightful place for most people was on their knees. Once long ago he had let a woman glimpse his deepest convictions, his ultimate pride, and she had recoiled in horror. This happened on the eve of the election in which he was humiliated. He had drunk too much, raved about his vision of a new race, and the task of subjugating it, and in a moment of passionate excess he had taken the woman, a highborn beauty, into his confidence. He had tried to show her his skill in his special theater, to demonstrate his theories, and she had become hysterical. Thereafter, he kept his knowledge to himself. It became his power, his weapon, his magic—which he worked over the length and breadth of the land.

Rocked gently by the hydraulic suspensors, Stoneman now allowed himself to visit this most secret depth of his being. The iron rails under him, rails that he owned, became in his thoughts a great causeway over the land and into the mountains where treasure awaited. But the treasure was guarded by an evil giant, who preyed upon the simpletons, the half-humans whose duty was to dig out the treasure and labor in smoke and fire-blast to render it pure. So he, as lord of the rails and ingots, had been called forth to subdue the giant. The pygmies and trolls that made up his legions were no match for such an opponent. The king himself must act.

Stoneman smiled to himself. His own genius, he had realized, dictated a daring attempt to capture this Big Foot alive. No triumph could be greater—nor publicity scheme more galvanizing—than to bend such a creature to one's will. Another vision floated up from the whisky glass as he stared into it, while the shadows of telegraph poles and cottonwood trees shuttered rapidly across the interior of the car. He saw himself with a whip, his boots gleaming in the dust, while a great shape cowered before him; he saw a post with chains, a gallery of spectators, the breeding pens, a long line of huge, bare-backed men who lifted track and ties as if they were toys . . . and now, again, the whip . . . the boots . . .

He shook his head impatiently, setting the whisky down sharply on the tray. It would not do to relinquish himself to dreams at this stage of the game. There was that infernal confidence man and his red-haired tart. He must at all costs reach the Finn before anything irremediable occurred. He had wired ahead to the military authorities, and a trusted railway agent in Salt Lake had begun soliciting the kind of hardened men who would be needed for the expedition against the outlaw band.

Stoneman was confident of his resources, his power, his shrewd knowledge of men and what money could make them do. With Fairfield's gift for blarney and his own immense prestige, he would have these provincials eating from his hand in a matter of hours. What troubled him was the matter of timing. All depended on the fate of that damned young philanderer, Evans. If he *was* alive, and somehow escaped or was liberated by the Army, then he would inherit the old professor's fortune, and the pact with the "widow" and her venomous escort would dissolve. The pair would still hold his note, however, a sufficient proof of his guilt should they choose to expose him publicly. They had probably devised a method of releasing the story of his unusual private diversions in the event of any harm to either. For that reason it was imperative to intercept the Finn.

He found an edge of zest now, cutting through both reverie and worry. It was the feeling, he recognized, that came closest to what others seemed to mean by the word *love*, the feeling that swelled under his ribs when he saw the figures posted on the board at the Exchange, or when he knew with certainty that a rival had taken a bait of preferred stock, or when he had first decided to gamble for political office. It was the peculiar combination of danger, challenge, and opportunity that fascinated him above all else.

He had of course done everything to minimize risk. Pinkertons from Omaha to Salt Lake had been mustered to proceed to the Idaho Territory and make circumspect inquiries after the Finn. A powerful senator, influential in the War Department, had contrived a communiqué to the field commanders of the Fifth Army, advising them to curtail patrols into regions threatened by hostiles, pending certain "strategic decisions." He had percolated money through a dozen brokers to begin the slow and devious process of inflating the price of silver.

In many of his dealings, such astute precautions guaranteed Stoneman his harvest of millions, but he found that sort of routine profiteering boring and debilitating. It was the unusual, the unbalanced, and the unforeseen that excited him: the situation that forged into one white-hot mass his love of gain, his dream of a new age of powerful rulers and their colossal servants, and the thrill of a fresh opponent on unfamiliar terrain. Looking out now at the rolling plains where the late afternoon sun created pools of shadow, Stoneman did not reflect with any pride that he owned half the land on either side of the tracks for as far as he could see, did not in fact see at all the domain of which he was already unchallenged monarch. He saw a far vaster landscape, desolate and magnificent, where, at one whispered word from him, hordes of men with flashing swords rode into a mad and bloody fray. In his very bones, without putting the sensation into words, he knew already that he was voyaging toward the grandest of triumphs, or the most stunning of reversals.

[20]

TO LYDIA it seemed as if Providence had determined to transport her in one swift step from the Inferno to Paradise. The name of the establishment where Mr. Baldo had found her lodgings was in fact the Eden Hotel. If the wallpaper and veneer fell a little below the standard of the Original Garden, at least with the shutters closed and drapes drawn, with her private tub of gleaming copper and a fresh counterpane upon the bed, she could almost believe herself again in a civilized land.

The nightmare journey by stagecoach from Salt Lake to Idaho City had obliged her to suffer conditions rude beyond belief. The meals were hardtack, black beans, and a horrible concoction of sulfur-cured fruit covered with suet in a basin of dough, identified as "pie" by the leering, toothless mulatto who claimed the title of cook at the Iron Creek station. For much of the trip she had been the only woman passenger, and sometimes only a makeshift curtain of cheap blankets, drawn around a cot, delineated her quarters from those of the male travelers. Most of these slept on tables or on the floor in the station's low-ceilinged main room, whose log walls were nearly black with smoke and grease. At night she would hear snores and curses, the patter of rats' feet above and below her, and sometimes she nearly gagged at the odor of rancid fat, unwashed bodies, and open tins of lard and kerosene. It was often a relief to return to the crowded coach; though it jolted over the rutted tracks, or swayed sickeningly on its thoroughbraces while it filled with a fine fog of dust, the compartment was nonetheless open—when weather allowed— to the sunlight and air.

Had Mr. Baldo not been always there to assist with a polite word and a quick hand, she would not, she believed, have been able to withstand her despair and homesickness. Both feelings were intensified by the terrible wasteland she traveled through. It was a landscape of burned rock and twisted trees, yawning chasms and jagged peaks, whose few inhabitants appeared crude, unclean, and misshapen. But by a wonderful fortuitousness Baldo—"One name is enough," he said with his slight smile— was traveling on an itinerary almost identical with her own. He was a representative of a large firm in the East, seeking to make contact with speculators in mining and commercial properties in these remote regions. He referred with circumspection to his employer, and Lydia understood that the enterprise was a confidential one. For her own part she had been equally reserved, and more than a little deceptive. She had mentioned family business, a visit to distant relatives, one an invalid.

She sat before the mirror of the cheap vanity, applying a hint of rouge to her lips, and first questioned, then reaffirmed her decision to place even more trust in her Good Samaritan, who would be calling on her in a few minutes to escort her to dinner—her first decent meal, she calculated, in two weeks. She had determined to tell him, without any mention of painful details, that her journey was not after all at the behest of her family, but made in spite of parental will, and involved defending a young man's honor. In her efforts she might well find useful the assistance of those financial and commercial interests with whom Baldo had dealings. She could hardly solicit such aid directly, not only because she was a woman, but because her family's name could be known even here.

Her new friend had shown interest when she mentioned her father's university post. He remarked that his employer was a well-known patron of the scientific investigations at that distinguished institution. Baldo himself did not have the air of a learned man. There was a slight foreignness in his speech—Scandinavian, he said—and a total absence of figurative language or bookish allusion. Her one reservation about the man derived from this spareness of speech; it was as if he waited always on the words of others. When he did speak, his intention and his presence were more powerful than his language, and rendered it like the purring of a cat or the trill of a bird. She found it hard to remember anything he said.

The little bell by the door jangled, a signal from the desk clerk that Baldo awaited her in the lobby. She rose lightly, feeling for the first time in many days a pang of delightful anticipation. She turned from side to side, examining herself in the mirror—restored as she was to her natural condition: a pretty, cheerful young woman with bright lace at her throat and a clean starched bonnet on her arm. Soon she would be attended by a strong, considerate, and well-dressed gentleman. She smiled at her image, relief and hope flooding back into her heart. She had found a friend.

On the walk to the Café Moderne she was brought back rudely to the actuality of this place, its outlandish barbarity. Jefferson "Avenue" was a wide strip of churned mud where wagons, riders, and stray dogs jostled one another in a loud, never-ending hurly-burly of motion and noise. On the sidewalks of rough planking laid over railroad ties, a stream of humanity coursed in both directions, and sometimes a pedestrian darted away across the street, dodging the hooves, whips, and curses of the traffic there. At intersections they had to pick their way through the muck, and she steadied herself on Baldo's proffered arm.

Miners, in riotous, unkempt beards and coarse clothing, hurried along like men possessed. Lydia found their gazes either insupportably impudent or completely blank, the look of men blind or quite mad. Here and there a Chinaman slipped by in the current, eyes downcast, pigtail bouncing, feet lifting in small, quick steps; or a derelict squaw huddled against a building, begging, a child wrapped like a small mummy beside her.

At her involuntary gasps Baldo murmured inconsequential encouragement, until they reached a towering, three-story building with an imposing false front. The building was situated between a blacksmith shop and a dry-goods store, both of which were plying a busy trade. The street-level floor had been divided into two long rooms, one housing the Gold King Saloon, the other the Café Moderne. As they approached the ornate door of the café, the heavy boots before the dry-goods store shuffled aside to make way for them, and the men fell silent. Cheeks burning, Lydia kept her eyes fixed straight ahead and fought to keep from shrinking against Baldo's shoulder.

A young man with a beard halfway to his waist sprang in front of them, swept his hat from his head, and threw open the door for them. Murmurs of appreciation and envy came from the others. The Finn nodded at the youth as he passed, and Lydia gave him the swiftest and smallest of all possible smiles. When the door closed behind them they heard a chorus of whoops and laughter.

"Polite ruffians!" Lydia said between her teeth.

"No matter," Baldo murmured.

The maître d'hôtel approached, a tall, quick man with the hunched shoulders of a heron, and a waiter closed on them from another flank. In a moment they were seated at their own table and presented with menus. The alacrity and flourish of the service made Lydia smile. It was an exaggeration, a baroque form of the attendance one would expect in a fine restaurant in New York. The accoutrements, too, were almost parodic. A false ceiling of cheap wooden scrollwork contained an oval central mural depicting Aphrodite being born from the waves with the aid of delirious seraphim. A crystal chandelier hung on each side of the mural, and gilt-edged mirrors—far too many of them—lined the walls. Imitation Oriental carpets were laid end-to-end on the floor, despite wildly conflicting designs, and carved teak screens encircled certain tables.

"I hope it is . . . acceptable." Baldo removed his hat, and again Lydia had to consciously avoid staring at his extraordinary ears. The eyes in the small head, round as a cannonball, were a clear, pale gray.

"Charming. I think even quaint." Lydia smiled and reached for her napkin, then hesitated, seeing a flicker of movement in a far corner of the room. All at once her amused, patronizing smile vanished. Briefly but quite clearly she saw a rat—quite a large one—waddle along the wall and disappear beneath one of the tables.

Precisely with the sharp intake of her breath, a heavy curtain on the inside wall was swept aside and, along with a cacophony of sound, a group of people boiled into the room. Lydia understood then that there was converse between the café and the Gold King Saloon. Through the opening she could see men ranged along a bar of dark, polished wood; under a haze of tobacco smoke, others were seated at tables playing cards. There were women, too, in ruffled gowns, glittering with jewelry.

One of these women was in the group that had broken in on them. The bright rouge on this creature, her bare shoulders and only half-concealed bosom, the oversized stones flashing from her throat and ears, all proclaimed her profession clearly enough to Lydia. She had never before seen, at this proximity, one of her sex who had fallen so low. This vixen was not, she judged, much beyond her own age, yet she moved with the provocative insouciance of an experienced courtesan.

Her escort had apparently once found fortune, for his gray suit, though soiled, was of good quality, and the purple tie was affixed to his boiled shirt front by a pearl stickpin. He was of dark, Mediterranean hue and sported a tremendous moustache black as a crow's wing. Peering about the room, he gave an immoderate laugh, apropos of nothing. His bloodshot eyes seemed to dwell on Lydia.

"Evenin', ma'am," he boomed, and converted a lurch into a bow.

The "bird of the night"—Lydia had acquired the term from a novel—was staring at her frankly. All at once the creature advanced, pushing aside the maître d'hôtel, who had rushed up to intercept the new party. Lydia was aware that others had entered from the saloon and were watching this tableau.

"Good evenin', dearie." She addressed Lydia with an insinuating familiarity, then glanced at Baldo with a look of bold calculation. "Got yourself a sport, have ye? A right smart one, too. A right smart nob, he is." The woman coughed then, a deep, racking cough, and smiled a fierce smile.

Lydia still had not recovered her breath, and managed to gasp out only a weak "Beg pardon?" At a near view she perceived that the woman was very beautiful beneath her makeup, and very pale.

Baldo, who had held the menu suspended before him, now set it carefully on the table and shifted in his chair, as if to rise. The woman put a hand on the tabletop and leaned toward Lydia.

"What's the matter, love? Cat got your tongue?" She reached toward Lydia's cheek.

She did not see Baldo move, but his hand was all at once intercepting the woman's hand and turning it back. There was a small popping sound and the woman squealed, caught her heel somehow in the ruffled hem of her gown, and fell full-length on the floor.

Lydia herself uttered a sound, a tentative shriek, as the dark man attempted to run at their table; but became entangled with the woman thrashing on the floor. Now Baldo was on his feet and moving toward the other man, who had bent suddenly in a low bow. When he straightened, there was a sliver of brightness in one hand, and under the great black wings of the moustache a dazzling grin appeared.

Baldo crouched and glided to the right away from Lydia. His hand darted behind the flap of his coat and reappeared gripping a dark, dangling object. She was absurdly reminded of a sausage. With the other hand he gestured, beckoning the man who held the knife.

"Come," Baldo said in a voice still soft and polite, "come along."

The woman on the floor twisted suddenly, arching her back, and uttered a sound hardly human—a hoarse, rattling snore. Her eyes had rolled back in her head, leaving only white slits like the blank eyes of a statue, and the heels of her shoes began a staccato hammering on the floor. Horrified, Lydia stared at the contorted features, at the bubbles of spittle oozing between clenched teeth.

"Hold on, you fellers! She's a-havin' a fit!" a man called out, and there were gasps and murmurs of alarm.

The maître d'hôtel moaned aloud as more men intruded into the room from the saloon, excited by the disturbance.

"Stand back!" someone commanded, and two men stepped between Baldo and his adversary.

Lydia found herself on her feet, fumbling with a handkerchief. A man knelt and placed a knife against the woman's bared teeth. He pried sharply, then nodded at Lydia.

"Stuff it in thar," he said gruffly.

Trembling with fear and revulsion, for the grimacing and gaping beneath the knife blade were terrible to see, Lydia folded her kerchief and placed it in the woman's mouth. The blade was removed and the jaws closed with a muffled click.

"Now git out'n her way," the man said, rising.

Lydia too stepped back. A ring of curious onlookers now surrounded the woman on the floor, who continued to tremble, her back arched. On opposite sides of the ring Baldo and the dark-complexioned man regarded each other, but their hands were now empty. All at once the galvanic force contorting the woman seemed to relax. She became limp and soft, pale as death. Her eyelids fluttered.

"She's a-comin' around," someone exclaimed. "He'p 'er up," someone else urged, and people surged forward with extended hands.

"Stay back!" commanded the dark man. There was no longer any trace of intoxication in his manner, and Lydia noted that his voice was strong and well-modulated. He pulled off his coat and knelt to prop up the woman's head. "Give her time to recover." Others also removed their coats, and soon the woman reclined in a veritable nest. Her eyes were open now, blinking at them as if she were awakening from a dream. She had removed the kerchief from her mouth, but pressed it again to her lips as her body was racked by a deep cough. With a shock Lydia noted flecks of red clinging to the linen.

"The poor thing," she said. With a sudden pang of grief she thought of Willard, who, would have ministered with sure confidence and strong hands to this suffering creature.

"Like hell."

Startled, realizing she had been overheard, Lydia turned to find at her elbow an old man whose grizzled, seamed features were fixed in a sardonic leer. He jerked his head at the woman on the floor.

"She hain't even sick. I seen this pair a-workin' before."

He was wearing the canvas trousers of his profession, held up by wide suspenders, and a greasy buckskin shirt, but he flaunted also a neat bowler hat, at least two sizes too small, which he tilted and replaced quickly, like a valve letting off steam.

"Beggin' yer pardon, ma'am, but this pair o' rattlers will bilk you blind. I seen—" He broke off, for Baldo had appeared beside her.

"We should go," he said, and she felt his thick, powerful forearm brace against her own.

"But—" Lydia glanced again at the woman on the floor, propped to a sitting position now, the stained handkerchief clutched to her bosom.

"I tell ye I seen 'em afore," the old man hissed. "She had red har two weeks ago in Silver City, and he was playin' like her uncle. Hain't no such a thing. They got a hunnert deals, all crooked as—"

"Red?"

For the first time Lydia heard Baldo's tone change. The single word was like an ingot of iron.

"Yessir. And yaller afore that. She's slippry as a skillet full o' hog fat."

The woman moaned, then coughed again, a ragged, half-liquid cough.

Lydia shook her head and stepped forward, a bottle of smelling salts in her hand, like a talisman against distraction and confusion. "The poor creature is very ill, whatever her condition in life," she said firmly, and knelt beside the woman, extending the vial. The poor creature lifted her gaze, and in those green depths Lydia saw profound supplication, as if for salvation from a whole life of hardship and degradation.

[21]

September 4—

Frost almost every morning, and two days ago the slopes above us were white with snow. Parties of men depart daily to hunt. We butcher the deer they bring back, and dry strips of meat over the fire. Still, by the poverty of our stores I foresee extreme hardship in this climate and terrain. Occasionally a small party arrives with supplies and information. These visitors belong to portions of the Shoshoni tribe which are held in a government camp to the south, guarded—imperfectly, evidently—by a detachment of the Army.

As I wrote earlier, my return from the raid, with Cole's raw scalp dangling from the saddle, inaugurated a new phase in my captivity. The savages are now quick to assemble for my measuring sessions, and insist on teaching me words in their language, which, to my considerable surprise, I find regular in its declensions, not unlike Latin. When Jacques is nearby they cajole him into rough translations of their long harangues and interminable questions. They understand that my aim is to determine "character" (as I somewhat euphemistically term it) by reference to the conformation of the cranium, and this proposition seems infinitely amus-

ing to them. They insist, often with coarse gestures, that measurement of other portions of their anatomy would provide a surer indication of worth. They say also that there is no need for the calipers and tape, that they will tell me all I wish to know about themselves and their habits, and so I have had to listen to repeated yarns about the slaying of enemies and the hunting of bear, buffalo and wild sheep.

I am called "Peekchur Man," and the camera and developing trunk, though never deployed since that first photographic venture, are held in reverence. I am also addressed sometimes as "brother," and because of my crime of homicide am clearly on a more equal footing here. Such is the mad inversion of morals in this savage society! And how much I have discovered of the treacherous and labyrinthine corridors of the human heart, heretofore entirely hidden to me! I catch myself smiling, even laughing, at their simple badinage, at the eagerness with which they watch my face when I read the scale and make an entry. In spite of every cell of my being, bred and cultivated in an environment of high purpose, purity of thought, compassion, and respect for justice, I discover a growing kernel of sympathy for these depraved natives.

I have thought long and deeply . . .

But must stop here. I see men taking horses from the picket line and packing their belongings, so we are to move.

September 6—

The new camp perches on a steep and dangerous abyss—fitting metaphor for my existence now. The rocks pitch downward from barren ridges to a stream far below, and much of the day the canyon is in shadow. There is little firewood except the ubiquitous sagebrush. Each day four men must descend with water bags, and how they make their way over the precipices and desolate spurs of stone I cannot imagine. I thought from the beginning that the band decamped arbitrarily, with little regard for weather or threat of attack. This suspicion was confirmed a few days ago in one of my sessions with Nampuh.

His strategy, it falls out, is determined by the small pouch of buttons, bits of bone and bright pebbles which he has collected. Each of these objects has markings on top, bottom or sides, and each signifies a location, season, or direction. Apparently each is associated also with some important experience or revelation, which may indicate attack or retreat or holding fast. The giant throws this collection of icons on his bear hide and reads them like dice.

He demonstrated the method for me, pointing out how a bit of antelope horn with a crude cross etched on one surface "told" him that he could move eastward to the country of the antelope and expect a meeting there, an intersection with a party moving from north to south. Another pebble, however, qualified this information, for it signified winter. Of course practical matters like the weather, availability of water, and size of his armed force must be taken into account, he explained. But particularly in doubtful circumstances, when arguments between his lieutenants seem unresolved, he consults the oracle of chance.

For this reason, he said with great humor, the Army has never caught him. White men, he claimed, think only one way. If it snows early and pasture is scarce, they expect him to move to lower slopes, like the deer; if there is much traffic on a particular trail, they lay their snares along it, convinced that he will come as to a bait. They do not understand that there are always too many choices, as many as there are stones in the river, so a warrior must have a way to weigh them, a secret way known only to himself.

It is probably true that his capricious system has baffled the authorities who are attempting to capture him and his band. His followers, believers as they are in his shrewdness and strength, as well as his strange manner of determining an itinerary, lend force and momentum to whatever enterprise is so settled upon. I note that when a move is decreed, the men spring to their tasks with alacrity and speak encouragingly of their prospects. The ponies are rounded up and packed, fires extinguished, guns cleaned and loaded, and scouts sent forth in an almost holiday atmosphere. There is a certain value, as Nampuh claimed, in decisiveness for its own sake.

September 9—

A light drizzle is drumming on the tarpaulin which I have spread over my hovel of woven branches, and through the ghost-like veils of rain I can barely make out the rocky promontories of the opposing canyon wall. There is a dreariness in the scene that corresponds to the desolation within me.

I am not alone. Beside me, in a heap of blankets and an old buffalo robe given me to ward off the growing chill of these autumn nights, is an Indian woman—a girl really—still sleeping off the effects of strong drink. Her bare brown arm is only inches from my knee, and I would to God it were a poisonous serpent that could strike and so end this sickening vortex of depravity. I thought, with my taking of a man's life, that further degradation was impossible. But the terrible shocks, the ghastly paradoxes of this chapter of my life seem to go on and on.

*A moment ago I thought of Lydia—sweet, innocent, noble Lydia!—
and was conscious of the horror of such a thought in these circumstances.
Twice, now, I have dishonoured her in the foulest way known to man.
Twice I have had carnal knowledge of another woman. And last night the
crime was committed with drunken lust, in the company of a lewd savage.
It would be easy to claim that I acted under duress, that my own life hung
in the balance. But to cede to such coercion—was this not the behavior of
a coward and scoundrel? It might have been viewed as an opportunity to
quit this wicked life with a shred of honor, but instead—and here is the
utter horror of the act—I found myself borne under by my own bestiality.
Not once, but thrice I allowed myself the awful transports of licentious-
ness! My brain aflame with the cheap whisky supplied to these people by
dishonest traders, I lost all self-knowledge, all self-respect.*

*Oh Christ! I have glanced over what has been written, caught sight of
my own hands—rough, now, and baked brown by the sun, not so very
different in hue from those of this sleeping girl—and want to hurl the
notebook out into the empty air of the canyon! Hypocrite! All this blather
about "depravity" and "horror"! Where were such words when this miserable body was wrenched by the oldest and basest of passions? How have I
not seen that, day by day, I grow coarser, ruddier, more inured to this
harsh existence; how in fact I have come to revel in it at times? There are
evenings when, after a hard ride, I take my portion at the fire and eat with
good humor, trading with my cohorts the few words I know, laughing to
see their enactments of my posture when I dismount or throw on a saddle.*

*In this mood, yesterday, I watched a large contingent of visitors arrive.
They were all Indians from the regions around Fort Hall, who had slipped
away from the Army's surveillance to bring supplies and information from
the world at large. This time, however, the supplies included a small keg
of whisky and four women, two withered hags and two girls surely no more
than seventeen. There was much gabble and showing of goods, a bazaar
in fact, with trinkets, cheap clothing, knives and the like spread on blankets. The men began to gamble and drink, and the advances of the women
made perfectly obvious their purpose in coming.*

*One of the girls began to talk to me and pull at my sleeve, and my
embarrassment attracted general attention. I prepared to withdraw to my
own tent, but one of the visitors, an old man with many feathers and a
necklace of bear claws, accosted me and made a long speech directly into
my face. I understood nothing of it of course, and he commenced pointing
first at the girl, then at me, then at my tent. I pretended not to grasp his
meaning and again attempted to retire.*

At this moment I detected a change in mood throughout the group. Nampuh arose from a gambling game and approached, his countenance somber enough. Jacques stepped to my side and whispered rapidly that I had committed a grievous error, had insulted the old man by declining to accept his wife. To refuse a woman was, in fact, the most dire affront possible. There were still some in the band, he added hurriedly, who thought I was an evil medicine man and had taken the photos in order to put a spell on them. If this faction gained influence, I could be executed and left for the vultures.

I tried to placate the old man, tried to explain, through Jacques, my position as—yet another grotesque irony—a married man. My interpreter, I am sure, was not honest, and twisted my words to suit his own designs. The old man insisted that I drink whisky with him and listen to more speeches about his prowess as a hunter, and to an embarrassing catalogue of his wife's charms. Others gathered around, and I was continually plied with drink. The old crones began singing and shuffling about the fire in some kind of dance. Their movements were salacious and met with high hilarity from the men, who forced me particularly to observe.

The young woman became ever more insistent and suggestive, while my reactions were assessed instantaneously by the crowd. If I demurred, there were grumblings and insidious whisperings, presumably among my detractors; if I showed myself amenable to her solicitation, there were grunts and whoops of approval. At some point I was pulled to my feet and, unsteady as I was, propelled into the firelight. The old hags and the girl danced about me, looking like minions from hell with tongues of flame darting along their bare thighs. The others began pounding the earth with heel and fist in an infernal rhythm, and in spite of myself I staggered to its pulse. Perhaps, to be most truthful, I must admit that the coarse cries of encouragement from spectators somehow infected my blood, and I did not resist when, finally, I was whirled off into the darkness between the girl and her husband, with Jacques and Wart behind me.

What ensued in the darkness of the tent I need not elaborate, though perhaps the pain of recollection would in some small way purge my spirit. I resisted as well as I could, but though little more than a child, this dusky trollop knew all the wiles of the courtesan, and was as active and strong as a little panther. Also, many of the men remained but a little way outside the tent, and the hussy would call out to them, without shame, whenever I balked; and hearing their jeers—the tone of the jeer is comprehensible in any language—I was goaded beyond myself. What more is there to add? The flesh—with its terrible, ravening appetites—had its way.

There are stirrings about the fire site, now that the dawn is here. The rain has ceased but the sky is overcast, and wisps of cloud yet move through the canyon like wraiths. I suppose the visitors will be gone soon, and Nampuh will throw his little kit of symbols to determine our course. I have inadvertently received intelligence of impending danger to the giant and his followers, and to myself as well, I suppose. One of the newcomers brought a few combs and strings of beads wrapped in a sheet torn from a newspaper from Boise, and I seized it to read—my first communication with the life I once knew and took for granted.

A few paragraphs on one side of this sheet, a continuation of an article that must have begun on the front page, make mention of the arrival in the territory of Mandrake Stoneman. He has come to launch some mining and railroad enterprise in Silver City, and also "to lend his wealth and influence to the campaign to rid the mountains of the giant Shoshoni, Big Foot, whose notoriety has now reached the East." I cannot but marvel at the strange turns of fate since I shared fine cognac and cigars at Stoneman's table, planning my expedition to collect the remains of this same giant Neanderthalensis. Now I am in a quandary as to whether I should speak to Nampuh of this development, whether it would make him more cautious in his forays, or yet more daring and desperate. I almost wish I had a medicine bag of my own, full of bones, stones and coins, that would indicate my course of right action.

[22]

LYDIA had insisted on seeing the woman to her quarters. Baldo and the swarthy fellow arrived at a truce with the same mysterious rapidity that characterized the eruption of hostilities between them, so all four proceeded together—the weakened woman supported by the two men—to the El Dorado Hotel.

The woman, whose name was given as Theda, walked with faltering steps to the bed in her room and sank onto the coverlet with a murmur of gratitude. Lydia shooed the two men toward chairs in a corner and set about preparing a compress and a tincture of ammonia. Her patient's surroundings, she noted, were as dismal as her lot in life.

The El Dorado was primarily a saloon, with a few rooms above it whose purpose Lydia could all too easily surmise. Besides the decrepit bed with its cheap and garish coverlet, the only furnishings were a trunk with drawers, a clothes rack, a nightstand with pitcher and basin, a large framed mirror, a wooden table, and the two chairs the men now occupied. A brush, a bottle of cologne, and a few underthings were thrown carelessly over the trunk, but with this pitiful exception the room contained no indication of the history or purpose of its occupant.

As Lydia bent to apply the compress, the other lifted a pale hand to grasp her wrist.

"Dearie," she whispered. "Listen to me. You are an angel, a sweet angel. You think—" She coughed, twisting her head on the pillow. "You think we are wicked, my brother and I—yes, my brother—but we have known . . . a better life."

"Hush." Lydia removed her hand from Theda's grasp and poured a glass of the ammonia water. "You must rest."

Theda took the glass and sipped, her eyes closed. When she opened them, Lydia was again struck by their green blaze; they were like the sun through ice. Behind the mask of rouge and kohl was a countenance of great beauty and intelligence.

"We are of good family," Theda went on. "My brother was at the finest university in Europe—though you may not see signs of it now. We have had to . . ." She turned her face momentarily to the wall, clenching her lower lip between her teeth. "Alfons is not suited to rough work, and in this inferno there is no need for his learning or refinement. I am much more . . . valuable." Her face registered a bitter grimace.

Lydia gazed past the woman, a tiny frown creasing her brow. Something had tugged obscurely at her memory. She shook herself abruptly, and replaced the glass on the nightstand. "You must rest," she repeated, but without conviction.

For some minutes Lydia had been aware of another change in the mood of the two men across the room. Baldo's movements, by some subtle process she could not particularize, had become ever more catlike. His eyes, without blinking, possessed a peculiar glitter, and his hands, in gesturing, made the soft, quick strokes of a paw. Alfons seemed animated, intense. All trace of his former inebriation had vanished, and he spoke in an almost cultivated tone, insistent and rapid.

At first, from what she overheard, he had narrated a story much like Theda's, but after a question or two from Baldo the conversation began to digress in a most puzzling way. She caught the word "expectations," and then the phrases "contested estate" and "widow's mite."

"How unfortunate," Baldo said in a colorless tone. "So you have worked at many things?"

"Ah yes." Alfons grinned, tapping first his right arm, then his forehead. "With brain and brawn. Like you."

"The butcher and baker, cooper and clown." Baldo also smiled. "Perhaps a miller?"

"You mean grinding wheat? Crushing? With great . . . stones?"

Baldo did not answer. The glittering eyes were steady on the face of the other.

"You speak as one who knows. Are you a man of stones?"

Baldo laughed, and a moment later Alfons joined him, but to Lydia it seemed a laugh without mirth, a mere exchange of explosive hisses.

"There is no harvest here. This is a desert. You should perhaps go far away. Perhaps Europe. *Ein kleiner Ausflug.*"

"Ah, but my expectations are here, with my sister. *Nicht?*"

"It is most unhealthy here. You say you await the resolution of an estate, which will make you rich. But there is no need to wait. I can propose . . ." Baldo stopped, aware all at once that Lydia had paused in her ministrations. He rose quickly and nodded at the door. "Let us retire to your room."

He moved to the bedside and placed his hand on Lydia's shoulder. For the first time there was something in the gesture she did not like—a trace of familiarity or insinuation—and she felt her back grow tense.

"How is our patient?" Baldo bent and seemed to examine Theda intently. She murmured something and coughed.

"You must rest yourself," he went on, speaking to Lydia. "You have had a most exhausting evening. I shall be back in a moment."

Baldo and Alfons glided swiftly out, shutting the door behind them.

"Now, dearie," Theda said abruptly, and sat up. "The menfolks are off having a chat, and so will we. Where is your gentleman friend from?"

"I think . . . that is, New York."

"You haven't known him long? What's his business here?"

"He works for a firm, a large firm. What was that about an estate?" Lydia frowned again. Her patient seemed abruptly recovered, her voice strong and her eyes bright.

"Oh yes, I was married," Theda replied. "And widowed within the fortnight. What my brother said is true. His relatives have contested the estate and we are waiting—"

"Married?" Lydia reached for the bottle of ammonia, took it up, stared at it, replaced it.

"It was a bit of foolishness. A young man who ruined himself. No matter now." Theda turned again to the wall and underwent a tiny convulsion. "But he left me a certain sum—enough—if his estate could be cleared. We have spent everything defending my claim, and now just as—"

"Legacy?" Lydia said idiotically. She looked at the corners of the room, though they were bare.

"With a little money for passage to the East— Oh, but what am I thinking?" She coughed and fell back weakly on the coverlet. Lydia stared at her fixedly. "What—what is it?"

"Your hair. That man in the saloon said your hair was red."

Theda smiled faintly. "Black," she said. "Black as your own."

"The young man who was ruined"—Lydia could hear her voice rising in pitch, as if she were slurring through the scales, but she could no longer control it—"what was his name!"

Theda hesitated, arrested by the swift changes in Lydia's expression. From blank distraction, she had passed through a sudden flush of dismay to a preternatural intentness, fierce and cold. She drew away from Theda, gathering a fold of her skirt into each white-knuckled fist, her eyes riveted on the other woman's lips as if a snake, rather than a word, might issue forth. In the sudden silence they heard a solid, muffled thud from the alley outside the window.

Theda slid quickly from the bed and jerked aside the curtain. She gave an abrupt, sharp cry and then uttered an oath so foul that Lydia was stunned quite out of her train of thought. Theda left the window and ran to the trunk, betraying no sign of her previous weakness. She swept the bottle of cologne, hairbrush, and clothing from the lid, threw it back, and began rummaging furiously through the contents.

Lydia stepped to the window, glanced out, and saw, in the dim light filtering into the alley from the street, a man lying sprawled in the mud. She drew back, her fists still buried in her skirt, and tried to breathe, but there was a dreadful constriction in her throat, a power that would not permit her to speak, to utter a single sob, to form a thought. The door to the room swung open and Baldo entered.

He was smiling, his coat open, and Lydia saw the tip of the black sausagelike thing protruding from one pocket. Two steps into the room he came to rest, again with that delicate feline suddenness.

"Ah," he said.

Lydia saw that Theda had risen from the trunk; in her hand was a derringer, so small its two barrels, one atop the other, barely extended past her clenched fingers.

"He fell," Baldo said, tilting his head slightly. "He had drunk too much."

Theda uttered the oath again, and Lydia shuddered as if she had been doused with cold water. She began speaking all at once, in a torrent.

"This woman is an imposter. She is the woman who tricked my fiancé and ruined him. Her name is Elizabeth Miller and that man is not her brother. They are confidence—"

"Easy." Baldo shifted his eyes to Lydia, and their strange, steady glittering stopped her. "Now think," he went on. "You would have to kill her too. They would catch you in the wink of an eye. Everything lost."

"Stoneman sent you," Theda/Elizabeth said in a voice small and dull with hatred. "That slimy, lying bastard. We'll do for him."

"Ah," Baldo replied, his voice quiet, almost friendly, "not so easily done. Not so easily done. Anyway, you should be partners."

Elizabeth's eyes flashed and for a moment the fist around the tiny gun wavered, as if a wind had come and gone in the room.

"Partners? We were partners with that snake. We had a deal with him, the devil's own deal. And he—"

"You mean you squeezed him," Baldo interrupted. "Not a smart thing to do, try to squeeze a stone."

"You don't know, do you? That treacherous bastard, he's had you too."

"Mr. Baldo," Lydia said firmly, "what is the meaning of this? I demand you tell me how you know these . . . persons."

Baldo ignored her. He pursed his lips, speculative. "So you expected me?"

"You were to bring money and the contract. It was all set. We were waiting, and down to our last dime. Wolf saw this little piece—Elizabeth twisted the gun momentarily in Lydia's direction—"and thought she'd be our mark, the last one, until the boodle arrived."

"Ah, I see," Baldo nodded, smiling slightly. "So he was off his guard. Expected me to buy him. I thought it was a cock-and-bull tale—this deal you talk of—but perhaps not. Too bad. Too late, now."

"Too late for you." Elizabeth darted her tongue between her lips, as if thirsty.

"No, no." Baldo smiled more broadly. "Think, now. We must work together. It is unfortunate about Wolf. A good man, but he should not have played with his little blade in the dark. Here we are, you and I. The deal can still go through. You are twice a widow now, and could use some help. It is not certain, you know, that one of your husbands is entirely dead. That is a job I can do."

Elizabeth shook her head. "Trust you?" She gave a quick, fierce laugh. "I can shoot you and tell them you sapped my brother. I have an idea Miss Priss here might have to back me up."

"Two little bullets?" Baldo laughed soundlessly. "I have eaten bullets like those before, my dear." He rocked a little on the balls of his feet, the wide, thick body weaving slightly, light as a boxer's. "I could still break your pretty neck."

A silence fell; the three people remained transfixed in attitudes of extreme attention. Then, all at once, Baldo relaxed. He smiled, even closed his eyes, as if savoring something on his tongue.

"My God you're ugly," Elizabeth said. "Like a hog. Christ. I suppose you could do a job, all right."

"Oh yes." Baldo looked genial, calm, much as he had looked when Lydia found him by her side at the stage depot. "We shall see." He walked quite naturally forward until the derringer was a scant inch or two from his broad chest.

Elizabeth laughed between her teeth, and swung the gun again toward Lydia. "Her?"

Lydia took a faltering step toward the door. "I am . . ." she began, "My father . . ."

"Be quiet, my dear." Baldo frowned. "Unfortunate that you have run away and gotten yourself in a muddle. But we shall take care of you until—" He shrugged.

They heard then a babble of voices from the alley, a shout.

"We'll give her to Mama," Elizabeth said rapidly. "She's got a boy or two to watch her. We'd better have a story for this."

"He fell." Baldo screwed his face into an expression of great sadness, under which was a shadow of terrible mirth. "Went out to take some air and fell. You must go and shed some tears. You know how. I have seen you do a job too."

Elizabeth looked at him with her great, green eyes. Lydia had never seen an expression of such lewd insinuation. Then, as swiftly as holding up a mask, she became someone else: her cheeks were sucked in, her brow lifted and contorted, she threw the derringer into the trunk, and her hands contracted to wildly beating claws. She was a woman distraught, wild with an impending realization, on the brink of hysteria. With a strangled cry she ran from the room.

Lydia took another unsteady step, and tried to speak. "I demand . . . if you are a gentleman . . ."

"Ah, you should not have come. Your young man is doubtless already a pile of bones. And now—" Baldo looked momentarily sad.

More shouts arose, this time from the corridor outside. Doors slammed, and quick footsteps came and went, then returned. There was a thin, high scream. Baldo cocked his head, listening, and when there was a soft rap at the door, he grunted and opened it a few inches.

Lydia heard only part of the low, rapid conversation, catching the words "runaway" and "lunatic." Baldo reached inside his coat and she saw the flash of bills in his hand.

"Stop!" she cried, but dread had squeezed her voice into a feeble croak. "They are criminals! They will kill me! He killed that man! They are all imposters!"

As she stumbled toward the door it opened, and an immensely fat woman entered. Behind her were two men—a tall, sallow fellow in a flower-print vest, carrying a satchel, and a shambling, heavyset youth with a face like a pitted apple.

"Give 'er somethin', Doc," the fat woman said and handed one of the cluster of bills to the sallow man. She moved then toward Lydia like a great ship, the heavy folds of scarlet gown billowing around her, jewels quivering and sparkling like droplets of spray.

"My, my," she said, and threw one heavy arm around Lydia's shoulders. "If she ain't a looker, too." The smell of perfume and rouge was suffocating, and to Lydia the room seemed to darken. Over the woman's shoulder she could see the sallow man bending over the open satchel, a syringe in one hand. She tried to wrench herself free, but Baldo had moved to her other side and she felt herself being propelled toward the bed.

"The sports get a look at 'er, she could make you a wad," the fat woman said, one hand toying with a curl in disarray on Lydia's cheek. "Once she's broke in."

"None of that," Baldo said sharply. "Just keep her tight."

Lydia was going under. She sagged to one side and felt Baldo's hand at her waist. He lifted her as easily as if she were only an empty dress he was laying carefully out on the coverlet. Her breathing had become so shallow she could get out no more than a groan.

Then the sallow man was kneeling beside her, stroking and pinching her arm, and behind him she could see Baldo's silhouette like a great block of darkness.

"None of that," she heard him say, stern but matter-of-fact. "Yet."

[23]

"WHERE IS SILVER GOING, then, Mandrake?"

Stoneman arrested the crystal goblet on its way to his lips, and gazed at "Colonel" Nolan across the table. All evening, such direct questions had brought an eddy of respectful silence in the room.

A heavyset man with the rough features of an Irish miner, Nolan affected a bluff and open manner. He owned seven mines at Idaho City and four at Silver City. Backed by Huntington of the Central Pacific, he also owned controlling interest in a paper railroad proposed to connect Pocatello to Salt Lake. It was no secret to anyone present that one of Nolan's mines contained the new side vein of rich ore, and that Stoneman was interested in buying it.

"You've got it backwards, Colonel," said an old man, a banker, in a dry and sardonic tone. "Better ask where Mr. Stoneman is going. Your silver will toddle after."

There was general laughter. Before withdrawing, the Chinese servants had noiselessly removed the debris of the banquet and set forth decanters of brandy, along with ivory and teak cigar boxes. Nolan had tricked out his small but elegant mansion in an Oriental motif, with lavish carpets, silk screens, and tapestries. For this occasion he had had a jeweler cast tiny, solid silver pagodas to grace the setting for each guest.

Stoneman found these examples of barbaric taste amusing, but in the genial laughter and banter around the table he detected a shrewd company, their manners unpolished but their minds crafty and alert to advantage. These men, he sensed, also viewed him as a chance to test themselves, to risk—with or against him—their fortunes; and the lively discussions and anecdotes of the last hour had whetted an appetite to begin the subtle maneuvering of their common game.

"As you see, gentlemen, I am here with you." Stoneman raised his goblet with an easy gesture. "To Idaho."

"Hear, hear!"

"To the territory!"

"Milk and honey!"

Stoneman nodded, almost imperceptibly, to the governor, who beamed at this unexpected deference and tossed off his glass to lead the toast.

"You can't get off so easily, Mandrake," the colonel went on, after the smacking of lips and the rap of returning glasses. "Tell us our future."

"Oh, I've done that," Stoneman said, glancing swiftly around the table. "Silver goes where the railroad goes, as does coal and iron, and oil and cotton, and pork and beans. You recall my story about Cooke and the Northern Pacific? A hundred million in bonds—overnight?"

"But the cat's out of the bag there," the old banker cackled. "Can't do it that way ag'in. These damn newspapers run by the unionists and free traders—" He fumbled for an imprecation, his wrinkled cheeks shaking with the effort, and could find no oath sufficiently strong.

"It will be done," Stoneman said, and there was enough of the biblical in his tone to bring a hush to the assembly.

"I know you have all heard that the fever for rails is over—the Erie gang and Cooke and Commodore Vanderbilt have gotten a gutful, milked the thing dry—but don't believe it. Oh, it's true there won't be anything like the Transcontinentals again, but a man can do nearly as well gathering up the little ones, consolidating, settling up this country."

"The Transcontinentals," someone intoned reverently, "God's own horn of plenty, that was." There was a silence, in which some men appeared to be looking far away, across the mountains to those distant ribbons of steel that soared over plain and river, crag and gorge.

With the self-control that made him famous on Wall Street, Stoneman managed to refrain from grinding his teeth. He saw from the corner of his eye that the banker was watching him closely. The old cock knew. In his career Stoneman had made one serious, unforgettable error. He had not fairly judged the extent of the craze for rails in the western territories. Others had. Some seven years ago, Stoneman had watched a band of brash newcomers create, miraculously as gods, a tremendous fortune from nothing but dreams, and build at the same time a thousand miles of railroad out of more durable material. They not only kept their fortunes, wrung from public funds, but crowned them with popular acclaim. "Empire-builders," the press trumpeted, and Stoneman had seethed in the shadows, nearly mad with rage and grief.

Now he smiled again, imperiously.

"Some of you know I have learned my own lesson at considerable cost."

There were polite laughs and knowing winks; inwardly Stoneman writhed, but he broadened his smile.

"I wasn't wrong about the risk—remember, Cooke's bubble burst for good—but I should have taken it. Look here." Stoneman moved the tiny pagoda far to the right of his plate. "Mineral here in the mountains." He placed his glass, napkin, and an ashtray to his left. "Over here cities in the East, manufacturing everything." He pushed a plate to the middle of the table. "Down South we've got cotton and corn." He pulled a coin from his pocket and dropped it directly in front of him, so that it rang briefly on the table.

"Capital," the old banker said. "Capital to dig it or cut it or smelt it or move it or sell it."

"Especially to move it," Stoneman said, nodding with apparent respect to this opinion. "The manufacturer and the international banker need the minerals from the mines; people in the towns need food from the farms; everybody needs something from somewhere else, and they need more and more of it every year. The rails are your bottleneck. Everything must pass through, and pay its way. Control the road, you control the price." He turned to Nolan. "A fact perhaps you know well enough."

"Christ!" Nolan made a face, to another chorus of laughs. They all knew how Pacific Central had put the screws to him for illegal rebates, refusing to handle the ore from his mines until he paid.

"They all discovered it," Stoneman went on. "Carnegie saw that to make steel he needed coal out of Pennsylvania and ore from Minnesota, so he moved into rails. Vanderbilt did the same to protect his steamships, and Rockefeller—now there was a smart young fellow—started with a railroad line and used it to break the oil producers, buy them out and start his Anaconda."

"A miner ought to have his own line, for damned sure," Nolan said. "Otherwise they can wring you dry." He lost his easy manner for a moment, and spoke almost harshly. "But I'm a miner, by God, first, last, and always. And I've heard you've got some interests that way yourself, Mandrake."

It was an abrupt approach, and the atmosphere at the table changed subtly. Nolan knew he sat athwart what good ore was left in the Owyhee lode. And only he knew how much that amounted to. The fate of everyone else in the room, except Stoneman, depended upon that knowledge, for when the silver was gone the boom in stocks, bonds, notes, mortgages, and short-term loans would collapse instantly. These investors, if they waited too long, would be ruined utterly, but as long as rumors of new strikes could be fanned, as long as a reasonable tonnage of ingots emerged from the smelter, the chance for another lucrative round of speculation persisted. So a mixture of wariness and greed kept them close to the mines, fighting to hold on to Nolan's coattails.

Stoneman was, he knew, a mystery to them. They were aware that, in the whole scheme of his empire of banks, rails, mines, and factories, they would be a minor enough project. He could, if he wished, buy the assets of every man in the room without serious disruption of his operations. Why then had he come so far, with such a retinue, agreeing to banquets and receptions in these out-of-the-way places, when he owned the reputation of a recluse? They were simultaneously flattered and suspicious, watchful as carrion birds for what scraps might be gleaned from his conversation.

"I have indeed such interests," Stoneman replied finally. "We heard that the mines out here were exhausted—until this new vein opened up. But your problem is still freighting. As it is, you have to refine the ore at the shafts and ship the concentrate by wagon. If you had rails to Pocatello, you could put a smelter there, haul the raw ore out, and cut your costs in half."

Men nodded appreciatively. Nolan appeared to be considering deeply. "But that involves major investment," he said, "both for a railroad and a smelter. This vein—" He threw up his hands in mingled affection and frustration. "We simply don't know. A gamble, Mandrake, I tell you frankly."

Nolan was shifty, fabricating his case well and carefully. He did not know that Fairfield had already corrupted his chief mining engineer with a two-thousand-dollar "fee" for reviewing some worthless claims adjoining his employer's mines. Stoneman already could predict the day when the side vein would be exhausted, already knew that two out of every five tons of ore were being sent back down at night into an abandoned shaft for stockpiling, to spin out the prospects of the property a little further. The main mines—the Highpocket, Gem, Little Joker, and Yellow Dog—were already doomed as producers of silver. The copper ore, on the other hand, was almost limitless, and the engineer had confirmed that no one showed marked interest in the future of this ordinary metal.

Nolan also did not know—though he would discover it in a day or two—that the price of silver was going to drop steadily for a while, as long as Stoneman's brokers threw blocks of stock on the market. He might be astute enough to realize that he was being squeezed, in which case,

Stoneman had determined, he would arrive at one of two strategies. He could force the bargain early, selling a controlling interest at a modest profit, guarding enough shares to ride the bull when Stoneman reversed the trend in the silver market; or he could take his adversary into his confidence, reveal the scheme to hoodwink his followers into believing the vein still rich, and count on Stoneman's name and influence to inflate the profit even more, agreeing to split the harvest between them. Stoneman's own plan was based on the assumption that Nolan would ultimately choose the second alternative, thinking it both safer and more lucrative.

The first element in his plan was a diversionary maneuver, which Stoneman now launched.

"Railroads are not a gamble anymore, properly handled. We're interested in your problems here, gentlemen, because they're a place to try out a theory of ours. Mr. Fairfield can explain it, even better than I."

"Oh now, Mr. Stoneman . . ." Fairfield, far down the table, went through a brief rhetorical flourish of modesty and self-deprecation. "I'm new at it, gentlemen, but I shall endeavor to sketch the question. You think probably that the railroad would serve your mines, by hooking up with the smelter and lines to the East, or south to California. So it would, so it would. But that's not the heart of the thing, no sir. I venture to say, gentlemen, that even if that vein of yours peters out *tomorrow*, it would be worth laying the track."

"I'd advise then," Nolan said with elfin malice, "that you float the bonds tonight."

During the ensuing laughter Fairfield kept his good-natured grin; when he could be heard, he went on smoothly.

"We did that, sir, three days ago. And I'll wager any man here we drive the first spike inside the month." He paused to savor the subtle but definite consternation in the room. "I'd have laughed too, gentlemen—awhile back before I joined up with the Mohawk & Massachusetts, with Mr. Stoneman—but not anymore, no sir, not anymore. I want you to remember for a minute that just one century ago there warn't a man—a white man—within a thousand miles of this spot. There warn't a telegraph, nor a railroad, nor a mine this side of the Mississippi River, nor would anyone go across it except the trappers and squawmen, people like the French who have not got much in the way of civilization to start with."

The company laughed again, some settling back comfortably after refilling a glass or lighting a cigar. They enjoyed hearing this speech by a

young zealot. They had heard it before, had even pronounced it themselves, as younger men.

"And now what have we got?" The blond hair dislodged a little from
its careful pompadour as Fairfield glanced rapidly from face to face.
"You're living proof of what the country can do, gentlemen! Gold and
silver and lead and iron, stores and factories and great houses such as this
very one we're in, orchards and forests and vineyards!

"It's a whole nation getting built, and you—we—are the builders.
People are coming west, and they have to be fed and clothed and housed
and run from one place to another. But they come for the gold, you say,
or the silver, or the good land. Without those the whole shebang would
stay in the hands of the savages, who have no more idea what to do with
it than a pack of jackrabbits. Maybe that was true in '49, but no more,
gentlemen, no more!"

A few men around the table shook their heads, disgruntled. This
recitation of familiar dogma had taken a false turn.

"Got to have the goods," a little bald man objected. He owned a
thousand shares in the Joker, a hardware store, and two bordellos.

"I tell you if the people come, they will *find* the goods," Fairfield
insisted. "Once you strike the rails through a territory, the thing gets
going—like a locomotive! You mark out townsites, build a store and a
hotel and a blacksmith shop, and people will come, gentlemen, yes they
will. If."

Fairfield stopped and passed a hand through the cowlick that had
fallen across his brow. His stare was so animated and intense that men
looked away.

"If?" the bald man inquired finally.

"If there's two things." Fairfield quite unconsciously had risen to his
feet. "Romance and opportunity."

"Romance?" Nolan laughed and looked aside at Stoneman, to see if
there was a hidden joke.

"I mean something . . ." Fairfield grasped his coat lapels and closed
his eyes, searching. ". . . something *legendary*. Now in California they
had the giant trees and whales and hot water right out of the ground,
and so forth, and in Virginia City the big Rocky Mountains. I don't
mean they weren't rich diggings—richest in the world—but that wasn't
what it was that decided all those folks to light out West. They kept
comin', gentlemen, even after any man with a lick of sense knew the best
claims were gone and the Chinee had the worst ones. They came to *see*,
just damn fool curiosity if you will, because people still believe in mar-

vels. They want something to tell their grandchildren about, gentlemen, and they'll risk life and limb to find it. Now right here, in the Owyhees, you've got one of the wonders of the world, if you treat it right."

Again Fairfield paused, scanning the assembly of guests.

"What might that be?"

"For damn sure not any big trees," the banker observed drily. But there was no derision left in the murmur of laughter he evoked, and a couple of men near Fairfield's age looked impatient.

"You have in these hills a rare critter, hundreds of thousands of years old. A throwback. A scientific marvel. A giant!"

There was a stunned silence. One of the younger men looked disgusted. "Aw shoot," he said loudly. "He means old Nampuh."

"Yes, Nampuh the Shoshoni giant." Fairfield beamed down at them. "A surefire curiosity if I ever saw one. Perhaps you gentlemen already know the tragic story of that young man who came all the way out here from Harvard University to study this phenomenon? I can tell you that right now, in this city, another perfesser—mighty famous—has arrived to continue his researches. This big Siwash, gentlemen, that you take for granted and want to do away with, is an authentic descendant of Neander man, a wild and primitive type—stronger, faster, and meaner than any human being ever was."

A stir of interest swept through the group. This speech had indeed taken a turn into unforeseen territory. "You don't say," said one. "That devil!" another cried. "Evolution!" the old banker burst out. "Goddamn it, that's *Evolution!*"

Fairfield shook his head, lifting his hands to quiet the little storm of agitation. "You can believe it or not, gentlemen, go with the apes or the angels, but the fact is the critter's here, right in your backyard, and the world has found out about it. And they want to *know.*" Fairfield pushed his chair back and took two strides to the left. "Now you could do one of two things. You could send out the Army and pay taxes for them to corner him and shoot him like a mad dog, or you could see the second thing I talked about—opportunity." He strode now to the right. "Another thing you've got to have to settle up the country is labor. Strong arms and strong backs. Some of you gentlemen are from the South, and you know what happens when a labor force is taken away and corrupted, turned into a gang of idle thieves and drunkards and worse."

"That's true," the bald man said, "you can't find a hardworkin' nigger anymore." Others shook their heads, muttering accord.

"And your Chinee laid a lot of rail, I'll give 'em that. But you all know how, just as soon as they get a nickel to the good, they'll quit and live on their own in a dry hole rather than do a day's work for a day's pay. Now suppose—just suppose—that instead of wasting the tax dollar to hunt the Siwash down there was a way—a scientific way—to make use of 'im. Now what?" Fairfield wheeled to the center again and gazed up and down the table, but every face was an expectant blank.

"Here's where the man of genius steps in," Fairfield said in a softer tone, with a tactful tilt of his head toward Stoneman, who sat impassive through this speech. "Because the man of genius grasps how what looks like danger and loss can be turned to a profit. Suppose again, just suppose, that we *caught* this throwback and showed him off to the world. The Owyhee giant! That would bring in your rubes, gentlemen! But we don't stop there. We turn old Nampuh over to the perfessers and think in terms of a labor force. I don't have to tell you what the Unions and Socialists are up to, how they plan to ruin this great country"—he was briefly interrupted by another flurry of imprecations—"but I can tell you how far ahead the man of genius sees. The perfessers believe you could breed the mean streak out of these Neanders, make 'em docile as a Morgan horse, and think of that, gentlemen! A labor force to work your Unionist right into the ground, and whale the tar out of him besides!"

The group was spellbound yet, here and there, agitated. Some men looked at each other covertly, tempted to believe but fearing to appear ridiculous.

"I don't know," spoke up the one judge present, "if the law would allow that."

"Scientific purposes," Fairfield shot back. "We're performing one of the great experiments in human history—turning Evil into Good. Your legislatures will see that, and if they don't the newspapers will make it hot enough so they do!" The judge retired with a sagacious nod, aware that Stoneman owned half a dozen newspapers.

"Hold on!" Nolan's countenance was brick red with drink and confusion. "It'll take a hundred *years* to breed a line of these critters."

A silence fell, and some shook themselves as if awakening from a dream. There was a tentative laugh or two. The banker looked angry.

Fairfield smiled. "We're not dealing here with reg'lar human beings, gentlemen. The Neander is like your nigger and your Injun in that respect. A squaw's ready for service when she's twelve—maybe eleven. Four generations in fifty years. But even if the gentleman is right, say a hundred years, what of that? Civilization, gentlemen, started with the Egyptians and the temples of the Greeks. Mighty peoples, but not much when you think of what we can do here. We've got steam and steel, gentlemen, and oil and electricity are next! Oh, I know a lot of you think nothing will come of those, they're just playthings that won't ever threaten coal, but your Egyptian didn't even have kerosene, never even dreamed of it! And think what your Roman emperors could have done with the repeating rifle! What these peoples *did* have, gentlemen, was cheap labor. That's how they built the mighty tombs and crypts—dependable labor, bought and sold! Now what could a modern emperor do, if he had both the advanced machine and the giant worker, big as a house but quiet as a lamb?"

"Just a damn minute." The old banker focused blearily on Fairfield. "Stand still just a damn minute. Before this Nearender or whatever he be gets bred up, how are folks goin' to get by in these jackrabbit hills? When the silver's gone?"

"It isn't gone *yet*, sir," Fairfield said, "and I tell you people will come to see a land of giants, and I'll tell you further that once here they'll *find* a way. They'll hunt these hills for everything—mineral and pasture and timber—and they'll find it. They always have. Once you got a town going, and a rail line, they'll move the damn mountains if they have to. They'll find maybe more gold and silver, maybe iron or even oil, maybe lead." He saw in the faces before him a familiar flicker of greed, and he leaned forward, bracing his arms on the tabletop. "Maybe tin, maybe chalk, maybe co—" His eyes darted to one side and intersected with Stoneman's murderous, warning stare. "—co—co—" The syllable was caught, became a racking cough, seemed to be choking the young man. His face bright red, he sank into the chair and a man on one side pounded him on the back.

"What is it, lad?" Nolan leaned across the table.

"Co—confidence," Fairfield whispered, and his roving look skipped past Stoneman's face like a dog scrambling to avoid a heavy, onrushing carriage. "Confidence—that's it."

"More like capital," the banker said. "To float such an enterprise. Got to have loans."

"There will be loans," Stoneman said. His voice, though not loud, appeared to fill the room, everywhere and nowhere at once.

"Depends on that vein," Nolan said. "What this young feller says might assay out a little further on, when the territory ain't so damn lonesome—and this experiment with Big Foot is interestin'—but for right now silver's what we got and silver's what we sell. Maybe, Mandrake, you'd like to take a gander at the property?" Nolan squinted at

Stoneman like an old powder monkey examining a seam for the best place to plant his charge.

"Of course." Stoneman nodded, and then detonated his own. "I would like especially to have a look at the shafts where you have suspended operations. Four at the Jewel, or number six at the Highpocket, perhaps."

The secret nighttime deposits of ore were made in shaft six of the Highpocket. Once again, Stoneman allowed the other a measure of respect. Nolan's eyes widened slightly and within a few seconds a fine sheen of moisture developed on his brow, but he gave no other sign of shock.

"My pleasure," Nolan said heartily, and then turned to listen to his butler, who had entered with a murmured apology and bent to his master's ear.

"Mandrake," he said then, "your man outside says there's a visitor who won't go away, says you will want to see him. Fellow's name is Baldo and he sent in this." He waved at the butler, who handed an envelope across the table.

Stoneman slit the flap with a table knife, glanced at the note, and replaced it in the envelope, which he pocketed. All eyes in the room were on his expression, which was that of a man who has just remembered that he has a pot of geraniums to water. "Will you excuse me, gentlemen? A little business." When he was on his feet he turned back for a moment and remarked, with a slight smile, "An excellent brandy, Mr. Nolan. If you will pour me another glass, I'll be back to talk mining with you."

[24]

September 24—

A fine muddle now. As our band of traders and harlots was about to leave, I determined on a course of action. I told Nampuh that an important chief of the whites had come from the East with a vow to destroy him, and that I wished to send a message back with our visitors, the message being merely that I was yet alive. I hinted that my family might pay much money for my ransom.

The giant appeared to consider this opportunity, but I divined that he was angry. He said at first that he could not risk being pursued. If it were known that I was alive the Army might send out a search column. Then he said that no one knew what to do with me: perhaps it would be better to abandon me, or collect ransom and then shoot me. He would throw his medicine bundle, he averred finally, and discover his course. Saying all this, he watched me closely, and it came to me in a flash that he acted from sheer pique. I was sure that he had come to anticipate and enjoy our discussions, and no longer thought of me quite as his captive.

When he emerged after consulting the oracle, he said he would allow me to send the message, but in turn I must submit to an ordeal of initiation, usually inflicted on a young brave. In this manner I would take the place of the man I drove away from the band. Also, Nampuh has got it into his head that I must not only learn the ways of the Shoshoni, but live them, if I am to remain here. Perhaps, he says, I may reach sufficient understanding to cast off my evil obsession with my ancestor's bones. In fact, I believe he means to punish me. But this "initiation" could also prove to be an opportunity for escape!

September 28—

This notebook was forbidden, as well as all food and weapons, and I was given a single blanket. But before the final ceremonies I managed to secrete the book and a stub of pencil in a crevice of rock on the far side of the ridge, and on my way out I retrieved them.

I am exhausted from a long day's walk, and light-headed from hunger. The situation is quite bleak. At dawn I was driven from the camp, and from the time I lost sight of the sentinels I was persona non grata, prohibited from returning for at least five days, charged to avoid all encounters on pain of disgrace and, in my case, probably execution. The proposal that I submit to this rite de passage *was furiously debated after Nampuh announced it, for there is still a contingent here that thirsts for my blood. They argued (not without logic) that I was by definition a traitor, since to become an Indian would presuppose forsaking my prior allegiances.*

The canyon west of camp is well-nigh impassable, and toward its lower end lies the country of the Paiute, a people hostile to the Shoshoni, who would kill me on sight. Hunting parties are being sent to the north and south, so my route is restricted to the east—a steep, barren wasteland with little water, stretching for who knows how many hundreds of miles. Still I have a fair idea of the location of Fort Hall, and will gamble on travelling far enough east to turn the flank of the hunting party before proceeding south. I may strike an Army patrol or a prospector before my strength is gone.

September 29—
  The most miserable night I have ever spent. Very cold, soon after sun-down. Wart had whispered to me at one point during the purification rite (I was sweated and regaled with chants and bone-rattlings) that I must "sleep in sun." I see now the reason, but at night I could scarcely make progress for fear of falling into a ravine or losing my bearings. So I sat with my back against the lee side of a rock, shaking like a man with ague, the poor blanket clutched around me. I had terrible memories, terrible, fitful dreams. Now light enough to proceed, so I make for the highest point I can see, a bald dome-like mountain—how far? Twenty miles, fifty miles?

September 30—
  Cannot move from this place between two rocks. Last night worse. Sounds, things moving in the darkness. The sun warming a little now. All day to get warm as stone. A small spring near—cupful of numbingly cold water. Laughing a long time at my idea of escaping. They knew. Three days with no food, no sleep, and how far? Up and down up and down, my feet seeming far away, and sometimes they simply stop. Twenty, thirty miles—the bald mountain scarcely nearer. But that dead branch, the green pebble—they seem closer. Things move when you are not looking at them. Impossible of course. Sun through the rock now just a little. Warm.
  Five, six hours I slept. Shadows coming, I have to move to keep where the sun strikes. Feel feverish. Should I try to walk farther tonight? No. Hopeless. Last night I thought about the ritual against ghosts. They burned grass all around me and spit water at me. Nampuh told me that spirits would come, and to beware the spirit of the man I fought with and drove to suicide, for he would come. I know this is balderdash, rank superstition. Small birds are arriving to roost in sagebrush. Eyes like tiny drops of black water. They cheep frantically at me, telling me I am too close. They flit like broken bits of shadow in the lattice of branches. Light now heavy gold, a little red.
  Odd, but no hunger now. Very alert, though weak. I write easily, though soon it will be too dark. Scenes appear and vanish quickly in the mind's eye. I see Baum, as if he were near. Nampuh also, permeating everything. Ah! A deer came, a pale gray shade, and drank from the spring. Six steps

away. Watching me all the time. Thought of Lydia. Dear Lydia. Silly. Stars out, a wind rising.

October 1—

   It was true. They came. I cannot explain this. Dawn now. I can hardly believe it. Too tired to think. Must gather grass. No fire. Wave the grass, spit the water. Spit again and again and again, all night.

October 5—

   I have not much time, and no great wish to describe what took place, but habit, I suppose, impels me to say a few words. Nampuh says "Talk no ketchum," and I know now he is right. Language will not convey what I have gone through.

   When I returned yesterday morning I must have looked a fright: thin, hollow-eyed and raving like the Ancient Mariner. There was an immediate conference to interpret those ravings; then I was given a sweat bath, more songs, a pair of feathers, and a benediction, before being sent to my tent to rest. And a name, of course. I am now Little Bird. Tomorrow I will begin certain tasks given to the least of warriors—tasks formerly carried out by the man I defeated in combat.

   How do I account for Little Bird? I cannot, in the terms by which I have been accustomed to explain "phenomena." For my own reference, I shall describe what transpired.

   I was of course deprived of food and sleep for several days, and under such conditions men hallucinate. Usually one thinks of the term as meaning the seeing and hearing of things not actually present. But I first noticed that other beings—notably the birds, insects, a deer, squirrels, and a coyote—were merely present in a much more intense way. I was aware of their awareness of me. They seemed to "draw near" without moving; that is, I could distinguish individuals by a blemish in fur or a ragged feather, and see their slightest movement. The air seemed to throng with life— gnats, grasshoppers, vultures, bats, spiders floating on their silken strands —at all hours of day and night. I could perceive each living being, without losing my awareness of all, and gradually became convinced that this rich swarm was not arbitrary: I was in fact the center of a vortex of attention, or attraction.

   I next perceived an amazing interplay between my internal visions and this gathering of attention. Half-dreaming in my exhaustion, I would imagine my former life and simultaneously become aware of an anthill a few steps away, pulsing with tens of thousands of scurrying workers, or I would see Lydia, anxiety and yearning in her expression, just as a deer stepped from the shadows (this happened three times!) An old badger lumbered by, and he was Baum, even to his nearsightedness.

In this way, gradually, such dream-visions fused with the life around me, and I understood for the first time how narrow my notions of existence have been. I had always assumed a world peopled with objects of study, things and beings whose behavior would illustrate rational principles, but never had I apprehended the intelligence, the spirit, that also inhabits them.

The small birds in the thicket of sage became insistent in their presence. There was no doubt that they were attending me. I made the effort to walk some distance, perhaps a quarter of a mile or more, and sat on a little knoll, bare but for the skeleton of a juniper tree. In a few minutes they arrived with a clamor, a whirling cloud around and through the dead branches. Go back, *they said,* go back to the rocks! Go back to water! *Not in so many words, of course. The idea of "talking" with animals I have always interpreted too literally. What they "say" is clearer than words. Words no ketchum. The communication is instantaneous and perfectly clear, much clearer than a "statement."*

By nightfall of the fourth day I felt these birds to be almost an extension of my own nerves. When their fluttering and cheeping grew anxious, it was an infallible sign of the approach of some other animal, and every movement of mine, especially when I crawled to the tiny spring for a mouthful of the icy water, caused a flurry of activity among them. Near sunset, I noticed them bobbing along the ground, pecking at pebbles, and —again without words—I understood that the night would be very cold, that I must gather a ring of stones still warm from the sun and huddle inside it.

I recalled then a distant, trivial incident which occurred, I believe, the very same morning that Baum proposed this expedition. I glimpsed a thrush in the foliage surrounding the college chapel and felt an oddly personal connection to it, a feeling which I dismissed at the time as idle fancy, an impediment to my serious work! At that time a number of strange moods had beset me, and I worked to purge myself of their charm. Now it is clear that these "lapses" were overtures from a whole universe of subtle intelligences. It occurs to me that had I not tarried to wonder at this small bird, Professor Baum's messenger might never have caught up with me that day, and I might have proposed to Lydia on our boating jaunt.

But that fourth night, as the stars came out, the birds did not grow quiet as usual; they became restive, shrill, and finally frantic. I felt a powerful, nameless apprehension, for they were warning me with every fiber in their bodies. They "told" me to remain inside the ring of stones, to tear off a few handfuls of the sage and rub it on my skin, to spit water in the four cardinal directions, as I had seen done at my ceremonies.

The apprehension grew into dread. The inimical spirits about whom I had been warned were approaching, hovering. A coyote that I had spotted in the morning set up a yapping nearby. I cannot justify my knowledge that it was the same coyote, that it was in fact Nampuh, but I was as sure of these facts as of my hand before my face. The voice of this coyote was neither threatening nor comforting; there was a kind of mocking joy in it, an anticipation of combat, a heralding that it was to be a night of dire struggle for a soul.

Then, all at once, the yapping and the continuous chirping of the birds ceased. A wind came up, and the sage and few junipers nearby began to gyrate wildly. There was a sliver of moon that made a moving pattern of shadows and blades of light, and in and through these patterns I saw shapes of men, a horde darting and hiding among the screen of branches and the bulking rocks. They surrounded my little enclave, and a whispering and gibbering was distinctly audible. When I spit the spring water at them they would draw back a few steps, but as soon as I turned to another quadrant they surged forward again.

The danger they represented was indefinable. I can only describe it as a tide or current that drove against me, as if to push life and consciousness out of my body. At one point, their insane whispering rising almost to a shriek, I felt paralysis in my left hand and arm, which I could not lift from my side. The terror at this moment was so great I felt myself losing consciousness, and knew that I should never regain it. Just then the birds erupted from their hiding place, keening like tiny banshees, and began to circle, flashing between me and the advancing shapes. These shapes at first shrank away, then rushed as a group, melting into one another. They became a huge figure, looming high, a thing larger by half than Nampuh, and this figure hurled itself at me. I spat a cloud of water into the dark face and grappled with my arms.

A shock went through my entire being—body, mind, and soul. The wind and darkness seemed to be rushing through me, carrying me aloft at tremendous speed. In the sky I saw a tumult of scenes, forming and fading away as swiftly as clouds. I passed—flew—among them so rapidly that I registered only a few: a locomotive that blew smoke and fire like an angry demon; a figure I at first took to be Lydia, pale as death, but who turned suddenly to reveal not the long hair at the back of her head but another face, also a woman's, with wild eyes and teeth bared; and finally a great herd of horses galloping into a cave from which issued horrible squeals and sounds of slaughter.

When I "awoke" I was lying still in the ring of stones, the night now quiet, and overhead in silhouette sailed a great, silent owl. The occasional chirp from the small birds in their bowers told me that the assault was over, that I would live.

For the next two days I remained untroubled by such visitations. In fact, I felt myself surrounded by benevolent agencies, and at times my mood became ecstatic. It is again not possible to describe adequately how this transformation came about. I know only that my awareness of the world had sharpened to a heretofore unknown intensity: my skin recorded the slightest change in temperature; I saw every movement of bird, beast, or even plant; I continued to feel a deep kinship with my small, feathered companions. It was now easy for me to distinguish the soft rustle of wings agitated by joy from the restive fluttering of alarm.

So it was not surprising that I became a Little Bird myself. The council which listened to my report seemed to think it a natural conclusion. However, they impressed upon me that I have yet much to learn. As Wart phrased the matter, the lonely journey of initiation is only to "find out how find out." Indeed, I count as my principal discovery the simple realization that science does not, cannot give a full account of things. I have until now ignored another world, as real and powerful as the one we measure, perhaps even more fascinating to investigate. I anticipate such exploration, for surely there are "more things in heaven and earth than were dreamt of in my philosophy."

[25]

"LET ME TRY to explain it, gentlemen, in terms of geography."

General Howard rose from his desk and, with the one good arm that remained to him, gestured at a map hanging from the log wall. "This is the portion of the Idaho-Oregon Territory served by Troops L and F of the Fifth Army. It extends from north of the Snake River south to the Humboldt, and from Fort McDermitt eastward to the Yellowstone country. Notice that except for a spur from the Salt Lake line, no rails penetrate this area. And except for the wagon road into Silver City and another now being cut out of Winnemucca, we have no routes along which to move ordnance or supplies."

The General smiled faintly at his guests. "Though we understand that Mr. Stoneman is acting to rectify this situation."

Opposite him, in black broadcloth and white linen, the three men from the East did not return the smile. Braddock and Baum had asked most of the questions, Stoneman guarding an Olympian silence. The professors had come to petition the Army's assistance in locating a daughter who had run off after the young fool who had been captured by Big Foot. Stoneman had become acquainted with their mission, and wished to organize a volunteer militia to rid the area of the giant outlaw and rescue the captive. All these goals were, in the general's view, preposterous, but he was perfectly aware of the combined influence these men could bring to bear on him.

"We foresee rapid development," Stoneman said at last. "There will indeed be roads—safe roads—as well as farms, towns, and eventually cities. But this matter is urgent. You must act immediately, General, and authorize a militia. I will see to the arming and supplying of a large force, and keep them on the trail of this dangerous beast until he is hunted down. Once we know the fate of young Evans—alive or dead—I am confident Miss Braddock will rejoin her family. In the meantime I have a squad of Pinkertons ready to search high and low for a trace of her."

"We are most appreciative of your generosity." Professor Braddock turned in his chair and bowed slightly toward Stoneman. "At the same time I would hope the effective power of government here—represented by your troopers, General—could be summoned to the aid of a young woman of good family." He frowned severely at the old, one-armed man in the rumpled blue coat. "As I believe you remarked, policing such an extensive territory is an impossible task, and it would seem wiser to assist the citizenry immediately at hand."

"That is our aim, sir." The general found himself unable to hide the asperity in his tone. "We have gold shipments to guard, outlying ranches to patrol, freight stations that rely on our protection. If you send a posse after Big Foot—however well-armed—you give me simply one more duty: that of keeping informed of your whereabouts and maintaining a reserve guard to hurry along if you engage the enemy. As for searching for Miss Braddock, we have no men with that sort of training. You are better off with the Pinkertons." He glanced at the empty sleeve neatly pinned at his side. "It is a bad joke, but my hands are tied. I may tell you as well that I believe your chances of locating Nampuh are somewhat worse than those of turning up a needle in a haystack. This terrain is forbidding as well as immense, and the savages know it up and down and across. They will raid one day at the forks of the Salmon and two days later trade their booty to the Bannocks a hundred miles south."

The general continued in a voice at once calm and faintly menacing. "I know of course that you will proceed, my authorization be damned. I suppose if I withhold it some of the newspapers—your newspapers—will draw attention to that fact. So I will have a letter prepared to accord you permission to form a militia. It would follow that I also furnish you with a couple of scouts—Shoshonis who know the country—and if you need a support column and can get me the request in time, I shall send it. But I intend to word this document most carefully, Mr. Stoneman, so as to leave no doubt that the responsibility for this militia, and its fate, are not under my control. If they perish, one and all, you must bear the blame." The general again smiled faintly. "In my profession that is a matter of paramount importance, and I would advise you to consider it deeply before you act."

"So dangerous!" Professor Baum burst in. "Can it be so dangerous? I fear for Willard. In the fighting he could be killed!"

"We cannot be sure he is alive," Professor Braddock said bluntly, "given the source of the tale."

"Perhaps," the general said, "but the information that comes to us through the Shoshonis around the fort is generally dependable. The photograph, for example. Also, there was a mention of ransom, so we have really no reason to suppose that the young man has been harmed. I suspect he himself somehow begged or cajoled them into sending the message."

"Possibly he has become one of the outlaws himself," Professor Braddock sneered.

"Roland!" Baum groaned, and tugged his beard in embarrassment.

"In any case I believe the well-being of my daughter to be a matter of overriding importance," Braddock went on. "Surely—"

"Surely you will have the cooperation of my command when it is appropriate," General Howard interrupted testily. "In the meantime there is a federal marshall in Boise who has charge of this matter. If there is . . ." He stopped, blinked, and looked away. "You will pardon me, sir, but Miss Braddock undertook this dangerous expedient because of a rumor concerning young Evans, I believe? He had gotten himself ensnared by a confidence team out here, a man and a woman?"

"It is not necessary to review his abominable character," Professor

Braddock said in a cold and hollow tone. "I beg your discretion in mentioning our family's name in connection with this—"

"The odd thing is," the general continued, his look still searching an inner horizon, "Lieutenant Murdoch investigated this Evans affair in June. He knew of this pair of swindlers from a business in Lewiston, and just yesterday he mentioned to me that one of them, at least, had come to a bad end. The man—he's sure it is the same fellow—was found in an alley with his head broken open."

"You do not say so!" Baum looked thoroughly alarmed.

"No sign of the woman, I believe," the general said, and shrugged. "Perhaps coincidence. She was apparently successful in entangling Evans in a marriage, but her motives are by no means clear, since the young man was apparently without fortune. Still, an odd thing, is it not, gentlemen?"

Baum stiffened in his chair and cast a furtive glance at Stoneman. "What . . . what was the name of this man who broke his head?" he asked, his voice quavering.

The general frowned. "Don't know as the lieutenant said. Would that information assist you, gentlemen?"

Baum jerked his head once, violently. "He is, I fear . . . known to me."

The general groped behind his back, found the wooden handle dangling from a cord that led through a hole bored in the wall, and pulled sharply. They heard the distant, dull clatter of a bell. The aide who appeared was given two orders, one for tea and the other for Lieutenant Murdoch.

"How might you know him, Professor?" said the general, turning his attention back to Baum.

"He—if it is the same man—is also from Germany, and his family and mine were—how do you say—in rivalry. He was at one time a brilliant medical student, but he went down into the dogs."

"A habit of young men of a certain type," Professor Braddock interjected bitterly.

The general noted Baum's injured and reproachful look. There was, he was sure, rather more to this affair than met the eye. All the region was humming with rumors of Stoneman's arrival, the new vein in the mines, the projected railroad. Yet here was the great man, preoccupied apparently with the chase after a renegade bandit, ready to take tea and listen to gossip about a runaway brat from Boston and her lost beau.

The aide had barely set out the plain china cups and pewter pot when Lieutenant Murdoch announced himself with a sharp knock.

Murdoch was a tall, rangy officer with a bristling moustache the color of wheat and salt. His pale blue eyes were shrewd, slightly amused, as he saluted and cracked his heels.

"Lieutenant, this is Professor Baum, from Harvard College. Professor Braddock. And Mr. Mandrake Stoneman of New York. They'd like to hear about this fellow who was involved in the matter of young Evans' disappearance. The confidence man, you recall?"

"Yessir, I surely do. A rare bird he was. The lady too."

"What was his name?"

"Oh, they had a dozen of 'em, sir. He was Alexander in Lewiston, when I first run on to 'im, and she was Ophelia. But around Boise he was Mr. Miller, and I heard 'im called Wolf, too."

"Wolfgang," Baum whispered.

"Sir?"

Baum hesitated. "A tall man with black hair and eyes? A peculiar . . . manner?"

"That's 'im. To a T. Couldn't say about her. She was a redhead one time, and corn-yellow the next. She looked healthy as a cow sometimes, and other times half dead. And him—he was a gambler one time, and a preacher or a doctor the next. They was pretty good actors, sir."

"You believe their performance took in Willard Evans?"

"Yessir. You remember my report, sir, wherein I cal'clate they thought Mr. Evans was a rich young sport and laid a trap for 'im. Also . . ." The lieutenant trailed off, covered his mouth with one large fist, and gave a slight cough.

"Yes, Lieutenant?"

"I was about to say, sir, that some of the miners swore that the pair of 'em could convince the devil himself to wear suspenders. They had a way about 'em, sir. And she was . . . well, sir, quite a looker. In that way that leads a man down the garden—"

"I believe the lieutenant has given us a quite sufficient report," Professor Braddock broke in. "You are satisfied, Dieter?"

"I am sure it must be Müller, the foul hypnotist." Baum put a trembling hand to his brow. "Even a dead man, he is still doing much evil."

"Is that the size of it, Murdoch?"

"That's it, sir." Murdoch returned the salute, his heels snapped again, and he left, winking at the impassive aide on his way out.

"I hope you gentlemen will excuse me." Stoneman stood and bowed, first to the general and then to the two professors. "I have an appointment to inspect Mr. Nolan's mines, and cannot stay for tea. I shall send my man Fairfield to accept your letter acknowledging formation of the militia." He looked intently down upon Baum. "I assure you I shall do everything possible to rescue your young friend, as I know the extent of your . . . interest." In the dark suit Stoneman resembled a huge raven; he turned to Braddock as to a less desirable morsel. "I shall detach a squad of detectives to assist your search for your daughter, and offer also a reward of five hundred dollars for her discovery. I can do no more, but I extend my sympathy for your suffering, and urge you to take courage."

The two professors rose as one. Braddock glanced at the general with an expression of mingled reproach and triumph, then spoke pointedly to Stoneman.

"We are deeply grateful for your assistance, and wish you luck in the campaign to rid this place of a monster. Thank heaven for your kind of man."

"Yes," Baum added, a little dubiously. "I wish also."

"There you have it, gentlemen." Howard got to his feet and shook hands perfunctorily with all three men. "I shall be glad to hear from you in the course of your investigations, and be assured I will help within the limits of my duty and ability." He winced almost imperceptibly.

Without replying, the three turned in a flutter of black coattails and glided from the room. General Howard waved the aide out after them, and sat down alone to his tea. He lifted the cup and blew reflectively over its steaming, quivering surface. Well named was Mr. Stoneman, he thought, well named. Then the faintest shadow of a most curious feeling passed swiftly through him, accompanied by a mere phrase: *poor damned red devil.*

[26]

HER DREAM seemed to last forever. She wanted it to, because it had brought back her loved ones. Besides Mr. Baldo and Theda and Mama and the lumbering boy and the doctor, she had seen her father and Professor Baum, only for an instant, from the window. They were passing in a carriage on the main street, which she could just glimpse at the intersection of the alley. She knew it was her father by his erect posture and the line of his cheek, and the rotund figure and thick white beard surely belonged to Dieter. She tried to tell them, tried to urge them to call out, for she wanted to see her father, but the doctor had just given her an injection and she was so comfortable . . .

At first Willard had come, when she was afraid of the others, but her conversations with him were interrupted. She cried, asking him why he had left, why he had—but then Theda told her not to listen and not to cry, that would be bad, and she was a good girl, now, resting and taking her medicine. Before she had been sick, had been bad, thinking that people did not love her and want to help her. She knew that was right. She had been very sick, she had felt bad, and she did not want to go back to the awful dream, where Mr. Baldo looked so strange with the black sausage-thing in his pocket and Theda had said something terrible. She could not remember what it was and did not want to, for it made her so afraid.

Theda talked to her every day about how she would go back soon to Boston and her family, wearing a beautiful new dress; they had opened her trunk and tried on the dresses one day, like little girls. And her locket, she had given her locket to Theda to keep, even though one of Willard's little curls was inside, so she would not break the thin gold chain when the bad dream came back and she tossed in her bed. Theda said once that Willard had been untrue and a deceiver, but that upset her and so now he was all right but far away and could not come any-more because of his important work, which Theda said was just like the men, wasn't it.

Theda's voice was so sweet she loved to hear it, only sometimes with the light a certain way she looked different, her eyes wide and strange like a cat's. Theda talked and talked about her and her dresses and how she was good now, had only misunderstood that night when she got so sick, so sick she had accidents with herself after the doctor gave her the medicine, but now she was getting well to be ready when Mr. Baldo took her to her father again. But she was afraid of her father. She had run away. But then Theda said he would forgive her if she was good and did not talk about Willard, who was so far, so very far, and would not come back.

Sometimes there was only the big boy with the little dents in his face who watched her all the time. She did not like him so much, because he came to the bed sometimes and looked and looked at her, at her stomach and her knees and her neck, making a little sound like a dog that has been left in the basement. Mr. Baldo laughed at the big boy and made him run out of the room. Mr. Baldo had such small ears, like little pink shells, they looked absurd on a man so big. He did not look big but he was big.

Now she especially liked to see the doctor, because the medicine was so good for her. At first it made her dizzy and there were bad dreams, very bad, but then Theda told her wonderful stories and sang lullabies and the dreams became one dream, a wonderful dream, only if the doctor was late it made her nervous because of the light too bright and the coverlet full of burrs, scratching and pricking her skin; and the bad dream would come again, with the man lying in the road, something wrong with his head. She was so glad to see the doctor that she would smile and pull up her sleeve.

Mama visited her too, plumping up pillows behind her head and pulling her locks down over her brow. Mama said she was the prettiest girl she had, and she should put on her fine dresses and talk to her friends who were all gentlemen. But Mr. Baldo said she was not rested enough yet and needed more medicine and they would wait and see about some things, so he gave Mama money. She wanted to talk to Mama's friends and Theda said it might be a good thing, they were all like her father and Dieter and Mr. Baldo. Theda asked if she kissed her father and she said she did, giggling and telling how she liked how he smelled, books and dried roses and tobacco, and Theda said the friends were just like that, like her father, like Mr. Baldo. Mr. Baldo laughed and Theda said see now watch and she kissed Mr. Baldo, kissed all over his face and his neck and even his fingers and bit them a little and Mr. Baldo laughed as she had never seen and Theda said see now you try this is your papa kiss papa and I did and it felt so strange, hurting a little because he hadn't any lips, only his hard teeth.

[27]

TWO MEN stood in the shadow of a tiered structure of weathered wood and rusted iron, not far from the derrick positioned over the dark socket of the mine shaft. A crew of workers swarmed near a corral and chute where four mules kicked and brayed. One of the mules was goaded into the narrow chute. A gate dropped behind it, and one worker slid a wooden bar across the mule's neck to prevent it from rearing, while another fastened a leather shackle to a forefoot.

"Damn it," the younger of the two men expostulated in a voice squeezed small by urgency, "we don't *want* to know anything about her. It's all mucked up, now. Her father and that old Hun are putting the screws to everybody to find her. How you do it is your own affair, but it better be soon."

For several moments the other man did not respond. He stood with legs apart in a posture of easy alertness, his wide, square body turned a little toward the activity at the corral.

"Well," he said finally, "in a few days she won't remember much about it. Or anything else."

"No." The young man shook his head. "We can't chance it. You were seen together when you first arrived. If the marshall finds you he'll grill you good. Also, you came to Nolan's that night, so they know you are connected to . . ." He trailed off, with a nervous glance over his shoulder at the party of workmen.

They had captured all four feet now, and by means of ropes attached to the shackles they jerked the animal to its knees. The mule honked and wheezed in terror, but in another moment went over on its side. Men hauled on the ropes to truss the hooves tight against the belly, and the derrick swung overhead, a leather sling dangling from the log boom.

"I had to. There were things I was not told."

"He couldn't. The pair of them hatched their business after you had left. It's a miracle things aren't worse. You're sure Elizabeth is with us?" He peered at the squat man, who turned his gaze from the mule, cradled now in the sling, and smiled a little.

"We have an understanding. If anything happens to her, the story of the theater will find its way to the newspapers. If the posse does its work and she becomes a rich widow—and a partner too, I gather—we will of course restore the affidavits and forget the whole matter."

The young man drew in his breath sharply. The steam engine hissed and thudded, and when one of the workmen eased a lever backward, cogged wheels began to ratchet and squeal. In small jerks the sling and its cargo rose from the ground, the animal's head lolling over the lip of leather, eyes glazed milk-white.

"We?" the young man whispered. His hands began to dart in and out of his coat, as if seeking a pencil or watch.

The other, still smiling, turned his attention back to the derrick. Guided by cries of the workmen, the winch operator swung the mule over the shaft and, working the lever with both hands, eased pressure on the drum. The mule began to slide down again, toward the square, black hole that was just large enough to allow its passage.

"He'll be down there for seven years or more." The man moved his broad shoulders as if shrugging off a slight burden. "And never come up."

"What?" The other seemed dazed.

"The mule. They go blind often, down there, pulling cars of ore. But well fed. They have carved out whole barns in the rock with straw and salt and the lot."

The young man was breathing heavily, and looked wildly from his companion to the scene before them, as the mule passed out of sight to friendly jeers from the workmen. "We, you said *we*. You mean—"

"I have done what I was paid to do. Now I understand there is a partnership. Common interest. Mrs. Evans has engaged me to . . . to verify the death of her husband. The partnership is, I believe, founded on that verification?" He cocked his head at the young man.

"I—" The young man raised both hands in supplication. "Great Jesus! What a—" He stopped and lowered his arms. "You play a close game, Finn. I hope you know what you are doing. Anyway, you're right that this . . . verification . . . is the first thing. But you can't join the posse. He's going to lead it himself. I don't see—"

"We have a way to make him come," the other said in his quiet, almost idle way. "He and the big fellow too, perhaps. If you hold the posse ready, we will trap them."

"How? How is that possible?"

"Little Miss Braddock has made herself useful."

There was a long pause, while they watched the second mule twisting its body in the dust, trying to thrash erect without use of its legs. "How will he know . . . ?"

"We shall send a sign. Also some gold, a pledge for ransom, and instructions for meeting."

"But he can't get loose, surely?"

The other man laughed, a low, soft sound. "He has survived for three months with them, taken their pictures, traveled with them, and now he has a message sent out. Also, they say that for love and for gold, men will do anything."

"But how can you get close enough? He is recruiting forty men, all with Henry rifles. You can't put them in your pockets."

"Only she need be close. She can do the job."

"She?" The young man stared at him. "Ah. The widow Evans," he whispered. "Black widow, eh? She must be quite something."

"She is." The Finn shifted his shoulders and laughed softly again. "She is. Anyway, the big fellow will run with the gold, then, so the posse must move in fast and follow close. I trust they will be good men, on good horses."

"Oh yes. He'll have the best." The young man uttered a wild little laugh. "Quite a hunt. He'll have sharpshooters to wing the big ape or knock a foot out from under him. Some of them are a match for you, Finn."

"All the better. You should go along."

"Got my hands full," the young man said with a touch of self-importance. "I'm going to start a railroad."

"So? Good luck to you. Now, the money for the medicine and lodging?"

The young man pulled a thick envelope from a pocket of his coat, and with a glance at the workmen, who had rolled the bound mule into the sling, he handed it to the Finn. "So you will contact us in Silver City— but not in person? After this other problem, the Braddock girl is taken care of?"

The Finn glanced swiftly at the contents, nodded, and slipped the packet inside his own coat. "Soon. My respects, and assure him that all is well. The woman is with me."

The young man hesitated, wetting his lips.

"You have nothing to lose by doing so," the Finn said easily, "do you?"

The two men looked at each other for a long time, before the younger one shook his head and threw up his hands again.

"Tight to the chest. You're a cool one, Finn. As far as I know, everything is on grade. Just be careful with the girl."

"Nothing to worry about. It will all come about quite naturally." The Finn turned and walked away then, keeping in the shadow of the great building.

After a moment the young man wheeled and set off in the opposite direction, toward the offices of the mine. Neither looked back when, its muzzle gyrating and drooling strings of saliva, the last mule vanished into the earth with a bleat of terror.

[28]

Oct. 12—

There was a heated debate at the evening meal. Some of the scouts, among them Wart, argued that the movement of birds had for some days heralded the early onset of winter. We should, they urged, set up a second deer camp to enlarge our stores. A man named White Hawk rejected this theory with loud speeches and satiric pantomime. The storm to the south was a fluke, he claimed, and besides, what we needed most was gold to purchase ammunition and flour, and therefore we should range westward to raid pack trains or stagecoaches on the road to the mines. The opposition countered that some years ago a blizzard had struck at this season, and if such a sudden change caught us now, we might starve before spring.

Nampuh listened closely to these opinions, making no comment himself. A kind of parliament, I gathered, was in session, and I began to grasp the urgency of the question. It has indeed gotten very chill at night; a few weeks more could well bring bitter cold. Our tents, buffalo robes and blankets are barely protection enough, and we must spend much time on the move to avoid detection, which exposes both men and horses to the severe weather. To sustain such effort, a man must have a daily portion of meat. On the other hand, Broken Arm fears that General One Arm is waiting, cunning as a wolf, for our cartridges and stores to run low. There has been no patrol for many days, he said, and that may be a sign that some attack is being plotted.

There were subtle motives underlying these positions. Some of White Hawk's loudest supporters I recognized as those who drink and carouse most when the traders from the fort come. This commerce involves coin or dust, so one element of the band presses for the raids out of mere greed for gain. A couple of those in Wart's camp, on the other hand, are generally in charge of hunting parties because of their skill at bringing in game, and when we are short of meat they have great authority, and are treated with deference. The majority appeared to listen, noncommital except for an occasional "Ho!" of approval for a well-argued point.

It also was brought home to me that even in this seemingly vast and trackless wilderness we are like rats in a cellar, who may survive only by constant stealth, vigilance and movement. Especially movement. In the course of this parliamentary discussion rude maps were drawn in the dirt, and I saw how we are encircled by roads, mines, ranches and army posts. And now there is rumor of a new threat. Two days ago one of the pickets encountered a hunting party of Shoshonis from the fort. They said camps are being set up on the west bank of the Snake River for the building of an iron road through the mountains. I felt a secret shock at this news, recalling all at once the vision of the locomotive that came during the night of spirits.

Looking about the fire at this ragged and motley assembly, I can count thirty-three able-bodied men and two derelicts who are too old to do much but tend the fire and mind the horses. Although every man is armed to the teeth, some with two rifles and several revolvers, they are a pitiful force compared to the deluge of humanity in Idaho City and Boise, where a militia of hundreds, even thousands, could be mustered. Even Nampuh, an imposing figure by any standard, is but one man, and his whole empire can be put on the backs of three horses.

Toward the end of the debate, Nampuh interrupted, laying out his hand like a great scythe. He said my name in Shoshoni, and indicated that I should speak. There was a murmur of surprise, and then silence. I had, in fact, been thinking to myself that some combination of the two courses of action should be feasible, if a small detachment were to be sent out hunting and a spot chosen for a later rendez-vous. I was momentarily off-guard, and as embarrassed as a schoolboy by this sudden introduction into the council of elders, but managed by means of broken phrases and much pantomime—as well as a hasty sketch in the dirt—to convey my meaning.

The argument burst out anew then, more heated than ever. I sensed that my plan found favor, even though there was an instinctive bias against dividing the band. Some hinted that I was plotting escape, was an agent for my white brothers, and would steer them into an ambush. I have identified the group who wishes me ill. They are, I believe, the cronies of the man I fought and drove to his suicide. Chief among these is White Hawk, whose paler skin and pug nose indicate that he is himself, ironically enough, a mongrel.

Jacques broke in to say with some fervor that he was born a white man but had become their brother, and had taken the scalp of many bluecoats. Little Bird, he went on, proved his heart when he killed the thief with the small head. Here he launched a long pantomime of the raid, impersonating my clumsy movement with the .45-70, my reeling backward after firing the weapon, my expression of terror and amazement—all exaggerated for comic effect. His performance brought loud shouts of mirth from the rest, and I was the object of some good-humored raillery.

Then Jacques struck his chest and proclaimed that the heart inside was an Indian's heart, and he would match it against White Hawk's, which was the color of his name. Without a word White Hawk rolled away from the fire and came up with a blade in his hand. Jacques sprang to his feet, reaching for his own knife. There was a general hubbub, over which struck Nampuh's deep voice. At this command from their leader, the two crouching men seemed to freeze, their eyes locked in an intent stare. There was what seemed to me an interminable pause, when I could hear nothing but the sound of breathing and the crackling of the fire. Then Jacques grinned, sheathed his knife, and said simply, "Wahan," which means twice. White Hawk after a moment nodded, repeated the word, and slipped his weapon out of sight. It was explained to me later that this was the second altercation between them, and that at the third they would fight to the death, and no one, even Nampuh, could then interfere.

The giant spoke again, saying that he would consider the matter of raiding by himself, and that we were not to argue anymore like children. He looked at me then, and said that it was true I needed experience. I would begin training immediately in the skills of combat, and—here he pointed at Jacques—my white brother with the Indian heart would be responsible for my education. There was no room for women and children in his company. None of us would live very long, he pronounced, wrapping his blanket around himself and rising to his feet, and it would behoove us to die like men, fighting the enemy, and not yapping at each other like starved dogs. He stood at the edge of the firelight for a moment, like a great pillar, and his followers stared, silent, into the fire. Those who were ready to die tomorrow, he said finally, were his people, and those who wished to live like dogs should leave at dawn.

Oct. 15—

All the above, of course, is my version of what Jacques translated for me the day after, but it has turned out to be substantially correct. The following morning one of the old derelicts saddled his gaunt pony and left without a word, and my daily lessons in the art of war began. It is not the sort of learning I would wish to pursue, but there is not really any choice. Because I boxed as a lad, I have some ability to launch or intercept blows, but all my training as a pugilist assumes a contest by rules. In this business there is only one rule—to live by virtue of an opponent's death.

My first task is the grisly one of mastering the garrote. I have been given *a rawhide thong secured at each end to a wooden peg. Approaching from behind, I practice throwing the looped thong around Jacques' neck, twisting it tight and simultaneously knocking him to his knees. He wears a leather collar, of course, and is of a compact, sturdy frame, so there is no danger of seriously hurting him. A certain stance, crouching and quartered to one side, protects one from retaliative blows or kicks. We trade places then, and I practice defensive manoeuvers, the most effective being a rolling over backwards to aim one's feet at the attacker's face.*

With the knife I perform better, since this sort of combat approximates a match in a ring. We use wooden sticks instead of steel, of course, but even so my ribs, knuckles and forearms are bruised mightily. It is not so difficult to follow Jacques' instruction to watch an opponent's feet, which he tells me is the first indication of intent. If the other is reacting to one's own footwork, then one may feint, too, merely by shifting his stance slightly. My teacher seems satisfied with all but my state of mind, for he detects the reluctance with which I strike.

The conflict between my own character and the mentality of these outcasts has never been clearer. Jacques demonstrated for me every kind of treachery with cold steel: a handful of sand scooped up suddenly and flung at an opponent's eyes, the ingratiating smile or cringe as prelude to attack, the feigned retreat. All these are worthless, he tells me impatiently, without the will—nay, the hot desire to strike. He has shaken me, spat in my face, shouted into my ear in the attempt to purge me of that trace of humanity to which I cling. The hesitant, he insists, will always die. You must kill, he tells me with his evil leer, as you make love, with a perfect blend of skill and passion. What, in God's name, can I say to such an unspeakable proposition?

[29]

ONE OF THE OLD MEN spat at a large fly and watched it spiral away from the board sidewalk. His companion on the bench outside the Silver Monarch Mercantile had been whittling on a stick, and now stopped to examine his handiwork. They had both been observing the four men unsaddling their horses at the livery barn across the street, the third such group to arrive this day.

"Hard cases," the spitter finally observed. His wide-brimmed hat was tilted low over eyes bright as a squirrel's.

"Wouldn't cross 'em," the whittler replied. His long ivory beard tumbled down between wide suspenders the color of mustard, coming to rest on a belly small and round as a melon. Between them on the bench was a brown bottle with a bit of corncob for a stopper.

"Don't look much like a buffaler," the other said.

"Tain't a buffaler." The whittler blew on the piece of wood between his hands. "Sheep."

Two of the four men crossed the street, angling for the Lucky Lode Saloon, through whose open door came the ring of glasses and a murmur of voices. They were dressed like drovers, in spurs and high boots, and one wore a buckskin coat. Both had long-barreled Navy Colts in holsters tied down with a thong.

"Seen the Mucky-Muck since he come in?"

"No sir. Perkins says he took up the whole damn hotel. Fourteen flunkeys and four, five straw bosses."

The spitter wrapped a gnarled hand about the bottle, removed the stopper with the other hand, and took a long swig, his Adam's apple pumping like a goat's.

A freight wagon behind four mules rumbled down the street, and here and there smaller spring wagons were drawn up before stores, loading or unloading goods. A half-mile away, up a steep mountainside, there was more activity. They could hear the occasional squeal of an ore car, or the dull thud of an underground blast, and from the high, many-leveled building came the rapid, steady thumping of the stamp mill.

"Silver City never seen his like afore." The carver placed his bit of wood and knife carefully on the bench and received the bottle from his companion. He held it a moment meditatively. "Maybe 'nother boom."

"Mule shit." The spitter let fly a brown stream at another of the flies. He was so wide of the mark the insect merely tilted and flexed its wings. "Nothin' left in there to carry on 'bout. Nolan's got hisseff a sheep for shearin'. Big ol' Eastern sheep."

"They're layin' track already, got a camp at Kuna station. Ain't layin' track jess for the hell of it." The carver lifted the bottle to his lips and closed his eyes.

"Hell, that feller, old Stoneballs, he don't mind doin' nothin' for the hell of it. Little piss-ant railroad like that—he'd eat it for breakfast."

The other smacked his lips and belched. "Rotgut," he said affectionately. "Hogs wouldn't drink it if they could git shit."

"My my, what gentlefolk we got here." The spitter inclined his hat brim imperceptibly to the right.

From a boarding house near the end of the street a man and woman had stepped into a buggy. The woman wore a hat, and her face was masked in a dust veil. The man was dressed in common clothes, broadcloth and wool, but they were new. He was compact, agile, and handled the reins and whip with a practiced touch.

"Damn town's full up with strangers. Them two been ridin' out ever' day to that Injun camp on the Murphy road. Her too. Got a fancy dress under that coat."

"Don't say."

"Do say."

"Hell, he ain't even white."

"Don't look it, do he?"

"Kind o' Chinee look to 'im."

"Damn funny ears."

"Crossed a mouse and a bull." The spitter gave a wheezing laugh, and reached again for the bottle. "Damn town's got a freak show."

"Them riders come here huntin' that big freak," the carver said, picking up his work again. "How the hell they goin' to split two thousand dollars forty ways."

"Stoneballs is payin' 'em. He wants ol' Big Foot, personal. Fellers in the Lucky say they're goin' after 'im alive."

"The hell." The carver paused and for the first time turned and looked at the other. "What the hell fer?"

The spitter shifted the lump of tobacco in his cheek and looked away for a target. "Hooker says—" The brown stream spattered on the boards; this time an insect dragged itself in a small circle through the midst of the dark mess, emitting a frantic, intermittent buzz. "—he wants to breed 'im to a big ol' nigger sow and git a litter. Make spikers and rail hogs and gandy dancers outen' 'em."

After a moment the carver leaned back against the wall of the store, his melon-belly jiggling with silent laughter, making the ivory beard bob wildly.

"You think that's hum'rous," the spitter went on after the other had wheezed himself almost out of breath. "I don't think they was a-shittin' me."

The buggy wheeled off the main route onto a side road that was merely a pair of ruts. The woman had pulled away her veil to take the wind in her face and speak freely, while the man reined the horse in a bit to ease passage over the rougher ground.

"When will the posse move?"

"Tomorrow. They'll head south for a day, as a feint, then double back at night and make cold camp an hour's ride from the spring. The next day, if you miss, and I miss, they will take him."

"If he comes."

"I think he will come. You have heard what our friends say."

She laughed. "What a fool. He makes it easy."

"Anyway, even if he's forgotten his little belle, they'll come for the gold." The man tapped his coat pocket. "I'm sending a little sample."

They lapsed into silence. Gray sage and dun earth rose gradually to a horizon of black mountains. The landscape was empty but for the creak of harness leather and the swirl of dust from their wheels. After an hour they stopped by a creek. The woman removed her coat and let down tresses of long, black hair.

They drove on for perhaps another hour, until they topped a small rise and saw below a larger stream and, near a stand of cottonwood trees, a gathering of tents and tipis. Horses grazed along the stream, and a group of women knelt there pounding clothes on boulders. As they approached, some children saw them first and ran shouting toward them. The woman reached in a capacious carpetbag and withdrew a handful of taffy balls.

"Little rats," she said softly. When the children were running beside the buggy, hands outstretched, she threw the sweets to each side. They left the clustering swarm behind and drove into the shade of the cottonwoods, where an old man stood ready to greet them.

"Ho," he said, and raised a hand.

The driver of the buggy replied with the same gesture.

"They are here," the old man said, his wrinkled brown face contorted in a smile. "We talk."

The man helped the woman from her seat. Together, following the old man, they walked through the dappled shade to a bridge made of two logs side-by-side across the creek. On the other bank they made their way through more shouting children and yapping dogs to a large tent.

Inside they were seated on folding stools of Army issue, reserved for distinguished guests; opposite were two Indians who sat cross-legged on a faded, threadbare blanket. The Indians did not look at the man and woman, or at the old man who squatted on his heels at the entrance of the tent, but stared downward into some invisible pit. One was missing an eye, a shriveled lid drooping over the empty socket, and the other was a rarity among his people: a very fat man of middle age, wearing many bead necklaces and bracelets. They were famous as traders, the one-eyed man for his shrewd bargaining, the fat Indian for his stock of finery, horses, whisky, and squaws.

One-eye began with a long speech, his hands making occasional abrupt movements. At intervals the fat Indian uttered a "Ho!" or added a few phrases for emphasis. When they were finished, the old man explained to the man and woman that the thing they had asked was plenty hard, impossible, for no one knew where Nampuh would be at any time, and it was dangerous to try to find him. Also, these traders did not know whether the man and woman were from the government and trying to lay a trap; and although Nampuh was an outlaw, and not a good Indian as they were, he was of their blood and they could never betray him. And beyond that, even if they were not from the government, the government had spies everywhere and might follow them, so they would betray without even meaning to. And finally, they were good traders and did not want to be in any trouble with the Army, which had given them blankets and food, sometimes.

The man listened carefully and nodded pleasantly. He told the old man to tell the other two that they were only sending a package and a message to the white man that Nampuh had captured, because this woman was that white man's woman and wanted her man back and would give much gold for his return. The man took a packet from his pocket and opened it to show the others a little locket on a chain, a letter, and a small but bulging canvas pouch. There would be fifty such pouches to trade for the white man, alive, the man said. In the letter was the name of a place where they could meet, a safe place far in the mountains, and nobody would come there but the woman and himself and one other with a mule to carry the gold. In two days Nampuh could come with many soldiers to a certain hill where he could see everything. He could send one man to take the gold across the valley, while the captured white man rode to their side. Then they would all go away and not tell anyone what had happened. Even if they did, the certain place was far enough away so there would be plenty of time to ride away with the gold.

When the old man had explained all this, the fat Indian gave another speech, shorter, with many smiles. He said that this procedure was very dangerous and Nampuh would have scouts all around this certain place and would discover any trap and kill the white man immediately, if he was not already dead. If that happened, the old man could never again go into the mountains to trade, for Nampuh would hunt him down and kill him too. Nampuh was like coyote, everywhere all the time and doing mischief. It was much too dangerous for them to try to do this thing, so he was sorry for the woman who would not see her man again. They were only poor Indians and could not do such important things, even if they wanted to.

The man listened again and continued to nod his approval. Then, taking another canvas sack from another pocket, he said that he would pay much gold to get this package to the white man, even if Nampuh did not come to the certain place to trade, even if he played a trick and killed the white man. Lydia—he repeated the name three times, gesturing at the woman—would take this chance because of her great feeling for her man. If they could not take the package—the man thought they could because they were well-known traders and good Indians— then he would try to find someone else in the camp to do it. If the package was delivered then the white man could write a letter for the messenger to take back, and he would give that messenger twice this much gold.

There was a long silence. Then the old man, One-eye, and the fat Indian talked for a long time. The old man said the two were fools if they did not take this crazy woman's money. Probably the white man would die soon anyway, and they could have the gold even so. He had found out in Silver City that this man and woman traveled alone together, and nobody had seen him talk to the Army. The man by himself had gone out for two days with another Indian, Spotted Bull, and some maps, and had looked at the Little Duck Valley. This was surely the certain place he talked about, but they could see how the man was careful not to tell them where the place was, so they could not betray him either.

One-eye said he did not like it anyway. Nampuh would kill all three of them if he knew they were talking this way. The fat Indian said that was true, but if that was so they had already taken a chance and should get the gold. The old man suggested then that they take the first pouch, and on their next trip to Nampuh's camp they could take the packet and decide then what to do. This plan seemed the best, though One-eye was still reluctant and said they were maybe going to have plenty trouble.

The old man told the man and woman that these two traders would be brave and try to deliver this message, although it was probably impossible. They liked the man and felt sorry for the woman, so in spite of how poor they were they would try to find a way to do this work. As for him, the old man added, he was also very poor and had too many children, so they were hungry all the time, but even so he had worked hard for them three times now, talking for a long time each time even though he should be hunting or moving his horses.

The man took a gold coin from his pocket and gave it to the old man. Then the packet and pouch changed hands. The man and woman got up quickly, the old man after them, and left the tent. After a while the traders heard the children shouting again and the buggy rattling away. The old man returned and poked his head into the tent. The fat Indian had opened the pouch and was uttering small grunts of interest. One-eye continued to stare glumly at the earth.

The old man smiled. "Anyway, we do not live very long," he said, and withdrew again to go and see to his horses.

[30]

THE EL DORADO SALON sported divans and armchairs, silk lampshades, and a stereopticon through which maidens peeked lasciviously through a turn or two of gauze about their persons. Several of the nightbirds, resplendent in velvet and lace and large, bright, artificial stones, sat with gentlemen, cooing and trilling. An older woman, her withered cheeks thickly rouged, carried bottles and glasses on a tray.

"I say, the nobs are 'ere tonight," the South African muttered. He inclined his head toward a group at the far end of the salon. Five men sat at a table, their apparent geniality not quite masking a common restlessness. All wore fine suits of dark wool, silk vests, and collars fresh as new snow. Bits of gold flashed from hands and shirtfronts. "That there one with the red face, that's Nolan."

"Our establishment is frequented by the finest in the territory," said the woman who had introduced herself as Daphne. "I believe you all know Mr. Nolan?"

The South African looked at his companions and they laughed. The old man with the pink, bald head picked up his glass, arm cocked and little finger crooked aloft in an exaggerated pose of delicacy.

"We has been associated in the same enterprise," he said in a mincing falsetto tone. "Employed as I be in the freight business. Howsomever, we seldom meet in sassiety."

"Only side you see of the business is the backside of a mule," the Californian said, and Daphne frowned. It had been her bad luck to be assigned to this gang of ruffians, who certainly could afford little beyond the minimum. She observed covetously the table of gentlemen, as Mama approached it with loud and gay greetings.

"How come these chaps keep to themselves?"

Daphne sniffed. "Our clientele—" she began, and then her face underwent a swift convulsion. "They want to bid on a new one. The *virgin.*"

"Virgin?" The man from California stared at her, a laugh beginning and then ebbing away in his throat. "Don't pull a man's leg."

"Honey, you need a drink." The older woman, sweeping by with her tray, veered their way and bent over Pee Wee, whose bleared blue eyes, when he raised them, viewed first her dugs, still heavy and full under skin dark and freckled as a toad's. He raised his glass absently, maintaining his gaze across the two inverted hillocks, as if scouting there for sign of distant campfires, while the woman smiled fondly down at him and poured from a bottle as slowly as possible.

"You got a hell of a knock, there, honey," she said and laid a painted nail by the white scar on his bald head. "Poor thing."

"Ain't nothin' damaged," Pee Wee said grandly. "The main goods is all there and a-workin' fine."

"I'm Grace and I don't doubt it the least little bit," the woman said. "Neither of us ready for the barn yet, sweetheart." She handed the tray to Daphne as she talked. "Take over for me, dumplin', I got to run the feed line upstairs, and maybe this young feller wants to come up with me."

Pee Wee lurched to his feet, discovering that his height was such that he need only look straight ahead to keep in view the ample knolls of pleasure. "Gracie," he said gallantly, "lead on."

Tilted slightly backward, so that his feet seemed to be walking out from under him, he followed Gracie out of the salon, down a dim hallway to the kitchen where a Chinese man, bare to the waist and sweating, handed her a tray of smoking potatoes and corned beef. Balancing the tray on her shoulder with one hand, she trailed the other behind her, fingers entwined in one of Pee Wee's suspenders. She led him up a narrow flight of stairs to the third floor where she went to the end of the hallway and rapped softly, four times, at the last door.

A key grated in the lock, and when the door opened she shouldered it aside and pulled Pee Wee in behind her. Inside, a lamp was turned low beside a narrow bed where a young woman sat, looking at them with eyes huge and dark as a deer's. The man who had admitted them, his sleeves rolled up to his elbows, frowned and shook his head.

"Ain't supposed to be no sports in here yet," he said sternly. "She's just comin' around."

"Don't fret yerself," Grace said cheerfully. "He's just a tagalong. Now dearie, we've got some hot vittles for ye." She moved across the room and set the tray on a low table by the bed. The young woman caught at her sleeve with a pale, thin hand.

"My papa," she whispered, "where's my papa?"

"Don't you worry none, honey. He be back right soon."

"My medicine," the young woman said. "I want my medicine."

"Hush, now." Grace turned to the man in shirt-sleeves, who was still frowning at Pee Wee. "You got ever'thin' you need?"

"Yes," the man said. "You git on out now."

The young woman finally turned her gaze on Pee Wee, who had taken a reeling step in her direction. He blinked back at her, and saw her face alter from its blankness into the expression of one trying to recall a name, a dream. "You," she said. "You said . . ."

The man in shirt-sleeves stepped between them. "Git him on out," he warned. "Mama don' 'low no sports here."

"Oh hellfire," Grace said pettishly, and turned to hook Pee Wee again by the suspenders. "Come on, honey."

She pulled him into the hallway and the door clapped shut behind them, the key grinding again in the lock. She led him back down the stairs to the second floor, where they were jostled by other couples on their way to the rooms, from behind whose doors came muffled laughter, thumps, and artificial shrieks. Grace's room was barely large enough for the bed, dresser, and nightstand, and was decorated by two cheap reproductions, one of a lurid sunset, the other of a maid with a broken water pitcher and bare breast.

Grace poured a basin of water from her own enamelware pitcher and stirred in a tablespoon of Mercury salts. "Git off them britches," she said over her shoulder, and rapped the spoon smartly on the rim of the basin.

His brow wrinkled in concentration, Pee Wee fumbled with the snaps of his suspenders. Clucking in motherly remonstrance, Grace tipped him over onto the bed and wrestled off both boots and trousers together. When he was clothed only in his long johns, gray from many washings in lye soap, she unbuttoned these and peeled them from his boney shoulders.

"That there woman," Pee Wee said, "that there's the virgin?"

"You jes fergit that now, honey." Grace picked up the basin and a cloth and knelt before him. As she washed him she looked up and laughed. "This little feller's got a gray beard. Looks a mite like you."

Pee Wee rubbed a knuckle in one eye as if at an irritation, and did not smile.

When Grace finished her ablutions she shoved the basin under the bed, and lifting the little feller with one finger, she kissed his crown lightly. Then she cocked her head at Pee Wee inquiringly. "What's the matter, honey?"

Pee Wee shook his head, as if a bee were flying about it. "Damn funny," he said, "somethin' damn funny."

[31]

October 21—

Everything again in turmoil. My God, since my undergraduate days I have not known such riptides of passion! Where to begin? My whole former life crumbled away after my initiation into the world of Little Bird, who forsook tape measure and calipers for the knife and gun. My depravity was complete, and I abandoned myself to it—murderer, whoremaster, associate of the lowest races and castes of men—with a kind of fierce joy. It was rare enough that a vision of my former life troubled me. I dared not think at all of my engagement to Lydia: to utter her name, in this camp of outlaws, would have been sacrilege.

Now I can think of nothing else, and have left the fire to sit alone amid these old stones, like a ruined cathedral, and to repeat that name over and over like a litany, reading again and again by the day's last, red light, this note from her own hand. She is here! Not forty miles away! And she forgives me! The alternate joy and dread that sweep through me at the prospect of seeing her can scarcely be borne.

It came about this way. Jacques was giving me another lesson in knife-play, a rare trick he claimed was known only to himself. One feigns a loss of balance to the right, then tosses his weapon to the left hand and whirls in that direction to drive the blade into the ribs of a lunging opponent. I had mastered the manoeuver fairly well and we had taken a moment's rest when we saw two of the fort Indians ride into camp, a lone pack animal behind them. They disappeared into Nampuh's tent and in a few minutes I was summoned.

Nampuh was examining a heap of gold dust that had been poured from a pouch into a clean pan, and merely indicated for me to take a place opposite the two men. Then he tossed a small packet into my lap without comment. The visitors—a wrinkled old Shylock with one eye, and a rather sleek fellow who gave me a fair facsimile of a tradesman's smile—sat expectantly as I opened the envelope. The first thing I saw was the locket I had given Lydia on the first anniversary of our engagement, and the shock struck me quite dumb. With trembling fingers I pressed a catch which released the cover and found inside the lock of my own hair. There was also a letter, and it took every ounce of my strength to withstand the storm of feeling aroused by the mere sight of her handwriting. Only the presence of these strangers kept me from being overcome.

Although her penmanship seemed a bit more ornate than I remembered, she was brave, firm, and clear as always. She had come to Idaho against her father's wish, in the hope that I was yet alive. A gentleman had befriended her, and with his help she had found these intermediaries who might convey to me a message. Nothing meant so much to her as my life, whatever our misunderstandings might have been in the past. She had managed to raise a considerable sum and proposed to exchange it for my release. She knew it was the slightest of chances, but she would attempt to arrange my ransom, for there were plans afoot to make an attack on the savages who held me captive, and she feared for my safety. Mr. Baldo was to append a careful description of the plan to effect this ransom, which would transfer a cargo of fifty sacks of gold into Nampuh's hands and allow me to ride free.

Blinking back my tears as best I could, I looked up to find Nampuh watching me with the alertness of a great cat. He shook his head and frowned. "Hoor," he said. "Puta."

I shook my head in turn, violently. "No," I said. "Wife."

Nampuh's eyes turned hard and he stared into mine so that I felt the shock of his displeasure almost as a physical blow. I remembered then that in our conversations together I had once said, in my despair over the madness with Elizabeth, that I had no "woman." I looked away and searched for a word or phrase that would convey my meaning, but the giant interrupted me, slicing his hand through the air in my direction.

"Wahan," he said softly. "You ketchum?"

The second lie. I opened my mouth to protest, to placate him, but I knew with a sudden clutching of my midsection that this would be a grave error, might be in fact a third and fatal lie. His eyes did not move from my face.

"You ketchum?" he repeated.

"Ketchum," I said, and it was the right thing to say, for he sat back, cold and formal. Henceforth, we must be utterly honest in our dealings, or become mortal enemies.

I had no time to reflect on this awesome condition, however, for my brain was already busy with the prospect of release. I asked the two visitors to tell how they obtained the locket. At the description of the woman who had come to beg their assistance, I nearly broke down again. It was certainly Lydia, with her luxurious black tresses, habit of clasping her hands in her lap, and erect posture.

The giant roused himself from a long meditation on his great toe, protruding like a mushroom from his worn moccasin, and pointed at the letter. I translated its contents as carefully as I could, and he listened, again watching my expression intently. When I was finished he grunted, and looked again into the pan of gold dust.

"One white man, ketchum fifty sacks," he said. The sleek Indian nodded and said that the man who came with this woman had much gold.

"This man, you, brothers?" Nampuh asked me.

"No," I replied. "No sabe."

The one-eyed man said something to the effect that the woman was crazy, as she could take this stranger and his gold rather than risk everything for one white man who had only three horses. Nampuh nodded, saying that white men and their women did not have good sense, but he too was surprised that a squaw would pay so much for an ordinary man. It was most likely an ambush, he said. Other fort Indians had told them already of the many white men coming with guns to Silver City.

I followed the discussion so far, and interrupted to point out that Lydia herself warns him of this danger in the letter, which she certainly would not do if any ambush were contemplated. Also, at the first hint of such trickery, she would expect me to be executed summarily. The one-eyed Indian nodded grudgingly at this and added that the strong man—the one who came with the woman—had said the very same thing.

Then, without any explanation, Nampuh brusquely ordered the two traders to leave. We were left alone, opposite each other on the bear hide. For a long while he did not speak, and when he did it was only to ask me to read from the letter the description of the meeting place. When I had done so he traced with a stick in the dirt for a while, seemingly deep in a consideration of strategy.

"Little Bird," he said suddenly, "How your heart?"

I looked at him blankly. "No ketchum."

He waited, frowning. I noted at this moment a gauntness in his features, as if the coarse skin were shrinking over the heavy brows and cheek-bones, drawing tight to his skull. In spite of his tremendous size, and the absurdity of the notion, there was something almost ethereal about him, a frailty or mortality enhanced by his still, intent manner.

"Two hearts," I said then, remembering the stern necessity now for honesty. "All mix up."

He grunted. Demmy-injun, demmy-white man. No good. You want ketchum squaw, white squaw?"

"Yes." I nodded and made the gesture with the hand like a cutting blade. "Yes. Yes."

The giant went back to his meditation over the sketch in the dirt. "Trap," he said finally. "Bushwhack." He looked at me with the trace of a smile. "You trade Nampuh for squaw?"

Our language of discourse allowed only for nuance of tone and gesture. "Acai-sua," I said, "Not happy," and struck my breast. It was true, though I did not know it until I had spoken. However criminal and base this small band might be judged by a company of civilized men, they had fed, clothed and protected me for months, and I had come, through their instruction, to understand something of the beauty and strangeness of the cruel world they inhabited. Incredibly, beneath my delirium of relief and joy, I knew a pang of regret.

The giant regarded me for a good while, but there was neither suspicion nor hostility in his look. "Picture-man," he said then, "Little Bird. Too bad. You go, ketchum squaw. Ketchum grandfather head. No more scalps. Too bad. Acai-sua, pia-Nampuh." He too struck his breast with clenched fist, and we sat for a time in a strange silence. I felt again, fleetingly, the presence of those shadows that had come to me that night in the wilderness.

"This man ketchum your squaw how?"

I shrugged. "No sabe."

"Plenty trouble. Ketchum plenty gold how?"

"No sabe."

"Trap," Nampuh repeated, as if to himself. "Bushwhack. Nampuh ketchum."

"No," I remonstrated. "Squaw good. No lie." I pointed at the pan of dull, dirty yellow dust. "Squaw gold."

"No." The giant rapped the stick on my knee. "White Squaw ketchum money, picture money."

I pondered momentarily, for the point was well taken. It was not usual to see a woman with a pokeful of dust. The man must have acted for her. Generosity of such magnitude was not, indeed, common.

Nampuh held up one finger. "This man want squaw." He extended a second finger. "Bushwhack, kill you. Ketchum gold, ketchum squaw." A third finger. "Ketchum Nampuh, ketchum more gold."

I could of course see his reasoning, but the chance of Lydia's falling victim to such a schemer seemed too remote. The giant saw the skepticism in my expression.

He drew a line in the dirt from a central circle and marked a fork at its outer end. "Go pronto, stay here. Canyon, plenty deep. Come in, no sale. Some guns this place." He pointed at the circle. "You go, squaw maybe come, this man. Maybe good. Nampuh ketchum gold, you ketchum squaw, go away. Maybe not. Maybe bushwhack." He drew a larger circle around the first one. "Run this way, to canyon. They running after, ketchum bullets."

He threw down the stick once more, closed his eyes and, rocking back and forth slightly, began to sing in a high, almost keening tone, yet just loud enough for me to hear. I sat, enthralled, for he had an expressive voice. The melodic line was intricate and vigorous, strangely moving, though I could understand only a few words. When he had finished he opened his eyes as if waking from sleep, and the peculiar impression of frailty was enhanced by an almost child-like slackness of features.

"Bear song," he said. "Winter coming now. Last winter. Snow coming. Like white men." He yawned then and got slowly, almost painfully to his feet. He threw back the flap of the tent and went outside, where, as if to emphasize his words, a cold wind fluttered and snapped the blanket around his shoulders. I followed him and saw the rank of clouds gathering over the mountains to the West, the invisible sun behind them making a dull red slash across the sky.

He called out to three men at a tipi nearby, telling them to move quickly to gather the horses. To others, huddled by the fire over the traders' goods, he gave the order to collect and pack gear. At first light tomorrow we were to set out for a rendez-vous. There was snow coming, and we must travel ahead of it, so we could not be tracked. The two traders hastened to fold up their little stock. They looked frightened and relieved

*when Nampuh dismissed them with a few curt words, and were soon
mounted and gone—bearing to my dearest Lydia the news that her devotion and daring has succeeded!*

*This entry is then probably the last I shall make in this journal—the
little photographer's notebook is quite stuffed at any account—for my
thoughts now fly ahead, too swift for mere words, to the vision of Lydia
once more in my arms.*

[32]

THEY ERECTED THE TENT, a huge affair with collapsible cross-
beams of steel tubing, on the brow of a small hill, and set up the folding
chairs and shooting stands in front of it. Three men manipulated frames
with targets tacked to them at the crest of an adjoining hill, perhaps
eighty paces away. The rifles had been loaded and now rested in their
racks, while the marksmen took a light meal and refreshments. A steady,
mild breeze flapped the white tablecloths under the heavy pewter plates
and crystal glasses, and above them a hawk balanced on broad wings, as
motionless as if nailed to the sky.

Nolan fidgeted with his glass of whisky and soda water, not even
attempting to hide the glum indifference with which he contemplated
the bleak landscape. The insufferable young man, Fairfield, continued to
blather on about the brisk sale of townsites and rights-of-way, even chiding him with hearty familiarity as if they were now equals. Meanwhile,
Stoneman sat in Godlike somnolence, belching occasionally, scarcely appearing to attend the conversation.

They had him in a fine fix now. Nolan had come along on this re-
hearsal for the impending hunt, hoping to conclude the sale of a controlling interest in his mines and railway franchise, but saw soon enough that
Stoneman intended to play cat-and-mouse still. Nor was there any further doubt about who was cat, and who mouse.

"Opportunity unbounded," Fairfield went on. "Nolan, a man's a fool
not to invest up to his eyebrows. And the alternative"—he favored Nolan with a sly smile—"bankruptcy."

"Damn it, man," Nolan exploded suddenly, his face turning a shade
darker than mere sunburn. "You know I'm short. I have to sell stock to

get capital to invest. The mines are good enough—I've shown you the lot—to get us through the winter and spring."

"Ah, but silver is down just now." Fairfield shook a playful finger at him, and Nolan's knuckles on the chair arm went white with the effort of curbing his impulse to seize that finger and break it off like a twig. They all knew that silver was down because Stoneman had driven it down, by selling short massively. "And we don't know where she'll turn the corner."

Nolan drank quickly from his glass to disguise the unsteadiness of his hand. Stoneman knew very well when the corner would turn, and he would make his ludicrous offer at that point. Nolan would have to sell to avoid ruin, and he would get in exchange for his mines and franchise only stock in the new railroad. Then, he knew, the financier would begin buying to drive the silver market up again, and when it was high enough he would unload the mines. Even if the ore petered out altogether and the crash came, Stoneman could abandon the rail line or sell it for a song, leaving the investors he had sucked into his orbit holding worthless stock for the cash they had put up.

Even the small pleasures he permitted himself were threatened by this madman from the East. The new girl at Mama's, already a fascinating legend, would strain his cash box now. A ravishing girl of good family, it was said, taking perverse vengeance on a harsh father. But expensive. A doctor and attendant went with her.

Nolan frowned and shook off this diversion of his thoughts. "We ought to work together, Mandrake," he said, with an attempt at his old bluff manner. "You know you can reverse this drop, and I'm not asking to hold on to the controlling interest . . ." He trailed off as Stoneman lifted his goblet and drank the dark, red wine.

"They will set up the tent so, on a slight promontory," Stoneman mused aloud, "and the forces will engage below, on the plain. If he can be maneuvered into position, I will be able to shoot myself." He nodded as if at an invisible interlocutor. "The finest markmanship, if we are to avoid damaging his progenitive parts." He uttered a kind of pleased growl.

Nolan glanced covertly at Fairfield, but the young man seemed perfectly at ease.

"Oh yes, sir," he said with a gay laugh. "Opportunities of every kind. Investment, sport, romance. Everything, I swear, in the Land of Giants. We'll catch him alive, you know," he said then to Nolan, matter-of-factly. "He'll be an exhibit for the whole territory. A true giant. Scientific curiosity. We've got agents already drumming up settlers in Minnesota, showing hand-painted slides, the artist's version, through magic lanterns—brand-new brass ones from France!" He clapped Nolan on the shoulder in his enthusiasm. "They'll be here by the boxcar loads, big dumb Swedes with dollars in both fists!"

Nolan recoiled in disgust. "Listen," he said tightly, "Mandrake, let's talk business, for the love of Christ. I've been straight with my proposition, told you about siphoning off concentrate and sitting on it, now—"

Stoneman turned abruptly, and regarded him as if seeing for the first time a pesky insect. The indifference and contempt in his expression struck Nolan like an avalanche. The financier jerked his head at Fairfield. "Buy him," he said shortly. "Eight dollars a share."

Nolan gagged. The sum was so absurd he was struck mute. After a moment he tried to laugh, but the sound was of a man choking.

"Have the papers signed tomorrow," Stoneman went on with evident distaste, "or we will tell the whole story of the siphoning and say we want no part of such a crooked deal. Leave him ten percent of the stock, so he won't be tempted to play tattletale himself."

These instructions completed, Stoneman emptied his glass of wine and hailed the small group of attendants relaxing after their lunch some distance away. The men moved with alacrity, some trotting down the hill toward the targets, others hurrying toward the tent. The hawk overhead veered sharply away.

"Choose a rifle," Stoneman said, almost affably, "and shoot first. A twenty-dollar gold piece for the closest to the bull?" He looked out over the low hills, squinting a little in the pale, lemon light.

Nolan reeled to his feet. "You can't be serious, man," he whispered.

Stoneman merely glanced at him. Fairfield laughed delightedly, as if at some clever scene in a play.

"Very well," Stoneman said and got to his feet. He approached the rack and selected the longest, heaviest rifle, its ornate stock inlaid with ivory and mother-of-pearl. An attendant positioned the stand, an iron rod with a sharp pin at one end and a velvet-lined crutch at the other. Then he stood by attentively, holding ready an open case containing cartridges and cleaning and adjusting tools. Another man, well dressed with a neatly trimmed moustache and sideburns, stepped up beside Stoneman and doffed his bowler hat.

"This is the weapon for the lion and buffalo?" Stoneman asked.

"Yes sir. She's got a kick, sir. Brace yourself well. The ball is eight hundred grains, you might want to go just a hair high."

Stoneman lifted the barrel and settled it in the crutch, then drew back the hammer with a loud, clear snap. He looked casually over his shoulder. "Is our wager on, Nolan?"

Nolan's complexion had gone a faint, vitriolic green, and he seemed to be stooping slightly, as if a cramp had developed in his bowels.

"Eight dollars," he croaked. "That's ruin. What about the copper. The copper . . ."

"Copper?" Fairfield interjected with a cheerful hoot. "Piffle."

"Baxter," Stoneman said, as he settled the heavy stock against his shoulder and began to sight down the long barrel, "take the buggy and give Mr. Nolan a ride into town. He has a bit of business to do, and he is . . ." The barrel wavered, stopped, swayed ever so slightly, then stopped again. In the silence they could hear nothing but Nolan's shallow breath and the tablecloth still snapping faintly in the breeze. Then there was a tremendous, booming explosion, simultaneous with a great plume of gray-black smoke and a dart of fire from the mouth of the gun. Stoneman staggered slightly, then righted himself. He lowered the rifle from the crutch and handed it to the waiting attendant. ". . . indisposed."

Fairfield, still laughing, was on his feet pumping Nolan's lifeless hand. "I'll pass by your office in the morning, old boy; we'll do up the papers. You're a lucky man. You'll see." With a pat on the shoulder he sent Nolan after the driver, who had donned his bowler with a firm tug, and the mine owner stumbled away with the step of a man suddenly old.

Fairfield said, as the buggy pulled away smartly, "There's just nobody like you, sir. It's a plain fact."

Stoneman was watching the small figure of the targeteer on the nearby hill. After a moment the man turned to them and they heard his faint cry.

"Second ring! Whisker off'n the bull, sir!"

Stoneman turned then to look at Fairfield, while the attendant worked busily to swab out the barrel with a linen patch on a ramrod. Until recently, even with his hair hanging like thick wheat-grass over his eyes, the young man could seldom withstand the intensity of his employer's look. But now he dragged the cowlick away from his brow and gazed back, unblinking, with a strange, concentrated passion of his own. He looked, Stoneman imagined, like those Indian fakirs who gazed adoringly at the sun until it blinded them.

For his part, Stoneman now granted Fairfield an occasional wintry smile. Partly through circumstance and partly through his own persistence, the young man had made himself indispensable as an intermediary. He worked at the shadowy margin of the Stoneman empire, yet bargained adeptly among the stockjobbers of Wall Street. With his own shrewdness at estimating men, Stoneman detected in this bumptious, talkative youth a steel spring of vigor and resolve, and a hint of that messianic quality that sets true titans apart from the merely greedy.

The attendant slid another cartridge into the chamber, closed the breech lock with a well-oiled click, and handed the rifle to Stoneman.

"You wish to try?"

Fairfield shook his head.

"The bait is out, you say."

"So our man tells us. He expects the game to come day after tomorrow. We're not to worry about the young fellow at all. That's taken care of."

Stoneman grunted, lifting the rifle again to its velvet cradle. "The brute will expect an ambush, of course."

"The main group will make a feint to the south tomorrow. Tomorrow night they'll double back and take up positions, well hidden, in the hills around the valley. You'll set out the morning of the second day with a smaller bunch—the Pinkertons mostly, dead shots all of them—like a hunting party. They'll spot you, of course, but that ought to help draw them in."

The barrel began its weaving again, describing an ever-smaller arc until it held steady. Again came the boom and flash, and Fairfield heard this time echoes receding swiftly into the distant hills.

"Perhaps," Stoneman said with a shrug. "If the creature is a great ape, stupid and impulsive, as that old lunatic of a professor tells me. If not, we shall go in and root him out. General Howard will give us assistance —reluctantly."

"Oh, you'll get him first, sir," Fairfield said fervently, "your man has set it up just right."

"Bull's eye! Bull's eye!" came the targeteer's cry, wavering on the wind.

"You see, sir?" Fairfield gazed at him with all the pride and devotion of a child whose father has just ascended a throne. "Luck is with you. We've got the mines and the rails in our pocket. The trouble with that young man will soon be finished. And when we have this Big Foot in a cage there will be a boom like—oh, like nothing ever was!"

"Electricity, eh Fairfield?" Stoneman said with a certain indulgent contempt.

"That's it, sir, electricity! You mark my words. Someday a machine will send a man's voice through a wire—copper wire—and someday it'll be photographs, too. Someday—"

"You're a fool, Fairfield. But your wild guesses may attract some investors. God help them."

The attendant stood ready again with the loaded rifle, but Stoneman glanced at the sun, now almost touching the stark black line of distant mountains, and waved him away. "Remarkable," he said, as if to himself, "how quickly it gets cold here at sunset. Peculiar place."

"Yes it is, isn't it sir." Fairfield rose quickly to his feet and motioned the other servants to begin dismantling the tent and hitching the team to the coach. "But exciting in its way, don't you think?"

[33]

THE SNOW BLEW DOWN in light dry flakes that caught in eyelashes and forelocks, so men and horses seemed to peer through lace masks. By mid-morning the crowns of the sagebrush were edged in white, and the higher elevations were a pure and dazzling sweep, speckled here and there with black juniper, like pepper on cream. Nampuh's band climbed the first range quickly, the horses invigorated by the keen air, and then wound down a long valley to a region of barren hills split by two narrow canyons where small streams ran.

Here the snowfall was lighter, so they hurried into the steeper of the two canyons. At the head of the canyon the little stream bounded, smoking, down a series of stone steps. The walls on either side rose in great fractured plinths of discolored rock, their bases sheathed in ice formed by the mist from the waterfalls. The canyon floor still showed patches of thin, dry grass, so they picketed a few of the horses and turned the rest loose to forage.

Then four men rode back to the mouth of the canyon. These scouts cut sagebrush and, when the snow reached the right depth, they swept over the sunken tracks and obliterated them. Then they rode forth in different directions, cutting wide arcs around the Little Duck Valley, scouting for sign of an ambush. Wart, Broken Arm, Jacques, and White Hawk were given this duty.

The light snow continued through the night and into the next day.

There was little talking or movement. Two men were sent on foot to make their way to the canyon rim. Every two hours these sentinels were relieved, for in the cutting wind that blew there a man's eyes soon began to play tricks. The others built crude shelters of willow and sagebrush and crowded into them four and six in a heap, clasping each other like lovers under the buffalo robes. Twice the packs were opened and jerky distributed. Besides the dried meat, they took nothing but mouthfuls of snow.

In late afternoon the clouds were torn to reveal a sky of dark, brilliant blue. The wind died, and in the clear, empty air of the canyon there was no sound of bird or squirrel, only the dash of water and an occasional snort from one of the horses, or the click of a hoof against stone. Just before sundown the scouts returned. Each told the same story, in few words, to the others crouched in a half-circle about them. Nampuh squatted a little in front of the others, and occasionally asked a question.

The white men, armed with repeating rifles, came fast this morning, all together, as far as the bank of the Wickahoney, where they divided into three groups. Each group made cold camp on the far side of a ridge or hill bordering Little Duck Valley, hiding the horses well on picket lines in the brush. There were forty-two of them, including two scouts, probably Shoshoni, and some carried two rifles. Another party, with many pack animals, had come from Silver City and set up a camp on the highest hill, plainly visible. They were very awkward on horses, and seemed unaware of the other white men hiding over the ridge.

After these reports, a muttering grew among them, interrupted by an occasional loud, angry oath. The winter had come early, as some had predicted, and would be severe, but instead of retreating into the mountains after game they were chasing gold and skirting an ambush. The white man, Little Bird, had led them to this evil. He should have been killed and scalped at the very first. He had squeezed like a weasel into their hearts with the intent of tricking them this way. Who could believe his story of the rich squaw? Had he not a few days before advised them to split into two groups, to make themselves still weaker? Had he not sworn his squaw would come with the gold and nothing more?

Finally Little Bird leaped to his feet. Except for the palms of his hands and the shadow of his eye sockets, he looked little different from the rest. The sun, dirt, and smoke had cured his skin to a deep red-brown, and braided in his hair were the feathers given him after the initiation ceremony. He swore brokenly that his squaw knew nothing of this ambush, had been tricked herself, but he would ride out tomorrow to meet her all the same. If he died, he would be glad, for he was already like a dead man, without wife or relatives or children. They could leave him there and go home now. If the white men did not kill him, he would take the squaw and go back to his place, where he had come from.

Some of the others began to jeer at him, saying that he was a baby who must need his squaw's teat, that he was perhaps himself a woman, that he talked like a snake, twisting this way and that. Some began openly to discuss killing him on the spot, arguing over who should get his horses, who his old rifle, who the picture-thing.

Then it grew quiet, for the change had occurred in Nampuh's eyes, and he stared at all of them at once. He began to speak. He had thought they were no longer children, but they were showing again how small they were, squabbling and insulting each other. They had come two days early to this place to lay their own ambush, and now when the enemy came they talked of running away, of killing Little Bird not for something he did, but for his woman's treachery. To have such puny men—if they were men—in his company made him ashamed. Now, finally, the whites had brought them a large number of horses and rifles, perhaps even the gold, and instead of taking this rich gift they wanted to hunt a few miserable deer in the snow.

Perhaps he would do it himself, with a few warriors if any were there, since it was so easy. The woman was to ride into the valley with only two men, bringing the gold first. If there was no gold they could cut Little Bird's throat and send him to his squaw that way. If she brought the gold they would let him go. Then, when the white men came after them, they would lead the enemy into this canyon. The white men would be trapped, with no cover from which to fire. He would lead them himself, for of course the white men wanted *his* head, and not the heads of women, rabbits, moles, mice, little snakes, or his so-called warriors—all creatures afraid to come out of their holes.

There were forty-two of them, and they carried better guns, White Hawk said. And maybe the others, the hunters, were part of this ambush. What if the Army was waiting to join the fight, too? What if the white men did not follow into the canyon but camped at its mouth and on the rim and waited? In three days they would be eating their own horses. They would all die there, either starving or trying to fight out of a hole. Many men grunted in agreement with this speech.

Nampuh said this was very true. It was also true it would be a very bad winter. They would get hungrier, their horses poorer. The pack trains into the mines would be few, and well guarded. They would use up ammunition hunting and raiding these trains. When they were weak, some time in the spring, they could be sure General One-Arm would come after them. Then the bluecoats could shoot them down in the mud like rabbits. He, Nampuh, preferred to take this chance, either dying here with his arm still strong and a fat pony under him, or taking their guns, gold, horses, and scalps.

Favor seemed to shift again, but the discussion went on for another hour, until the light began to fail. Overhead the clouds visible in the crooked crack of sky had turned red and bright gold. The faction that urged a quick return began to lose spirit. Riding away into the bitter cold night did not seem so appealing. Finally the group elected to stay, and Wart delivered a speech, exhorting them all to give up grumbling and dire prediction, to face the oncoming sun with leaping hearts, for if it was their last day, they should be happy to die here, by the water, fighting the white men. Ho! The whole company roared its approval.

In the morning, it was agreed, Little Bird, Nampuh, and four others would ride out to meet the squaw and her escort. Until then, Little Bird would sleep bound by a braided thong rope to a guard, for he had shown himself a white man, and was their prisoner again. No one was to talk to him, to give him anything, or to take anything from him. He protested, but was met by silence and averted eyes. They tied him to Broken Arm and retreated then into their shelters, the great, dark heaps that breathed white vapor toward the stars now emerging to glitter in a sky of steel.

[34]

THEY CAME SLOWLY on a game trail, visible because the snow melted first there, making a dirty, broken line between two hills. The woman's muffler covered her face even though the sun had begun to warm things through the chill air. She rode sidesaddle, her voluminous skirt cascading nearly to the ground. The heavyset man was next, his sheepskin coat thrown open to reveal the revolver at his belt, a woolen cap pulled tight on his head. Behind them came a man in the rough garb of a drover, who held the halter of a pack mule loaded with securely tied leather panniers.

A little way into the valley they stopped. Even from a great distance their voices could be heard, though the words were unintelligible, and also the occasional clink of the Spanish bit on one of the horses. Perhaps two miles away, from the top of a high bluff, a broad canvas fluttered, and on the slope below several horses grazed. The man took a bronze eyeglass from the pocket of the coat and squinted through it for a time, but said nothing.

They waited. Around them wisps of steam rose from the dark stones exposed by the melting snow. A few yards away a rabbit broke out of one clump of sage, made a few zigzag bounds, then stopped, invisible, in the shadow of another bush; and at one edge of the horizon a kestrel coasted rapidly near the ground on its narrow, sharply angled wings. Otherwise the valley was utterly still and empty, the sun burning fiery diamonds in the snow.

Then, three quarters of a mile away, they saw six riders on the crown of a low hill, moving at an easy trot. When the six drew to a halt, they were still too far away to be recognized, or to hail the group on the valley floor. The heavyset man raised one arm high and moved it back and forth in a wide arc. After a long moment, one of the riders responded with a similar movement. The heavyset man turned, said something, and the drover began to ride slowly toward the six on the hill, leading the pack animal. When he was perhaps two hundred yards distant, they called out to him and he stopped. Two of the riders advanced at a canter, separated, and approached the drover and his cargo from the flank. Both held rifles and, reining to a walk, kept them pointed at the drover until they were an arm's length away. Then the drover raised one hand, spread and empty in the air, and with the other handed the lead rope to the nearest rider. They waited, the rifles following like compass needles, as the drover wheeled and spurred his mount to a brisk trot. When he was out of range, they returned with the mule to the others.

Two of the men dismounted and untied the flaps of the panniers. They began to remove the canvas sacks, handing them up to the mounted men, who jerked open the tie-strings with their teeth and peered inside. Then they swung the opened sacks by their strings, estimating weight. After the inspection, the sacks were secured again and stowed swiftly back into the panniers. Four of the riders, one leading the mule, set off the way they had come, first at a trot, then with sharp cries moving into a lope. One of the remaining two began then to angle toward the three in the valley, and a figure detached itself from this group, moving to meet him. It was the woman, recognizable by the dark puff of skirt on one side of her horse.

Even a half-mile away, Willard recognized the dress and the bearing, the light, erect, birdlike motion of the head. His heart felt like a struggling animal, clawing to escape from his body, and he found his vision blurred by a surge of tears. All during the last two days in the icy canyon, he had been an outcast, had felt himself more lost and alone than ever before. For he saw that he belonged nowhere, was neither thief nor gentleman, and his heart was bewildered by a turmoil of shame, yearning, remorse, and wild hope. He knew only that one pure soul in all the world had maintained faith in him, had sacrificed all to win him back.

The horseman behind him now advanced on Willard's trail a little way, keeping him within range of the rifle crooked under one arm. It was Jacques, whom Willard now heard shouting to him.

"Lentement, mon ami. Attention, plenty slow, *regardez-bièn."*

Grinding his teeth, Willard kept his pony under tight rein, for every nerve cried out to whip the animal into a gallop and throw himself at Lydia's feet. It was the figure approaching him, however, that broke into a swifter pace, and he heard a faint cry, clear as the note of a flute. It was his own name he heard, and the syllables, unheard for so many months, were strange to him. Behind the woman the two men now began to advance, moving apart to position her between them.

"Attention." The voice behind him was further away, as if Jacques had halted. "Theez fort-two mens—*comment ça?* Bushwhack! Beeg fool!"

He heard the firing begin then, beyond the first range of hills at the point where the four men and the laden mule had galloped away. The reports of the guns made a continuous sound like flame crackling through dry branches. From further away, from the bluff where the tent swelled and flapped like a great brooding bird, came the periodic roar of a heavier caliber weapon.

Willard urged the pony forward into a swift trot, and as he did so a shadow flitted beside him. He blinked back his tears, shook his head, and looked up automatically. The kestrel wavered in the air above him, not twenty feet away. He could see the feathers of bright reddish gold with black bands, the pale underside of the wings, and even the hook of the little beak, gaping wide as the bird uttered its thin, scraping cry. He stared at it, tightening his hands on the reins.

Again he heard his name, and looking down he saw her now perhaps fifty yards away, the black hair tumbling down her shoulders, a white hand reaching out to him. The two men were still behind her, ranging further to the side, coming at an easy gallop. Something powerful, unnameable, wrenched at his heart. He leaned forward and tried to cry out, but the sound was throttled into a sob. The bird shrieked again, and he heard a thin whistling of wings. The figure before him seemed to enlarge suddenly, with an unnatural clarity. He saw the foam at the horse's bit, the eyes hooded by a fold of the muffler, the white hand disappearing into folds of the skirt spread now like a turkey's bustle.

All at once the shadow darted at him and wings clapped about his head. His pony shied, and as he lurched to recover his balance he saw the woman's fist emerge from the skirt, something bright perched on it. An instant before the muffler dropped away from the grinning mouth, he saw again the vision that had come during his vigil, the two faces on one head, and the shock galvanized him into movement. He was turning, rolling to the side, one arm around the pony's neck, when the little flame flicked like a serpent's tongue from her hand. He heard her scream and the kestrel's shriek. The tongue flickered again and a hot lash went across his shoulder. The pony bolted and he lost his grip, falling flat in the dirty snow.

He heard the rifle crack behind him, then the terrified squeal of a horse. When he had wiped the muddy grit from his face he saw her for a moment, green eyes wide with anger and surprise, a small red blossom on her white shirtfront. Then the horse danced and humped, pitching her to the ground in an explosion of ruffles. The rifle cracked again. He raised his head and shoulders, propping himself on his elbows like a lizard. When he turned, he could see Jacques crouched over his pony's neck, stretching at a dead run back toward the hills, while a scatter of riders galloped to cut him off. The pounding of hooves and occasional gunshots receded, and Willard became aware of the faint sigh of wind through the sagebrush, the fall of droplets of water from leaves. Then he heard the soft footsteps behind him.

The man had dismounted, leaving his pony with reins dangling to the ground. He stood a few feet from Willard, a cocked revolver in one hand. His flat, ruddy face was smiling, an odd smile of anticipation. Feeling something on his skin, Willard glanced aside to see the soaked shirt, a trickle of bright blood winding through the hairs of his right forearm. He moved his fingers a little in the mud, then pushed himself slowly to hands and knees. Staring down at the patchwork of snow and earth, he breathed heavily for a few moments, then raised his head and gathered one foot under him.

The man continued to smile, and lifted the barrel of the gun in encouragement. Staggering a little, Willard hoisted himself erect. He slid the knife from his belt and held it awkwardly, the thread of blood crawling between his knuckles and down along the blade. The man laughed aloud, a heavy, soft burr in his chest. He raised a thumb, care-fully released the hammer of the revolver, and holstered it swiftly. With the same hand he then lifted from his coat pocket a tube of black leather, a whipstock packed with lead shot, which he draped into his other palm with a light slap. He moved his shoulders inside the coat, stretching and settling them, and took a quick, gliding step toward Wil-lard.

"Come now," he said in the same soft, heavy, humorous tone. "Come here."

Unsteadily, Willard edged to his right. The man circled with him, the limber bludgeon alternately dangling and flexing in his hand. When Willard stumbled once, the man laughed again and the whipstock swished lightly around and tapped his shoulder.

"Come now," the man repeated, with a little sigh of impatience.

Willard seemed to stumble again and lunge ahead, the blade jabbing feebly once and then flashing as he appeared to lose his grip on the handle. The man sprang forward like a cat, the whipstock curling over his head in a blurred arc, but as he did so Willard caught the knife with his left hand and shifted to his left. The man tried to adjust his swing, but the descending stock only raked Willard's shoulder as he wheeled to drive the blade up and in. The man grunted in surprise, then stepped back, righting himself, and for a moment they stared at each other.

The blade in Willard's hand was smeared bright red, and even as he crouched and began to circle again, he saw the man smack his lips and cough. The whipstock hung limp for a moment, and then the man retched suddenly, a gobbet of blood spilling from his mouth down his chin. He dropped the whipstock to claw again at the holster under his coat, taking an uncertain step backward.

Willard moved after him and stroked hard with the blade across the knuckles of the hand clutching the gun-butt. The man uttered a sound unnaturally high in pitch, like the voice of a thwarted child and tried to ward off the attack with his other hand. Willard brushed the hand aside and drove the blade directly into the broad chest. It passed halfway through the breastbone and then stuck. The man tried to run backward and fell. Willard, still wrenching at the knife handle, was dragged over with him. Straddling the thick chest, Willard worked the handle back and forth while the man beat at his face, the stubs of his severed fingers spattering both of them. Finally he pulled the blade free and immedi-ately drove it into the hollow at the base of the man's throat. The body under him arched in a powerful convulsion that bucked him to one side. As he rolled away, the knife came free with an odd sucking noise.

The man bent double, then slowly uncurled. The sound of his gagging was loud and continuous. His two hands, one of them seeming to sprout red flowers, flailed aimlessly. Willard began to crawl toward him, the knife upraised, but in a moment he stopped, for the man had begun to jerk and tremble all over, no order in his movement. His gagging became sporadic, then ceased.

When the man was still, Willard went to him on his knees. After wiping the blade on his sleeve, he clamped it in his teeth and went through the coat pockets, removing a wallet and watch. He examined the revolver for a moment, then jammed it in his waistband. On his feet, he sheathed the knife and approached the pony, who was complacently cropping a few strands of seared grass. Taking the reins, he moved toward the dark heap of the woman a few yards away, but the wind puffed and rustled the skirt and petticoats, making the animal shy. He could see her face anyway, fixed in its grin, green eyes staring at the horizon. Elizabeth, now with black hair. His dead wife.

In the sagebrush flat three riderless horses now trotted erratically. The drover too had apparently been shot out of his saddle. Then he saw another rider galloping along the crest of a hill, doubling back. The figure halted for a moment and danced sidewise, looking his way. It was Jacques. Willard waved with his one good arm, and after a moment Jacques raised his rifle aloft. A faint cry, perhaps a hoot of laughter, came to Willard on the wind. Then a volley of shots sounded behind the hill and the figure broke again into a gallop, veering away and out of sight.

The gunfire became sporadic and distant, and except for the riderless horses, now grazing, the valley was again empty. The kestrel was gone; even the sky was bare. He stood for a moment, touching the shoulder which pained him. Then he spoke quietly to the horse, steadied it, and mounted. He bore west and north, away from the sound of the guns, toward Silver City.

[35]

GENERAL HOWARD had commissioned a corporal in the Quarter-master's to sew a brass hook on the side of his field coat. He could hang his sword belt on this hook, then reach behind his back, catch up the belt, and buckle it in front with one hand. He had begun this operation when his aide informed him that the two men would not go away. They insisted on seeing him, and the taller one had a telegram from Washington, from some senator or other. Also, the two survivors who could still get to their feet had been sent up from the medical post, and were ready to talk.

The general threw the sword and belt on his desk, startling the two orderlies behind him, who were working furiously to pack a trunk. Around them were strewn maps, a brass compass, writing pads, a chipped shaving mug, leather razor case, and a stack of oilskin bags.

"Goddamn it, Lieutenant, throw those two old fools off the post, and kick their behinds on the way out." He leaned over his desk, as if looking for something. "Where is my mirror?"

"Here, sir," said one of the orderlies, reaching into the trunk and rising with alacrity to replace on the desk a small, silver-backed mirror on a stand.

"Sir," the aide began nervously, "they—"

"—have a telegram. I know that. But goddamn it, it is against regulations to admit civilians into a column during active maneuvers."

"Unless to protect them, sir."

"Lieutenant . . ." The general bent toward the mirror, arranging his moustache with his thumbnail.

"They say they are going, with or without us, sir."

The general straightened, and after a moment with eyes closed, he sighed and smiled tightly. "Then show them all in, Lieutenant. The boys from the posse as well."

When the two men entered, he could see by their pallor and clenched jaws that they had already heard about the woman. The little German, his beard tangled and damp from weeping, was absurdly dressed in twill jodhpurs and a calfskin hunting jacket, and he carried a leather quirt as awkwardly as a stalk of celery. The other, the girl's father, looked like a cadaver. Flesh had sloughed from his bones until they appeared ready to poke through his dry and withered hide. He bore the telegram, already unfolded, in one hand.

"General—"

"I know, Professor Braddock. Lieutenant Phillips has told me about the message from the senator, and we intend to investigate this report of a young lady at the scene of the engagement. You will be informed immediately."

"We are going ourselves," Braddock said in a voice so harsh and loud the orderlies paused again in their labor. "My daughter may be seriously wounded or . . ." His breath failed him.

"Your assistance is for us necessary," Baum interjected, "most necessary."

"Gentlemen, we are in the midst of preparations, at all possible speed. I have a troop of cavalry to muster and deploy to the rear, as well as a flying column to get on the trail of this gang of murderers."

The door stood open and through it came another aide, who saluted smartly and began to speak even before the general's nod of acknowledgment.

"They're here, sir. Patched up pretty well. Lieutenant Murdoch wants to know if the men to escort the supply wagons should come from his company, and should he fire the field pieces before securing the caissons. They haven't been fired for a long time, he says, sir."

"Take the men from Company C. Don't do any firing, for the love of God. All the horses on the post are out of their corrals and half-hitched up. Murdoch ought to know better. Yes, send them in." The general dropped into his chair, and indicated other chairs to the visitors, but they ignored him. "These men managed to survive the attack—God knows how—and have given reports to my chief field officers, but I wish to hear some particulars myself. Please, gentlemen, allow me to ask the questions and do not interrupt."

Both of the survivors were bandaged, and one dragged a leg stiff as a post. He leaned heavily on a soldier who accompanied him, and groaned when he was eased onto the bench before the general's desk. Their features were dark with grime and burnt powder, streaked with rivulets of dried sweat, but he could see what kind of men they were. The younger of the two, whose mat of dull brown hair, like old hay, was caked with blood from a scalp wound, nodded deferentially in the direction of the two professors, then addressed an awkward salute to Howard, palm outward in the Confederate manner.

"Jim Crawford, suh. Reportin' a massacree. A good many men gone, suh. I tolt yer decamps all 'bout hit, suh—"

"Kilt 'em ever' goddamn one, General," the older man interrupted. He had a narrow hatchet face under straight black hair. "That murderin' Siwash, he done it. We was—"

"I've heard the report," Howard cut in, a little sharply. "We are moving post-haste to get troops into the field and bring vengeance down on this monster's head. I need to know, very quickly, please, the number of the enemy you observed, where you saw them last, and your estimate of their armament."

"General," Crawford said with a sudden, ill-humored laugh, "them's hard samples to assay. I never seen most o' 'em atall. We had that little pothole valley plumb sewed up. Forty-two men, good men, with Henrys and Winchesters and Colts. Two groups equal on each side of this yere valley—Little Duck, they calls it—"

The man with the hatchet face broke in, agitated. "And Mr. Stoneman, there he was at the far end with ten Pinkerton boys and rhinoc'rus guns and I dunno what-all. We—"

Crawford shot his companion a warning look and resumed his narrative. "We couldn't git too clost, though, or they would spy us, so we was back in the hills when they rode in. Six o' 'em, and one was big's a house."

"Yes, yes." Howard grimaced. "I have heard, but how—"

"We never knew nothin' 'bout how nor why they showed up, 'cept it were a ransom deal. We wa'n't to take no pris'ners, 'side from the Big Foot. It did *look* like, from a consid'able ways off, they was a woman in this bunch that come to the other end o' the valley, but I sho' couldn't swear to't. So anyways we was to wait for the palaverin' to git over, and when the Injuns lit out fer home we come after 'em. We got two, and had 'em pinched up tight 'tween our flanks when they run into this little canyon, jest wide 'nough fer maybe eight men to go at once.

"Bill here 'n I come last, and 'fore we got a hunnert yards in we heard the shootin' bust out. But I could tell it wa'n't no six Injuns in there, so I held back a little, and when I come 'round the last bend—" He shook his head and looked at the general, then at the professors. "They ain't no words could tell."

"Try," said General Howard acidly.

"What kilt 'em," the older man said, picking up the thread, "was the goddamned ice."

"An' the horses," Crawford reminded him.

"And the horses," the other continued. "It were a box canyon, or damn near, and the rocks was straight up and down, and slicker'n Satan with ice from a crick. The Injuns was all up in them rocks. Couldn't see nor hide nor hair on 'em and they could shoot right down a man's throat. Some of the boys got off'n their horses 'n tried to git up them icy rocks . . ." He, too, stopped to shake his head.

"And they had them hosses o' their'n penned right at the bottom of the canyon," the younger man said, tilting forward and running his fingers through the matted hair, "and when they seen us tryin' to git off'n ourn to find cover they sent two braves to spook the whole herd right through us, and goddamn, they was horses 'n men 'n guns a-flying ever which-a-way. We was at the back and still mounted, so we run with the herd, and when we come to the mouth o' that canyon, here come two more Siwashes to turn the bunch back. They never seen us through the dust, so by Gawd we put holes in them two, at least, but the horses was turned and we heard 'em a-stampedin' back down the canyon, crazy as crazy could be, 'n I bet they tromped near as many as the Injuns kilt."

"Jim here 'n me was both hit twic't, so we jest rode fer all we was worth to git back. We seen them men gettin' blowed right out'n their saddles and floppin' 'round under all them horses—"

"I understand, Mr. . . . ?"

"Kittredge, sir. I come from Indianer."

"Yes, thank you, Mr. Kittredge, but we must not waste any more time. How *many* of the Indians took part?"

"I swear, Gen'ral, they ain't no tellin'. I seen maybe six 'sides the two we shot, but they had to be twic't or three times that many, one way or 'tother."

"Their guns?" Howard asked, rising.

"Couldn't say, General. I heard a few Sharps and an old .45-70, but they was some repeaters, too."

"Sure as hell got repeaters now," the young man said with an edge of admiration in his bitter tone. "Forty o' em."

The general had picked up his sword belt again and secured it on the brass hook. He glanced at the soldier from the medical post, still at attention by the door.

"Take Mr. Crawford and Mr. Kittredge back to their quarters and see to their needs. Thank you, gentlemen."

Behind him one of the orderlies, also standing, cleared his throat.

"Oh, yes. Load it in the wagon, boys. And you"—the general looked then at the aide, who was holding an attitude of respectful parade-rest—

"send the clerk here double-quick. He should bring the seal. Tell Captain Matthews to have the men load and saddle, and to send someone here with two additional mounts." He finished buckling the belt and picked his hat from a wooden peg on the wall. Outside they could hear the creak of wagon wheels, the slap of leather, and the ringing of steel, punctuated by shouts and oaths.

"We must insist again, General—" Braddock began in the same harsh tone, but he stopped when Howard turned on him. Along with the sword and hat, the general had taken on a different bearing. Under the wide, rolled brim his face had lost all trace of politic deference. His glance was keen, unblinking, without humor or pity.

"You have a half hour to ready your gear, gentlemen. I hope you have your own coats and weapons."

Baum and Braddock exchanged startled looks. "General—" Braddock began again.

"I will have you sworn in as a citizen's militia when the clerk gets here. You will be absolutely under my orders, and required to keep up with the column—if it kills you—until we engage the enemy. I warn you right now, gentlemen, that this campaign has as its object the extermination of Nampuh. You heard these men. The beast has perpetrated the most savage and bloody massacre in this territory's history. I will not rest until the creature is dead and under six feet of God's good earth with his head in his lap. We will do our best to investigate this business about the woman as we go, but there will be no—I repeat, *no*—deviation from our ultimate purpose. Is that clear?"

After a long moment Braddock looked away. "I understand your duty," he said, his voice subdued. "Surely, you understand mine, as a father, to come to the assistance of my child. We shall respect your orders, sir."

"Yes," Professor Baum nodded vigorously, "certainly so. But, Roland, must we have with us these large guns?" He regarded the quirt in his hands with apprehension.

"I will sign a requisition to the armory if you wish," Howard said, turning slightly to beckon the clerk, who had paused in the doorway with his writing-case. "And you may ask at Quartermaster's for what small items you may need. I would advise"—he glanced at Baum's jodhpurs—"different apparel."

The clerk, studious and efficient behind his steel-rimmed spectacles, listened carefully to his instructions. When the general had departed with a spare salute, he opened his case, removed the proper papers, uncapped the inkwell, and picked out a pen with a silver point.

"Well, well, my bravos," he said to the two professors, dipping the point into the ink. "Off to war, is it? Well. Full names?" The pen waggled in his hand and he smirked a little. "Just in case. Next of kin, and so forth."

[36]

THEY SAT uncharacteristically forward, elbows on knees, swinging their heads to follow the hectic traffic, or to hail an acquaintance from the throng to discuss the events of the day. The carving lay untouched beside the knee of one, while the jug passed often between them, sometimes being handed to passersby who stopped to converse. Without the soporific thudding of the stamp mill, the atmosphere was charged with excitement, even gaiety, as if for an impending festival.

"Anybody come out o' the hotel yet?"

"Nope."

"Lickin' their wounds."

"Hell, he never got none. Perkins says the Pinkertons all wanted to ride after the posse, but he was agin' it. Sat up on the hill like the Sultan o' Singapoor, waitin' for them to bring back the big 'un. Only thing come back was horses with blood on the saddle."

"They say two got away. All shot up."

"That damn Siwash is smart as a damn coon. But I doubt he be long for this world. They're callin' in all the railroad gangs and shuttin' down the mine for a week." He glanced to the far end of the porch, where an Indian huddled in a ragged blanket. "If I was him I'd skedaddle for the tipi quick 'afore some of the boys has a notion to take revenge right yere."

"Well, ol' Stoneballs won't git no breedin' stock now. Fellers git holt o' that big Injun they'll geld 'im first thing. Jest to start the ceremony." The carver waited for an opening between pedestrians and then spat a rusty stream of juice into the dust.

"When them wagons come in with corpuses 'thout no scalps, they'll be a hell of a militia signed up," the other man agreed. He tugged a strand of his thick white beard. "If I weren't so damn old and stove up I'd ride 'long to watch that."

His friend sighed and shook his head regretfully. "They say they kilt a woman, too. Fellers'll be fit to be tied."

"She ha'nt no business bein' out there."

"This whole shitaree makes me 'spect somethin'. Stoneballs comin' to town the same time. This yere railroad. Town's full o' whores 'n sharpers 'n galoots." He tilted his head toward the figure crouched below the sidewalk. With a striking motion like a snake's, he ejected a wad of tobacco that arced into the street only a yard short of the Indian, but the man did not move. "And these varmints."

" 'Tain't bad," the bearded man said with admiration. " 'Nother stride an' you'll git 'im. Hey there, Pee Wee!" He motioned, and a man crossed the street toward them.

"Howdy gents," the newcomer said, nodding and reaching for the jug. "Mighty nice o' you to invite a thirsty trav'ler to this yere drawin' room."

"You j'inin' the posse? Old boar like you cattin' 'round doin' everything else, we hear."

"Don't b'lieve all you hear," Pee Wee instructed, and tipped the jug over his cocked arm into a mouth already working in anticipation.

"Go easy there, young feller," the bearded man admonished. "We got to git through the day on that."

Pee Wee lowered the jug, smacking his lips. "Mighty fine. You gents heerd the news?"

"Hell of a massacree."

"Ain't the last, neither."

"Damn certain." The man chewing tobacco shifted his cud from one cheek to the other. "Mighty peculiar."

"I been thinkin' the same," Pee Wee agreed. His eye fell on the Indian a few yards away. "Somebody ought to tell the chief here to git his tail back to the fort 'fore somebody shoots it off."

"Yer closest. Anyways, we hear you been to the cathouse, but they wasn't no gal that small a gauge so they give yer money back."

"Jealous, ain't ye Abe? Been so long ye can't recall how to go about it."

They cursed each other genially. After a pause the bearded man went on. "Speakin' o' which, they any truth to that rumor Mama's gonna auction off a certainteed virgin?"

Pee Wee frowned. "More shenanigans." He reached for the jug, then seemed to think better of it. "I'm headed down to the Lucky Lode and listen to the jawin'. Thankee, gents. Don't fall off'n yer log."

He turned and sauntered down the sidewalk, snapping one gallus with a hooking thumb, the only indication of deep thought. He did not notice the Indian get to his feet and shuffle along behind him. Within a few strides, however, he felt a hand pluck at his sleeve.

"Git off, ye red devil!" he said angrily, and kicked out with one foot. The Indian dodged and kept pace, a hand extended open-palmed. Pee Wee stopped and jabbed a finger at the beggar, who masked the lower part of his face with a fold of blanket. "Git home! Bad medicine here! Ketchum foot!" He kicked out again in illustration. The dark eyes stared at him, unmoving.

"Goddamn it! Stinkin' red beggars." He dug in one pocket and withdrew a handful of coins. Selecting two large copper pennies, he dropped them into the man's palm. "Now git on with ye. Ketchum plenty trouble!" He made a shooing gesture with both hands and turned back on his way.

"An extremely rude manner to adopt with a former employer."

Pee Wee stumbled, righted himself, and whirled about. He could see no one but the Indian. An alley opened to his right, but it was empty except for a scatter of chickens. He took an uncertain step backward.

"If you intend to kick me, you had best advance."

The blanket had fallen away from the face, and he saw indeed that the voice came from the Indian.

"Holy Christ!"

"Hold your voice down." The Indian looked over his shoulder. "Your friends may think I'm trying to rob you."

"Goddamn Jehosophat! It's you! I'll be—" Pee Wee veered to the corner of a building and supported himself against it. "I thought you was sure as shitfire a dead man. Ever'body did. How in Creation— nobody ever come out o' Big Foot's camp alive. How . . ." He looked Willard over from head to foot, carefully. "What's the matter with yer shoulder?"

"A slight wound—a scratch, really. But I had no proper bandage."

"How come yer done out like a Siwash? You kin git kilt in that getup."

"I have no other clothes, and I was not sure I would be any better off as . . . as a white man." Willard smiled a little. "Things have rather changed." He looked up at the sky. "But I can't explain that now. I need your help. I want to know about the man and woman who were killed in the battle at Little Duck Valley, and the other young woman—"

"Some damn funny busines," Pee Wee interrupted. "Yer damn right there is. But hell, man." He shook his head. "We cain't go into no saloon together. A Siwash don't talk to a white man thataway. You got to get some decent duds."

"All right." Willard reached under the blanket to his belt and removed a wallet. From the thick sheaf inside he took two bank notes. "Will this do?"

"Jesus wept," Pee Wee whispered, awestruck. "Where did you—"

"We can talk then." Willard pressed the bills into the old man's hand. "Where can we meet?"

Pee Wee thought briefly. "Outside o' town, goin' east, there's a wagon road cuttin' to yer left. Little clump o' trees there, and an old fell-in hay shed beside it. I'll git ye some pants and boots and socks and a shirt, maybe a proper bandage. Be there in maybe an hour."

"Capital." Willard automatically thrust out his hand, then quickly withdrew it. He winked at Pee Wee, then turned to squat again with his back against the sidewalk.

After two steps, Pee Wee stopped, considered, and asked over his shoulder in a hoarse whisper, "What size boots?"

They were of thick, stiff cowhide with an iron shank in the arch, and pinched his feet painfully, for he had been in moccasins for months. The English words, too, seemed unwieldy. Men at the bar or tables stared at him covertly, he knew, for his skin was burned an unusual shade of umber, and the brand-new clothes were striking in a company where stains and patches were the rule. The whisky in front of him he sipped very carefully, a few drops at a time, listening for the most part, prodding Pee Wee with an occasional question.

The old man, halfway through his third drink, snapped his galluses from time to time as he talked. Willard's expression unnerved him. The frank, open countenance he remembered had given way to a flat, neutral look, behind which he detected a dangerous intensity of purpose. He supposed that being held captive in the outlaws' camp had affected the young man for the worse. Also, he believed privately that the blow on the head from the horse's hoof had altered his friend's character permanently, had "teched" him.

"It don't 'ppear likely atall," he said, "that yer intended could be this yere gal at Mama's."

"But you admit that when you first saw her, in the company of this foreigner, she was—as I have described—beautiful, and—as you say—high-toned?"

"As best I rec'llect," Pee Wee rejoined, "but I was three sheets in the wind and rudder up. I was shore took back to see her in that crib, though."

"You are sure it was the same woman?"

"Yep."

"It had to be. I recognized the dress, and the locket—there could be no mistake." Willard pushed aside his glass, still almost full. "I must free her."

"Whoa, now, Willard." Pee Wee shifted in his chair and passed his gnarled hand quickly over his pate, smoothing invisible hair. "They got her under lock 'n key, 'n a pair of bravos standin' guard."

"We shall enter as customers. You direct me to the place, and I shall see to the rest. With three fast horses standing by—"

"Whoa, *whoa*, young feller! Yer talkin' a holdup. That there girl has got a board 'n room bill. She's jest as much propitty as . . . as a prize mare. Stealin' a horse is worse, a-course, but stealin' a whore is—" He stopped, seeing a change in the other's face. "I mean, I take that back, 'pologies, but that's the way Mama's goin' to look at it. And her an' the marshall and the judge is all thicker'n thieves. Anyways, where you goin' to hide?"

Willard looked away from the table, out a window into the street. "I know places," he said.

"Whoa," Pee Wee repeated, this time as if the man opposite him were, indeed, a large and dangerous animal. "Yer not thinkin'— You ain't goin' back to ol' Nampuh's camp?" He peered at Willard's face as one examines a wall for cracks. "Gen'ral Howard is takin' ever' able-bodied man he's got into the Owyhees. Man, yer talkin' like a lunatic! I know from what you tolt me that they treated you square, but they're savages, damn it!" Willard did not respond. Pee Wee groaned. "Don't be thinkin' damn fool things like that!"

"I've told you the situation," Willard said evenly. "She is surely being kept against her will, for the most despicable reasons. If the laws of . . . property, as you put it, imprison her, then we are better off with Nampuh. Also, he bargained in good faith with me and I—it seems as if I betrayed him."

"Betrayed? Lord, Willy, he's an *outlaw!* A damn murderin', thievin'—"

"So am I." For the first time Willard smiled at him, a broad but bitter smile. "So am I. Anyway, I am not suggesting that you and Lydia accompany me so far. I can find a safe camp for you, and go the rest of the way myself. But I must get there ahead of General Howard." He pulled the wallet from his pocket and removed a half-dozen of the bank notes, tucking them under Pee Wee's glass. "Agreed?"

Pee Wee writhed on his chair, both thumbs jammed in his suspenders. He looked alternately from the bills to Willard's face. "Lord," he whispered. "Lord help me."

"He helps those, I am told, who help themselves."

Pee Wee sighed. Hesitantly, delicately, he slid the money from beneath the glass. "I'm too old for this malarkey," he said wistfully. "Too goddamn old."

Willard stood up quickly. "The horses," he said. "We need good ones."

[37]

"EUROPE, SIR, I think Europe would be best."

Fairfield lounged in a cheap imitation of a Queen Anne chair, while his employer stood at a window, hands clasped tightly behind his back. In an adjoining room they could hear the muffled thuds and exclamations of the servants, as they packed trunks in utmost haste.

"The scoundrels. Vermin, human vermin," Stoneman muttered. His broad chest heaved once, then again, convulsively. "Nothing in their effects, you say."

"The Finn had an account book. A few sums and some initials. No names."

"So he betrayed me." Stoneman ground his teeth audibly. "The swine."

"Well, there's no knowing, of course, if they were really blackmailers. The whole thing might have been a bluff. But if you were out of the country . . ."

"And this . . . operation? This nest of snakes you have gotten us into?" He glared at Fairfield for a moment, but the young man only smiled, and Stoneman looked away.

"It's not so bad, sir. General Howard has taken the field. The railroad gangs have been armed and moved to a camp in the hills, ready to march. Unfortunate, for our reputation, about the posse—but they'll catch that big devil for sure now. We won't get the carcass, of course, with the Army involved, and it will take a while for the settlers to start coming in again . . ." Fairfield shrugged. "But I have faith it will work, sir. Especially the copper."

"And what about—damn it, man! Wipe that infernal smile off your face—what about the allegations about . . . the theater? If there are affidavits . . ."

"You are a man of great importance, sir. Sharpers are always after such a man. And if you are already in Europe when the papers—"

"Damn it! The wretched hacks! They'll print anything. The governor has not responded?"

Fairfield shrugged again. "He has his reputation to protect too, sir. But this will all blow over." The young man laughed. "One bright spot, you see, is that after word of this massacre, trading in the railroad stock was halted on the Exchange. Rock bottom, sir, eight dollars a share."

"I fail to see the good fortune of that. Perhaps you can enlighten me." Stoneman's hands twitched in barely controlled fury.

"Well, sir, I think it would be best if you got out of this business here —I mean formally, sir—because after this massacre . . ."

"My name is a liability."

"Not exactly, Mr. Stoneman, but say that we've lost our head of steam on one track. But you know, sir, I've got a bit put aside, and some friends, and if you could swing us a little loan—through the Philadelphia bank, perhaps—we could maintain a controlling interest in the rail and the mine both. Very cheaply. Under another hat, so to speak. Sir."

Stoneman unclasped his hands, balled them into fists. He took a step toward the young man, who straightened in the chair and lifted his own pale, plump hands in a gesture of gentle remonstrance. "You, Fairfield? Your hat? You little pup!" He raised one of his heavy fists.

The young man slid from the chair, hands now crooked as if to catch something thrown. "Mr. Stoneman, you know I look at you as a father. More than a father. And you know, sir, I have worked mighty hard, and I know things pretty well. I'd say inside out. You wouldn't want me . . . outside? Would you, sir?"

Stoneman paused, weaving a little from side to side. He unclenched the raised hand and touched it to his brow. His voice, when he spoke, was dull.

"What is it you are saying, Fairfield?"

"I'm only saying, sir, that until this little business blows over—and it surely will—perhaps it would be better to transfer things onto my shoulders. I know you could just chuck the whole kit and caboodle, but I know too, sir, how you hate to miss the bull's eye."

Stoneman noticed, all at once, that the young man's four-in-hand of scarlet silk was secured by a glittering stickpin, a diamond of impressive size. He watched the smooth, fleshy face with interest. The eyes, blue as cornflowers, looked back at him with a pure zeal.

"I can do it, sir. I know I can. The rail stock will come back as soon as the Army brings in that big Injun. The papers are going to make Nampuh known across the land. And the copper, sir—I'm sure of the copper. Oil and copper will be the stocks to trade, and they'll go cheap when the silver peters out. You can trust me, sir. Absolutely certainteed. Just like a son."

Stoneman grimaced and walked to the window, keeping his back to the room. In the street wagons were drawn up, ready to load his trunks and valises. He saw a horse try to kick at a man arranging harness, who then seized a wagon pin and struck the animal under the belly. A slight shudder passed over Stoneman's frame.

The prospect of riding, even in a closed coach, through the muddy streets of this miserable town, while the residents—people of the lowest character—regarded him in contempt or even called out in derision— this prospect made him faint with shame and rage. Fairfield had known this, and knew as well that he cared nothing for the loss of a few millions, but abhorred above all the ignominy of defeat. So he offered this straw of hope; and it was not, Stoneman admitted to himself, a bad plan. Through a joint-stock company, acting secretly in his interest, Fairfield might finagle the vultures into a vengeful bear raid, and later catch them out when the copper began to pay. Then he could step in, the worm would turn . . .

"You would not betray me, Fairfield?" He spoke into the window glass, where he could see the ghost image of the young man staring at him.

"Oh, sir!" The ghost waved a hand and laughed silently.

"You know there are others like the Finn, ready to take on his duties?"

"Of course, Mr. Stoneman."

He watched an old man gesticulate at an Indian cowering in the street, then take out coins and drop them into the beggar's palm. He grimaced again at this transgression, however small, against the iron rule of Nature. Behind him, Fairfield cleared his throat.

"All right, Fairfield. I will have the papers prepared, the securities transferred, as soon as I am back in New York. You ought to give the railroad another name, by the way." His lips drew back from his teeth. "So as not to be tainted."

"I've thought of that, sir. I'm going to call it the Owyhee Giant." The young man began to pace a little back and forth. "I can see already the opportunity for some feeder tracks and a hook-up eventually with the Northern Pacific. Villard will lose some sleep over us, sir, you can bet on it! I'm tremendously grateful—"

"I am tired, Fairfield," Stoneman said and touched his brow again. "Leave me."

"Oh yes, sir." The young man strode to the door, turned its handle, and then stopped. He looked over his shoulder and his ruddy features seemed to pale momentarily.

"I—I—sir, I—"

"What is it, Fairfield? Stoneman wheeled from the window and squinted at him.

"I—that is—" The pallor was followed by a sudden rush of color. "May I call you . . . M—M—Mandrake, sir?"

[38]

GENERAL HOWARD had finished logging his daily report and his orderly had brought a mug of hot tea, but he continued to toy with the pen, forming simple designs and then scratching them out. He was waiting, he knew, for the sound of Lieutenant Murdoch's patrol returning. The two men in an adjoining tent were also waiting, of course, and in much greater apprehension than his own.

The general had seen carnage before, fields of it, at Bull Run and Phillipsburg. In the campaigns of the Dakotas two years ago, when the Sioux had taken to the warpath, he had seen the awesome sight of men without their scalps, without their tongues, without their private parts. It disturbed him far more, though, to assume the burden of communicating such tragedy to the living, and it would be his duty to speak to the girl's father.

He made a wry face, watching the steam curl away from the cup of tea. The woman was foolish beyond belief to have ridden into that region. It also confounded him that Stoneman's posse had been so perfectly disposed to encounter her. The shadow of suspicion had appeared in his mind—an obscure connection between the financier and the runaway girl. Had he enticed her into serving as bait for his trap? Or simply followed her, trying to effect her rescue and the ambush at one coup?

Stoneman was an odd duck—those mad theories of breeding the lower races as one breeds cattle—but he was known to be a gentleman and philanthropist. His scheme to capture Big Foot had gone awry, had effectively ruined his much-ballyhooed plan to launch a new boom in Silver City, but the general took no satisfaction in having warned the man of his foolishness. Forty men were dead and probably a woman as well because of this preposterous enterprise, and he was now under great pressure to wipe out the nest of Shoshoni renegades for good and all. If he failed, the settlers were likely to take out their own vengeance on the fort Indians, and that, he knew from experience with the Sioux, could be an ugly business.

And then the damn, treacherous weather had gone against him. The light snow had melted, creating sudden streams and mudholes, and the field pieces had bogged down on the wagon road out of Kuna station. They had camped far short of Swan Falls, and would have to ferry the guns over the Snake tomorrow. He hoped Nampuh's band was bloated in victory and would spend a day pawing over their booty. He felt the knife of winter in the wind again, and hoped for snow this night, which would make it easy to track the band and the horses taken from the posse—a total of nearly a hundred head.

Outside he heard a sentry call, and a murmur came from the men at the campfires. In a moment his orderly shook the flap of the tent.

"General, Lieutenant Murdoch has come in. He'll be along as soon as he gets the saddle off."

Howard grunted and threw down the pen. He could not decide whether he wished that the lieutenant had discovered nothing, or that their worst fear was confirmed. Were he Professor Braddock, he supposed the latter would be preferable, for no agony approached that of ignorance, of always suspecting, and never knowing, the terrible truth. He himself had lost two brothers in the Great War, and had seen his mother undergo a kind of relief when the letters came at last to verify their deaths.

Finally Lieutenant Murdoch entered, bearing a set of dusty saddlebags on one shoulder, his face sterner than usual. He saluted, and in that movement the general could see the man's weariness, and something more.

"Bad news," the general said quietly.

" 'Fraid so, sir." Murdoch glanced over one shoulder. "I guess they're waitin' over there, sir, so I'll make it quick." He slid the saddlebags from his shoulder and began to fumble with the buckles of one flap.

"Wasn't much left, General. In the valley there was a body, one of Nampuh's men, but some joker from Silver had been there and took the head. Inside that canyon"—he paused, and his mouth tightened, as if he remembered the stench—"the Injuns scalped ever' mother's son of 'em, and cut 'em, too. No tellin' about the Injuns, they would have taken their dead out with 'em."

He had the flap open and removed from the bag a swatch of cloth, torn and spattered with dark stains, then a woman's high-buttoned shoe, mud-caked and misshapen.

"So," the general said even more quietly. "You found her."

"Not much, sir. She wasn't as big as a man, sir, and the coyotes got to her . . ." He stopped, holding the bit of cloth and the shoe over the general's field desk.

"Yes, put them there."

Murdoch deposited the items carefully on the scrubbed plank.

"So you buried her there."

"It seemed best, General. You couldn't have told anything, and her father being here and all . . ."

Howard nodded almost imperceptibly. "I trust your judgment, Lieutenant. I think under the circumstances we should report to Professor Braddock that the body was simply . . . not recovered."

"Right, sir." Murdoch swayed slightly, the open saddlebag dangling from one hand. In a moment he said, "Your tea's gettin' cold, General."

Howard, too, stared at the cup, still brimful. "Thank you, Lieutenant. You must be ready for dinner and a bedroll. Good work. Get on with you, now."

Murdoch saluted again and left, the saddlebag still gaping from his hand. When the orderly looked inside, the general spoke without looking at him. "Send them in," he said.

Professor Braddock, entering the tent behind the older man, saw over his friend's shoulder the torn, stained garment and the shoe. He tried to speak, but what emerged was only a low bleat. He stopped at the threshold, pawing at the flap of the tent for support. Baum also seemed shocked into silence. General Howard hurriedly began the brief, painful speech he had composed in his mind.

"A patrol has scouted the area, and I am sorry to say their report does not leave us any hope. We could not recover the remains, but the woman was wearing these. Can you say if they belonged to your daughter?"

Braddock tottered forward, his face gone slack, and with the extended fingers of one hand stirred the bit of cloth.

"Oh my God," Baum said hoarsely, "merciful God."

"Her—" Braddock began, then bleated again. He touched the shoe and it fell over on its side.

"These belonged to Miss Braddock?" Howard spoke doggedly, between clenched teeth.

"Her . . . things." The slack features convulsed, formed a mask of ghastly calm. "These are . . . her . . . things. This black dress, she took it when she . . ."

"Roland! Roland! We cannot know in this world, what is for all the best." Baum threw an arm about his friend's shoulders, though he had to rise on tiptoe to do so.

"I am sorry, Professor, most sorry. I can tell you very little now except that the two men who accompanied your daughter are both dead. They were apparently trying to help her arrange ransom for . . . the young man. Evans, is it?"

Baum nodded wordlessly. Braddock groaned and another spasm passed over his countenance.

"What you see here is all that could be recovered. I am deeply sorry, and I can assure you"—the general's voice changed, became softer, colder—"that we shall not rest until those guilty of this despicable act are dealt with. And our vengeance will be swift, sir, and terrible. Depend upon it." Howard got slowly to his feet. "You have my word."

Braddock heaved a long, shuddering breath. "Thank you, General," he whispered.

"If you would like to return to Boise and await our return, I can send a detachment with you tomorrow as far as Kuna."

"I want to come with you." Braddock's tone had taken on a hint of color and strength. "I want to be there."

"I also," Baum interjected staunchly. "We shall fight. We shall shoot them all."

"As you wish." The general bowed. "I sympathize with your feelings. At the same time, my conditions are the same. You will be obliged to observe regulations, as civilian militiamen." He glanced at Baum. "The business of war has its rules, and is best carried out by those who know them."

"We are at your disposal, General," Braddock said and bowed in return. His face was still pale, but set now in grim determination.

Howard thrust out his hand. "I know the sorrow you must bear. May God bless you and give you strength. We must think, now, gentlemen, of vengeance. Of vengeance alone." After shaking hands he stepped back, erect, his gray head poised like a hawk's.

"There is nothing," Baum said then, "nothing recovered. Is there but a chance she . . . they took her and—"

The other two looked at him, and the ferocity of their gaze startled him into silence.

"No," Braddock choked out. "Not that. She is dead."

There was an uncomfortable silence. Braddock made a slight gesture with his hand, which was visibly trembling.

"Good night, gentlemen." Howard stepped back to his desk and bowed again as the two left the tent.

[39]

WITH TWO of the three gold coins remaining from the morning's horse trade, Pee Wee had bribed Grace to give his friend, a young sport with more to him than met the eye, just one glimpse of the guaranteed virgin. The young buck had struck it rich, the old man leered, but preferred to disguise himself as a square-head, and might come up with a bid to match Nolan's. Grace finally shrugged and told them to wait a bit in the salon.

Things were slow at the El Dorado, as they had been since the first rush following the massacre, when customers had flocked in to celebrate both the tragic heroism of the dead, and their own good fortune in not belonging to that illustrious company. Also it was mid-afternoon, and the stamp mill had resumed operations with a skeleton crew, all other able-bodied men having joined the new militia. Except for a humpbacked old mule skinner and two youths barely out of short pants, Willard and Pee Wee found themselves alone in the salon. Through a curtain drawn aside, they could see two of the girls playing a game of cribbage, yawning and arguing over points.

Pee Wee was drinking nervously in swift, long gulps, but the glass before Willard remained full. The old man thought his companion looked far too outlandish and sinister, even though the new clothes were creased and rumpled now, since Willard had slept in them. His hair was still too long, his skin too burnt, his face too empty of congeniality or even interest. The young man had changed, had lost something that Pee Wee could not identify, but whose absence disturbed him profoundly.

"So what did them Siwashes make you do—if'n you kin talk about it," he said lamely.

"Do?" Willard examined him absently. "Oh. We moved around. Raided two or three times. Traded with the fort Indians. Hunted."

"I mean . . ." Pee Wee frowned. "They didn't *torment* ye? Make ye eat vile m'terial, er drink . . . blood, or nothin'?"

Willard laughed shortly. "No. I had to fight a man once."

Pee Wee looked about nervously. "Jesus, I hope we don't have to do no fightin' here. This yere is a foolish thing to do, Willard. I tolt ye—"

"I know." Willard looked at him with an invisible change in his countenance, a subtle hardening of features, and the old man looked away with a mournful sigh.

"How long me and the gal got to wait fer ye in this camp? I only got supplies in them saddlebags for maybe five days."

"That should be quite long enough. If I don't come back in four days, take her back to Silver City and contact Professor Braddock. I expect he will reward you handsomely."

"Ha! Stretch a rope is what I'll do fer a reward. Lord, I never been such a fool. Anyways, how come you don't take 'er direct to the perfesser yerseff?" Pee Wee drained his glass and tilted it accusingly at Willard.

"Professor Braddock and I are not on the best of terms, and I need to speak to Lydia . . . at some length. And before that I must reach Nampuh."

"I don't see how you owe that damn Injun bull anythin'. You say he figgers you lied to 'im. Well, hell—" He stopped, for Grace had entered from the hallway and was beckoning them.

"Come along," Grace said briskly. "I had to give one of them twenty-dollar gold pieces to the Doc, and you got five minutes." She extended her palm, and after a moment's fumbling, Pee Wee got out the third coin and passed it to her.

She led them up the two flights of stairs and along the dingy hallway to the last door, where she rapped softly four times. After a long pause they heard heavy footsteps and the door opened a few inches. A whispered argument transpired through the dark crack.

"He says they's two of you, and he wants another twenty."

Willard nodded imperceptibly, and in a moment the door swung wide enough to admit them one by one.

Looking at her, he realized she did not recognize him, and her own appearance was a shock to him. She was thin, pale as milk except for the bright dabs of rouge on her cheeks and lips, with eyes huge and unnaturally brilliant. They had garbed her in the one expensive gown she had packed, of wine-red velvet with pale gold brocade, and had hung about her throat a strand of imitation pearls. With a bright but utterly vacant smile, she turned from them to the doctor, who stood protectively by the bed, his long, dour face contorted in an anxious frown.

"Papa?" she said in a voice that Willard did not recognize, a cool, clear, but empty tone. "Is this my new papa?"

The Doctor strode from the bed to the door, which he bolted with a certain stealth. "Take a gander and then gimme the twenty. This ain't usual, and Mama wouldn't like it."

Willard stepped to the side of the bed, where she reclined on pillows. From his coat he took the locket and held it in his open palm.

"Lydia," he said softly. "My dearest Lydia."

She sat up as if slapped, peering at him with the great, glittering eyes. "Papa?" she whispered.

"Willard," he said. Taking her hand, he folded it around the bit of filigreed gold. "It's Willard."

She shuddered, and in swift succession her face registered several emotions: sly suspicion, uncertainty, ecstasy, horror. "What?" Her voice was suddenly sharp, high, the yap of a fox.

"What the hell—" The doctor whirled to Grace, who had in turn rolled her eyes in reproach toward Pee Wee. "Who are these—"

"Willard?" She clutched at the locket, two large tears rolling suddenly across her cheeks. "Is it . . . ?"

"Gawddamn! Wait—" The doctor tried to thrust between them. Willard released Lydia's hand, dodged, and drew from his coat pocket a coil of rawhide thong tied to two small sticks.

"Damn your hide!" Gracie swung her fists at Pee Wee, hammering at his chest.

The doctor, attempting to shove Willard toward the door, found his adversary had vanished like smoke, gone under his arm, and was then behind him. The thong, now a loop, flipped over his head, while a blow from a knee directed between his legs nearly collapsed him. He drew his breath to emit a tremendous bellow of pain and rage, but the thong grew taut with an audible snap and there came forth only a faint squealing.

He went to his knees, hands clawing furiously at his throat, while his face grew dark and swollen with blood.

Pee Wee, arms raised to cover his head and deflect Grace's windmilling fists, moaned in despair. All at once her assault stopped, for she had glanced over her shoulder and seen the two men, one standing with jaw clenched in effort, the other on his knees and sagging now to one side, eyes bulging like boiled eggs.

"Sweet Jesus," she whispered, "don't."

Lydia had crawled to the corner of the bed against the wall, where she huddled and watched them. Willard released the thong, and the doctor pitched forward on his face, legs unbending slowly. Pocketing the thong, he went to the closet and removed a coat and scarf. He approached the bed and spoke to Lydia in a low, soothing voice, holding out the coat. She shrank into the corner.

The door handle rattled then, and a voice called from the hallway. "Doc? Doc? What's a-goin' on in there?"

Pee Wee reached into his waistband and withdrew an ancient, long-barreled Colt. He stepped behind the door and waggled the barrel at Grace. "Let 'im in," he said.

"You damned old fool." She shook her head, smoothed her hair with an automatic gesture, and unlatched the door. The young man with the round, pockmarked face stepped over the threshold. He looked questioningly at the doctor on the floor and opened his mouth to speak, but Pee Wee reached from behind the door and rapped him on the side of the head with the gun barrel. The young man turned, lifting one hand, his mouth still working. Weaving slightly, he pawed the air with the hand. Pee Wee rapped him again smartly, the metal ringing against bone, and gently as a lowered flag the young man slid to the floor.

Willard had lifted Lydia in his arms, the coat draped over her. "You'd better give us five minutes," he said to Grace.

Pee Wee had restored the pistol to his waistband and looked apologetic. "He's a damned young fool," he said, "but he loves this yere girl. She don't b'long here, anyways."

Willard crossed the room and stepped into the hallway, and Pee Wee turned to follow. "That there gold piece is still in his vest pocket," he observed as an afterthought.

"Yer both damn fools," Grace sniffed. "But what could a body do, overcome by desperadoes?" She edged toward the doctor.

"Nary a thing," Pee Wee said and shut the door behind him.

They moved swiftly down the stairs, took a corridor into the kitchen, and walked by the two surprised Chinese cooks, one of whom toyed briefly with a boning knife in his hand before looking away. In the alley they pitched Lydia onto the smallest of the three horses, hiking her gown to her hips on the man's saddle, and quickly securing her waist to the cantle with leather belt. She clasped the horn and stared at them in mute terror, while Willard mounted swiftly and led her horse at a trot down the alley. In a few minutes they had crossed the town, keeping always to back streets, and reached an old, disused trail to the Murphy station.

Above them the clouds had thickened to a gray, roiling mass that already obscured the mountains to the east, and the wind had begun to sting with cold.

"Oh damn gawddamn," Pee Wee moaned. "It's gonna snow agin. They'll track us, sure as the Lord made little green apples. If they find me with this yere gal . . ." He jerked down the brim of the old hat he had donned to hold fast the strip of wool about his ears. "Gawddamn *gawddamn!*"

Willard did not even look at him. He had dropped back beside Lydia, who still sat stiffly erect, her hands fused to the saddle horn. But when she turned her face toward his the blank terror had receded, and there was a flush in her cheeks, beneath the rouge. He smiled and nodded at her. After staring at him a moment longer, she looked away over the sweep of plain rising to the clouds, and uttered a faint cry, like that of a small creature at its birth.

[40]

THE HORSE'S HOOVES made no sound flailing in the snow, but Wart could hear the harsh labor of its breathing over the tinkling of water through ice-rimmed rock. He held a bead a little ahead of the rider, the rifle cradled on a rolled blanket he had lain over a flat stone. A very fine snowfall, like dust motes, swirled in the air between them. Flexing his forefinger several times to work out any stiffness, he curled it around the trigger and began to slow his breathing.

But the rider drew up, just beyond an acceptable range, and was staring into the rocky draw, as if he knew someone was watching. He took off his hat and shook out his hair, very long hair for a white man.

He waved the hat. Then he waited, the horse's sides heaving, vapor jetting from its nostrils. Wart waited too. He frowned, unable to guess at first how this lone rider—clearly not a scout, for he carried no rifle—could know of his presence.

The man shouted, a startling sound in the wide, white stillness. It was the Shoshoni word for friend, and when he heard it Wart knew who the rider was. He stood up behind the flat rock, keeping the rifle at his shoulder. The man immediately dug his heels into the pony's belly, coming again at a lope.

When he was ten yards away, the man raised a hand and tried to speak, but Wart shook his head and trained the rifle at his face. Then he stepped carefully around the horse, looking intently at the saddle, the man's boots, the pockets of the coat. Finally he lowered the rifle and told Little Bird what a great fool he was to come back.

"Ho!" the man answered, so emphatically that Wart smiled.

"Ketchum trouble. *No vale* fifty sack?"

Little Bird smiled at this, then laughed outright, but an instant later his expression was somber. He began to tell about the soldiers, the militia, the railroad camps, straining for words and making quick, violent gestures, but Wart interrupted to say shortly that they knew all that. They were waiting for the soldiers to come now, and he had thought Little Bird was a scout for them at first, since One Arm was moving from the north, with the storm at his back.

Why were they not moving too, Little Bird asked, twisting uneasily in his saddle. The fine snow had begun to whiten his hair, as he still held the hat in one hand. Wart said there was nowhere to move to. With so little game now in the mountains, they had had to return to the deer camp on the canyon rim. Also, some of the others wanted to spend the gold. These had ridden away, each with his scalps and a new gun and a sack of gold, all of which they would have to hide before they slipped into the fort like beaten dogs. What good was a scalp, Wart wanted to know, if you could not wear it.

How many were left, Little Bird asked. Eleven. Eleven? Did Wart know how many soldiers and militiamen were coming? The Indian shrugged. It made no difference. There was nowhere to go. For a time neither spoke, while they looked out over the ridges. Those farther away grew dim and indistinct behind the veils of snow, disappearing finally into gray nothingness. Little Bird said then that he wanted to tell Nampuh what had happened with the woman. He had been betrayed. Wart shrugged and remarked that a man of Little Bird's age should know this risk. Then he went back to the place he had swept bare behind the flat rock, and did not look around when Little Bird rode past him.

Most of the men were asleep or in a drunken stupor when he rode in. Each tent or tipi was surrounded by a heap of saddles, guns, clothes, and boots taken from the dead. Already, it appeared, traders had come like vultures after the gold. A woman, her face puffed with bruises, lay beside a smouldering fire with an empty bottle under her arm. A lone man guarding the horse herd had signaled his approach with a shout, but no movement followed until he was within a few yards of Nampuh's tent. Then the flap was thrown back and the giant thrust out his head, blinking in the sudden light. When he saw Willard, he watched him until he had reined in the pony, then abruptly withdrew. Willard dismounted and stood quietly, waiting.

There was a rustling of garments, and then Nampuh emerged from his tent. He had knotted the three eagle feathers in his hair, and from his belt dangled a cluster of scalps smoked too hastily, so that they had curled into tight cocoons. A new blanket was drawn over his shoulders, and he carried a new Winchester in one hand. The bones of his face had grown even sharper under taut skin. The giant regarded him with eyes sunken in the cavern beneath his brow, and Willard could not fathom his expression.

Before he could speak Nampuh gestured with the rifle.

"Pitchur," he said, and following the line of the barrel Willard saw his photographic trunk under a pair of saddlebags. "Ketchum pitchur."

"The squaw—" Willard began, but Nampuh shook his head and waggled the rifle barrel vigorously.

"Pitchur," he repeated sharply. "Plenty goods. Plenty scalps. Seven guns. Pitchur. White man sabe Nampuh ketchum plenty."

"One Arm and the soldiers—" he began again.

Nampuh interrupted. "Snow coming. White men like snow. Over everything, kill everything. *Pronto*. Ketchum pitchur." He turned and reentered the tent, where Willard could hear him gathering the rifles together with a clash.

The trunk open, he saw that the remaining plate was intact, the gear strapped into wooden cradles as he had left it. He set up the tripod swiftly and mounted the camera on it. As he was arranging the black hood, he heard the distant report of a rifle, dull and without echo in the snow-laden air. Then came several shots in succession. He looked anxiously at Nampuh, who sat now in a packsaddle amid his possessions, the rifles stacked across his knees, but the giant seemed not to hear. Ducking under the hood, he measured the salts hastily in a beaker and stirred them into the side tanks. Then he dipped the plate and loaded the dark slide, cursing when he could not find the brass pins to secure the cover.

There were more shots, suddenly loud, and he heard horses neighing. As he found the pins and twisted them tight, the hood gave a flutter and a pale finger of light darted through a small rent and touched his sleeve with a bright spot. The gunshots were now continuous, like popping corn, and he heard light thuds, a ring of metal, a series of sudden, hissing whines. He ripped aside the black cloth, and the sudden blaze of whiteness made him squint. There was an acrid stench of burnt powder in the air. At his feet the snow scattered in little puffs.

Nampuh grunted something. He sat motionless in the same position, staring into the dark hole of the lens.

"Go! *Vamos!*" Willard shouted, waving the slide, but Nampuh did not move. He heard a crack of wood, and the tripod shuddered slightly. One of its legs sprouted a small growth of splinters. With a muffled groan of rage and panic, Willard threw open the back plate of the camera and jabbed at the gear knob with half-frozen fingers, bringing the image into focus on the glass screen. Nampuh took shape there, a figure only four inches high, with toothpick rifles in his lap. Willard removed the glass screen, inserted the dark slide, and fumbled with the brass cap until he had covered the lens. A moment before he removed the slide cover, Nampuh lurched slightly. He heard at the same time a solid slap, and a moment later saw a stain appear on the giant's blanket.

He folded out the slide cover and uncapped the lens. In the interminable seconds of waiting for the image to register, he looked wildly around. A little away from the camp he could see a man firing over the belly of a dead horse, and a little beyond that another man lay still and huddled as if against the cold. Someone was screaming and someone else singing. Through the veils of light snow he could see men on the hills above them, their blue coats startling and distinct: most were on foot, crouching and running. Plumes of smoke erupted from rocks and clumps of sage, and the firing now sounded to Willard like one continuous explosion.

He jammed the cap on the lens, closed the slide cover, and jerked the exposed plate from the camera. Running to Nampuh's side, he heard a loud clang from the brass body of the instrument. Nampuh looked up wearily, holding the blanket tightly with one arm against the side now soaked with blood. "*Vamos,*" he said, and handed one of the rifles to

Willard, allowing the others to topple to the ground. He stood and moved toward the canyon rim at a heavy, shuffling trot. Glancing over his shoulder, Willard could see the tents and tipis being plucked here and there, in many places at once, by invisible fingers. The whole hillside bloomed in fire with corollas of black and gray smoke, and the brush around him seemed alive with wasps, the fluttering of clipped leaves, and tiny avalanches of snow; when he scrambled over the rim behind Nampuh the grass itself was shivering and whispering with sudden messengers.

He clambered after the giant, who kept well ahead without appearing to hurry, over the sharp and broken rock of the canyon wall. After perhaps a hundred yards of steep descent, they angled along a deer trail, barely wider than a man's foot, that wound under an overhanging shelf. Here they were protected from view from above, but between gunshots Willard could hear shouts from the canyon rim, and behind them a shower of pebbles dribbled over a sheer stone face, indicating that they were pursued. Near the end of the shelf, the trail pitched sharply down again, following a cleft in a stratum of basalt. The cleft ended in a ledge from which Willard could see no exit. The stone shafts on either side were without purchase for hand or foot, and the lip of the ledge overhung what appeared to be a sheer drop of a hundred feet or more.

Nampuh leaned his rifle against the rock wall and walked to one end of the ledge. From behind a tangled clump of foliage growing in a crack, he produced a heavy coil of braided rawhide rope. He shook it out, gathered it in the middle, so both ends hung over the ledge, and then draped the loop over a smooth knob of rock at the brink of the narrow shelf. Adjusting the length of the two strands until he could hold the short end in his hand, he wrapped the rope once around his torso and tied it fast. Willard heard him take a sharp breath when the rawhide drew against his wound, but the giant did not falter. He shoved the rifle into one of his leggings, lay down on the ledge, and, gripping the long strand in both hands, he wriggled over the brink. The rope tightened against the stone knob and then began to slip gradually as he lowered himself. He looked up once as Willard leaned over the rim to watch, but said nothing. When he was perhaps halfway to the slope visible below, he pushed away from the cliff with his feet and began to swing slowly back and forth. The rope slipped another few feet, and then the giant disappeared into the wall of the cliff. In a moment the rope swung back, empty and slack.

There was, then, a crevice or cavern in the rock face, invisible from above, and probably from the side as well. Above him, Willard heard voices again, men shouting to each other from various points along the canyon wall. He pulled up one end of the rope and secured it around himself. Then he buttoned the rifle and exposed plate into his coat, the barrel of the gun projecting absurdly through his collar and along his cheek. He crawled over the lip of the shelf as Nampuh had done, and began releasing tension on the rope. He dropped in short, sickening jerks into space. Once a few feet down he saw the little cave that opened in the rock, a niche barely big enough for two men to squat in. He did not have to swing out in order to gain momentum enough to arrive there, for Nampuh reached out and hauled him in by the feet.

Quickly Nampuh jerked the rope, and the loose end cleared and came snaking in after them. Willard fumbled to untie the other end from his chest, but the giant shook his head and raised a warning hand. Above them they heard the clink of metal, a scraping against rock, a man's voice calling "This-a-way! Over here!" Another voice called back something unintelligible, and then they heard several men slide the last few yards down the cleft leading to the ledge. The voices were abruptly loud, spoken as the searchers peered over the cliff.

"No sign of 'im."

"Couldn't git past!"

"Damn!"

"That sumbitch is like smoke."

"Well," one voice said after a pause, "we got 'm stoppered in this yere canyon anyway."

They heard the scrape of boot heels and rifle butts on the stone again, and the voices receded suddenly. Willard moved to wrench at the rope, but Nampuh clamped a hand on his wrist and shook his head. They waited for perhaps ten minutes, hearing only their own breathing and an occasional distant shout or gunshot. The snowfall had grown heavier, flakes wobbling down, filling the air until the opposite wall of the canyon was only a ghostly shadow of crevice and outcropping. Then they heard a slight sound over their heads, a pebble or twig dropping. A moment later the loose rock in the cleft stirred as someone climbed up and away from them.

Nampuh released his wrist. "Scout," he said.

[41]

WILLARD had tried twice to minister to the wound, but Nampuh would not permit it. Then he had explained about the treachery with the locket and dress, how the woman had not even been his squaw—though he stumbled here, for of course by another, earlier treachery she was—but the giant appeared uninterested. They sat cross-legged, so close their knees touched, facing each other. As the afternoon waned, they heard no more shots or echoing calls from the canyon rim. The snow fell steadily, in thick, heavy flakes that blew in on the stone floor of the cave. From time to time Willard beat his arms against his sides or rubbed his legs for warmth, but Nampuh did not change position. The stain on his blanket had dried black at the edges, but the center was still red and glistening.

Nampuh asked him about his Old Man God, and what was done for white people when they died. Willard told him that the Old Man would listen to confessions of bad deeds and perhaps forgive them, and that candles were lit, incense burned, and prayers said for the passage to another world. This was all good, Nampuh said, especially the candles, but did no one tell of the man's good deeds, his many battles, the many horses or women he had stolen? This was not done, Willard said, until the man was in fact dead. Then he could not hear it and be comforted, the giant protested. They smiled at each other.

After a time Nampuh went on to say that he had decided to confess some bad deeds. He had killed a white woman long ago for laughing at him, and this had begun his raiding. Other bad men, thrown out of the tribe or hated by their people, heard about him, his size and strength, and came to him. A big bear draws many flies. To survive and to maintain strength he had had to raid and keep raiding. But he had made a mistake by not becoming a greater chief who could lead many, many warriors—good warriors as well as bad—so as to kill more whites. He had killed very many, but not enough. His people were mostly gone now, the Shoshonis, for the Indians at the fort were not really Indians. His men might be bad, but they were at least Indians, who knew how to steal horses and hunt. It made no difference in the end, because there were as many white men in the world as there were ants, and they would eat everything up sooner or later, and finally eat each other, but he would have been a better chief if he had killed more of them.

Willard said nothing, and after a pause the giant added that he had at least one more chance. Here was one white man right here he could kill. They smiled again together. Too small, Willard said, too weak. Bears and Little Birds were not enemies. Anyway, Nampuh said then, you must take the picture back to show the other white people how I always am, no matter what they do. They can look at this picture and be afraid. Willard nodded, and the giant said then that he wished he could give something in return. He knew Willard wanted his head for measuring, but it was bad luck to have others look at you after death.

No, Willard said emphatically. He no longer was interested in heads. Maybe the medicine bag, the giant said, and took from under his blanket the deerskin pouch containing the odd bits of his divinations. He would not have any use for this bag, or the gold either. He took four pokes of gold from a larger sack tied to his belt. All these he could give away. Only the rifle would he like to have beside him. It was a new rifle, a good repeating rifle, and had been taken in battle.

He had fought many battles, Nampuh said in a louder tone, as if to compensate for the failing light. The snow was now gray as ash and they could no longer see the canyon wall opposite them. If there was no one there to tell of his deeds, he would have to do it himself. After killing the white woman, he had run for five days, on foot, with men riding after him on horses. He outran them, lost them in the mountains east of the Snake. Then he stole a gun and two horses from a prospector. With this gun he held up two freight wagons and a stagecoach, killing everybody except another woman and her small boy.

After that he had crossed to the Wind River country and raided the Blackfeet. There he met others like himself who had left their villages to be dog soldiers, living a day's ride away, watching for Crow, Blackfeet, or Paiute, taking women and hides as payment. But he saw that it was as his grandmother had said: the white men were deadly and they came like ants, in endless hordes, when they found something they liked. So he went back to his homeland, the Snake country, and killed as many as he could. He had killed maybe a hundred, which was not so many, but if every Shoshoni warrior killed a hundred, that would be something. He and Broken Arm together once killed seventeen, and they used only twenty-six cartridges.

Willard shifted his legs and swung his arms again, for the gray air was growing colder. Nampuh gestured at the five sacks beside them. Take them and go, he said. It is time. I wish we could keep talking. We could tell more about Coyote and your Old Man. I do not know so much about Coyote as my grandmother did. That old man who sneaked away for the fort, you remember, he knows much about it. Talk to him. Now I have to sing my songs, bear songs.

He straightened a little and began to sing, barely loud enough for Willard to hear. After only a little while he stopped, took a long, shuddering breath, and fell to one side. Willard reached to catch him, but the giant rolled against the rear wall of the cave, as if burrowing in for a long sleep. Willard listened at the chest and held a hand over the lips, but felt no stirring of warm air. He sat for a long time, crowded now to the very brink of the ledge where the flakes touched his face and melted in streams down his cheeks. He tried to repeat the melody of the song Nampuh had sung, mixing the few words he had understood with meaningless syllables. But after a while the crooning sounded strange, deadened by the snow and darkness, so he stopped.

Then he began to feel along the inner surface of the cave, prying loose chunks of rock and picking up those which had accumulated. He laid the rifle beside Nampuh and, after a moment's hesitation, placed the photographic slide against the chest, folding one great arm to hold it in place. He breathed deeply and closed his eyes, his lips moving but making no sound. Then he stacked the rocks against the body.

He gathered up the sacks and distributed them in his coat pockets, then shook out the rope again. When he had located a projection firm enough, he looped the rope around it and belayed himself down the cliff as before, until he reached the ground. Recovering the rope, he slung it around his shoulder and began a precarious climb deeper into the canyon. He was guided by the sense of his feet and hands against the rock, since he could see nothing in the gathering darkness but gray shadows of snow.

[42]

THE GIRL had finally begun to talk to him, and had stopped behaving like a madwoman. When they arrived at the abandoned cabin, she had been in a kind of trance, but after Willard left she had fits. Pee Wee did not recollect ever seeing a woman with such fits. She screamed at him to bring her medicine, mistaking him for the doctor, and twice ran out into the snow, where he had to wrestle her down and drag her back inside. Then she cried for half a day without interruption; but after that she came to the table, wan but calmer, and ate a few mouthfuls of beans and jerky.

Hunched over his own tin plate, he watched her covertly. She hesitated sometimes, a dazed expression on her face, the spoon poised halfway to her open mouth.

"We got a few dried apercots, ma'am, if'n yer still hongry."

"Yes," she said, and after a pause went on abruptly. "Willard. Did I see Willard? Or did I just have another dream?"

"No'm. It were Willard right enough. We come fer ye in that . . ." Pee Wee coughed and hurriedly worked with his spoon to herd together the last of his beans.

"Is he coming again?"

"Oh yes'm. He be back tomorree. If'n he ain't, I'm gonna take ye to yer pappy—"

"No!" She spoke so sharply he cringed. "Do not say that. Do not say pa—pa—pa—" She gasped like an asthmatic and her face flushed hotly.

"No'm," Pee Wee said anxiously, "no'm indeedy. Willard's a-comin' back. Sartinteed. Don't you carry on, now."

"Mr. Baldo, and Theda, they . . ." She frowned, still breathing rapidly and shallowly. "They didn't come back. They . . . they told lies. They told me Willard—"

"Don't you carry on so, missy," Pee Wee said in the same wheedling tone he used for large, troublesome mules. "Ever'thing is hunky-dory. Willard's a fine young feller an' he'll be back right soon. You feed up good now, so's ye'll be strong an' ready for 'im."

"Yes," she said, and dutifully scraped again at her plate with the spoon. In a moment she looked up at him with a shy smile. "This tastes so good."

Pee Wee looked nonplussed. "It do?"

"Oh yes. I'm feeling much better." She looked down at herself. "Oh dear."

"What's the trouble, ma'am?" Pee Wee peered anxiously at her. He dreaded the prospect of having to subdue her again. Her virginity had become notorious, and to touch the voluminous velvet with layers of rustling linen hidden beneath it made him shiver, as if he had been handed a gunnysack full of rattlesnakes.

"I must tidy myself up," she said pettishly, and plucked at the mud stains on her sleeve. Pee Wee heaved a sigh of gratitude. The idle, preoccupied tone of the remark struck him as utterly familiar, feminine, and normal.

"I've been sick, you know," she said matter-of-factly. "I had medicine." A fleeting expression of childish greed crossed her face. "Very strong medicine, the doctor said. Stronger and stronger. You don't—"

"No'm, shore don't. Little bottle of cod-liver oil is all. Willard said not to give ye nothin'. Jest feed up an' rest up." He fidgeted with the spoon and gave her a mournful smile. "I ain't much of a doctor, ma'am, 'cept for horses and mules."

"That's quite all right," she said and glanced around the room. "This is not much of a hospital, either."

He laughed, wheezing, his eyes screwed shut, and in a moment she joined him with a hesitant, lilting laugh that ended with a catching of breath, and then sobs.

"I'm s-s-sorry," she gasped. "It's not that . . . that humorous, b-b-but I h-h-haven't . . ." She put her head in her hands and her shoulders shook, from grief or from mirth he could not say.

"Now now," he said soothingly, and putting forth a gnarled hand he touched her hair gently. "Ye've had one helluva time, in places not fit fer a lady, but ye got to go for'ards. In a tight place, ain't nothin' else to do."

At last she seized a fold of her dress and dug at her eyes with it. "I'm being foolish," she said. "A little fool. But this is all . . . so different." When she looked up at him there was a smudge on her cheek and another on her nose, from the mud spattered on the gown. "I never got dirty in Boston," she said, "never. In Boston—"

For an hour and a half she talked to him, about people and shops and parties, about her family's interest in the textile mills, about how the leaves there were now a blaze of flame and gold. Then she told him of her journey, crossing the desolate plain, sleeping in the wretched coach stations, seeing the throng in the mining camps, where she had met Mr. Baldo and the strange couple. She had been following Willard's path, for he was not what her father said he was, she was sure. And yet—

"He . . . he seems quite different." She looked at him carefully. "Doesn't he?"

"Yes'm. 'Course he do. He's lived with the savages, et their grub, slept in their lodges. 'Course that 'ffected his mind some." Pee Wee reached over to collect her plate and spoon.

"He has terribly dark skin."

"Sun," Pee Wee said easily, moving to the bucket in a corner by the potbellied stove. "Jest a mite too much sun."

"And his hair—why hasn't he cut his hair?"

"Hain't hardly had no time fer that, ma'm. Nampuh don't go in fer haircuts. He takes the whole damn scalp, most times." He bent to dip the plates, cups, and spoons in the bucket.

Lydia walked to the tiny window, covered with greased paper that had torn, and peered out. In a moment she gave a little cry of surprise.

"Why, there are some soldiers!" She turned to smile at Pee Wee, who was frozen in a crouch with the tinware still clutched in his hands. "Quite a lot of soldiers!"

Pee Wee dropped the dishes with a clatter into the bucket.

"Lord Jesus Christ Almighty," he whispered. He scampered across the room like a goat that has blundered into a wasps' nest. Through the rent in the paper he could see the column, moving down a long slope toward the cabin; behind it, on the crest of the hill, was a long line of cavalry followed by wagons.

"Lord, Lord," Pee Wee moaned and stepped back from the window. "Ma'am, I got to—Lord help me—ask ye to keep a tight halter on yerself, please ma'am. And when ye was runnin' away out thar in the snow and I had to rope ye in—don't recall that, ma'am, if'n ye please. I warn't meanin' nothin'—"

She nodded and smiled shyly again. "Yes," she said. "You have been very good. Better than those people back there . . . I'm all right now." Her hands fluttered about her hair. "Goodness, I've not even a brush or a comb. We must ask them to come in, though, mustn't we?"

"Yes'm," Pee Wee replied in a hoarse whisper. "We surely must." He took a long breath, strode to the door, and threw it open.

Outside the weather had turned again, the sun warming the land through air cool and fresh. Great patches of wet, dark earth were emerging through the snow, and the horses under the approaching soldiers were steaming and caked with mud to the shoulder. One of the riders raised a hand and shouted a command when Pee Wee stepped from the cabin, and the column came to a halt with a jingling of bits and creak of saddles. In a moment four troopers detached themselves from the group and rode toward him. Pee Wee could see that they were weary from a long march, and one of the men had a dirty, bloodstained wrap of bandage around a foot out of the stirrup. He recognized also, at the head of the standing main column, the old man with the empty sleeve, the sun glinting from the silver handle of his saber. Beside the general were two men in long field coats, wearing woolen caps rather than wide-brimmed cavalry hats.

He heard the rustle of Lydia's gown, and she stepped over the threshold and into the sunlight. Even as the four troopers stopped at the dilapidated hitching rail, one of the men in woolen caps stood up in his stirrups, head thrown to one side as if an invisible noose had tightened to lift him. Lydia smiled at the young officer who approached them and saluted. Pee Wee cleared his throat, hoping that the words he yearned for would come quickly and surely; but before he could speak, the man above them on the slope, still hanging from the invisible noose, gave a strangled cry and slapped his horse into a run. The other man in a cap rode after him, bouncing high in the saddle.

"Is this your—" the officer began, but then he too turned to watch the approaching riders. They were old men, Pee Wee could now see, and the one in the lead was bellowing like a weaned calf, his mouth twisted in a terrible amazement. The rider behind him, white beard bobbing with the motion of the horse, was shouting something too. Pee Wee and the officer watched, transfixed, as the two rode up before the cabin and slid from their mounts. The taller one, gaunt and shriveled, staggered a few steps with outstretched arms.

"Lydia," he called, his voice all at once high-pitched and tremulous. "My child!"

Pee Wee felt the woman sway against him, her face in his shoulder. He glanced down, startled, and saw only the whites of her eyes through closing lids. Reaching hastily to put his arm around her, he just managed to catch her and lower her clumsily to the ground in a dead faint.

[43]

AN AMBIENCE of strained politeness had oppressed the early course of the dinner, which was the best the Continental Hotel could provide. General Howard had agreed to attend because he was curious. He had also a certain political interest to defend, in dining with Fairfield, for as word of the extermination of the notorious outlaw band reached Boise, this deceptively plain young man had put out broadsheets crediting the successful campaign to the "civilizing" influence of the new railroad. After the scandalous defeat of Stoneman's posse, this bit of puffery had at first enraged him. Then he had cooled into caution, for the move betrayed a boldness and cunning that warranted close watch.

The general was also titillated at the prospect of meeting the girl Lydia, who had undergone such appalling adventures, and he understood from the good professors that she was sufficiently recovered to at least put in an appearance at table. Beside Braddock, Baum, and Fairfield, the company included the mining magnate Nolan, the federal judge for the territory, and their wives.

To cover an uncomfortable silence, Howard had expressed his view that the Shoshoni were, despite the long and bloody history of Nampuh's band, a degenerate people, inferior in warfare to the Crow or Sioux. He then found himself fencing acerbically with Baum over the proper view of the bandit chief. The general held that the creature was no more than a freak, an outsized member of his race, but otherwise identical to the type, with its characteristic childishness and depravity. The professor asserted vigorously that the very facts of Big Foot's black career bespoke a rare measure of terrible, primal energy, as much animal as human.

Nolan had asked then about young Evans, who was thought to be the man who had vanished with Nampuh. The big fellow might be cunning and strong as an ape, but what of this young white man, allegedly brilliant but without common sense, who had also eluded capture?

Howard was aware that this mention of Evans cast a sudden chill over the table. He was also embarrassed at not having produced these two corpses. The wives, particularly, had shown disappointment, and the professors no little displeasure.

"Anyway, they are both most certainly dead," the general finished, rather lamely. "The canyon in which they were trapped has been under continual surveillance. One or both of them left blood enough in the snow to indicate mortal wounds, and in this unseasonable cold—they could never survive."

"Well, he's done it before," Nolan rejoined. "You know the story of how he outran twenty men on horseback."

"A badly wounded man cannot pass over snow without leaving tracks," Howard said shortly. "He most certainly found a hole in the rocks, crawled in and died. Young Evans, if the giant did not eventually kill him, froze to death."

Baum coughed and rubbed at his eyes with his napkin. He mastered himself then and turned to Howard. "About this other woman, Herr General—"

"What a loss," Fairfield broke in, his plump, pale face struggling with an unfamiliar emotion of grief. "That giant, if we'd been able to catch him alive—why, an eighth wonder of the world! A true scientific miracle, eh, Perfesser?"

Baum shot him a glance of manifest disgust. "—this other woman, how did it come to be for her to serve as doppelgänger?"

"The dress and the shoe were Lydia's," Braddock added sternly. "That is the point in need of explication."

"She was a sharper. Took young Evans in," Fairfield said easily. "Took your daughter in too, it looks like."

"Somebody is everybody taking in," Baum said darkly. The silence descended again on the table, magnified by the clink of heavy silverware on porcelain. Their table had been behind heavy curtains, and the few diners in the room beyond made a distant murmur of conversation.

"Oh, men are always fools for a certain kind of tart," the judge's wife observed, balancing a bit of the roast beef on her fork and swabbing it in horseradish. She was a heavyset woman with a faint moustache and small, shrewd eyes. "She was a great beauty, they say, and not an honest bone in her body." She glanced at Nolan's wife, a thin-boned, colorless being who kept her eyes on her plate, aware that everyone except the two scholars from the East knew her husband's reputation as a rake. "But she certainly got her comeuppance."

General Howard pushed back his plate with his one hand and lifted the goblet of wine before him. "I should like to propose a toast—to the prosperity of Mr. Fairfield's new rail and mining enterprise, to the quick recovery of the professor's daughter, and to the destruction of our great nemesis"—he paused as the others also curled fingers around the stems of fine crystal—"but I cannot decide whom to thank. One of our benefactors, at least, is not present. Mr. Stoneman, it was, I believe, who gave up a great deal—a tragic loss of life—in pursuit of the renegades?" He smiled thinly at Fairfield across the table. "He laid the trap, I believe, that brought us our prey?"

"Well sir, he did and he didn't." Fairfield waved his glass vaguely in an easterly direction. "He hired a fellow—a lot of fellows, Pinkertons mostly —to help find Perfesser Braddock's little girl. He was awfully disturbed, ladies and gents, at such a thing happening in this fine territory where he had in mind to make investments . . ." He looked significantly at Nolan. *"Considerable* investments."

"You refer to the fellow who was in the company of this Elizabeth Waring, or Theda Blanchard, or Eliza Cooper, when they attempted to free young Mr. Evans?" The general leaned back, his gaze steady on Fairfield over the rim of the glass, his empty sleeve swinging very slightly.

The young man's easy and genial manner vanished into a slight frown. He appeared to ponder deeply for a moment. "We believe there was a rotten apple in the barrel, General. It's a fact. This fellow only told us he had managed somehow to contact Big Foot himself and persuade him to ransom the boy."

"Somehow," the general repeated.

"Yes sir. Devil take him, he had apparently run into this woman—if it was the same woman; we hear that body's missing too—and rigged up a scheme with her to steal Miss Braddock's clothes."

"What, what is this?" Professor Braddock was deathly pale, and a muscle in his throat contracted.

"An impersonation," the general said softly. "Somehow. I wonder, Mr. Fairfield, if you have any notion of why your employee would venture such a scheme? At such expense? The gold, you know, was recovered from the savages."

"A rotten apple," Fairfield said, with a laugh that lacked gusto. "Anyway, you were making a toast, sir—"

"Wait! Wait, my good sir!" Baum's eyes were like two small, blue flames. "This rotten person could know of the legacy to Willard! Or Mr. Stoneman . . ." He stopped and tugged at his beard, a gesture reserved for the sudden emergence of startling hypotheses.

"Legacy?" The general turned to the professor with difficulty, for the new configuration of Fairfield's countenance greatly interested him.

"What legacy?" the judge's wife demanded stridently, and even Nolan's wife glanced up from her plate.

But the curtains had parted and a middle-aged woman in a plain dress now entered, followed by a waiter. The woman bowed to those at the table, and then addressed Professor Braddock.

"Lydia's dressed, sir. Would it be your pleasure to have her come to table?"

Braddock had half risen from his chair in evident confusion. "Is she—"

"She's pretty well, sir. We've given her laudanum, and the doctor says she'll be better for the evening."

"Fine, fine," Braddock said and dropped back in his chair. "Please escort her in." When the woman had withdrawn, he looked around the table. "I beg your indulgence in turning our conversation away from these matters—especially young Evans and that woman."

"Right enough," Fairfield said loudly. "A gloomy business anyway. Let's have that toast just to Miss Braddock, General, when she—"

"I don't think that would be appropriate," Howard broke in curtly. "The young lady has suffered quite enough attention."

"I only meant—"

"The old man," Howard went on, ignoring Fairfield to address Braddock, "is she still insisting on his attendance?"

"I am afraid so," the professor said with a wince. "I would like to have him sent to jail—to which I am sure he is no stranger—but she feels that he was a good Samaritan. I shall probably have to give him some money to leave us alone."

"Our territory is still in need of some cleaning out," the general began apologetically.

"You've got the job going, General," Fairfield said, again cheerful, his blue eyes wide with sympathy and enthusiasm. "Helping us get rid of that pack of cutthroats. We'll see the day when you ladies can sashay out to an opera right here in Boise, or the best dramatic plays from New York, and buy a dress brought by rail from France in less than a week. Why—" He stopped then, for the curtains had been drawn back by the waiter, and Lydia entered with slow, tentative steps. The men stood up, napkins draped like flags, and the women broke into a little chorus of murmured compliments.

"Lovely, my dear," the judge's wife cooed hoarsely. "You're quite recovered."

"I'm sure," Nolan's wife said with a puppetlike nod. "To meet you. Very charmed."

Lydia curtsied automatically and slid into a chair between General Howard and Professor Baum. Her plain black gown fell about her like a dark pool, her face floating above like a single, sad flower.

The men sat down again and there was an uncomfortable pause. Baum busied himself pouring a small amount of wine in a goblet before Lydia, the bottle rattling against the rim, and Braddock fussed over the roast, slicing a portion onto a bare plate.

"As this young feller was sayin'," Nolan declaimed with a show of what he hoped was nonchalance, "the territory is openin' up. Rich country, very rich country. Glad to have 'im with us as a pardner." He acknowledged Fairfield with an expansive smile. He was nearly overcome with relief. After an instant of awful apprehension, he had seen that Lydia did not recognize him as one of those who had been privileged to glimpse her at the El Dorado. "Between the likes of these new boomers from the East and ourselves, Judge, we'll have the riffraff on the run."

The judge grunted, somewhat derisively. He was a scarecrow of a man, alcohol having burnt away his flesh and left him a face permanently inflamed under a thin patch of white hair. Like the general, he was curious about the young woman, whom he knew very well to be the same piece of goods who had been offered to a selected public at Mama's, and about what sort of business Stoneman had been up to involving the legacy. He saw no prospect yet of a legal proceeding, but the odor of scandal was certainly rank in the air.

"I hope, ma'am, you'll have a chance to take some air soon and see our exhibits," Fairfield said with a bow to Lydia. "We've got a new land office down the street a piece, and I'd be glad to show you the place, top to bottom."

Lydia said nothing, her lips set in a polite, empty smile. The general noticed that she did not look at her father, who had placed the plate in front of her with the smallest of portions huddled in its round, bare expanse. Her reactions to the conversation lagged, so that she often stared disconcertingly at the others long after they had spoken. Periodically she turned to watch for some moments out the window, where nothing was visible but a net of bare branches and an occasional flash of wings.

"It would do you good, my dear," Professor Braddock was saying gently. "When you are a bit more rested."

"Atmosphere," Baum agreed, smiling at her gallantly. "You must intake the clean atmosphere, get ready for the trip back to Boston."

Her face registered a slight shock, and she turned a little toward him. "Dieter," she whispered. "I—"

"Yes?" The old professor leaned anxiously toward her, and the table fell silent again, all of them sobered by the odd timbre of her voice, the voice of one who has wakened from a deep coma. "I do not want . . ."

"Lydia!" Professor Braddock peered insistently at her face, but she did not look at him.

"I do not want . . . Boston," she said and then choked slightly.

"Here, *Liebchen*," Baum said, his own voice trembling as he extended to her first a napkin, then, absurdly, a spoon.

All at once there was a commotion somewhere in the dining room beyond the curtains. "Stop him!" a man shouted, and the subdued murmur of voices ceased. Then the curtains flapped, shook, and flared apart. One of the two men who stepped into their compartment was spat-

tered with mud to well above his caked boots, and the sleeves of his coat
were likewise smeared, in places torn. His greasy hair hung below his
shoulders, framing a dark, intent visage. He looked swiftly around the
table, then riveted his gaze on Lydia, who stared back at him, lips parted
and cheeks suddenly aflame. The other intruder was a sprightly old man,
bald and sunburned, who looked up at the ceiling as if in fervent prayer.

"*Grösser Gott!*" Baum dropped the spoon on his plate with a clatter,
and pushed back his chair to rise.

General Howard pawed instinctively for his absent saber, but before
he could speak the curtains thrashed again and the maître d'hôtel, his fat
cheeks swollen in outrage, thrust his way in.

"Out!" he bellowed. "You *sabe*, out! Ketchum jailhouse!" He waved
his hands frantically at the table. "Ladies and gentlemen, my sincerest
apologies—" Behind him two waiters appeared, sidling tentatively
through the curtains, one bearing a meat cleaver. "I've sent for—"

Now two orderlies in regulation blue trousers and black boots, but
without coats, crowded behind the waiters. Both looked stricken. One
had a stained napkin still tucked under his chin, and the other pointed a
large, cocked service revolver at the ceiling, then, vaguely, at the whole
table.

"Willard! My boy, my boy!" Baum cried and threw his arms about the
newcomer. He stood back then, his small portly figure in an attitude of
rigid attention. "My God, my son, what has happened to you?"

Howard had managed to get to his feet. "Put that away, Turlock, for
the love of heaven." He surveyed the man in mud-stained clothes, who
still stared at Lydia, and she at him.

"Willard Evans?"

The man glanced at him and gave a just perceptible nod, a gesture of
cold formality. "General."

"Pee Wee Sullivan," announced the little bald man.

"Well I'll be a monkey's uncle!" Fairfield cried and uttered a long,
jovial laugh. "If it ain't the wild perfesser! Back from the dead!"

There was a murmur of incredulity and excitement from the company
of guests, while the maître d'hôtel looked nonplussed. "I say," he began,
"not in the hotel, no coloreds . . . General?" He looked pleadingly at
Howard, then at the orderlies, who were trying to look polite and stern at
the same time.

"It's all right." The general gave a perfunctory salute of dismissal.
"This is Mr. Evans, and his associate. Our . . . unannounced guests."

"But—" The maître d'hôtel peered at Willard, then sighed. "As you wish, General." He made a small gesture of resignation and, ushering the waiters and soldiers ahead of him, he departed with a long look of suffering indulgence over his shoulder.

"Willard, you have made this miracle how?" Professor Baum's face had grown ruddy, and his chest heaved with emotion. "We thought—"

"Mr. Fairfield, General." Professor Braddock had put aside his napkin and now rose, like a ruler unfolding. "Ladies. You will excuse us." His face was drawn, and the muscle in his neck now jumped rhythmically. "Lydia, we shall retire now. As for you, you contemptible serpent, never come near me or my daughter again." His voice shook with the effort of restraining his fury. He walked stiffly around the table extending one trembling hand to touch Lydia's shoulder, but she shrank from him, and in an instant was out of her chair, eyes wide with dread.

"No!" Her voice was all at once harsh. "I do not want to go . . . back there. No more. No more . . ." She swallowed. "No more medicine."

"Lydia!" Willard had stepped past the table on the other side, but the general arrested him with a raised hand.

"Gentlemen! Please!" He inclined toward Lydia. "Miss Braddock, your father is concerned for your welfare. Surely—"

"Beggin' yer pardon, Gen'ral, they got 'er cooped tight as a chicken under a bucket." Pee Wee jabbed a finger at the two professors. "They fiddle-diddled around 'n this yere girl would o' been lost, 'cept Willy here got 'er loose from them crooks at the El Dorado." The finger swung next toward Fairfield. "And this yere gent, I 'spect, knows somethin' consarnin' that. Ye better ask him 'bout that red-haired woman and how they come to git skinned 'long with that posse. 'Tain't no coincerdance they all shows up together."

Fairfield appeared at once haughty and confused. "Blarney," he said loudly. "A man gets a bit ahead of the game and every lunatic in creation accuses him of something. General, I ordered this table for a spot of privacy, and if you don't mind . . ." He fumbled in his pocket to produce a silver cigar case. "Maybe Mr. Evans has some business to state, and could go his way then. Perhaps to the barber." He flipped open the lid of the case and selected a fat cigar, but General Howard noted that despite the sneer in his tone the tip of the cigar was not steady.

"I am here to take Lydia with me," Willard said evenly. "Now."

"General, this bounder, this degenerate, is guilty of breach of promise, of professional misconduct, of behavior so foul I cannot give voice to it here." Professor Braddock spoke rapidly between great gasps.

"Now Roland," Baum remonstrated, his beard waggling in agitation, "he was subjected to torture. A terrible experience."

"Got kicked square in the head by a horse," Pee Wee volunteered helpfully.

"He can return to his career," Baum went on, and laid a tentative, restraining hand on his colleague's sleeve. "He has no doubt some data . . ."

Braddock shook off the hand. "Lydia," he said, and the word was lead, hooped with iron. "You must return to the hotel, to your bed. We are taking the next train to Boston."

"No!" The young woman veered away from him, brushing the general's empty sleeve, and took a step toward Willard. "I want to . . . to go with them." She swallowed again. "I am of age."

"You cannot!" Braddock's face was wrenched by a mighty crosscurrent of passion and fear.

Involuntarily the general looked at the judge, who hunched his narrow, sharp shoulders like a crow.

"No law agin' it. No dowry, though."

"Damn shame," Fairfield said with a little pout of disgust, and struck a match to his cigar.

"Lydia!" Braddock cried, the iron hoop snapping.

"I'm sorry, Dieter." Willard moved to the young woman's side, and taking her hand, placed it on his arm. "I have no data. I'm afraid I see our work rather differently now. We never thought of measuring what's inside the skulls, and that's where things are. Things that matter. Little Birds." He smiled swiftly. "Our grandfathers are not just bones, you know."

Baum blinked at him, stunned. "But this Big Foot . . . your theory . . ."

Willard smiled again, a little sadly. "He was a bear."

"General!" Braddock struck at the air with his clenched fist. "My daughter is not well. She is my charge. This man—"

"Calm yourself, sir," the general said, a little peremptorily. He turned then to Willard. "I doubt, young man, that you are considering the consequences of subjecting Miss Braddock to further hardships and possible dishonor." He found that the young man did not avoid his stern regard, but waited calmly for him to continue. "I understand you have undergone an ordeal. How you came here alive—a miracle, as the professor says. The fact that you may be guilty of treason and can be put in irons I shall leave aside for the moment. But you clearly have not her father's blessing, nor does your equipage appear very promising." He stopped, aware that the heavy irony of his tone made no alteration in the dark, still face or the impenetrable eyes.

"His prospecks ain't so poor, General," Pee Wee offered, sauntering to the other side of Lydia. "We got a new spring wagon an' a team and two good saddle horses outside, an' three months worth o' grub, too."

"Lord," said the judge's wife in the tone of one announcing a military triumph, "they're elopin'!"

"But Willard to you I have given . . . you know I have some property," Baum moaned. "And to them—to this young jackanapes and to Stoneman—I gave the property, as a legacy to you for your work—upon your marriage!"

Willard looked away from the general to Fairfield, now obscured by the cloud of smoke from his cigar.

"Yes, fine securities, all in rails," Fairfield said in a tone of blustering optimism. "Down just now but bound to rise. A sound investment, Perfesser, as I told you long ago. However, I understand there was a prior marriage—yes indeed." His tone grew sly, containing a trace of secret glee. "Don't know the particulars, if consummated and so forth, but legal status uncertain, I would say—"

"Indeed," the general interrupted. He gazed steadily at the blond young man who puffed the cigar now a little wildly, bloom after bloom of smoke rising between them. "I begin to see."

"I don't want your money, Dieter," Willard said quietly. "But you might wonder how it was that Stoneman and his crowd came here, and one of them fell in with the woman who led me to betray myself. I have wondered at the value of my ransom, but now I believe I understand." He inclined his head slightly toward Howard. "Had the strategy been successful, General, I would not be surprised to learn that my fortune reverted to Stoneman. As it is, I would rather not be a corpse of great value." He smiled without humor. "Good evening, ladies and gentlemen."

"One question, sir." Howard stopped him with a raised hand. "Nampuh?"

"You will never see him again."

"You saw to it?"

"I did."

They locked eyes, and finally the general raised his hand the rest of the way to his brow in a slow salute.

"Wait!" Professor Braddock's voice cracked, the force draining from it. "He is married, he—"

"Widower," Pee Wee said confidently. "Man's a widower. Independent as a hog on ice. Let's git."

"Good-bye," Lydia said then in a low but firm voice. "Papa, I shall write, and I—" She took a step toward her father, but he recoiled, turning away from the table toward the wall. She lifted a hand toward him.

When the professor spoke his voice was metallic, like the tumblers of a lock falling into place. "Leave me," he said. "You are not my child. You are an ingrate."

Lydia's hand fell again to her side. "No," she said, and there was something of wonder in her voice. "That's true. I am not a child."

She turned then and the three of them passed through the curtain, which swayed to and fro after them. The group at the table watched the fabric's undulation, mesmerized.

"Well," said the judge's wife with a deep sigh. "Such is life in the Far West."

[44]

LYDIA occupied the narrow board seat of the wagon and held her head high, spots of color already in her cheeks. Pee Wee climbed up beside her to take the reins, while Willard mounted one of the two horses and secured the other by its halter to his saddle horn. It was early dusk, the air chilling suddenly in the last light, and from behind the seat Lydia drew the buffalo robe to wrap about her. On the street a few other wagons or coaches rattled by, and men passed to and from saloons, their silhouettes sharp before the soft yellow light of lanterns.

"We got to make tracks," Pee Wee said to Willard, who was riding beside and slightly in advance of the lead wheel. "In them hills she's blacker'n the inside of a stovepipe, and we got to find that cabin tonight. Tain't much, ma'am, but better'n that hospital we was in afore."

She smiled at them both. "It doesn't matter. We're out here." She gazed at Willard, then ducked her head shyly into the robe.

They came to an intersection where an imposing three-story structure of brick was brightly lit, its courtyard crowded with people. A bonfire blazed on the cobblestones, and tables had been set up under the trees. Over the gate was a large wooden sign, freshly painted.

THE OWYHEE GIANT RAIL & FREIGHT COMPANY
Newly Reorganized
and
THE SNAKE RIVER LAND COMPANY
Present
All Properties! Townsites!
Good Farms! Grazing Land!
Historical Museum!

They slowed, and saw that at one of the large tables a clerk had been established, his seal and documents before him, a line of customers waiting for his services. Beside the clerk was another man, a heavy iron box open in front of him, and behind this pair stood four others bearing shotguns. A man by the gate, resplendent in otterskin coat and bowler hat, hailed them as they slowed to observe.

"Step right in, laddies and ladies—you've found it! The God's green paradise promised to Moses, available right here as low as ten dollars the acre! The Owyhee country! Home of the giant Nampuh—but that's ancient history now—the outlaw band is ground to dust before the iron wheels of the modern age! A survivor is right here to tell the awful tale!" He extended an arm theatrically, leering up at them as they drew abreast of the gate.

Resting on one of the tables where a group of men and women had gathered, chattering and pointing, was a pile of rags, an old hammerlock rifle, some battered and twisted pots, and a large glass jar.

"Take a look, gentlemen, madam. All free, including beer and crackers—courtesy of the Owyhee Giant!" The man stepped aside from the entrance with a sweeping bow.

"What the hell izzat?" Pee Wee peered into the darkness, halting the team with a tug of the reins.

Willard urged his horse forward and rode through the gate to approach the table. The firelight flickered on the surface of the jar, so at first it seemed to contain ghostly blazes within, but when his own shadow fell over the glass the face appeared, tilting a little, seeming to stare up at him through the gloom.

It was Jacques, grinning widely, his hair and moustache floating free in a clear, yellow liquid, as if lifted in a faint breeze. His expression was a familiar one of ribald glee, strange only in its fixity. When Willard turned, by some trick of the light, he thought the head rotated slightly also, keeping its gaze on him as he rode back through the gate.

"Give the lady a gander, mister," the man in the bowler cajoled as he passed. "Wonder of the world."

Willard fell in beside the wagon and Pee Wee clucked the team back into motion. They turned off the main street and passed through a section of miners' hovels, then through a Chinese quarter with its pungent odors and figures crouching over iron buckets glowing with coals. Above them, a star or two pricked through the violet sky.

"What was in there?" Pee Wee asked finally, as they rolled by the last row of tents, the wagon wheels biting into the dust of a plain that stretched to black humps of hills etched against a red sky.

"Nothing," Willard answered. He did not look away from the horizon. "Nothing to speak of." He rode in silence for a time and then began to hum to himself, a high, strange melody. Pee Wee frowned and clucked at the team with a shake of his reins.

Lydia had retired from the seat to a place amid the flour sacks and bedding rolls, where she was curled up to doze. She uttered a low sound then, muffled under the robe, the sound of an animal drawn up safe in its burrow to embark on a long and refreshing sleep.

Baker, Will
Track of the giant